T0129106

DRAW ME WITH YOUR

A NOVEL BY **SHONELL BACON** AND **JDANIELS**

A STREBOR BOOKS INTERNATIONAL LLC PUBLICATION
DISTRIBUTED BY SIMON & SCHUSTER, INC.

Published by

Strebor Books International LLC
P.O. Box 1370
Bowie, MD 20718
http://www.streborbooks.com

ISBN 978-1-59309-000-5 ISBN 1-59309-000-5
LCCN 2003100151

Distributed by Simon & Schuster, Inc.
1230 Avenue of the Americas
New York, NY 10020
1-800-223-2336

Cover Illustration: André Harris

First Printing June 2003
Manufactured and Printed in the United States

10 9 8 7 6 5 4 3 2 1

TO ALL MY FELLOW AUTHORS, WRITERS AND POETS
who are striving to achieve the same reality that I have been blessed to achieve. When you reach upon a star, when you persist in it, those wishes really do come true!

—JDaniels

AS ALWAYS, I WOULD LIKE TO DEDICATE THIS NOVEL
to my trio of love: My mother, Brenda Henson; my grandmother, Audrey Bacon (1931-1998); and my grandfather, Charles Bacon (1929-1998). Your love and inspiration means more to me than you will ever know.

—Shonell Bacon

Acknowledgments

JDANIELS

I always thought that by the second time around I would have gotten used to the wonderful feeling of sharing and having readers and friends reading and enjoying my work, but the elevated sense of joy has not diminished. In fact, it's grown even stronger with the release of ***Draw Me with Your Love***. So I want to thank you all for your support of Shonell and me.

Special thanks to the following stars who light up my life: My **mom and dad**, for your love and support. **Usted es mi fuerza, y las paredes que me protegen.** You are my strength, and the walls that protect me… **My siblings and all my immediate family**, you are too numerous to name, but I love you all. **My close friends**, you know who you are, thank you! **Shonie**, what can I say? We've penned these words of love together for the second time, and my love and awe for your talent has only grown. God shined on me the day I met you in that chat room. **V. Anthony Rivers**, you know what you mean to me, my brotha. Thank you for your encouragement. You are my kindred spirit forever. My agent, **Sara Camilli**, I've put my career in your hands, and so far it has been more than a pleasure. Thanks for all your encouragement and pep talks. **Brandon Massey**, thanks for all the late night chats and advice. You make me feel like the little engine that could, because when I doubt and feel like I only ***think I can***, you are right there behind me, giving my engine a strong push with, **"YES U CAN!"** **Darrien Lee**, how can I forget you? Love you, girl! **Miguel Wilder**, **Kat**, and all the rest of **my TNC familia**, ONE LUV!

And last but not least, the incomparable **Zane**, I will ALWAYS be grateful and appreciative of your faith in us, and for your allowing us to grow to incredible literary heights with Strebor Books International. You're a one in a million you! The second time around with SBI is a hundred times sweeter. I love you.

SHONELL BACON

Wow. Who would have thought two books in two years? There are many people responsible for my joy, first and always, **my mother**, who has allowed me to follow my dream despite the path's uncertainty. I give big ups to **Zane** (and the whole Strebor Books organization) who took on my and JD's dream and made it a reality. Zane, there will never be enough words to tell you how blessed I feel for meeting you. **JD**, my ace boon coon, who- despite the miles that separate us-continues to be a great friend and a wonderful partner in literary crime. I love you! **André Harris** gets all the love for making a slamming *Luvalwayz* cover and an equally wonderful DRAW cover. Your talents are da bomb, Dré! Praise goes to all the book clubs, organizations and bookstores that have carried our books and have helped make *Luvalwayz* a building success. It is our words but your love that keeps us writing and getting people to READ us! To all my friends-literary and not-who have listened to me gripe and complain about making it, yet you loved me anyway: **Darrien Lee, Anthony Rivers, Kat Lavache, Miguel Wilder, Pam Osbey, Jacquelyne Jermayne**; to those who have supplied me with valuable knowledge through talks and interviews: **Bernice McFadden, Margaret Johnson-Hodge, Gwynne Forster**, and so many others. To those not mentioned: you *know* writing is my heart, my very lifeline, and you have continued to help me and nurture my talent. I could write a book to all those who have helped me get to this next step but to save space, I will simply say thank you from the bottom of my heart.

DRAW ME WITH YOUR LOVE
(ROXY'S SONG)

One day, you find that special one,
the sparkle in your sun,
just when you've given up...
And you know that finally the gods they
smile on you...yet it's so hard to
believe it could be true...

Boy I'm your easel, draw me with your
love...the love I've dreamed of,
paint me with your touch...

And we know that we'll be artistically
one...just draw me with your love...

I close my eyes and I see you...
designing on my heart...
The magic that you do...
And you washed ashore and brought me
more than I've ever had, never felt oh
so adored till I met you!

Boy I'm your easel, draw me with your
love...the love I've dreamed of,
paint me with your touch...

And we know that we'll be artistically
one...just draw me with your love...

(Repeat chorus till fade)

Boy I'm your easel...(paint me)
draw me with your love,
the love I've dreamed of,
(draw me) paint me with your touch...

And we know that we'll be artistically
one...just draw me with your love...
draw me with your love...
draw me with your love...
(till fade)

CHAPTER One

Roxy

"I want you two to leave, now!" Thomas said. He waved a revolver around in the dense air of the hotel room. "Roxy belongs to me. I paid for her services, and she is going nowhere!"

I stood, shaking in my sister's arms as the man I thought I loved swung a gun between my sister and me.

Stephen, my sister's friend, laughed off Thomas' gun and attempted to take over the situation. "Why don't you put your water gun down?" Stephen asked. "You don't want to go there with me."

Thomas' eyes bore into mine, and despite my wish to leave, I felt a tug in my chest. It wasn't his fault that he paid for a woman who didn't know what she really wanted out of life. I thought France would awaken my artistic passion. I thought it would solidify my relationship with Thomas, but all that it had really done was allow me to see how much I had messed up my life.

Tears trickled down my face, mingling with the sweat. Stephen and Thomas were at a stalemate, each staring the other down. I sniffed and Thomas glanced my way.

He was shaking, tears dripping from his eyes. His hair was pasted to his scalp. "Don't go, Roxy," he said with a voice full of pain. I trembled. "I love you!" he cried out.

My sister guided me to the bed where she began to throw my clothes into a bag.

"Don't listen to him," Dee growled.

"Roxy." Thomas' voice went up an octave.

"Please," I cried, "I want to go home, Thomas. I'm sorry."

"After all I've done for you?" He pointed the gun directly toward me and suddenly the room went still, voices hushed, breaths silenced. "I gave you money," he continued. "I gave you France. I gave you love and the chance to paint. And now you leave me?"

In that moment, before I could respond, my so-called life flashed before my eyes and for a split second, I wanted Thomas to pull that trigger. Wonderful family, all-American sister, and me, the fuck-up. Instead of trying to be as good as my sister, I rebelled against it and became someone I hated. Selling my body and my dignity and now I had a gun in my face.

My mouth began to form the words, *shoot me*, but instead, I spoke, "Thomas, I'm so sorry. If you love me, you'll let me go."

I could literally see Thomas fold upon himself as if air simply vanished from his body. He held himself up against the wall, weeping from his gut.

"Thomas," I whispered. Dee grabbed the bag from the bed, snatched my hand and pulled me toward the opened front door.

"Get out of here," Stephen called out. "Now."

My heart and mind were playing tug-of-war with each other. I wanted to escape Thomas and to forget what he represented. I wanted to erase the black eye and swollen cheekbone of abuse he had given me when I begged to leave. At the same time, a part of me wanted to stay and accept the only love I had ever received.

At the threshold of the door, I looked away from Thomas and began to follow Dee out the door.

"Roxy!"

I turned and looked at Thomas. His eyes were wide and frightening. The gun rose and leveled off directly in line with my heart.

"I can't let you live without me," he said slowly. The gun, the animate seemed to quiver as if alive while aimed at me.

Before Stephen could pull out his own weapon, Thomas fired. A yellow-gold flash erupted, and the bullet, in a slow haze, came toward me. I could hear myself scream "no," and heard the high-pierced yell of Dee, but I was frozen in place. The bullet ripped through my tee shirt and plunged...

I screamed, springing up from my sleep. Sweat dripped from my body and my skin was boiling hot. I gulped air in like I had been in a desert for weeks without water or oxygen. I blinked for several minutes, taking in snapshots of my bedroom. I saw the NYU banner taped onto the mirror of my dresser and slowly, my breaths came to me.

I snatched my cordless phone off its base and punched in a number. It rang three times before a gruff male voice answered, "Yea?"

"Steve," I whispered, "it's me."

"Roxy, what's wrong?" Despite my sweating, I dug deep under my comforter.

"I'm sorry for calling you this early. I know you're leaving for Cali today."

"Don't worry about it." He yawned. "What's going on?"

"I had the dream again," I whispered, still shaking. "I got shot."

"Oh Roxy, honey." Steve sighed. "Did you, um, die in the dream?"

"Close." I wiped my tears away with the sleeve of my tee shirt. "Last time, the gun went off and I woke up. This time the bullet hit me, but I woke up before it went into me."

Silence. Heavy breathing. Sniffling.

"When is it going to end?" I cried, one hand holding the phone while the other wiped away tears, pushing my stringy hair from my face. "The dreams are just getting worse and worse. I might die in the next one."

"Babe, you won't die. You didn't die. Thomas did. He shot himself."

"I know." I fell back onto my pillows. I coughed up a sob. "I know he's dead. I helped kill him. It should have been me. I ruined him."

"Stop it, Roxy! I don't want you to say that again. Ever. You got me?"

I nodded, though I knew he couldn't see me. "Yes, yes, I have you," I whispered. "I'm sorry, Steve. I heap all this shit on you. It's not fair."

"I'm your friend. I don't give a shit about what's fair or not fair."

"It's been a few years now. I don't think I'll ever let it go."

"Don't cry, Roxy." I could hear Steve sniffling. "You want me to come over?"

"No, but thanks. I need to get up."

"First day at Visions?"

"Yep. Full-time, no less. I guess I really impressed Charlise during my temp gig."

"Of course, you did. Roxy, you are a very talented woman. I know she loved you."

"Aww, you are so sweet. Better be glad you're already taken." We laughed.

"Seriously, Roxy. You're strong, and you're going to get through this."

I took a deep breath and let it out. I batted away tears and promised myself that no more would be shed today.

"Thank you, Steve. I can't tell you how much it means to have you as a friend."

"Same here. If you need me before I leave, call. And just because I'll be three thousand miles away doesn't mean you can't call if you need to. Even collect."

"Thanks, 'cause you know I'll be broke for a while," I said with a laugh.

"I love you, Roxy."

"Love you, too, my friend. Wish me luck."

"You don't need it."

I hung up the phone and tried to push Steve's love and positive voice inside me for safekeeping. I always found it ironic that the only person I could trust with my past and my pains was a man. Steve just walked into my life at the right time, for me anyway. I shook my head and began to peel my comforter from me. I slipped out of the bed and planted my feet on the floor. I sighed wearily. When would I be able to have a full night of sleep without dreams of my past, dreams of gunfire, dreams of a fatal attraction that unfortunately or fortunately, ended the way it did?

Before it rang, I banged my hand atop of my radio, turning the soon-to-be-buzzing alarm clock off.

"Okay," I whispered. I stood up and flattened my hands over my tummy and thighs. I had an hour and a half to shower and dress before I had to be in SoHo to meet with Charlise, the owner of a chic, small but quaint art gallery by the name of Visions. If anything, my new job at Visions was a positive in my life. Especially at a time when I was about to be kicked out of my NYU apartment and needed a job to pay rent and to utilize my interior design degree. Not only would I be getting paid to design the new bookstore café, but I would also be able to dream of art and painting, my secret loves.

I walked over to my dresser and pulled out panties and a bra, and then headed over to my closet to select an outfit. A Sunday paper was on the floor, glaring at me. It was open to the real estate section where I had been looking for a place to live.

"You'll find a place to live," I told myself, though I had been looking for three weeks and had found nothing. Now that I had a job that paid, I couldn't find a place to sleep. Figures.

I stood at my dresser and applied my makeup and jewelry. A picture of my sister Dee and me caught my eye. We were hugging fiercely, me in my cap and gown, her in a pale pink summer dress. Even on my graduation day, she outshone me. My faint smile faltered a bit. I swallowed a few times, trying to squelch the jealousy that threatened to come up.

"Not on my first day," I gritted out. "I love Dee. She loves me. She's a great person, and so am I."

Self-affirmation. Something I had to do every day to reassure myself that I was worth something. Sometimes, it didn't work.

I riffled through my top drawer to get my silver watch and stopped. A white tee shirt. Emblazoned on the front: *Viva la France!* I gripped the dresser and tried not to think of *him*, but I failed. High school graduation, college in California. Bad things passed through my mind, leading up to Thomas Dugué—a man who would change my life in more ways than one.

He was debonair and witty and his French accent drew me in with a tenacity I hadn't seen before then. His words lulled me in, and before I knew it, I was being asked to travel to France with him, for a fee and the opportunity to leave France whenever I wanted to. "But," he had said, one of his sly, come-hither smiles falling upon his lips, "once you get there and feel your painting muse flow, you won't want to leave."

He was wrong. Steeling myself against painful memories, I grabbed my purse and headed out the door.

"Girl, you are the best decision I've ever made," Charlise said as she tossed her flaxen blond hair over her shoulder. I chuckled at her use of *girl*, almost sounding like a sister, despite her debutante appearance. Body-wise, Charlise could have easily been a model. Tall, svelte with a walk that made her appear to glide across the floor as opposed to walking like us mere peons. One could easily tell that her passion was art and painting, as she stood before me, dressed in white overalls with splatters of colors all over her. The only thing in place was her hair, for even her face, the right cheek to be exact, held a spot of emerald-colored paint. She made the perfect image of the *perfect* artist.

"Thanks for the compliment," I replied. I moved along the gleaming hardwood floor as my eyes took in the splashes of colors that adorned the bright white walls of the gallery. "I am so happy to be here," I added. "To be around such beautiful artwork really feeds into my artistic aura."

"Wanna see my latest piece?" Charlise asked. Beams of light bounced off of her.

I nodded anxiously, and she guided me down a hall that gave way to a newly structured escalator. We went downstairs where the café would be located. I smiled when I entered the large space, watching construction workers smooth walls in order to place oak wood paneling onto them. I had suggested to Charlise that with the brightness and colors that permeated the gallery, a more classic coloring of oak, hunter green and burgundy would go over well in the bookstore and café. The fact that she took my advice made me swell a little in pride. I swallowed and continued to follow her down another hall to a door on the left.

"This is where I do my painting," she said before flipping on the switch. I sighed when I spotted her painting resting upon an easel in the middle of the room. She was an abstract painter, like me. It took a keen eye, and some knowledge of the artist to understand the abstract painter's work, but I got this one, no problem. Upon the pristine white canvas laid colors of emerald, navy and a chocolate brown, strokes of colors so smooth, it was as if the grace of a swan painted the lines. I could smell the Earth resonating from her painting, her love of Earth, the emerald representing the growth of life, the navy reflecting the oceans and the brown imitating the soil, the life force that helps to make the things we need grow. I was impressed.

"Wow," I said. I sidled up beside a grinning Charlise.

"You like?" she asked, hugging herself and rocking back and forth on her heels.

"It's incredible, girl."

"I've been on such an artistic high since I went on this cruise a couple months ago."

"Cruise?"

We left the room and made our way into the space that would serve as the café. Kitchen materials were already set, and Charlise poured us both a steaming hot cup of coffee. Black, just like I like it.

"Yea, I went on a cruise called The Art of Life," Charlise said. "For an entire week, we sailed the beautiful waters, ported in Cancun, although I believe their next cruise is going to the Caribbean. Got to hobnob with the hottest new artists out today, learned some new strokes, read up on new opportunities during the workshops, and even got a second to do a little painting."

"Whoa!" I exclaimed. I sank into a thickly pillowed chair and slipped one leg up under me. "That sounds so incredible. I wish I could do something like that. I mean yea, I have my degree in interior design, but art has always been in my heart. It would probably awaken the artist in me to surround myself with other lifescapers."

"I like that. Lifescapers."

We both smiled for a moment before Charlise jumped into the chair beside me, as giddy as a child on Christmas. "You can go!" she squealed.

"Go where?" I chuckled as I warmed my hands on the ceramic mug. "On the cruise?" Charlise nodded enthusiastically. "I would love to go. Let me go pack my suitcase!" I noticed Charlise's huge grin and decided I'd better hook her to reality. "Sike! Girl, I have no money, feel me?"

"Oh, come on, Roxy, I could give you a week or two's pay upfront."

I shook my head so hard, it damn near fell off my shoulders, my streaked hair flipping back and forth across my lips. "Unh-unh, I'll need that to get me a new sleeping pad. I'm trying to prove to Deandra, that's my sister, that I am a responsible person. I've been doing well so far this past year. Blowing two weeks' pay on a trip would be above and beyond irresponsible."

"Surely your sister knows how important art is to you?" Charlise questioned. "This is a once-in-a-lifetime cruise."

I blinked a few times, understanding what Charlise was saying, and wanting to tell her that she didn't know the entire story, but I bit my lip. Deandra had very valid reasons for not believing or trusting anything I did or said.

"The next cruise is in a week," Charlise added, perking my attention back up to her. "I know it's late, but if you could get the money, I could probably sweet-talk someone into getting you aboard. They do the cruises four times a year, but this would be the perfect time for you to go."

"She's not going to give me the money." I shook my head and took a sip of coffee. Charlise completely ignored me.

"It could refresh your whole outlook and rejuvenate and escalate your appreciation for the arts."

By now, I was moaning. I really wanted to go on this cruise. It felt like something I had to do, but I had no way of paying for it myself, and knew of no one who would be even willing to unload that kind of cash for me at a moment's notice. Except, well, hmm, not even she would do that, I didn't think. Besides, Deandra had given me an iBook for my graduation gift just a week earlier, so I knew giving me money, when her wedding was at the end of the year, would be a big no. Then again, I wouldn't know for sure unless I asked.

"Hold up, sis! I have to get something to clean my ears out because I know you are not asking me for that kind of money!"

Oddly enough, I was hurt by Deandra's outburst. I mean, hell, I would have been like *what the hell*, too, but I had barely gotten the question out. First, I wanted to tell Deandra about my great job, and then reintroduce her to my love of painting before I mentioned the cruise. By the time I finally got to it, she had put two and two together.

"Sis," I said, half-whining, half-crying, "you know I wouldn't even ask you this unless it was an emergency."

"A cruise?" Deandra asked blandly. "A cruise is an emergency? If that's the case, sign my butt up for one also because I've been working sixty-hour weeks for the Orioles lately and could use a vacation. Excuse me, an *emergency*."

I kicked off my shoes, padding along my apartment, pacing actually, praying and hoping that I could find the right words to sway Deandra over to my side of the fence. "I'm sorry, Deandra," I said, in a clipped, professional tone. "It was rude of me to call and ask you for money. All you or Mom and Dad have asked of me is that I try to put my life back together, to leave the past in the past and move on. I think so far I've done a good job of that."

"You have," Deandra said. The high-pitched shrill became a soft, mellow yell. "We are all so proud of you, sistergirl! Couldn't you tell at graduation?"

I smiled at the memory, thinking back to how gleeful everyone was to see me walk across the stage in my cap and gown. They all laughed when

I snatched up my degree and did a little happy dance. That day was a good day, most definitely, despite my feeling second best at my own graduation.

"I saw how happy you guys were," I admitted. "Made me happy to know I could put smiles on your faces. It meant a lot to me."

We both sat in silence until I spoke again. "My boss offered to pay me two weeks upfront, so that I could go on the trip." Even through the phone, I could feel Deandra's eyes widen as she sucked her teeth. "I didn't take her up on her offer," I added, smirking because I knew Deandra would be blushing with embarrassment right now.

"Deandra?"

"Yea, babe?"

"For real, I do want to go on this trip. Don't ask me why because I just found out today, but it's like, I love painting, I love art, and something inside of me is saying, 'Go on this trip, Roxy!' I think I could find myself there, reconnect myself with things I threw away, trying to forget them."

If anything would get Deandra, it would be the truth. More than anything, I *knew* I had to be on that cruise come next week. Like it was destiny, something I never listened to in the past, but was trying to befriend as I *grew up*.

"You really want to go that bad?" Deandra asked. Her voice had softened considerably.

I sighed, answering, "I know, under the circumstances, I don't deserve shit, but yes, I really do want to go that bad—bad enough to take a loan from you if you have the extra cash. Once I move out of my apartment and get into a new place, I will hook you back up with *all* your money, sis. I promise."

"I don't want to regret this later," Deandra said, almost in whimper tones.

"Deandra, you won't," I said, practically skipping around my tiny apartment. "Will Stephen get mad that you gave me the money?"

"Hell no." She laughed at me. "I have my own individual account with a little sumptin' sumptin' in there. He doesn't even bother to ask about it."

"Thank you so much, Dee Dee," I said. I wanted to cry at the Hallmark moment we were having. "Um," I added sheepishly, "can you wire the money to me? Like today?"

"Damn it!" Deandra joked. "You beg for almost an hour and now you're being Miss Dictator. Fine, I'll have it wired to you within the hour."

"Oh, my God!" I squealed into the phone, running and sliding along the floors of my apartment. "I think this experience will change my life, girl! Call me crazy..."

"And you know I already think you don' lost it!"

"Hush. For real, Deandra, this means a lot to me. I'm going to come back from this trip a whole new woman. Just you wait and see!"

CHAPTER *Two*

ANTOINE

The tiny outdoor café in Manhattan was crowded, everyone obviously getting his or her eats on before finishing out another busy workday in the Big Apple. I felt jumpy as I looked down again at the gold quartz watch that my parents had given me for my twenty-fifth birthday two months prior. Let's face it. I was just a jumpy somebody, period–at least that is what Nicky always said. Nicky is my twin of hearts, and the love of my life. No, she isn't my lady; she is more than that. She is my kindred spirit. We had been the best of friends since pre-school. She is also a lesbian. I had to smile when I thought about her and some of the *'let's discuss this thing called life'* convos we'd had zillions, and I say, zillions of times.

The sound of someone clearing their throat jarred me from warm thoughts of my Nicky. Lynn Johnson. I had been waiting for this moment for Lord knows how long. I stood up and smiled warmly as he extended his hand.

"Antoine, how are you?" he asked, giving me a firm, warm grip.

"I'm good!" I exclaimed. "I've really, really been looking forward to this meeting, Mr. Johnson…"

"Call me Lynn," he cut in.

"Okay, Lynn it is."

As we sat down at our table, I gestured to the waitress for service. She came over instantly with a warm smile. Lynn ordered rum on the rocks, and me, a cranberry juice. I had never been a drinker, never really understanding what the hoopla was about. I had never been able to savor the bitter flavor of beer nor liquor. We sat in comfortable silence for a moment after the waitress took our order, and then I figured it was time to get down to business.

"I was hyped after our phone call last week when you told me how much you all liked my art line. This is something I've been working on for a long time," I said.

Lynn ran his hand through his short blond locks, which were receding slightly from his forehead. I took him to be maybe in his mid-to-late thirties, but then it was always hard to tell with fair, Caucasian people, who tended to age a bit quicker than darker- hued whites, and especially quicker than people of color. "You do good work, Antoine. You're an extremely talented young artist, and you're going to go far in this industry."

"Thanks a lot," I said, flattered by his praise. I pulled out the leather folder I had brought along with my contracts for Lincoln Galleries on hand. "I brought the contract and some other papers that I thought you might want. Now I can guarantee you the originality of each and every piece of work I do for you. Each piece will be painstakingly done to perfection. I don't sleep. I paint while normal folks sleep." I chuckled. Just then our waitress showed up with our drinks. I watched the odd look on Lynn's face as he thanked the waitress, and then looked down at his rum and coke as if there were a piece of lint on his glass.

"Antoine...I don't know how to tell you this, but there's been a change in what we originally had planned."

"Okay, what kind of change?" I queried.

Lynn cleared his throat, took a sip of his drink and looked up at me, not quite meeting my eyes. I started to get a not-too-good feeling about this meeting, which was a complete turn from how I was feeling when I woke up to the morning sun hidden behind the New York smog.

"It's not your paintings. It's nothing to do with you actually. But the owners of Lincoln want to make some cutbacks, so a couple of days ago they informed me and our other buyer to put all of our up-and-coming deals and contracts on hold for a few months."

"A few…? Wait, wait," I put my hand up, breathing deeply. This could not be happening! "We had a deal; I mean this is not a sudden thing, Lynn. I showed you my work months ago. I presented the idea of a Cherokee line to you back in February, and you said that Lincoln needed and wanted something fresh. Well this is as fresh as you get, man!"

Lynn took another slow gulp of his rum, while I felt a burning in the pit of my stomach that was getting hotter and hotter, waiting for him to say something, anything to help me understand what the hell was going on.

"Antoine, you are not new at this game. Shit happens, especially in our line of work and you know it. All of us are struggling. It's the art world, and it's our karma, you know?"

I felt my face getting hot. "Man, I don't wanna hear that bull. Look! Why did you even show up for this meeting, if this is what you were planning on telling me?" I felt totally frustrated. "We talked just two days ago. You could've told me then, so what was the point of all this?"

"Because I wanted to do this the right way. I know that it has been almost a done deal, and I know how you must feel."

I laughed sarcastically, bitterly. "No, you have no idea how I feel, believe that."

Lynn looked down at his watch and sighed, standing up suddenly. "I'm really sorry. Like I said, I'm not saying no. We still want to work with you, and we are still interested in your art line. Just not right now, okay? I'll be in touch in a few months."

Lynn extended his hand, which I took grudgingly. I didn't want to seem unprofessional. The art world was a small and exclusive one. And as pissed off as I was at Lynn Johnson, and the cracker-shit Lincoln galleries he was buyer for, I couldn't afford bad press to go around about me. Not a struggling Manhattan artist like myself.

I laughed bitterly to myself after Lynn had departed, and left a crisp ten-dollar bill on the table. "Mofo didn't even pay for his own drink!"

My day was done. I had no intentions of going back to work on the painting that sat quietly in my studio awaiting my touch. I had pre-named it, *A chief and his princess*, and right now, as far as I was concerned, the chief and his princess could kiss my...well, you get the picture. I felt like burning the whole collection of Cherokee art, the collection that was supposed to get me what I had been dreaming of. A bigger studio, the relaxed feeling of being able to breathe a little easier financially speaking, and also the confidence of finally being able to say I had reached a goal.

I walked into my small Manhattan apartment, which actually was a small two-room dump over top of my studio that the artist in me was able to decorate until it was livable and cozy. I didn't need much. I had always been happy with just a small space and an easel, brush set, paints and chalk. That alone made me a happy man. I immediately stripped out of my shirt. It was a hot day, and an inner burn was making me feel even hotter. I looked at my reflection in the huge mirror over my pullout sofa, which I had left pulled out and unmade from the morning.

I loosened the rubber band from the back of my hair. Soft, baby-fine black tresses fell to my shoulders, with only a hint of curl. The hair had been a gift from my full-blooded Cherokee mother, along with the strong, sharp nose, and deep black soulful eyes, reminiscent of ancient Cherokee warriors of long ago my mother would always say. My dark chocolate complexion spoke another heritage though, as did the full lips, black man lips, my daddy's lips. Rev. Charles John Billups, longtime pastor of Mount Phillips Baptist Temple in Queens, New York.

I'd grown up an only child, but with strong deep love, commitment and family values. My parents had never really gotten any stink about their biracial union, being that my quiet neighborhood in Queens was quite mixed in itself, so along with that they produced me, Antoine De'Ron Billups, the one and only spoiled rotten kid of their dreams. My mother had always said that I came out painting, an artist for life.

I studied art at the Manhattan School of the Arts. After I graduated, I got a small loan for my studio, and have been able to support myself with my paintings. That is something a lot of artists are not able to do, so I'm lucky, I guess. It's a cold, cruel world out there, especially when one does not have a conventional job or career.

I sighed. Now this rotten kid artist felt like crap. It wasn't so much that I'd lost the deal...okay, I admit, it was. But it was also that I had told so many people about it. Had already spent the damn money, which was a lesson in itself. *NEVER spend money you ain't got yet!* Nicky had warned me again and again about setting myself up for stuff, then not being able to stomach the fall. And now here I was again, looking like a fool, and no way was I gonna be able to face any of those people I had ran my mouth off to. It was not that I was conceited about my work. I was simply convinced. And I must admit, having Lynn Johnson tell me that Lincoln loved my painting and wanted me to do an entire line was a booster for sure.

The ringing of the phone woke me from my thoughts.

"Hello?"

"Well?"

"Well what?"

"Antoine, sweetie, baby, BooBoo, you *know* what I wanna know. How did it go?"

It was Nicky.

Nicky had planned on running a small café beside my new studio. We had already scoped out the spot together so I knew my news would disappoint her.

She was a caterer and pastry chef. The sistah could gourmet cook and bake her sweet ass off. And we had sat up together many a night, and fallen asleep on my sofa bed, as we did on most occasions, discussing how we were going to work out our dreams for both of us.

"Antoine?"

"It didn't."

"What didn't? Didn't you tell me that you had the meeting with the buyer today?"

"Nicky, he said that Lincoln changed its mind about the deal. Maybe in a few months, he said, but as for right now, no, they aren't buying." I breathed deeply, sensing Nicky's instant disappointment. "I'm sorry. You know I wanted this for you as well as for me."

"No, suga, this wasn't about me. Don't worry, I'll get my café, bakery, pastry shop or whateva you wanna call it, but I know how much this meant to you. And I can tell how upset you are."

"Nicky, I'm just tired of trying. You know? Don't get me wrong. I have no intentions of giving up. No good artist ever gives up over a setback. But I need a vacation, I'm tired and I was thinking about just...I don't know, going somewhere."

"I think that's a marvelous idea," she said brightly. "What about that cruise I mentioned to you a while back? The one for artsy people like you? Remember I told you about that? The *Art of Life* cruise, I believe it's called."

"The Caribbean? Come on, I'm crying about not having any loot now and you're talking about me spending more. How much is this cruise?"

"Baby, baby, boy, I got it all right here; all the numbas and figures, and the travel agent who could hook you up, too." Nicky giggled sweetly. "I done told you, I lubzz ya, honey, and I watch out for my baby. See, if I didn't prefer Vanessa over Denzel, I would've been jumped your cute, Indian bones!"

I laughed heartily at that one, blushing slightly. "You're a nut!"

"No, I'm a squirrel," she purred. I could almost feel her winking over the phone.

"No, you're a trip!"

"Nope, what am I?

I laughed again, shaking my head.

"*ANTOINEEEEEEEE...*"

"All right, all right. You're a vacation!"

"Sho ya right, and I'm on my way ova. Get your credit card out and pull out your suitcases. Your boat is waiting for you, Captain. Buh bye."

I hung up the phone, trippin' as I heard the theme song to *Titanic* buzzing around in my head. I said aloud to myself with a laugh, "I just hope my boat has a much safer sail."

I have to admit I was excited. My cruise was a Holland America theme cruise nicknamed: The Art of Life. Six days and five nights of pure excitement at a bargain price. When Nicky says she's gonna hook a brotha up, she ain't kidding! I felt totally relaxed as I got off of my flight in Fort Lauderdale. This was one of the first spring cruises leaving from the Florida docks, and I was really lucky to have gotten a ticket.

I had packed a little heavier than normal. Really, my preference in clothing stayed at jeans and tee shirts, but I didn't know what kind of people would be on this cruise, and I didn't want to appear too out there. I had a small, private room, second- class and not overly ritzy, but good enough. Anything was better than sharing. Being an only child, I had never been used to having to share anything, let alone my space.

I moaned as the hot water washed over me in my shower, thinking about how good it felt. I'd have to thank Nicky and do something really nice for her when I got back to Manhattan. She always had all the answers. That's not to say that a week away was always needed. But it sure as hell made everything, every problem and worry momentarily fade. I dressed carefully for dinner. I donned a dark green pair of slacks and a beige silk shirt. Instead of pulling my hair back in my traditional ponytail, I decided to let it hang and be a black Fabio for the night. I brushed it until it gleamed and shined like black velvet. My mother had never cut the length of my hair when I was growing up, except for an occasional trim. I did cut it once when I was in art school, at the request of an old girlfriend who was into the fade thing. My mother was so horrified when she saw it and me that I never tried that again. I had always embraced both my heritages, never feeling that I had to choose one over the other. I was simply me, and that was good enough.

I stood for a moment at the dining room door entrance, feeling suddenly a bit awkward. Going solo had never really bothered me, but for some reason, as I looked around at the couples and groups smiling and laughing in front of me in the dining hall, I felt like the teenage boy I had been back in high school who didn't have a date for the dance. Oh, I had definitely gotten better in the looks department since then. I kept in tiptop shape body-wise; working out a couple of times a week if I could swing it. I had also lost the braces and replaced the thick-rimmed glasses with contacts. But I still felt somewhat the geek at times. I finally made my way slowly into the room, exhaling and trying to get up the nerve to actually do something with myself. I saw an attendant walking toward me and was just about to ask her where I could sit, or rather if there were assigned seating. Shoot, I didn't know anything about cruises, or how things went. I waited patiently as she made her rounds, knowing she would soon get to me.

"Lawd! I tell you I haven't seen so much white since *Snow White and the Seven Dwarfs* hit the theater." I looked around to see who was talking to me, when suddenly I heard... "We must be the only black folk up in here, dang!"

I found my eyes glued to a golden goddess with big huge almond-shaped eyes and shoulder-length light brown hair with golden highlights. She had tiny kiss-me lips, the bottom lip protruding in a cute pout. I was gawking like a thirteen-year-old, unable to close my mouth.

"Well?" she said, fanning a hand over my face as if to wake me from my daze. "Are we going to have dinner together or not?"

CHAPTER *Three*

Roxy

The more I fanned his face, the more he gawked at me. I wanted to laugh but I was too hungry to muster up the strength, so instead I gripped my newfound friend's hand and guided him into the dining room. I nodded and smiled, and secretly fawned over some of the most prolific retro artists in the industry. Already, I felt my engine running over with excitement at the opportunity before me.

Right now, however, I was more excited about the food that would soon be before me. "Ooh," I cooed, eyeing a long table full to the edges with mouth-watering treats. The table was laden with various seafood, salads, vegetables, breads, pasta, sweets, just about anything you could conjure up. And in my big eyes, that entire table was *mine*. "Come on," I said, continuing to drag an extra body behind me. Finally making my way into the line, I stopped, smiling and satisfied.

"So," I said, whipping around to come face-to-face with my extra weight, "my name is Roxy Winters, and you are?"

I watched the guy, about my age, trying to get his bearings. I was tickled. He was attracted to me. Unlike most men I have been in contact with, they knew whatever they said was golden, so they never had to act shy or care about being turned down. When you turn tricks, you do all kinds of 'em. When the line moved, I moved, but my focus never left the stranger's face, noticing his coal black eyes widen, his pupils dilate. He ran a hand through his silky black hair. My sight followed his hand, watching his fingers get lost in the silky cover of hair that lay upon and down the shoulders of this man. He was definitely different, I thought to myself, totally not the type who would go cruising one night to find a trick to entertain. This guy looked like he was in the right environment, an art cruise that is, but he looked almost wholesome. Well, maybe wholesome wasn't the right word for a guy as cute and fine as he was, but compared to me, um…

After much time and preparation, he finally answered my question. "I'm Antoine Billups." He raised his hand for me to take, and I did, pulling him along the line.

"Well, Mister Billups,." I said with a smile, slipping my arm around his. "It's a pleasure to meet you."

Antoine found his voice, and replied, "Same here." He bit his lip nervously. "I was hoping I wouldn't have to eat alone."

"Well, now you don't. I'm here!" I announced with glee.

"True."

He looked pleased. I gave his arm a friendly squeeze and said, "Let's get some grub and find us a table before they think we're the hired help and make us start bussing tables."

In the mere second it took me to reach for a plate, I had sized up Antoine Billups, from head to toe, to boxers or briefs, to left or right side of the bed, to doing it on top or on the bottom. It was a wretched gift I learned from back in the day, something that popped up when it felt the need, and looking at Antoine, it felt the need.

I guess my enthusiasm got the best of Antoine because he began piling up his plate, matching me spoon for spoon with crab imperial, pasta salad, and homemade rolls. By the time we scurried off to a table and sat down, we were both laughing, trying to figure out who had the largest plate. I did.

"Wow," he said, "are you going to eat all that? I mean, you're a little thing."

"Hey, good things come in small packages, and this here package," I said, pointing at my stomach, "is about to be *very* happy and stuffed." I watched Antoine stare at me in disbelief, but to prove my point, I snatched up a jumbo shrimp from my plate and dipped it into sauce before devouring it, sighing. "Mmm," I moaned, my eyes fluttering closed, "so good." When my eyes opened back up, Antoine was staring at me with his black eyes, and I blushed, even though it wasn't of my nature to do so. Playfully, I looked toward his plate and smirked, "What, no shrimp?" Picking one up from my plate and dipping it, I hoisted the shrimp to Antoine's lips. "Taste it," I said in a hushed voice, "I swear it's almost like an orgasm in your mouth."

Antoine choked on nothing. His eyes widened, his mouth gaped open, and his skin reddened. Sometimes I couldn't trust the things that came from my mouth. This was no exception. I chuckled, shrimp still in air. "Taste it," I repeated. Antoine glanced at me; eyebrow cocked as he leaned toward me, across the small table and opened his mouth to take the shrimp. I could see the smile forming before he finished chewing.

"See." I laughed. "That's the face of pure pleasure." Before he could respond, I winked at him, adding, "So tell me about you, Antoine. Where ya from, where ya work, any and everything."

Antoine grinned. "You are a very…vocal person."

"Hush and just answer my questions." With my mouth happily chewing, I listened intently to Antoine speak.

"Nothing much to say," he began. "I'm an artist from New York."

New York, hmmm. And as cute as he was? Probably had a million women jockeying for his attention.

"Get out!" I said. "I'm from New York, too. Well, Baltimore, but I live in New York now."

"Small world."

"Very." I dipped into my pasta salad as Antoine added, "My mom and dad are still in New York, and my dad is a minister."

"Preacher?" I swallowed the salad. "So, you're really religious, huh?" *No Antoine for me*, I thought, but I kicked myself for the thought.

Antoine chuckled, his full mouth showing a glistening set of teeth.

"Yes, and no," he replied. "I don't let it consume me, you know?"

I nodded, drinking from my wine glass. Talking to Antoine, I felt this oddness surround me. Since Thomas' death, this feeling of hatred rose from me, causing me to keep men at a distance, not even achieving a normal dialogue with one, unless it was school- or work-related. Yet here I was, ears opened, talking to Antoine.

By the time our plates were clean, I knew just about everything about Antoine–from his Baptist upbringing to his strict yet loving father who was a Baptist minister to his Cherokee Indian mother, who bestowed him with the hair and eyes and lashes and the smile, which right now was gleaming directly at me. All he knew about me? My name and that I was at NYU and about to work at a hip art gallery. After hearing about his father and his Baptist upbringing, the last thing I wanted to say was, "Oh, funny you should be a Christian, because I had men screaming the Lord's name in vain every chance I got! So I guess we have something in common, huh?"

We sat for a moment, sipping our drinks, me a white wine, and Antoine a mineral water. Our quiet time was interrupted by a lovely statuesque sistah who approached the table. "Hi," she said, smiling as she motioned her long, thin braids over her shoulder. "I was going to come over here earlier to introduce myself, but you two appeared to be having too much fun." I gave Antoine a sheepish grin. "There aren't too many of us here, and I wanted to give you all a holler before I retired for the evening. My name is Dyeese Tolom."

My eyes instantly popped open and I raised my hand to shake hers. "Wow," I gushed, "your piece, *Travesty in Black* is so unbelievably dope." Dyeese smiled. "Oh, this is my friend, Antoine Billups," I added, watching the two shake hands. Antoine gave me a smile and an odd look, but my attention was given back to Dyeese.

I felt my heart pumping quickly being in Dyeese's presence. I had seen her work in a small gallery in Baltimore before leaving for New York, and fell in love with it. With her right here before me, I saw the opportunity to talk her brains out. "Umm, are you really tired?" I asked Dyeese, giving Antoine the eye as he chuckled.

"Not really," Dyeese answered. "I'll probably walk the deck and mill around until I get sleepy."

"Would you like some company?"

"Would love it." That's all I needed to hear. I jumped up from my seat, drinking the last of my wine before turning to Antoine.

"Thanks for allowing me to drag you to dinner. Question, do you work out?"

He nodded in the affirmative. "A couple of times a week, at least I try to."

"Good! I heard the ship has a nice gym on the lower level, and I can't go a day without working out. Meet me there in the morning, seven sharp, and we can work out and eat breakfast together."

I laughed outwardly and loudly as Antoine slipped a *no she ain't dictating to me* look on his face. "I'll see you tomorrow morning, Mister Billups," I added with a touch more saccharine before winking and walking away with Dyeese.

The gym was tight with a capital "Damn." The steel of the machines glistened from being buffed and polished to a high gloss. At such an early hour, I was one of four people to venture into the gym. No sign of Antoine. I briefly wondered if I had been too forward with him the night before. Not everybody found my boisterous attitude as refreshing as I did, and he looked the type to be taken aback by my panache. I slipped my gym bag and windbreaker into one of the coin-operated lockers that lined the wall, and walked toward the track, which enveloped the machines. I began warming up by doing some bends and lunges.

I spotted the upside down Antoine walking in just as I parted my legs and bent down deep in the waist. He was looking at me...okay, well not at *me*, but my ass, so technically, it was me. Admittedly, I was checking him out also. He was wearing black shorts and a black sleeveless tank. He wasn't bulky in his muscularity. His dark brown body was well-toned, lithe, almost one of a dancer. His hair was tied back with a rubber band, but I could tell that his body also inherited the same black shiny hair, as sprinkles of hair came from his partially exposed chest, and his legs and arms had the dusting of similar hair. He really was a treat to look at, and for an ol' girl who hadn't looked at the opposite sex in a while, I had second thoughts about asking him to join me this morning, or being in this provocative position. I quickly stood straight.

"Good morning," I chirped, bouncing over to him and giving him a quick hug as if we had been friends forever. Funny, it did seem like forever…had I slept a lifetime away and didn't know it?

"Good morning," he replied back, just as enthusiastically. Plopping his gym bag down beside the lockers, he asked, "So what do you want to do first?"

A devilish smirk crept along my lips as I took in his body with one appreciated swoop. "Well, I usually run a mile or two, then work on my Stairmaster for about thirty minutes and then…"

Antoine held his hands up. "Just how long do you exercise for?"

"What, didn't you say you work out?"

"Yea," he answered, laughing. "I just felt you were going to tell me that you work out on about fifteen machines, plus the running and Stairmaster."

"Well…okay, you got me. Besides, we do have that workshop this morning, but tell me something, if you weren't expecting a heavy-duty workout," I said, smirking as the answer came to mind before I finished the question, "why did you come here this morning?"

Antoine's eyes held a twinkle to them as he showed me all of his glistening whites. A blush rushed across his face, and I felt this girlish giggle that wanted to erupt from me. I had never met a guy who had that cute…freshness to him yet at the same time held a sexiness, manliness to him that made you weak in the knees. Antoine had them both in spades. His twinkling eyes, teeth- showing smile, flushed face; all of it overwhelmed me and touched me. To keep from falling into the pit of Antoine, I glanced toward the Stairmasters, and nodded my head. "How about forty-five minutes on the Stairmaster?" I asked. "That way we'll have time to eat and check out the workshop."

"I think I can handle that," he answered. He looked hopeful–hopeful for what, I didn't know, but a part of me was interested in finding out.

"So," I puffed out as I pumped my knees faster, my arms moving with opposite fervor, "you think this morning's workshop will set a flame in our hearts to tap into our painting?"

Antoine had a small trace of sweat beading along his brow, but only the soft pants that emitted from his mouth gave detection of any exhaustion. "I can't wait," he answered. "What artist *doesn't* use self-reflection to paint their masterpieces?" He inhaled from the physical exertion, breathing heavy. "Art is the very essence of the soul."

I nodded, digging the soulful vibe that permeated from Antoine. "Actually, Dyeese is the workshop facilitator. She is about the most positive sistah..." I began, the beeping sound of the Stairmaster making me stop. I hopped off the machine, wiping it down with my towel, as I continued, "She's the most positive sistah I've met in a while."

Antoine simulated my hop and wiped off his machine. "So you two connected last night?" he asked, looking down at me with those black eyes. Before I could answer, a cramping pain erupted in my right calf. The pain weakened me, and I fell forward into Antoine's arms. Softly, Antoine lowered me down onto the floor. "Where's the pain?" he asked, concern written on his face.

"My right calf," I whimpered, the pain throbbing wildly. I oohed audibly as Antoine maneuvered his hands onto my calf, firmly yet gently rubbing and massaging it. Antoine's hands on my leg sent silent yet potent streams of pleasure up through my thigh, dwelling between my legs. I leaned back, masquerading the flush of excitement with my pain. I doubt if Antoine was getting satisfaction from rubbing my leg...to him it was simply helping me to alleviate pain.

As the ache began to subside, Antoine rested his hands upon my warmed skin, raising his eyes to me. "How does that feel?" he asked.

Oh…yea…the feelings weren't coming just from me. Antoine couldn't hold a secret under tight lock and key, especially if it happened to pass by his eyes. They told everything, and I could feel his interest in me resonating in them.

"Uh-huh." I nodded, bending my leg at the knee, watching his hands slip from my leg. In an instant, Antoine was up from the floor, helping me to my feet. "Lord only knows what would have happen to me if I had ran first," I said chuckling, trying to lighten the mood. Antoine smiled slightly, but didn't laugh. "Maybe we should have warmed up first."

"True, but anyhow, you're my hero," I crooned, bowing to Antoine.

"Just doing what any man would do for a lady in distress."

"You're a sweet one." I latched my arm with his. "Support an ol' sistah and join me for breakfast and learning to paint our lives."

With his signature grin, Antoine and I slowly went to retrieve our bags and head to breakfast.

"That thong tha-thong thong thong!"

"No you didn't bring back that song!" I screamed. "Years later and Sisqo still thumping a summer!" Dyeese and I were in the ladies' room, primping in our bathing suits. After our walking of the deck and sistah talk, she and I became fast friends, which got even faster and friendlier after Antoine and I took in her *Painting Your Life* seminar that morning. I was on Cloud Nine, wanting desperately to be in front of an easel, brush poised to create a work of wonderful art.

"You are really pulling out all the stops, huh?" Dyeese asked as she played with her orange two-piece, making sure the tennis bra-like top kept her full breasts in.

"What you mean?" I asked, twisting and pinning my hair up on top of my head.

"Girl, please! Antoine!"

I was never one to shy away from my body. I was blessed by good genes and exercise dedication, and believed in fully flaunting what I knew I had. That's why I stood there, checking the spaghetti straps of my white, two-piece *thong* bikini, making sure the small patches that were supposed to hold my breasts were strategically hiding my more aroused members. I turned to Dyeese, grabbing my sheer white sarong and wrapping it around my waist. "What about Antoine?" I asked, checking out my fully exposed butt. It had just the right amount of firmness and wobbliest.

"It's like so obvious that he has a crush on you…and maybe you on him?" Dyeese said, staring intently at me.

"Naw, it ain't even like that." I laughed, shaking my head no. "I met him last night, and he's my cruise buddy."

"Mmm-hmm, and it doesn't matter that he will drool or blush until he catches on fire when he sees you in this?"

"Dyeese," I said, slyly, "one thing you need to know about me…I do nothing for anyone, but myself. If Antoine gets a rise, well then that's on him. I brought this baby along before I even knew who Antoine Billups was. Sistahgirl is about to catch herself an Island man, so back up now!"

"Gon', Miss Thang!" Dyeese laughed as we both sauntered out of the bathroom that led us out onto the beach. For the afternoon, the cruise ship docked into St. Thomas, allowing us to catch sight of the beauty of the area. Dyeese, Antoine and I had already spent time at the Main Duty-Free Shopping Zone, a place that housed shopping of variable tastes. I had purchased a couple of tourist items for sis and myself like tee shirts, key chains, postcards, and local music. Now, we all were ready to catch some rays and water before we located back onto the ship for the next voyage.

My eyes found Antoine at the edge of the water, kicking along the sand. His body was clothed in black, baggy swim trunks, but his chest was out for all to see, and I did see it, watching the sun gleam off the silky chest hairs. The closer we got to him, the more silent I tried to become, the more Dyeese attempted for Antoine to turn and spot us. By the time he did turn, we were but ten feet away from him, and the look on his face made me blush instantly. Dyeese smirked.

"You don't care, my ass," she whispered under her breath.

Antoine didn't speak, just glanced at me. Inwardly I laughed at myself, seeing the oxymoron of having *me* be in anything white, and then to have the purity cloaked within a white string thong bikini. God himself should have come down and insisted I dye the suit fiery red like the hot lil' tart I used to be.

Why was I feeling so awkward? I thought to myself. Hell, I wore a lot less than this out in California, and Antoine was just a man. To fight the awkwardness, I stripped off the sarong and jaunted up to the water, kicking it toward Dyeese and Antoine. I tried to pretend that I didn't feel Antoine's watchful eyes on my bare backside or that I didn't feel a slight tremor thinking about what he might be thinking with me dressed like this.

Eventually, the tension in the air lightened and floated off into the blue skies. Instead, a playful banter between the three of us ensued in which we water-fought and swam in the azure blue waters. After just one full day of the cruise, I felt like a different woman. I still had my emotional baggage, and would probably have it until I died, but I forgot about all that and let the new me rise up. It felt good to be her, made me want to be her.

My mind was muddled with these thoughts, making it easy for Dyeese and Antoine to attack me and push me under the water. After an hour of taking in too much water, I swam back to shore, crawling to my sarong that still laid upon the golden sand. By now, my hair had fallen from my barrette, so I unhooked the it, allowing my wet curly hair to drape around my shoulders. I leaned back, resting onto my hands, and closed my eyes. I could hear people around me, laughing and talking. I could feel the sun against my golden skin, changing my color. I could feel this glow that rested in my belly, moving upward.

When the glow *kissed* my lips, I rocked my head back and shook my wet hair. Slowly I opened my eyes and found Antoine coming out of the water, his eyes glued to me. He had this look upon his face. I couldn't put my finger on it, but the look made me nervous, made me frightful because it looked like something I wasn't remotely able to conceive or give back.

In a flash, the look was gone, replaced by a soft one. I could feel the struggle on his face as he walked up to me, squatting down beside me. "You know," he began, his voice almost a quiver, "you need to be painted."

"What?" I asked, laughing.

"I was just looking at you now…you had this look on your face."

"What kind of look?" I asked, eyes wide, never knowing that others could detect my thoughts.

"You looked really happy, blissfully so. Shone right through your skin."

I fought to hide it, but couldn't. I licked my lips. "Believe it or not, Mister Billups, I feel kinda happy right now." Our eyes smiled into each other's. I warmed inside feeling like an orchestra was about to play some corny tune to cement this sentimental moment.

"Well, Miss Winters," Antoine said in a soft voice, "you need to hold on to that happiness. It looks good on you."

CHAPTER *Four*

ANTOINE

She's looking at me, and she's laughing at me. I know she is.

I felt tiny prickles of nervousness raining down my back as I applied strong intense strokes to my canvas, trying not to notice Roxy's glance, but it was hard. Not only was Roxy watching me paint, a whole group of ten other artists were watching me. I was in no way unconfident about my work, but I was used to working alone, not to an audience. This was an exercise in which we were to share some of our techniques with each other. Jeremy Guy, the art director of the cruise, just so happened to pick yours truly to be first.

We were on our fifth day of our cruise, all of us having learned a lot, and shared even more. This was more of a fun type of trip than what I had expected. And when I was able to keep my senses around a certain lady, and not seem like a complete idiot, I was doing all right.

"Notice the heaviness of his strokes and the intensity of his movements, ladies and gentlemen. The passion in his art, I love it!" Jeremy sung in an opera-like tone. The sounds of feminine giggles floated through the air.

I have got to finish this up and sit my ass down, I thought to myself.

I quickly finished up my sunset, eager to give some other poor fool a chance to be a spectacle. I breathed deeply in relief when Jeremy called up Samantha Lox, who was all too thrilled to show off her talent.

"Now Samantha is going to show us how to raise a mountain before Antoine's sunset, without diminishing its glow. I've seen and I'm sure most of you have also seen Ms. Lox's work. What I've been most impressed with is the bumpy quality that she is able to create on a flat surface," Jeremy announced.

I was settling down comfortably in my chair, when Roxy, who was seated behind me, whispered teasingly, "We loved the heaviness of your strokes and the intensity of your movements, Antoine."

Looking back at her, she gave me a cute wink, with Dyeese, echoing her with a wink of her own. Then both of them burst out in giggles again.

"Ladies, excuse me, but would you please focus on what we are doing here!" Jeremy exclaimed in a heated breath.

I smiled a little, watching him. If nobody else was into his little art lesson, he sure was.

After the group was dismissed, I headed toward the bar room, thinking I would have a cranberry juice and maybe lax out a bit before my dinner meeting with Samantha Lox. It was amazing that I would meet her on this cruise. Samantha Lox was one of the most well-known artists in New York. And I had been trying to get her attention and get some of my pieces submitted to her gallery, where she catered to up-and-rising artists like myself. After the letdown with Lincoln Galleries, this was a chance of a lifetime to get to work with her. So when she mentioned dinner, I jumped at the invite.

I settled down, ordered my juice and had just taken my first swallow when Roxy came bouncing in and plopped down on the stool beside me. "Sure, Mister Billups, you can buy me a drink. I'll have an umm…white zinfandel," she ordered, as the bartender nodded in her direction. "Hi!" she said beaming.

"Hi." I laughed.

"What are you laughing at?" she quizzed, punching me lightly on the arm.

"Well, somehow it always seems like you are just coming in from playing hopscotch or something. You're just full of life, aren't you?"

"Chile…" Roxy took a sip of her white wine. "It's better than being an old dead head, don't ya think? I mean I've had my ups and downs, but here we are on this beautiful boat, breathing fresh air and getting to meet new people who love what we love. So I can't help but feel like I'm floating on air. I'm having so much fun, aren't you?"

"Yeah, I am," I admitted. *Especially with you here.*

Roxy looked at me, as if she could read my mind. Or maybe she could read my face. I've never been a good one for hiding what I feel.

"You look so odd."

"Well, thanks!" The last thing I needed was for another woman to think I was *odd.* Odd was a description used for me back in my teenage years. Hmm. "Geez," I whispered under my breath.

"No, Antoine, not like that, I mean in a good way. I would kill for your hair and eyelashes; most women would. You said the other day that you didn't have a girlfriend, but do you date a lot? And look at you blushing!"

This girl was killing me. I couldn't help but wonder if she was interested, even though up until now it hadn't seemed like she was. Her comments about my appearance were starting to give me hope.

I looked at her and tried my best not to smile. "Now how do you figure I could blush? I'm not blushing, it's just...you talk a lot, do you know that?"

"Yada, yada, yada!" she spat. "Now answer me. Do you date? What kind of girls do you like?"

"Actually, I don't date much. And the last time I had a girlfriend was two years ago back when I was in art school. Since then my work has been my lady."

"So," Roxy's eyebrows rose naughtily, "what do you do when you get horny? Paint?"

I was sucking on an ice chip that I almost choked on, especially when I looked in her face and saw her tiny smile and the twinkle in her eye.

"You like picking on me, don't you?" I shook my head in amazement. I felt my groin tightening all of a sudden.

"No, I'm not picking. I like seeing what people are about, and you're so interesting. I've never met a brotha like you."

We were both quiet for a while, enjoying our drinks, a comfortable quiet though. I looked over at Roxy again. She smiled prettily. My groin tightened even more. I silently prayed she would get up before I did.

"Well, I guess I'm go get ready for dinner. Are you going to be in the dining room tonight? You can eat with Dyeese and me."

"Thanks, but I have plans. Actually I'm trying to work out a deal with Samantha Lox, maybe to get some of my pieces in her gallery."

"Ahh…"

Was that jealousy I saw on her face? "Well, do what you want. If you change your mind and want to sit with us sistahs, you know it will be cool."

I paid for our drinks and noticed Roxy exiting through the door. "Actually I do paint."

"Excuse me?" she asked, turning sideways to look back at me.

"You asked what I did when I get…you know, horny… I paint."

Her eyes met mine, as we stood there looking at each other. "I'll remember that, Mister Billups."

Samantha was an attractive lady, in her thirties. Blonde hair, gray eyes, she reminded me a little of Michelle Pfeiffer. And oddly, she didn't look like an artist at all. But in this case, looks were deceiving. There wasn't an art student in all of Manhattan who hadn't heard of the one and only Ms. Samantha Lox.

We talked as we ate dinner, discussing everything from art to politics. She seemed genuinely interested in me.

"Well, Antoine, I swear, I don't know how we haven't run across each other before now," she stated in wonderment.

"Well, I've been to your galleries many times," I admitted, "and even studied some of your work back when I was in art school." I looked over to the other side of the dining room. Roxy and Dyeese were in what appeared deep conversation with two men who had joined their table. Even though I was enjoying my dinner and conversation with Samantha,

I could have kicked myself for not being able to keep my eyes off of Roxy. She had an effect on me that was uncontrollable. Just as I was peeping over to her table, she looked up and smiled at me, as if she knew I was watching her. I glanced away quickly.

"Hey there, are you still with me, handsome?"

I was glad for Samantha's awakening call. "I'm sorry, I'm sitting here dazing. What was it that you said?"

"I said, dance with me." She smiled.

"Well, I've never been much of a dancer, but I could try," I said.

"Now you're talking." Samantha winked, holding her hand out like a prima ballerina as I stood up to lead her to the dance floor.

The music was a Natalie Cole duet with her famous father, Nat King Cole. Samantha's hips swayed seductively against mine, but I hardly noticed as I kept my eyes on one specific lady. Who was dancing with one of the guys she and Dyeese were sharing dinner with. Our eyes met and held as unspoken words seemed to fly between us.

"I thought you couldn't dance," Samantha said, turning my face toward hers with her long, painted fingertips.

I laughed. "Well, with you I have a great teacher. All I have to do is follow along."

"I heard you." She winked at me, and stared appreciatively. I hardly noticed her examination of my face. I looked across the room again to find Roxy, who had settled back down at her table, locked in deep conversation. As the song ended, Samantha yawned.

"I'm so whipped; it's been a long day. Do you mind if we call it an evening?" she asked.

"No, not at all," I stammered. "Do you want me to walk you to your room?""Ohhh, you're a sweetie. Yes, please."

Samantha grabbed her purse and we headed toward the twin doors. My eyes automatically made their way over to Roxy's table.

It was empty.

"Thanks, Antoine," Samantha said. She took her shawl from my hands as we stopped in front of her cabin door.

"Anytime. I enjoyed myself. And I really hope you give me a chance to show you my work when we get back to New York."

"Sweetie, I'm a woman of my word," she said, holding her hand to her heart. "I definitely want to talk to you some more when we get back to New York."

I smiled at her, thankfully. "Great."

"So, do you want to come in for a nightcap? I have some delicious blush chilling in my little fridge."

"Do you know I have never tasted wine?"

"Get outta here! You're kidding?" she exclaimed. "Then here is your perfect opportunity."

"Actually I'm a juice man; never touch the hard stuff, probably never will." I didn't mention that even though I wasn't necessarily religious, my father had somehow drilled it into my head that liquor was the devil's fluid and would probably rot my liver and send my soul to hell.

"Well, I got *juice* for you…" I looked down at Samantha, noticing her gray eyes had turned almost to a dark dusky appearance. Oh, Oh…

"Well…" I cleared my throat. "I better get going. It's pretty late." I turned to walk away when I felt Samantha's hand on my waist.

"Antoine…"

Just as I turned back toward her, she pulled my face close. I could feel her hand running down the front of my pants, squeezing. She whispered, "Remember, we have to be good to each other. I can really help you, okay? Goodnight, handsome…"

One more night before our cruise was over, and it went by fast as lightning. Too fast, as far as I was concerned. I didn't get to spend that much time with Roxy on the last day. It seemed to me that she was somewhat avoiding me. Or, maybe she was spending all her time with that dude she was dancing with at dinner the night before. I tried not to think too much about that episode with Samantha, or her insinuations that we be good to each other. Did she really want me to give up the goods for a spot in her gallery? I wasn't sure. Maybe it was just my overactive imagination. But I knew I hadn't imagined her hand rubbing my penga.

After having had dinner with a couple of sculptor dudes from Los Angeles, I lounged out on the deck our last night. It was amazing how many new friends I had made on the trip. A lot of us had already decided that we would plan to hook up again for an *Art of Life* cruise in 2002 reunion. I had seen a little of Roxy at dinner, but she was all into her friends. She didn't even appear to look my way. It was just my luck to be feeling someone who may be a flirt but who in reality had no clue that I was even alive.

I laughed sarcastically to myself as I leaned across the ship's rail, sipping on my iced orange juice, and watching the blue waves blanketing the ocean. *Some things never change much from high school.*

"Are you sad to be going home?" a soft voice asked, creeping up behind me.

I turned around at the sound of Roxy's beautiful voice. "Very much so," I said nervously. My heart started beating fast as she came closer to stand beside me at the rail.

She closed her eyes, and I watched her. She was so beautiful. With the ocean wind blowing her light-brown hair away from her face, the beautiful heart-shaped design of it was easier to observe. And maybe it was the artist in me. I had never been able to resist beauty. But it hit me again, the feeling that I had to paint her someday.

"I feel like I have a whole new grip on what I want to do with my life now," Roxy said.

"Why is that?" I asked softly, not even trying to hide my attraction as I soaked her in with my eyes.

She laughed, but I could tell that it wasn't with humor. "Antoine, I feel old. I've done so much, and yet so little that is worthwhile in my twenty-two years. See, you're different than I am. You knew what you wanted to do from the time that you were little. And you did it, you didn't just think it, but you actually did it. I envy people who are able to know their own minds like that."

"So what do you want to do?"

"Well." She breathed, trying to sound excited. "I just received my B.A. in interior design; even got a gig back in New York for it."

"No, what do you want to do?" I insisted.

She was quiet for a moment and then this radiant look of peace came over her face. "I want to do just like you. I want to paint and I feel so free saying that."

She looked at me with watery eyes. Something was going on deep inside of her. I had no idea what it was, but it was haunting her. I could see that much.

I reached out and smoothed the golden-brown strings of hair that had blown across her eyes. Eyes that were looking into my own. Something inside me wouldn't stop, wouldn't allow the fear of rejection to get the better of me this time. My long fingers streamed down her satiny cheeks, almost as if I were drawing her, but with love. *Love.* Had that thought really come to my mind? Was I drunk on the orange juice?

I couldn't stop touching her face, her lips. Running my fingers across her lips, I suddenly felt her kissing them softly as I watched her. I finally brought my lips down to meet hers, both of us moaning against each other's mouths, deepening the kiss, our bodies straining against one another at the ship's rail. When we finally broke loose from our heated kiss, both of us were breathing deeply, trying to catch our breaths. I knew damn well that she just had to see my heart beating against my chest. Because I sure as hell could see it, and feel it, rising and falling against my cotton shirt.

"Mister Billups, I do believe that after this ship docks, I'm gonna have to look you up."

When the ship docked the following morning, it was not just the end of our *Art of Life* cruise; it was the beginning of something fresh and new, and colorful.

CHAPTER *Five*

Roxy

The morning after I landed back in good ol' New York, I woke up smiling instead of my normal nightmare of Thomas. That kiss between Antoine and me had me wanting things that the old Roxy would have laughed at. I jumped up, feeling light, quickly grabbing up the classifieds from the newspaper while I went into my small kitchen to pour a bowl of Apple Jacks. I needed a place to live–and like soon. Charlise was the best boss an employee could want. She gave me my first two weeks' pay and told me to go get a new place to live so that could be one worry out of my hair.

I had already circled six choice apartments and was about to circle my seventh when I felt a warm throb on my lips. I expected Antoine to be looking back at me, but nope, nothing. I promised myself, after the "escort" business, after Thomas, that I was going to focus on me. I couldn't allow myself to get caught up with a man anymore. Nothing good could come from them. Besides, if I happened to meet Mr. Wonderful, someone like, oh, I'd say, Antoine, he'd leave me in a hot minute if he knew how I made my living. Back before I had actually *lived.*

A part of me hoped that Antoine would lose my number and my address and wouldn't bother to look me up. But after remembering the look in his eyes, the look of his face after we kissed, I knew that he would use my information as soon as possible. And admittedly, begrudgingly so,

I wanted him to. Being the aggressive sistah that I am, I thought why not call him up and see what was going on. Almost an entire day had passed. That was enough time not to appear anxious, right?

His phone rang three times before the machine picked up. I placed my receiver back on the base. It was only eight in the morning; maybe he was painting. Antoine told me on the cruise that when he painted he turned the phone off, only answering if someone was in dire need, like for a blood transfusion, a kidney, some body part that maybe he could spare.

Before even my brain knew what it wanted to do, I showered, dressed in a pair of soccer shorts, a tee shirt and Adidas. I placed a set of clean clothes into my gym bag, along with my toiletry essentials, grabbed up my keys and things, and was out my door. Stepping from the apartment complex, I stood on the sidewalk, breathing in the already warm air of a New York June day. I dropped my bag real quick, only to pull on the ponytail atop my head to secure it more tightly. Then I snatched up my bag and almost ran down the sidewalk, wanting to reach the subway and be at Antoine's place like yesterday.

My mind was still playing tricks on me, as if it were a ball in a tennis match, telling me to go to Antoine, express to him my interest in him, see where "this" could lead. The opponent wanted me to get my ass back into my apartment, lie in the bed, and have nightmares about Thomas...to do what was garnered *normal* in my life. What would I do–pursue this fine brotha until he fell in love with me, then drop the bombshell about me being an ex-ho?

Even now I shivered, almost convulsed, as I walked...and thought of what I used to be. No matter how good I cleaned up, how good I changed my appearance, my attitude, my lifestyle, I would always be a whore.

A whore, like her; I thought, right after I bumped into a streetwalker at the corner.

"Sorry, sistah," I whispered, looking into her eyes.

I quickly turned away from her, before hearing her say, "No problem, Girl. Just watch your way from here on in."

Just watch your way from here on in, she had said. I had been watching my way, trying diligently to keep myself to myself. With one cruise, I'd destroyed that. I allowed myself to think that I, Roxy Winters, slut-tramp-harlot-theotherwoman-whore, could have someone good, when all I had ever been was so horrifically bad. I was on my way to tell Antoine that if he wanted to hook up, consider me the line to his reel 'cause we were going fishing, but sistah stopped me right in my tracks.

Her big, brown, unfocused eyes; her soft, curvy, supple body; the face of a child; the body of a vixen. I had been her then, and I was still her now. It was just that now I covered up my past to make way for a supposedly better future. I quickly walked past the woman, giving her a smile before moving toward the subway. I still felt the need to see Antoine, but now, the reasons were so different.

I was right. When Antoine didn't answer the phone, he was painting. He invited me into his apartment with a warm hug and added pang to my heart. I laughed to myself at Antoine's weak portrayal of Robin Leach as he gave me the grand tour of his humbly petite abode. "I tried calling you," I said, after I came out the bathroom, upon the conclusion of my tour.

"I was painting…had this incredible urge to do something beautiful." I glanced up, anxious, wanting to yet not wanting to see any looks in his eyes. I saw something deeply resonate there, something that had my body tingling all over, but I fought to keep it down, and down it stayed.

"Oh, umm," I began, "I was wondering if you wanted to go work out with me this morning."

My eyes took in the sight of Antoine wearing a pair of loose- fitting jeans, hung low on his hips, the tight fit of his wife-beater tee shirt, and the blood-red bandana that he wore on his head over the beautifully shining black hair that hung loosely under it. He had the aura, the personality, the soul, the spirit of an artist. Watching him watch me so intensely, I secretly wished for him to have the power to draw me into him, or to erase me out completely.

"I can do that." Antoine smiled. "I just finished the painting I was working on, so lemme toss on some gym gear, and we're outta here."

I nodded, too afraid to say anything. I sat on his sofa bed, getting up the strength to tell him "nay"or "yay." I knew right then that I must have really cared for Antoine because telling people how I felt was never a problem for me, and now I sat there, on his sofa, almost in tears because I didn't know exactly what I wanted to say…or do.

"What's wrong?"

I turned quickly, finding Antoine coming from the bathroom, dressed in shorts and a tee shirt, a worried expression on his face. He had taken off the bandana and wore his jet-black hair straight.

"You and me. We can only be friends!" I looked around, searching for the person who said that. I blurted out the comment before I could think, before I could find a better way to word it, or decide if I would say it at all. Antoine's already dark brown skin darkened even more, a light having been turned off inside of him.

"Friends?" he asked, his eyebrow rose to me.

I threw my hands to and fro as I explained to him my rationale. I lied, telling him how I had previously been in a long relationship with a man who hurt me, who left me and broke my heart. The break-up left me with a strong distaste toward men, and I was in the process of learning to love myself again. I was trying to get myself straight, and that I didn't, couldn't subject my life on another person right now…they would deserve more, hence *he*, Antoine, would deserve more than I could give right now. There were tears in my eyes, but it was the only thing from the performance that was genuine. I don't know how I had managed to care for one person in such a short amount of time, but I had…and now, I was hurting him, and that hurt me like a bitch.

"It's cool, I mean I can understand how one could want to find themselves, and I won't push you. Friends then…" he said, fixing his expression quickly, but not quick enough. It hurt to look at Antoine. His whole "huggable" demeanor changed to a *friendlier* stature and, as we left from his apartment, I could already feel the change in what had been so magical on the boat.

CHAPTER *Six*

Nicky

"Damn it!" I exclaimed to myself. I was fuming over the two hundred-dollar food bill I had just gotten for the five hundred-dollar luncheon I had catered the week before at Ingles, INC. Adding it up, I could see that I had basically been gypped. I had to pay that lazy bitch Jennie her seventy-five. That left me with…grrrr, it was too indecent even to think about!

"These little luncheon gigs are just not panning out."

"Girl, are you in here talking to yourself again?" I turned around to see Mya's smiling face.

"Hey, baby girl," I crooned. "Damn, I've missed you!"

I swiveled over, slipping my hands around Mya's slim waist, lifted her chin up to mine and brought her thick juicy lips up for a kiss. Mya flickered her hot tongue against mine, causing me to give her tight little ass a squeeze.

"Mmmm…," she moaned. "You know you need to stop. You're making a sistah's body get to humming."

"Uh-uh, I'll make it hum all right." I smirked. "And what are you doing here anyhow? Hubby finally let you out the house?"

"Hubby ain't got shit to do with this," Mya said, smiling.

I had been bumping with Mya for about six months now, regardless of the fact that Mya was married to a man. That was her biz. Frankly, I didn't and still don't believe in relationships, not gay ones, not straight ones, nada. There were very few gay men or women that I knew of who were actually able to make a committed relationship work. And Mya's so-called marriage to her husband, yet her weekly coming by to hit it with me also showed that so-called he/she marriages weren't the scream they were made out to be either.

Mya wandered purposely into my bedroom, not even looking behind her. I smiled. *Cocky bitch, she knew I'd follow her sexy ass.* I stood at the door watching as Mya slipped off her thin, short summer dress, letting it slowly slip to her feet. She was looking good. Standing braless, with her perky high tits and black thong. I stood watching for a brief moment, seeing the heat in her eyes, before walking into the room, and pulling my DMX tee shirt over my head. I was about to take off my own bra and jean shorts before something in Mya's eyes got the better of me, causing me to swiftly walk up to her and fall to my knees where her hot, swollen love was sizzling before my lips. I pulled the crouch part of her thong aside and planted my lips against her heat.

It was gonna be a hot afternoon.

I plaited my final braid, and had just showered and changed into my regs. This time my EVE tee shirt, boy boxers with baggie FUBU shorts. I took a last look in the mirror and chuckled. I mean let's face it; I was not what one would call a girly girl by any means. Maybe I wasn't the smoking cigars, flipping people the bird, dyke type of chick, but I was definitely what was considered, *soft butch.*

I was headed down the cluttered hallway to grab my mail when the double doors to my apartment building came creaking open.

"Antoine!" I screamed.

Antoine's face lit up, showing me that famous ear-to-ear smile of his. Now Antoine was my BooBoo. Not my boo. See I didn't have boos, neither male nor female, but he was my BooBoo, my baby.

"Baby, you're back!" I ran down the stairs, giving him a big squeeze.

"Yep!" he exclaimed, hugging me back. "My plane got in last night. I had to pop by and see you, sis, and grab my mail also."

Antoine had this cute laugh and voice that sounded and had always reminded me of Larenz Tate. Now Larenz Tate, he was cute. I had always said that if I had ever been into dudes I would've had to taste me something that looked like him. My BooBoo didn't look nothing like him, but he sure sounded like him. Antoine was chocolate and beautiful, but what made him unique were his features. Most of them weren't black at all; just that deep brown skin and them fat ass lips.

"What you looking at, yo?" He laughed.

"Just breathing you in and thinking about how good you look, suga. I've missed you…" I touched his cheek. Damn, I loved this boy.

"Well, I've missed you, too," he said, his eyes getting a soft look in them as he gazed into mine. I was about to give him another tight hug when I sensed someone behind him. "And…," he continued, "I have someone I want you to meet. This is Roxy. Roxy, this is my sis and best friend in the whole world, Nicky."

The short, red-boned creature smiled a toothpaste cheesy grin at me, and it hit me as soon as I saw her. She reminded me of those girls who back in high school that used to make my life a living hell. The cheerleader types that would always call me names like "dyke" and "lesbo."

"Hello, Nicky, it's so nice to meet you. Antoine has told me so much about you," she cooed.

Something was happening; I felt my fingertips tingling as my invisible claws started making their way out.

Antoine, me, and his new *friend* were sitting comfortably at my kitchen table. I stood up to get some glasses. "So, do you drink, Roxy? I know you don't, Antoine."

"And you know it," he said smiling. "Got milk?"

"Yeah, I got some milk for you." I gave my breast a lil squeeze. Miss

Girl got pretty red in the face at that. That shit made me laugh.

"You're a mess, Nicky." Antoine laughed, shaking his head. "Roxy, didn't I tell you she was a trip?"

"Yes, you did," she said. "Do you have any white wine?"

"Nope; got sum Thunderbird and grapefruit juice. That's whatcha call ghetto-mixer. I take it that's not your speed, right?" I raised my eyebrow at her.

"I've had Thunderbird before. I may surprise you. So, Nicky, Antoine says that you're a cook?"

Why was my face burning? A cook? "I ain't no fuckin' cook, girl; I'm a caterer, and pastry chef; a *chef!* You understand?"

"Ah, okay."

The skinny bitch was trying to be cute. I hated when someone called me a cook. I had been to two different schools, one in Staten Island and one in New Jersey, mastering the art of cuisine. The last thing I would call myself is a damn cook!

"Well anyway, I'll take some of that ghetto-mixer," she quirked, with this amused look on her face.

After we got settled with our drinks and Antoine's milk, Miss Thang proceeded to tell me more about her. How she and Antoine had been working out and had met on the cruise and how they were friends. This bugged me the fuck out, like how she could sit here and tell me she was all friendly with my best friend, as if she were introducing him to me.

"So what, you two were kickin' it on the love boat, huh?"

Antoine looked at me with a *cut it out* stare. I shrugged and smiled innocently.

"The love boat, now wouldn't that have been fun," Roxy said animatedly. "Really, we are just friends. I just looked him up when we got back here, and wanted to know if he wanted to go work out."

"Well, you just got back yesterday. Didn't waste any time, did you, friend?"

Antoine broke in, changing the subject. "So what have you been up to, Nicky?"

"Well, working as always, and oh! You know you missed Dr. Dre at Jays the other night, boy! He was getting off. If I was ever into dudes, I'd have to do him!"

"Ever into dudes?" Roxy asked.

Damn, I had forgot that Miss Thang was sitting there.

"Nuttin, honey, just a figure of speech." I cheesed a smile.

The last thing I was going to do was tell some chick like her my business. I was just so used to being open and free with Antoine.

"Well, Antoine, I'm still feeling a bit jet lag, you know from the cruise and all. I'm gonna go catch my train, okay?" Roxy announced.

"Listen, why don't you let me call you a cab?"

I finished off the last sip of my Thunderbird, watching their exchange. Antoine was digging this girl, and there was something about her that I wasn't digging, at all...

CHAPTER *Seven*

Roxy

It took five "nos" to get Antoine to let me go home by myself. He offered to take me home personally, offered to call me a cab, but I glanced at the way Nicky was holding his arm, as if for dear life, and thought better of it. Sistahgirl looked like she was bench-pressing cars on her days off, and I didn't want to come between what was obviously a tight and loving friendship, or was it more than friendship? And if it was, why should I have even cared about that? Especially after my damn decision to keep Antoine and me strictly friends.

My mind battled back and forth, in and out of thoughts as I walked the block to the subway. But, instead of going underground, I crossed the street to the corner store, using the phone outside of it to call me a cab. I needed silent time to think on my way home, not the crowded, confined spot of a New York train.

Comfortable in the back seat of a cab that smelled remotely of rice and some foreign, fleshy meat, I tried not to gag. I closed my eyes and my mind to the cab and focused on why I had decided to nix a relationship or anything closely resembling a relationship with Antoine. I didn't even want to admit it, but the quiet yet deeply spoken and extremely attractive brotha had gotten to me on the cruise. So much so that not even a day had passed before he was monopolizing my thoughts. I kept picturing that perfect moment; us out on the ship's deck, Antoine's fingers on my hair, then my lips. I kissed them, his fingers that is, before he kissed me, and I kissed him, and we kissed each other, and the sparks that flew from that one kiss were more than I had ever experienced in my short, "experienced" life. Mr. Billups and his long, drawn-out kisses were definitely A+ material. But that was not important now; what was necessary was getting home and getting packed for my trip to Baltimore and Artscape.

Baltimore, Maryland...

I thought maybe the artistic ambience of Artscape and the gathering of sistahfriends–Dyeese, my sister Dee and Charlise–would put me in a happier frame of mind, but it didn't. I was getting better though. I was more adjusted to my new relationship with Antoine. After all, this past week, we had spent time together, and not once did he make me feel bad about my decision. I was beginning to enjoy the mere camaraderie of my time with Antoine, and I was anxious to get back to New York to hang out with him.

"Dyeese, Dyeese, I simply love this painting!" Deandra cooed, eyeing the framed portrait of a young black girl, sitting upon a grassy hill, and the visions—visually created–that flowed through her mind: a vile of crack, boys doing drugs, a girl selling herself as the last visualized thought from her mind was that of a young lady–an older version of herself—with a paintbrush in hand poised toward an easel. The portrait signified overcoming your adversities, the problems that already existed to take you down. As soon as Deandra saw it at Artscape, she pouted and whined about *needing* to have it don a wall of her brownstone.

Now it leaned along its new home, a bare white wall in Dee's brownstone. "Thanks, Deandra," Dyeese smiled, blushing, "I painted that about two years ago; it took me a while to bring it out."

We all sat in Dee's living room. Having spent the entire day at Artscape, buying art, schmoozing with the who's who and eating an eclectic array of food served there, we all came back to Dee's place to chill, each of us sipping on a glass of white wine.

"Why did it take you so long?" Charlise asked. "It's a beautiful piece."

"Because that little girl is me," Dyeese answered simply. "As a kid, every corner I turned, every door that didn't lead to my home was infested with devices that could keep me from realizing my dreams. I've always wanted to paint and prayed that I would live long enough to do that. When I painted that," she continued, pointing to the painting, "I was in a very joyful frame of mind, grateful to God for allowing me to reach that point. Took a while for me to want to share that particular part of my life with the world."

"I've always wanted to paint, too," I whispered, not knowing why I said that, but feeling the need to have my voice heard.

"Your sister is an excellent painter," Charlise praised. "I was surprised when she came to my gallery with her degree in interior design, especially after I saw her portfolio."

Dee glanced at me, looking proud. "After we get the new bookstore and café built, I'll have to make sure Miss Roxanne Josephine Winters is well-known for her art and not just her ability to design and beautify a room."

"Didn't I tell you she was a godsend, Dee?" I asked, smiling at the girls.

"You surely did. And I'm just grateful that someone sees your talents, baby sister, besides me that is. You may have always been a dramaful, but your artistic flair has always been on point."

"Oh, so ol' girl is a drama queen extraordinaire, huh?" Dyeese asked, playfully kicking at me.

"You don't know the half of it," Dee snickered.

"Well," Dyeese responded, hopping up from the sofa to lean toward the loveseat, where Dee was sitting. "Did she tell you about the fine ass man she met on the cruise?"

I also sat up and wanted to leap over and snatch Dyeese out of the room. I hadn't talked to Dee about Antoine. Hell, I had never talked to my sister about any men in my life. I had no idea how to go about doing that with her. And with my feelings already haywire regarding him, I thought best to keep things to myself. I had no choice but to 'fess up now.

"Uh, no," Dee said, eyeing me suspiciously. "My sister likes keeping me in the dark when it comes to matters of the heart."

"I'm your boss, and you didn't even tell me!" Charlise cried in mock exasperation, resulting in laughter from us all.

"It's nothing to tell, guys," I said. "We met on the cruise, he lives in New York also, but that's it. We've been talking and hanging out a little this past week, but we're solely friends, nothing more."

Dyeese's glance said she didn't buy it; Charlise looked disappointed that nothing more had transpired between Antoine and myself; but Dee...well, she had sisterly intuition, and that meant she would be re-asking questions pertaining to Antoine...and would want more elaborate answers then as well.

I couldn't sleep. It was still early, just a little after midnight, but Dee's place was silent. Charlise and Dyeese had already left, needing their sleep before the final day of Artscape. Dee was used to going to bed early, so she could rise even earlier. She and her soon-to-be hubby, Stephen, had been in bed since eleven. Without thinking, I jumped up and went to retrieve the cordless phone in the living room. I dialed Antoine's phone. It rang three times before the answering machine picked up. I sighed, placing the receiver back onto the base. Ashamed, I felt a pang of jealousy pulsate along with my heartbeat. Where *was* he at this time of night? Was he on a date? With his girl, Nicky? Or maybe he was home, painting feverishly. Either way, I couldn't be upset...he probably would have jumped at the chance to try and do a lil' sumthin' with me, but I pushed him away. Probably into the arms of another woman.

I walked around the downstairs of Dee's brownstone before opening the door and looking across the street to Joop's brownstone. I felt the urge to talk, and if Shameika were there, then I knew I could release everything inside of me to her. She was the type of person who would understand. Someone who went through hell herself to finally make her life right. There was no truck or motorcycle out front and all lights were out, so that nixed my plan to trot over in my pajamas. Instead I sat out on the stoop, letting the cool summer air infiltrate across my skin and face.

"Got some room on that stoop for me?" I nodded yes, as Dee stepped out and sat on the stoop, snuggling up beside me. "It's a little cool out here," she added.

"Yea."

"What's wrong, sis?" Dee asked, leaning her head on my shoulder. My eyes moved downward, connecting with her upward glance at me. We both smiled. "Is it about this new guy?"

"Dee," I whispered, "when was the last time I came to you, gushing about some guy or crying about him dumping me?"

"Never."

"You're exactly right; never. Now you wanna know why that is?"

Dee frowned, anticipating my self-loathing. "Why?" she answered.

"Because I was too busy fucking every Tom, Dick and Harry to be happy about being with any of them. I have no clue about what a real relationship is like, and with my past, I'll never know."

"What does your past have to do with you finding and meeting someone now?" Dee asked, leaning up from me to place her arm around me.

"Are you serious?" I laughed. "What *real* man will want to build a life with a girl who probably fucked every man in his family?"

"Stop saying fuck." Deandra frowned. "That's so vulgar."

"Sis, *I'm* vulgar, come on. I made a living out of being as vulgar as possible to as many men as I could. It's what I do. It's what I'm good at. I don't think I can learn to be anything but that."

"Not true," Deandra said, anger in her voice. "You went to New York and got your degree, Rox. You've been trying to get your life back on track, and you've done that, right?"

"But that..."

"But nothing, damn it." My eyes widened. Deandra rarely cursed, and "damn it" to Deandra was like me saying "fuck." "You messed up, yes. In your own words, you fucked up royally, but don't let that dictate how you live the rest of your life."

I sat silently as I rocked slowly back and forth, Deandra joining me. "This guy must be awful special if he has you this confused," Deandra added.

"Dee, I just met him. It was only a cruise. We didn't even have sex."

"That's going to be your biggest obstacle."

"What?"

"To not associate sex with love in a relationship. I mean yes, sex is great, but that real love, those deeper feelings? They come from the heart, from finding someone that shares your interests, makes you laugh, holds you when you cry, encourages you when you feel discouraged. You have a beautiful heart, Roxy. Don't let it run second place to what you think is more important."

"By the time I learn how to switch all these wires in my head, I'll be too old to be loved by anyone," I whispered, tearing up. "Antoine wouldn't want me anyway."

"So that's his name?" I sighed, pissed that I let his name slip out into this conversation. I nodded. "You know, you'd be surprised as to how the heart, how love, can make you understand things, forgive things that most would frown down upon."

"What are you saying?" I asked, looking at her.

"I'm saying, don't give up on Antoine. Or anyone else for that matter. You're a beautiful woman and a good person, with a good heart. Any man, including Antoine, would be lucky to have you in their life."

I looked away from Deandra, quickly and roughly wiping the tears from my face. I wasn't at her level of confidence in my goodness, in me having a good heart, in someone being lucky to have me in his life. However, it was a nice dream.

CHAPTER *Eight*

ANTOINE

The sounds of clapping, praising and singing filled Mount Phillips Baptist Temple with the Rev. Charles John Billups leading in worship. I struggled not to nod off. Not that my dad was a boring preacher; I just hadn't gotten any sleep the night before.

As I started zoning out again, I felt a sharp jab in my side. I looked up to my mom's stern reprimand.

"Don't you dare go to sleep, Antoine Billups," she whispered. "You know better than that!"

"I'm sorry," I mouthed back silently. Something told me I should have left that painting alone and got some sleep, but when the inspiration hit me, I was one who always had to let it flow. My mom had called me earlier in the day to ask me to be at church, complaining that I hardly ever showed my face anymore. And she was right in a way, but it wasn't that I was no longer a believer; I just didn't feel and had never felt that church attendance was paramount to my salvation. For as much as I loved and respected my father, I loved and respected him even more because of his never pushing me as far as the faith was concerned. I remembered once when we talked about it, and he mentioned my dwindling attendance record. It took only one time of explaining my position for the sincere hug and "you do what's best for you, son," to be said.

I have always felt that we all have a calling in life. Some people may be called to preach and others to teach. Others are blessed to sing, act, or maybe practice law. But in my case, I felt my calling was to paint. So while others may feel closer to God while singing at Mount Phillips, I feel closer to nature itself, and whatever form He presents Himself when I am painting nature, some of His creation, be it human or not. To be real about it, art was my religion, my worship.

After the service, I smiled at the familiar hellos and *oh my, it's been so long, Antoine* remarks I received. I was happy when my parents and I were finally home, downing the delicious curry chicken and rice lunch my mom had prepared. Of course, they wanted to know everything that I had been up to, especially about my cruise.

"I have always wanted to go on a cruise." My mother sighed, looking at my father as if hinting. "I guess someday, huh, Chuck?"

"You never know," my dad said, winking at me. If I knew my dad, he would be going online that night to look up information to fulfill my mother's dream. He spoiled her like a queen, which was fine by me. She was my queen.

"So was it romantic, dear? You know the eyes meeting across the room type of romantic?"

"It was an art cruise, Ma." I laughed.

"And? What does that have to do with it? Are you trying to tell me there were no lovely ladies on that cruise that noticed my handsome son?" she asked indignantly.

"I'm just saying that was not the point of the trip. It was to learn and enjoy studying the work of other artists. I met a lot of people though, male and female." I was not about to mention Roxy; after all, she only wanted to be friends, so what was there really to say?

"Hmm..." My mom started picking up the dirty lunch dishes. "I think it's just ridiculous. You need a woman, Antoine. God didn't intend for man to be alone. He says you need a woman as a helper, a complement of you."

I stood up to help her, knowing that her sermon was coming, the I think you need a woman, you are the only child we got and we want some grandkids, etc, etc, etc. My father sipped quietly on his cup of coffee as my mother rambled on. We both looked at each other and smiled wistfully—a smile that only another man would understand.

"Leave the boy alone," my father finally said. "He's only twenty-five. He has a long time to worry about the responsibility of marriage and a family."

"Well, twenty-five is not too young to get married. If he waits around, he's gonna end up doing too much shopping and you never know what diseases you'll pick up with these fast-tail girls out here nowadays."

Did we need a subject change or what?

"Y'all want cake?" she asked suddenly.

Thank God, she changed the subject.

I shook my head in the negative, hoping that my father would follow suit. He didn't. I was worried about him; he had been dealing with heart problems for the past year and needed to drop the weight. But how do you tell a fifty-year-old man that he needs to do anything, when it has been bred into him the words, *ain't nuttin' wrong with a lil' excess and spare tire.*

I hung around for a couple more hours, but needed to get back to Manhattan by six p.m., the time that Samantha Lox asked me to call her. She was my next big hope in getting my Cherokee line out, and I didn't want to blow it. I kissed my mom and headed out the door, followed out by my father.

"Listen, Antoine," he said on the front porch. "I didn't want to say anything around your mother, but I'm going to need some maintenance work done on this old heart of mine."

"Maintenance work?"

"Oh, it's nothing. Don't want to worry you. But they want to put a little clock up in it. You know what I mean? But it's nothing."

I started feeling an ache at the base of my neck. "You mean a pacemaker? Why, what's the problem now? I thought you got a clean bill with your last appointment?"

We both hushed when my mom came to the door.

"You better let that boy catch his train, Chuck," she bossed. "I'm really glad that you're leaving early, baby. I hate for you to be catching the train all the way to Manhattan in the dark. Got so many devils out here."

"It's okay, Ma," I assured her, "they come at ten-minute intervals." I gave my father a worried look. "Call me, all right?"

"Keep that phone on the hook and I will," he joked, giving me a punch on the arm. My mother stood at the door smiling, watching us. I wanted and needed to know more about this pacemaker thing, but now was not the time.

I couldn't help but be worried about my pops on the ride back to Manhattan. Whenever he said it was nothing that was sure proof that it was something. But the simple fact was there was nothing I could do about it now. I'd just have to wait and call him at his church office in the morning.

When I got to my place, I quickly rushed to check my messages. I was listening out for two people actually. Somebody who just wanted to be friends and somebody who I hoped would see me as a potential colleague. I got messages from both.

"Antoine, this is Roxy. I was kind of hoping that I would catch you home but anyhow, Dyeese sends her love. Remember her? And I picked up this beautiful charcoal piece that I know you'll love." I smiled at that. She had thought about me, maybe that meant… "I always try to get something for all my friends when I go away," she giggled in her message. Wrong again, Antoine.

"Anyway, stay sweet and I'll see you when I come back, tata."

I sighed. I swear I think I needed this break from her. It was allowing me to get a rein over my hopeless attraction. Almost.

The next message was from Samantha, asking me to come over around seven with one of my Cherokee pieces.

"Fantastic!" I shouted, rushing to find something to wear. I had about twenty minutes to get showered and changed and catch a cab, which in itself could take about thirty.

Samantha had one of those beautiful high-rise suites. All hooked up with an English-accented homeboy waiting at the elevator and everything. "What suite, sir?" he asked.

"Ms. Samantha Lox's, please," I said.

He dialed her up first, getting the "come on up" signal. The elevator opened right at her door, with her standing there with a big bright smile.

"Antoine! It's so good to see you again, handsome." She kissed me directly on the lips. "Oops, now you got red lipstick all over you." She wiped it away as she looked me over.

"It's good to see you, too, Samantha." I smiled. "I really didn't want to take up too much of your time. Thanks for inviting me over though."

"Too much of my time? What kind of nonsense is that? I have wanted to have you over ever since the cruise. Now, what would you like to drink? I have some delicious Moet that you just have to try."

"That's wine, right?"

"Yes, and yes I do remember that you said you've never had it. That makes this the perfect time to devirginize yourself," she said with a wink.

I gave her a crooked smile. "I guess, but just a little bit, okay?"

"Of course, just a little." She jumped up and headed off to her wet bar, giving me a little time to look around her place.

It was laid out, and I mean to the max. She was into white–from her soft white couch to the white carpet all the way to...hell, she even wore white herself.

She came back with the wineglasses and some cheese. I had brought along one of my paintings, of course, and felt thrilled as she gasped and smiled over the fine lines and uniqueness of them.

"You are so talented. It's amazing that you haven't ever sold a line before. Or is this your first attempt?"

"It is," I said, gulping down some of the Moet. It wasn't as unpleasant as I had thought. Actually it was a mix of bitter and sweet, which wasn't bad. "I had a deal with Lincoln Galleries in Atlanta for this line, but it fell through."

"They don't have you under contract, do they?" she asked, looking very businesslike suddenly.

"Oh, no, we didn't get that far. Actually we were just about to sign when they decided to put a freeze on new contracts until further notice."

"I had heard they were doing that." She nodded. "News gets around fast in this business." She crossed her legs, which caused her white miniskirt to hike up a bit, exposing up to her upper thigh. I swallowed the remainder of my wine. "Here you go," she said as she filled my glass to the rim. Her eyes widened at what must have been a goofy smile on my face. Damn, does one glass of wine make you feel tingles like this?

"I want to sign you, Antoine."

"Really?" I said in surprise. "I mean, just like that? You don't have anyone you need to confer with on it or anything?"

"No, of course not." She moved closer to me. "Antoine, I am Samantha Lox's galleries. What I say goes. There is no board of directors or anyone who has stock in my company. And you know that I have galleries in L.A. and in Chicago. This will mean big things for you."

"Wow, I don't know what to say. I mean, thank you!" I was almost speechless. I had hoped for something like this for a long ass time, but hope doesn't make dreams happen. People like Samantha Lox do.

"There's nothing you need to say. You're talented and you know it. I had almost decided to go with you from just what I had remembered before of your work, and with what I saw on the *Art of Life* cruise." She raised her wineglass. "Drink up, handsome. Here's to us, life, peace, happiness, and good art!"

"Good art!" I echoed back to her, bringing my half-filled glass against hers for a toast. We both kind of laughed after our toast. I was feeling a definite high, both from her agreeing to run me in her galleries and from the wine, my second glass that I was just about to finish polishing up. I decided that I wouldn't have any more that night. I could just picture the look that would've been on my ma's face if she could've seen me now.

"So what are you thinking about?" Samantha asked, running her fingers through my hair.

"I don't know. I mean my mind is a little befuddled right now." I laughed nervously. Her hand went down the side of my face, caressing my cheek.

"I had almost forgotten," she said, kind of whimper.

"Forgotten what?" I asked. My voice cracked on the word *what*.

"How beautiful you are." She ran her hands down to my chest, whispering in my ear, "I want you, Antoine..."

"You do?" I croaked.

She didn't say anything. Her fingers worked their way up to my lips, tracing the outline of them. I cleared my throat.

"Samantha...when you say you want to feature my line in your galleries, that isn't dependent on me and you kickin' it, is it?" I asked hesitantly.

"No. I'm a businesswoman, Antoine. One has nothing to do with the other, okay?" Looking at her, I could suddenly tell that she was being honest, which was a relief to say the least. "But outside of that? I still want you. Think about what I'm saying. I see the wheels rolling in that cute head of yours. If you don't want this, stop me. I won't be offended, but until you do..." She had opened up my shirt, playing with the hairs on my chest with her lips.

This lady coming on to me was now my boss. The wine was messing with my head. It had been a few months since I'd last gotten any, and...damn, her lips felt good. I moaned, realizing that she had removed her own shirt and was rubbing her soft, heavy breasts against my chest. Dipping my head down, I got a pink nipple between my lips and sucked hungrily.

"Oh, yesss...mmmm, baby!" she moaned.

She suddenly seemed to become another person, almost scary. Growling and moaning as she ripped at my pants zipper, then sucking and biting at my lower. Her bites were kind of sharp, painful, but at the same time I felt a burning of pleasure everywhere she touched. I gasped as her mouth engulfed me, fire licking at my loins. She moved up and down with her mouth, slurping, sucking, licking; shaking her head and swallowing with every downward movement. I coughed back the unmanly scream that threatened to fly out of my mouth. My mind was a blur as I sat up on my elbows, moaning. My hips rocked back and forth, thrusting up and down. I grabbed her blonde locks and held her there. I could feel the familiar "I'm about to get this nut" tingle in my testicles. It was building, climbing, calling me. Suddenly she stopped and slid her body up my torso. She slipped her tongue inside my mouth, stifling my protest.

"Please, don't stop," I moaned out when she stopped kissing me.

"Oh, don't worry. I'm just getting started." Samantha got up and removed the rest of her clothes, her eyes never leaving my erect manhood. She turned and walked toward what must have been her bedroom door. Looking back toward me, she said, "Come on, lover. Tonight this pussy has your name written all over it. You've got work to do."

"Thanks, keep the change," I told the cabby, thankful to Samantha for getting me one. She had gotten one in a matter of three minutes flat. We had spent the morning talking about my art line, eating breakfast, and screwing. I felt a little out of whack though. I didn't like getting off my schedule. Plus, it was already noon and I needed to call my father. I walked up the stairs to my apartment feeling tired and in great need of a shower.

"Hi, Antoine."

Looking up, I felt a mixture of surprise and pleasure. And guilt? Naw, I wasn't her man. We were friends.

"Roxy!" I said, walking up to give her a hug.

CHAPTER *Nine*

Roxy

On the flight home from Baltimore, I let the sound of Charlise's constant approval of my sister drone on in the background of my mind. I was beyond tired, and the little bit of energy I had focused totally on Antoine. Dee and I sat up most of the night, her holding me and me crying, trying to figure out what I wanted…and how to go about getting it. The last thing Dee had told me before I left Baltimore was that if I did in fact like Antoine beyond the friend stage, that I needed to tell him that…and while I was at it, I needed to spill the beans about my past, too. Now, I had never been a quiet person. A sistah likes to talk and never bites her tongue, but since Thomas died I had vowed to keep the past in the past. Why should it matter what I did then? It didn't define who I was now. Did it?

Charlise and I arrived in New York shortly before noon and as soon as I grabbed up my luggage, I hugged her, letting her know that I would be into work later that afternoon. I needed to drop my bags off at my apartment and I needed to see a special someone I had missed the previous weekend.

My special someone wasn't home when I got to his studio. I tugged on my jeans and picked on my baby tee, fiddled with my hair and whatever else I could do waiting for Antoine to come home. *Where was he?* I thought to myself. I shook my head. It was no business of mine where he was, and even if it was...

I heard footsteps coming and I immediately jumped up from my squat. "Hi, Antoine," I whispered, smiling from ear-to-ear as he came into view.

His initial response was a little less than happy. His black eyes widened, as if surprised...or caught? He replaced the look with a sincere smile as he stepped to me, enveloping me into his arms for a hard hug.

"You just getting back?" he asked.

I cringed. I was feeling lulled into him by his warm embrace, yet I was getting the distinct vibe of another woman bouncing from his body. The thought made me sick to my stomach. Without drawing question, I slipped from his hug and eyed him up and down. He looked calm, almost like he had released some pressure. *I just bet he had*, I thought to myself, rolling my eyes.

"Everything okay?"

"Yea," I answered, my mind still stuck on the *other woman*. "I just got in and came by to say wassup before I head over to Visions. Miss me?"

Antoine smiled, one that would have made me blush or feel young any other time, but now...now it just made me feel sad, like I was getting secondhand smiles, and his lady of the night was receiving the real deals.

"Of course, I did," he answered, opening his door. "Come on in."

Stepping through his apartment, my mind flashed *Nicky*. Could she have been the woman to place that satisfied look on Antoine's face? I quickly dismissed that idea. I couldn't put my finger on it, but something told me that Nicky wasn't digging men in the "traditional" sense. Then who could it have been? I plopped myself down onto Antoine's black sofa, pulling my leg up under me.

"So tell me everything about your trip," Antoine said as he sat down beside me. I turned to face him, momentarily lost in the strong, classic features of his dark brown face. *He could have easily been a model*, I thought to myself.

My mind was still set on wanting to know who this other woman was, but I answered his question. "It was really nice," I said, smiling at him. "Artscape was fabulous. Hanging out with the girls was wonderful. And getting to see my sister was great."

"You and your sister are very close, huh?"

I nodded. "You should see us. I'm the short equivalent to her. We look exactly alike except that she's tall and athletic, and well...I'm not."

"But like you said once, good things come in small packages."

I smiled, remembering the first night of the cruise, and the date between me and my tall plate of food.

"I did say that. Didn't know you listened to everything I said."

"Everything," he said, showing his pearly whites again. This brotha was making me fuzzy in the brain. I almost forgot the smell of another woman on his clothes...but not quite.

"Oh, I got you this bad ass painting," I chirped. "It should be arriving tomorrow sometime. I hope you like it."

"If it's from you I'm sure I'll love it, so thanks in advance."

He hugged me, and instead of feeling that confused rush of warmth, I felt the need to push myself from him and ask him about the perfume on his clothes. I didn't push him off, but I did wiggle from his embrace, placing the softest, most calm expression onto my face.

"So, where were ya?" I asked, lowering my eyes from his. "Had a hot date or something?"

I sat back, arms crossed. A series of emotions ran across his face. Shock, confusion, guilt, confusion again, and finally resolution.

"Um, yea. I was showing my artwork to Samantha. She's going to be promoting my Cherokee line through her galleries."

"Wow, that's great," I replied, feeling slightly disgusted.

As fine as he was, he would have to go and get his jollies with a pasty chick. I shook my head, trying to remove the bitter tone from my voice, but I couldn't. I was hurt but shouldn't have been. Antoine could screw every woman that came through his life if he wanted. Lord knows, I had endured my share of men. Antoine and I weren't kicking it, but I couldn't help the gnawing feeling that tore at my stomach, or my need to leave his apartment…it was closing me in.

"I think so," Antoine said, waking me from my thoughts. "I've been waiting for a chance to show my artwork like this for a while."

"I'm sure she loved your artwork," I retorted, a disgusted sigh following my statement. "Seemed like she *loved* your artwork on the cruise, too."

"What's that supposed to mean?" Antoine asked, looking at me as if I had lost my mind, like I was crazy for showing my anger. I was crazy for doing it.

"Nothing, Antoine," I answered, rolling my eyes. I catapulted from the sofa. "That really is great, Antoine." I turned to face him. "I know how important it is for you to get ahead, and Samantha knows all the movers and shakers to make that happen for you. So congratulations, Mr. Man."

"Roxy," Antoine whispered, rising up from the sofa.

He stared into my eyes and in that instant, I wanted to tell him about my talk with Dee, tell him how all I could do was think about him during the weekend, wondering what he was up to. Now that I knew what he had been up to, it almost pained me to look into his eyes, knowing that she had kissed his lips, and God knows whatever else.

He didn't touch me, but his eyes, those telling eyes, said so many things. We stood there like statues for what felt like an eternity but, in reality, was only mere seconds. I blinked back wishes and dreams, willing myself to give Antoine a big, cheerful smile of reassurance. I gave Antoine a playful tag on his left arm, really wanting to give him a tag to his lips with my own, but I squelched those needs. I shouldn'tve been feeling him anyway, or any man for that matter.

"Look, playa." I laughed. "I gotta run. I just wanted to touch base for a minute before I went to work for a couple of hours. I'll holla at you later, 'k?"

Antoine nodded, still looking as if he wanted to say something, do something. Of course he did nothing but stare at me forlornly, trying to find a smile that matched the brightness of my own. He didn't. With a wink, I trotted over to his door and quickly left. The farther I got away from his apartment, the better my breathing became.

Antoine and Samantha sitting in a freaking tree. Why did this have to happen to me?

"So?"

"So what?" I asked, maneuvering myself down into the empty vastness of the bookstore café area. The oak, hunter green and burgundy of the bookstore café gave off warmth that would draw people in, create a relaxing atmosphere conducive to wanting to chill and read, or parlay with your friends while drinking a cappuccino and listening to the live band or spoken words of the night. I felt jovial as I flipped through swatches, looking for material for the café's chairs and the bookstore's furniture. I felt like I was actually contributing to the creation of something great, and that thought almost made me forget about being depressed.

"Did you go and see Mr. Wonderful?" Charlise asked, sitting in a metal fold-up chair beside me. I had my legs crossed, a sketchpad perched atop my lap and a pencil poised over the paper, stroking a creation onto the paper.

"Mr. Wonderful, huh?" I laughed, but said nothing more, just continued to stroke lines onto the paper.

I had no idea what I was drawing. My hands just wanted to move along paper. Absentmindedly, I worked on my lines, the curves, while I looked around me, noticing the business of the construction workers who placed the oak wood paneling up onto the café's walls. In my mind, I estimated that in a week's time, give or take a day, we would have the walls finished, and could begin the sanding and shining of the floors before purchasing the material for the furniture. All these things and more were going through my mind when I felt Charlise softly shove me.

"What?" I asked, looking up from my sketchpad.

"Well, what did you tell Antoine? Did you get to talk to him?"

"I saw him, yes," I answered, raising up from my seat. Pad in hand,

I took the escalator back upstairs to the gallery with Charlise in tow.

"I take it things didn't go well, huh?" she asked.

"It went as well as could be expected. I mean seeing that he was just coming in when I got there."

"Ooh. He was with someone else?" Charlise's soft-featured face held a major pout. I gave her a small hug for the sisterly concern.

"He said he was with Samantha, showing her his *artwork*."

"Artwork, my ass," Charlise grunted in disgust. I had to chuckle. Her blond, blue-eyed self did not equal to her sistahgirl persona, and I was still getting used to her down-to-earth way of being. "Wait a minute!" she exclaimed. "Samantha...as in Samantha Lox?"

I nodded.

"Wow, she's totally bigwig, and so young, too! She's like my role model. She's only like two years older than me, but I feel like she's the 'mother' of all us young artists trying to make it out here."

"Yea, yea, yea, she's a freaking God. I got it."

Charlise laughed. "Wow, aren't we bitter?" I gave her a look, and sistahgirl shot me one right back. "I'm sorry," she offered. "I know you're bummed out, but come on, it can't be that serious. Maybe you still have a shot."

"Seeing that I didn't think I had a shot before, now that he's been with the Art God of New York, I doubt my non-existent chance is even still around."

I was holding my pad close to my heart, like it kept me from falling apart, like it was my lifeline. In the gallery, all the majestic colors gave me the strength to not let this setback hurt me. As long as I had art and painting, I felt like I could endure most anything. It still stung though...thinking about Antoine...and *Samantha*.

"Just don't give up, miss," Charlise insisted, throwing one of her slender arms around my shoulder. "You have just as much to offer as Miss Lox...besides," she added, leaning in to whisper in my ear, "you're a helluva lot cuter than she is."

"Thanks, girl." I laughed. "I need some ego stroking right now. Believe me, it's been a while since I've even given a man the time of day. I'm pissed at myself for fawning over some guy like he's all that."

"You know he's all that." Charlise sassed.

"Yea, well so!" I retorted.

Our laughter was short-lived when someone entered the gallery. We both stood there, eyebrows cocked as we watched a vision of beauty walk through the door.

Today, after having my ego bruised, my eyes were wide open to the tall, model brotha who came into the gallery. He was dressed in a chestnut-brown, double-breasted Armani suit, with matching color leather shoes, a soft beige shirt and gold tie. The suit complemented his chocolate complexion. He walked further into the gallery, finally making his way up to Charlise and me, who still stood there gawking. His head glistened with its baldness and his eyes were just as chocolate as his skin, but it was the smile that threw us both for a loop.

Charlise was the first to awaken from the stranger's spell. "Hello," she said, smiling, "I'm Charlise Timson, the owner of Visions. How are you doing today?"

"Very well, thank you," came the baritone voice. "I'm Jack Wilder."

I continued to stand in the background, eyeing the brotha, feeling self-conscious in my jeans and baby tee. After all, I was solely there that day to take care of some things in the bookstore café area. If I had known someone like Jack Wilder would be coming into the gallery, you best believe I would have been dressed to the nines. Jeans or not, I noticed Jack's glance float over to me, and I blushed.

"I'm looking for a piece to place in my office," Jack continued. "I work for Canfield and Hill, and now that I've just received a promotion and a larger office, I want something beautiful to view every time I step in there."

Dang, not only did brotha man look the part of a man with bank, but obviously he had bank. Canfield and Hill was one of the largest law firms in the state of New York. Impressive to say the very least.

I could tell Charlise was in overdrive, already racking up a commission in her head. "Do you have anything in mind?" she asked.

"No, but my friend, Deborah Wann, bought an exquisite piece last week. She told me that the artist's entire collection was equally wonderful."

"Yes, yes," Charlise cooed. "The artist is Suzanne Dalona, and we actually have her collection in a wing of its own."

Another patron stepped into the gallery, and Charlise looked from the patron to Jack to me. "I will escort Mr. Wilder to Dalona's pieces if you like," I offered, receiving a sigh from Charlise.

"Thanks," she said before patting my hand and wandering over to the new customer.

Jack gave me an appreciative glance as he followed me down a corridor and made a left. I had always considered the paintings of the young artist Dalona to be those of a florist. Her paintings were so lifelike, I once thought I pricked my finger from a painting of roses she created. I smiled as I viewed her paintings.

"She's good," Jack said, eyeing me as we stood side-by-side.

"She's wonderful," I concurred.

"Do you paint?"

"Technically, no. In my mind, yes."

Jack laughed. "That sounds like a night of explaining."

"It would take a lot longer than that." I chuckled. I continued to hug my sketchpad to my chest, rocking back and forth on my heels.

"I want that," Jack stated simply, nodding his head to the rose painting I had fallen in love with before.

I smiled. "Great selection."

"Now tell me, does this painting come with a date with you?"

My eyes widened as I looked up into his sexy face. The last thing I wanted to do was deal with a man, especially if it wasn't Antoine, but my ego was bruised. I had the blues, and a fine, well- dressed, obviously well-paid brotha wanted to dine me. Who was I to refuse such a proposition?

"Normally, no," I answered, giving him my serious look, "but if you insist on dinner, I might be persuaded to say yes."

Jack gave me a look that oozed sex appeal. Even though Antoine was imprinted on my mind, I was already thinking about what I would wear that night for dinner...with Jack.

After Jack left, Charlise came smiling up in my face, wanting to know every detail. There was nothing really to tell, but she squealed when I told her about the date. She hugged me so hard that my sketchpad, which until now was plastered against my chest, now laid upon the floor. Charlise picked it up and examined the sketch I was doodling earlier.

"Cute," she said as she handed me the pad.

I looked at the page I had been sketching and my breath caught in the back of my throat. Even though my mind tried valiantly to erase all thoughts of Antoine, my hand, my art, I guess my heart, were trying desperately to keep him in my mind. A sad smile touched my lips as I looked at the sketch of Antoine that I had drawn in my pad.

I thought I might get my ego stroked that night. I was so wrong. I went straight home from Visions and prepared myself for dinner. I took a scented bath and perfumed myself in just the right spots. I donned my silk, black sleeveless dress, and black high-heel sandals. My hair hung low and bumped under. I was looking lovely, feeling lovely and ready to be wined and dined.

Jack was on time and looking mighty fine in his black suit, a soft black metallic shirt and white tie. Together, we needed to be splashed onto all magazine covers for being the sexiest couple. We went to Houston's, which was great because I had a hankering for Chinese chicken salad. He greeted me with a warm hug and a soft kiss to my cheek. Told me I looked beautiful, a work of art.

The night went downhill from there.

My appetite was gone. I sat at the table, my head being held up by my left hand as the beautiful yet robotic Jack Wilder droned on and on about his life and achievements. Since his remark about how great I looked and my thank you, it had been "The Jack Wilder Show."

He was thirty-five, born and raised in Alabama, moved to Minnesota, where he received his bachelor's and law degrees before being recruited by Canfield and Hill right out of law school ten years prior. He had been there ever since. Made six figures, lived in the Upper Eastside, had an affinity for Armani fashions, didn't smoke, occasionally drank, and ...in my opinion... was an extreme blowhard.

"I play racquetball three times a week and jog daily," he continued, in between spoonfuls of his appetizer, cream of broccoli soup. I was eating mine, too, but I had *time* to do so since there was less talking on my part.

"Do you exercise?" he asked. "As great as you look, I'm thinking yes."

My spoon halted in mid-air, stunned he had even asked me a question. I quickly swallowed the spoon of soup, not wanting to miss my opportunity.

"Yes, I do," I answered. "I jog every day, and try to hit the gym three or four times a week. I take a TaeBo class, too."

"You know," Jack said, eyes wide, excited, "I know Billy Blanks..." and the words continued to flow from his mouth.

Dear God, I begged in silence, can You please make this night end...and quickly?

I restarted my process of tuning him out and going back to eating my soup when our entrees, his seared tuna salad and my Chinese chicken salad, arrived. Good, a new flavor of food to wash out the *bland* Jack. I took a strip of chicken and began chewing, damn near choking when I viewed Antoine and Samantha, along with an artsy-looking white male, come into the restaurant.

"You okay?" Jack asked, momentarily stopping his solo conversation.

I nodded, my eyes glued onto Antoine. I drew his attention to me as Antoine looked up and across the restaurant, spotting me. He looked really good, dressed casually in a pair of charcoal gray linen slacks, a black shirt unbuttoned at the collar, and a matching gray linen jacket. He wore his hair out, letting his silky locks flow against his lapel. I groaned, turning my eyes from him to dig into my salad. I refused to let him see me pissed at him being here with *her*, or me being so damn unhappy with Mr. *Let me tell you a bit about myself.*

I swallowed the delicious chicken and turned to face Jack, taking one of his hands in mine and stroking it playfully. "I just want to tell you that I'm having a really good time here with you tonight," I crooned, smiling at him.

He was definitely the type to expect women to fawn over him. This time was no exception as he dripped a come hither smile onto his lips and replied, "How good of a time are you having?"

"How good of a time would you like me to be having?" I hid my irritation with admiration.

"Good enough to want to divulge in a nightcap at my place?"

I was insulted. No, this high-class, highly paid, model brotha wasn't expecting a taste in the panties tonight! This...this was like, dang, this could have been a scene from my life not too long ago, and that thought sobered me up real quick. I took a breath, threw on a phony grin, and began to speak, "Look, Jack..."

"Good evening, Roxanne."

Antoine's voice eked up my back and rang like a symphony in my ear. I looked up to him as he glanced down at me, taking in my face as well as the view of my cleavage. I blushed, feeling my nipples harden. I quickly turned my attention to Jack to unstiffen them.

"Good evening to you, too, Antoine," I whispered, rising from my seat.

Without positioning myself first, Antoine slipped his arms around me, hugging me close for several seconds. I almost melted into the scent of him, silently moaning from the feel of his body against mine.

"You look so beautiful tonight," he said, without qualm of seeing Jack there with me or with Samantha shooting darts at me from across the restaurant.

"And you're looking quite dashing tonight yourself," I said, inching away from Antoine's heat. "This is my date, Jack, Jack Wilder. Jack, this is my good friend, Antoine Billups."

Jack stood and shook hands with Antoine, each sizing the other up. I wanted to laugh at the OK Corral feeling I was experiencing, but I kept all laughter in check.

"I saw you as I came in with Samantha, and I wanted to say hi." Antoine gave my entire body a once over. I shivered in my spot. "I don't want to keep you two from your date."

I wanted to kick Antoine, really hard. He was being so damn polite, so damn courteous, like he didn't care one way or the other if I was with Jack or fifty men at once.

I balanced out my anger with a smile as sweet as pure cane sugar.

"That was sweet of you, Antoine," I said. "Tell Samantha I said hello and I'll talk to you later."

Antoine's mouth opened into his normal, sweet, joyful smile as he hugged me again, this time, more intimate, as if he were parting from me for a distant journey. I couldn't hide the moan that escaped from between my lips. When he released me, he looked directly into my eyes and in a hushed voice, said, "Be good." Softer, he said, "But not too good." He eyed Jack and added, "Nice meeting you, Jack. You two have a good evening."

And with that, Antoine turned on his heels and walked back to join Samantha and the other man at their table. I watched him talk animatedly to Samantha and the man and my eye caught the few times Samantha managed to gently stroke Antoine's hands, like I had done Jack's earlier. I rolled my eyes and dug back into my plate, ignoring Jack's question about if he and I were going to do the nightcap.

Who needed a damn nightcap? To me, this capped off my night, horrifically.

CHAPTER *Ten*

Nicky

"You're a fuckin' trip!"

"I'm serious. That cat was hitting on me. I thought about kung-fuing his ass, but then a picture of my Nicky came flashing before my eyes, and I said…naw."

Antoine was in rare form. He was spitting and raving over some guy who worked for Samantha Lox's galleries that had made a pass at him.

Having a few of his pieces there was getting him seen and heard, and I couldn't be happier for him. But it appeared, I thought with a laugh, it was also getting him seen by some of what we affectionately called...family.

"Well, maybe he thought you were one of them thug-out, down-low brothas. You know many gay men find them sexy as a mutha."

"Do I look like a dl thug to you?" Antoine asked indignantly.

"No. Besides, you know I'm just joking with you." I pitched his cheek, teasing him. "Why didn't you just tell him you were straight?"

"I did tell him, but since when has that mattered to your umm…family?"

"Whateva." I smirked. "Well, you shouldn't be so sweet-looking and maybe the dudes wouldn't mess with cha. Besides, you're the one who chose the career of the *family*.

Antoine laughed and shook his head, getting up and changing the CD to one of my favorites: Ice Cube.

"Turn it up, BooBoo!" I shouted. "Well, hello!"

Antoine immediately complied with me doing a sampling of rapping that I felt put Missy Elliott to shame. She just got lucky, and I just hadn't been discovered yet, I joked. I swear I was a rap- loving fool.

"You keep it up, you're gonna have five-O banging at my door shooting me on the bottom of my feet and then doing a 'we shot him 'cause we thought his Coke bottle was a gun' thing."

I fell back into the soft covers on Antoine's sofa bed. "But that's aight, BooBoo. They fuck with you, they gotta fuck with me, ya heard me? Hell, I'll put a cap in dere asses!"

He laughed, mocking me with, "Aight, gangsta momma!"

We cuddled up into bed together, listening to music and sharing a half-gallon of Edy's cookies and cream ice cream. I hadn't seen Antoine much during the past week. To say I missed him was an understatement; it was catch-up time.

"So what else has been going on with you, other than your big break with that gallery?"

"Not much, you know me. I like to stay focused. Yesterday and today I took four pieces over to the gallery and got to know a few people there. In fact, Monday night I had dinner with Samantha and Gerald Heinz."

"O…K." I nodded. "And um…who is Gerald Heinz?" Sometimes Antoine would talk as if I knew all these artsy people he was affiliated with, I thought with a smile.

"Gerald Heinz?" He looked at me with astonishment. "Man, Gerald Heinz is a damn guru, a sculptor. He's even worked in the White House, with reforming some of the busts from back in Revolutionary times. He's in New York now visiting from Paris. I was starstruck when Samantha introduced us. She knows everybody."

"Sounds exciting." I grinned slightly. My sarcasm was not missed, however.

"See, now you're picking." Antoine laughed. "I can't help it. I get worked up over stuff like this."

"Ain't nothing wrong with that, suga. I know you, remember?" I reminded him. "So what's going on with Miss Thang?"

"Miss Thang?"

I rolled my eyes, handing him the ice cream carton. I was full to the max. "You know who I'm talking about. That high-yulla chick you brought by my place right after you got back from your cruise. I forget her name."

"Roxy."

"Okay, Roxy then," I huffed. "Are you still seeing her?" I couldn't help but notice the change in Antoine's demeanor at my mention of her.

"She was actually at Houston's. That's where I had dinner with Samantha and Gerald. She was there with this rich-looking dude..."

I raised an eyebrow. "Ahh...and how does that make you feel?"

"What do you mean, how does that make me feel? You sound like a shrink or something." He laughed. "I told you we are only friends."

"And I've known you all your life, Antoine Billups. I could tell right away that you had a thing for Miss Thang."

I reached across to the end table, grabbing a handful of jellybeans while Antoine finished off the last of the ice cream. This was definitely junk food night.

"I don't have a thing for her. I mean, I showed interested in her but she said friends, so friends it is. I'm not buggin'." I watched the array of expressions change on his brown features.

"So she turned you down?" I gasped. "Oh, hell no! Why in the world did you let some high-class yuppie chick diss you, Antoine? She should be glad you paid her some attention. The stank bitch!"

"Chill out, Nicky," Antoine said, looking at me disapprovingly. "I'm fine with us and the 'friends' thing, okay? For real, I'm not buggin' about it. In fact, I've been kicking it with Samantha Lox."

Shock! "You what? You been doing the wild thang with the white lady? *ANTOINEEEEE!* Like Whoa!"

Antoine laughed, having the nerve to look a bit embarrassed. "No, it's not like whoa. It's like it just happened. It was nothing but a physical thing, and had nothing to do with my working with her, and that's all to it."

"Uh-huh, if you say so, I believe ya," I said, tongue in cheek. "Well, anything is better than that Roxy. Can you believe she called me a cook? The nerve of her!"

I yawned, slipping underneath the covers. It was my way of making sure that Antoine was the one cutting the lights off and not me. I was sneaky like that!

"See, there you go again, trying to be slick," Antoine fumed with a sideways smile.

He knew me.

I giggled and pulled the covers over my head until heard him change to a soft R&B station, turn the music down some and click off the lights. Once he was comfortable under the covers, I curled up behind him in a spoon-like position. We always slept like that whenever one of us spent the night. We would cuddle and talk about everything. Or just find comfort in listening to each other's heartbeat. It was funny, the type of relationship we had. Nothing at all sexual about it, yet so close we almost always knew what the other was thinking.

"Nicky?" Antoine whispered.

"Yea?"

"I do care about Roxy, okay? And I love you, and you know that. I know you think you don't like her. But for me, give it a chance? We are friends, she and I, and you and me–well, you know what we are." I squeezed him tightly around the waist. "Play nice with her, okay? Please?"

I listened carefully to what he was saying, but listened even more carefully to what he was not saying. Those words spoke louder than any that he could have spoken vocally.

"How about you invite her over for dinner one night soon, and I'll cook? Just me, you and her," I suggested.

Antoine twisted around, hugging me close. "Thanks, Nicky. I love you, Girl," he said, kissing me on the tip of my nose.

"I love you, too, BooBoo..."

ANTOINE

Toward the end of the week, I found myself stuck up in my studio, *trying* to paint. I felt antsy. I hate not hearing from my parents, and I had been having a hard time catching up with my dad since he told me about his upcoming surgery in two weeks. It bothered me that he had not even told Ma about it yet.

Someone else was on my mind, too. I don't know how I kept a straight face at seeing Roxy with the fancy rich dude. I mean, she told me she didn't want to get mixed up like that, no dates or anything other than friendship. Yet there she was with him rubbing his hands and all. So to relieve my frustrations, I went home with Samantha and banged the hell out of her. The problem was that sexing Samantha left me feeling even more stressed than before. To be real, Samantha was not who I wanted.

I watched the busy world of Manhattan through the big picture window in my studio, having warmed up potpie for breakfast, and a zillion thoughts roamed through my mind. Those thoughts were jarred by a soft tapping of feet walking down the hallway toward my easel room.

Damn, I thought I had locked the door. I walked quickly to see who it was. You could never be too careful in a city like Manhattan. Just as I was about to peep around the door, Roxy's forehead bumped right smack into mine. She screamed.

"Oh, God, Antoine! You scared the shit out of me!"

I was holding my hand to my heart. What in the world was she talking about?! "I scared you? How do you think I'm feeling?" I laughed. "Come on in here."

I pulled her inside the door, closing it securely behind her. She turned around and smiled at me nervously.

"Hi."

"Hello, back at cha…"

"I know it's been a few days. I was off and I've missed ya and thought I would take a chance catching you home on a Thursday morning."

She seemed pensive, and I wanted very much to ease the tension between us.

"I'm glad you did," I told her, pulling her in for a close hug. We stayed that way. I definitely was in no hurry to let go; she felt so good.

She pulled back and laughed softly. "I knew you had to be in here, but do you really want to spend your day cooped up in here painting when you could be painting the town with me?"

An instant smile curled on my face. Was she asking me out? "What do you have in mind?" I asked her, trying not to seem too desperate.

"Well, it's early. We could check out the Met?"

I hadn't been to the Metropolitan Museum of Art in a long time, so she most def had said the magic words. "Hold up," I told her, running into my supply room. I came out with my camera and keys. "After you, Miss Winters." I winked.

"Well, thank you, Mister Billups," she purred back. We both laughed, heading out the door for a day of adventure.

"Oh, Antoine, I think I'm going to cry," Roxy exclaimed an hour later. We both stood in awe, having been lucky enough to get into the special exhibitions. We decided on *Painters in Paris* first. "Pablo Picasso..."

"Girl reading at a table," we both said in unison, laughing.

"So you're a Picasso fan, too, huh?" she asked me.

"Well, I have to be, but I became an even bigger fan after my trip to Paris," I said.

Roxy's almond-shaped eyes got huge. "Paris, I have always wanted to go there," she said hesitantly.

"Dang, you should. I mean an artist needs to visit the city of art at least once in their career. I stayed for two weeks and still didn't see all that was to be seen." We walked over to the next portrait. "This one is called *The Mountain* by..."

"Balthasar Klossowski," Roxy said, before I could get the words out.

"Well, for someone who has never been to Paris, you sure know the paintings." Her knowledge impressed me.

"Oh, I've studied about them in books," she said quickly, looking around suddenly. "I read a lot. And check out a lot of art books, too."

"Well, babe, you can't check these out in a book. You sure you've never been here?" I asked in puzzlement. She knew an awful lot about Paris art, more than I had expected.

"You know what? I may have," Roxy laughed suddenly. "I swear, half the time, I don't know if I'm coming or going."

"Well, I get that way, too."

I was enjoying her company. And I was happy that she seemed to be enjoying mine also. We took more time checking out the French exhibit before heading over to the African Arts. For some reason, Roxy seemed to become more relaxed then. Although in a way, I could understand. African art always moved me in its strength and the love that shone from it. Almost as if the artists were in tears as they painted.

After that, we followed the big white M and headed over to the Met store. I bought a book called *Assyrian Beliefs and Ivories in the Metropolitan Museum of Art*. I was a cheap mofo, but I really had enjoyed that exhibit and wanted to read more about it. Roxy was looking at some posters of the African and Egyptian arts, when something caught my eye. It was a beautiful, lush, cut-velvet scarf adapted from *Magnolias and Irises* by Louis Comfort Tiffany. It was long and thick and totally Roxy. I completely forgot about my cheap ways and pulled out the Visa.

As I walked out of the store, I saw Roxy looking around. I knew she was looking for me. I took the velvet scarf out of its bag and wrapped it around her shoulders, kissing her softly behind the ear. She jumped.

"Antoine, what is this?" she gasped, stroking its softness.

"It's for you," I whispered.

"But...but you didn't have to do that. I mean, I saw the prices on these scarves and they were expensive. Come on, I asked you out today, remember? You didn't have to do this."

"Okay, I didn't have to do it, but I wanted to, all right? And now that I'm broke, you can buy me lunch!"

She giggled, looking at me with sparkling eyes and shaking her head. Regardless of what she said, I knew she was pleased.

"Well, lunch it is, Mr. Man," she said with a smile. She was still stroking her scarf as we headed out the door for much needed nourishment.

I had almost forgotten how Roxy could talk and eat at the same time. She asked questions about my childhood and about how Nicky and I had hooked up. "You two do seem really close," she noted.

"Oh, we are. All the way back from grade school. In high school, she was my stick partner."

"Is she gay?" Roxy blurted out.

"Yea, she's openly lesbian. Always has been, even in high school. She got a lot of flack about it back then, too, which is one of the reasons we stayed so close. I was this scrawny, quiet dude that was always getting my ass kicked, and Nicky was this Queen Latifah-looking chick always kicking ass."

"Well, she seemed like she wouldn't have minded kicking mine that day. I swear she is protective over you, BooBoo!"

"Watch it now!" We both laughed, then looked into each other's eyes. I reached over for her hand. "So that's enough about me. You never really tell me much about you."

"Oh, come on. There's nothing to tell," Roxy said, chewing on her salad. "I'm just me. Little ol' Roxanne Winters."

I leaned forward, taking her chin in my hand and stroking it as if wiping a food stain. Roxy's eyes went soft. "Well, I want to know about this little ol' Roxanne Winters. So 'fess up."

"What?" she whispered.

"What? Tell me more, that's what." I bit my bottom lip, trying not to break into smile at how hard she was trying not to look at me. "Okay, so you told me before that you have only been in Manhattan for about two years, that you came here to finish up your degree. What were you doing before then? What made you take a break? Were you living in Baltimore then?"

"So many questions. My goodness." Roxy sighed and took a deep breath. "Okay, I just needed a break, needed time to find myself, you could say. So um...I did some, some modeling for a while."

"Really?" She was kind of short for a model, but she sure was pretty enough. "What kind of modeling did you do? For magazines or the runway?"

"Oh, uh, both." She looked up and exhaled. "Oh, I am soooo full! I, um, after that I did nanny work for a while. Modeling didn't really suit me. It was really exhausting and so competitive, so I went to Los Angeles and watched these two rich kids for this lady I had modeled with. Eventually, I decided that my education was more important, so I re-enrolled, and I haven't had an ounce of regret since."

I could have sat there listening to Roxy talk all day, and would have if she hadn't cut in with, "Chile, it is getting late, I didn't mean to kill your whole Thursday. Can you believe we've been running around all day?"

"I've enjoyed being with you..."

"I enjoyed being with you, too," she said quietly. We sat there looking in each other's eyes for a moment, neither of us knowing where to go next. As for me, I didn't want to push anything. After all, she hadn't said anything that would make me believe she had changed her mind about the friends-only deal.

We caught a Yellow Cab, her being dropped off first. She gave me a quick kiss on the cheek and headed out the door. After she left, I sat in the back seat of the cab and it hit me. All the orgasms in the world had never had me as relaxed and stress free as my day with her had been.

Nicky

One thing I was always sure about is when I was looking good, it was all good. I had just gotten my hair done up in micro braids, and had even put a touch of lip-gloss across my lips. Styling in baggy jeans and my loose-fitting "Hot Boys" with Juvi tee shirt, I was relaxed and rested. What can I say? I was in my environment, something that wasn't always an easy achievement.

I had been relaxing all of fifteen minutes, sipping on a drink at my favorite club when I spotted my pick-up for the night. Girlfriend had it going on. She was tall, slender, and an obvious femme; all qualities that I liked in my woman. The conversation wasn't too bad either, if not a bit too giggly for my taste. But that was okay. I hadn't spent twenty dollars on drinks and an hour of my time talking to let something as simple as a giggle or two get in the way.

"So how far do you live from here?" I asked her.

"Oh, I'm in the heart of Brooklyn—Crown Heights, about thirty five minutes maybe, depending on the driver," she said softly, blushing slightly as I continued rubbing her upper thigh.

The club was full, yet no one was really paying much attention to two women sitting close in a dark booth. I had finally found something to quiet her down, moving higher and higher up her thigh, until my fingers were rubbing between her legs. She gasped, parting them as I probed the out print swell of her. She sat watching me with her lips slightly parted, her hips moving, reaching as I pressed. I smirked as I watched her, her breathing deepening. I was going to make this girl come like putty in my hands.

"Let's get out of here," she said suddenly, surprising me actually in her swiftness. *But hey, that was okay, too,* I thought. I grabbed my keys and Bebe, the sexy piece I had just stroked to a feverish pitch, grabbed her purse and followed.

Just as we were going through the doors leading to the parking lot, two guys started walking up behind us. Bebe looked at me, then I at her, as if to say, do you know them? I know I had never seen them before, and really knew I hadn't when they started running off at the mouth.

"Check out the dykes," one of them said.

"Can we watch?" another shouted. "Can we come watch y'all eat da cat!"

Oh, shit! I thought to myself. *Don't tell me we are going to have to deal with this shit tonight…*

"Nicky…" I looked over at Bebe and saw she was scared. The guys were walking up faster and faster behind us. Thinking quick, I reached in my back pocket and pulled out my small pocketknife. I swung around at them.

"You want to watch?" I said in a low voice. "You want to watch, muthafucka?" I pushed the knife toward them. They jumped back quickly.

"Aight, shawty, we just fuckin' with you. Don't be trippin' now," one of them said.

Bebe and I got into my Ford Taurus, keeping a close eye on our so-called new friends. I locked the doors quickly, my fingers shaking uncontrollably as I put the key in the ignition.

"Who do you think they are?" Bebe asked.

"I have no idea..."

But funny thing was, as soon as I said those words, I noticed someone who did look familiar, standing outside of a Jeep. He seemed to give our two harassers thumbs-up. I wasn't sure, but he definitely gave one of them a high-five as they walked past his Jeep and got into the car parked beside him.

It was Winston Greer, husband of my once-a-week lover, Mya.

CHAPTER *Eleven*

Roxy

"I'm sorry, but I don't think I'm interested in going out with you again."

Here it was my lunch hour at Visions, and I was spending it on the damn phone with Jack, the all-about-me brotha. Silly me for thinking that not joining him for a nightcap the night of our date and telling him that I was seeing other people would be clues as to how I wanted him and I to part ways. Silly, silly me. For days, he had been calling me, showing up at Visions, offering to take me out for lunch, dinner, even breakfast, and this would be the very last time I would be talking to him.

Charlise waltzed past her office door, finding me lounging back in her chair, feet upon her desk. My face was one of disgust, and she fell out laughing. "Lover boy again?" she whispered into the office.

I nodded, as I heard her chuckle long after she walked down the hall. After another fifteen minutes of Jack's vocal resume and rationale for why I'd be crazy not to go out with him again, I asked, "You want to know the truth?"

"Yes," Jack answered, "because I have no idea why you wouldn't want to go out with me again. I've never been dumped."

You have, I thought. *You just haven't allowed it to sink into that thick ass head of yours.* "The truth is," I whispered, "I'm gay."

Charlise had just stepped back to her office door and froze in place, mouth open, alabaster skin red, eyes wide. I had to pray to God to keep from screaming in spastic laughter.

"You…you're gay?" Jack asked, stuttering.

Charlise ran into the office, jumping into the chair opposite where I sat, all smiles and waiting to hear more of my soap opera.

"You're one of the first to know," I began. "For years, I have been trying to hide my homosexuality, trying to keep up the persona of a straight woman." I sniffed, a gesture that had Charlise gripping her hands over her mouth to scream in silence. "I wanted so bad to be normal or what society deems as normal. When I saw you, I knew you would be the type of man I could change for…and when you asked me out, I thought yes, immediately.

"But I realize my sexuality, my being, is something that cannot be changed. I am who I am. Roxanne Josephine Winters. Lesbian. I'm proud of who I am, and I'm sorry for deceiving you."

Jack sighed. "I'm glad you told me the truth, Roxy," he said. "I was beginning to think my sex appeal was wearing." I stared at the phone in disbelief. I had just acted my ass off and this Negro didn't give a rat's ass one way or the other. I quickly said bye and hung up the phone, to rousing applause by Charlise.

"Utterly wowing!" she said, slapping her hand against the desk. "Your calling is acting, babe!"

I laughed, closing my eyes and shaking my head. "Yea, well, I'm here in New York, the perfect place to go into the biz. I'm just glad the nut case will leave me alone now. He was not the man I wanted to have on my mind." *ANTOINE*. Neon sign flashed through my mind since our outing the previous day. I don't know what possessed me to boldly go to his apartment and ask him to the Met. But I know I didn't regret it. I didn't regret the glances and stares or the smiles and hugs. I didn't regret him buying me the *Magnolias and Irises* by Louis Comfort Tiffany scarf either. I had worn it the previous night while I slept, wanting to remember him giving it to me and kissing me behind the ear. There were two things I did regret, however. One of which I hoped to correct; the other, I hoped would never come to light. I regretted not kissing him goodnight, that kind of kiss that leaves you both breathless and full of visions of intertwinement and complete satisfaction.

Painfully, I also regretted the lies. I never modeled, never took care of kids, lied about not having gone to Gay Paris. When he said he wanted to know all about me, I wanted him to know all about me. The good, the bad and the extremely ugly, but I was afraid to risk it. So, instead, I was a model and a caregiver.

"What man do you want to have on your mind?" I shook my head, awakening from my fuzzy thoughts as Charlise and her question came back into view.

"Huh?" I asked, rising from her chair.

"I asked, what man do you want to have on your mind?"

I felt my face radiate with heat as I blushed from Charlise's question. Despite my blush, I answered, "Nobody. You know I've got too much on my plate right now. Likeeeeee," I dragged out, "finding me a place to live. The classifieds have been my best friend, and when I'm not here I'm running all over New York City and Manhattan trying to find me a shoe box to live in. Gotta find something soon."

"You will, Girl," Charlise said, like she knew for sure that was true. "If push comes to shove, you can stay with me until you find a place. I have a nice size loft with an extra room that could be easily converted to a bedroom."

"You are like my fairy godmother, you know that, right? I seriously don't know what I would do without you, Char. Thanks for helping me out."

"Any time, mi amiga. I predict you won't even need to cash in my offer. You'll have new digs within the next two weeks."

"And how are you so sure?"

"Just trust me," she answered back.

"You haven't steered me wrong yet!"

"And I won't begin now, so, moving on...we're having an unveiling next week."

"For Destrani," I added, "yea, I was snooping on your desk."

"Uh-huh. Anyway, she'll be here the day before the event to meet you and me. She needs to get her pieces up on the wall, set prices, and all the other boring, technical jobs that need to be done before the actual event."

"Sounds cool, and you know if you need me, I'm here for you. The paneling is ninety-percent up, and I've already placed the order with the fabric distributor to send its material to Akron Furnishings. Within two weeks, we'll be in business, Girlie."

Leaning across the table, we high-fived. "So this is what you gallery people do all day!" Antoine. He was standing at the doorway, clad in loose-fitting jeans and a somewhat snug white tee shirt. I sighed. Charlise's eyes moved from me to Antoine, yet she remained silent.

"Hey, Antoine." I walked around the desk to him. He reached out his arms and took me in them, hugging me hard and long. I was getting used to such touchy-feely affection, even though I had the urge to add to the affection.

"So this is the guy Dyeese was talking about?" Charlise asked.

Oops! I wanted to jump across the office and make her vanish. The last thing I wanted Antoine to know was that he popped into conversations I had with other people.

He glanced down at me, a smirk forming on his lips. "So you talk about me, huh?" he whispered.

I rolled my eyes. "Whateva."

Taking Antoine by the hand, I brought him toward Charlise. "Char, this is my friend, Antoine, and Antoine, this is the best boss in the entire universe, Charlise." They shook hands.

"I love your gallery," Antoine said. "Just last week I purchased a print of yours online."

"We're online?" I asked, looking at Charlise.

"See, there are things I still need to teach you." Charlise smirked. "In fact, I got you your own Visions' e-mail account."

"What, roxywinters@visions.com?" I asked.

"Exactly," Charlise replied. "When you start getting out there in the art world, that's where all the bigwigs can reach you."

Antoine winked at me. "Now that I have a friend here, I'll actually make the time to patronize the physical place."

"Either way, we thank you for your support," Charlise said. "You know us artsy people have to stick together."

"Like glue."

"I'm gonna leave you kids alone to catch up," Charlise said. "It was nice meeting you, Antoine."

"Likewise."

I watched Charlise exit her office, but not before giving me the thumbs up and shutting the door. With her gone, I felt the proximity of Antoine there with me, and my body lit up. I leaned back onto the desk, glancing up at Antoine.

"Hey," I said, my voice in a soft, girlish tone.

"Hey," he answered back.

"To what do I owe the honor of your visit?"

"Several reasons…first and foremost, I missed you."

I blushed. "You just saw me last night."

"And now it's the next day–too long." Nimble fingers like a paintbrush, Antoine stroked his fingers across my cheek, against my hair.

"What were your…um, other reasons?" I asked, feeling my heart snatch up double beats.

"I can't remember them right now." I felt Antoine's breath against my cheek. Fear kept me from facing him…I knew I would kiss him if I did, and this was moving way too fast, even though it felt way so right.

"Antoine," I whispered, closing my eyes slightly to block him out, but his warm breath against my cheek and my neck alerted me of his commanding presence.

"You know," Antoine began, halting for a moment before continuing, "I thought about you last night."

"You did?" I asked, looking up and regretting doing so. His large ebony eyes held warmth in them and I couldn't look away.

He nodded. "Did you think of me?" he asked, his voice low and deep.

I didn't know where this bravado of his was coming from…or maybe I did. Our outing yesterday was perfect…all but one thing had been missing, the perfect night kiss. Was this Take Two of our kiss scene?

Instead of answering him, I raised my hands up to his face, drawing small lines with my fingertips before slipping my hands into his dark, silky hair, bringing his face even closer to mine. The weight of his body slightly pressed against me and I moaned, kissing his lips. The initial contact was soft, almost invisible, yet I trembled, feeling each pore go weak from the rush of emotions that raced inside of me.

"Roxanne," Antoine whispered against my lips, prompting me to kiss him again. This time his moan bombarded my lips, parted them and allowed his tongue access into my mouth.

Feverishly, we kissed like teenagers for the first time. Our tongues tangling up with each other, our moans almost like pants and grunts, our fingers not wanting to leave the body of the one we were kissing. I felt Antoine's hands move along my jean-clad thighs, lightly stroking them. I purred against his mouth. My fingers braided themselves through his hair, pressing his lips closer to mine.

Knock-knock. As quickly as our kisses began, they ended as we jumped from one another, feigning innocence when Charlise opened the door, a wicked smile on her face. She knew, despite our trying to act otherwise.

"Dyeese is on line two," Charlise said. Every last one of her glistening white teeth were showing.

"Thanks," I whispered, clearing my throat.

Shutting the door, my attention went back to Antoine. "I'll let you answer that," he said, hunger written on his face. I swallowed hard. "But I did remember another reason why I dropped by."

"And that was?"

"Nicky wanted to cook us dinner tonight…at my place…you, me and her, say seven-ish?"

I was in a daze. It didn't matter to me at this moment that his girlfriend hated me. I just wanted to be around him…and if that meant I had to be cool with his girl, then I would do it.

I picked up the phone. "I'll be there…definitely."

Okay, so Nicky was not a cook. She was a bad ass chef with skills that left my mouth watering for more. She prepared Focaccia bread that was used for sandwiches of Italian roast beef with tomato dipping sauce. Sun-brewed iced tea was the beverage of choice with this meal, Nicky had told us. Antoine's place was small, but Nicky worked it out with his small dining table, covering it with a hunter-green tablecloth and bringing her own fire-red dishes to set off the colors within the meal. I wanted to take a picture of the table and the food; it was just that perfect.

If dinner was delicious, Nicky's homemade pineapple upside-down cake with homemade French vanilla ice cream was the crème de la crème of a wonderful dining experience. I was expecting a bill after finishing my dessert.

"Girl!" I cooed, biting into a spoonful of cake along with ice cream. "You make me wanna slap my mother with this cake, okay!"

Nicky looked on approvingly across from me at the small table. As a culinary artist, I knew she hoped for rave reviews, and I wouldn't disappoint. I had to give her major props. She was really trying to be nice to me, and I just made that easier on her by truthfully commenting on her wonderful culinary talents.

"Thanks," she said. "I just wanted you to know I could cook, but I wasn't some cook!"

"I got you, Girl. Point taken and highly noted."

I glanced over at Antoine who had made me his object of viewing all evening. I enjoyed it, but wondered if his attachment to me would mean a detachment from Nicky, and would she hate me because of it. I wouldn't look at Antoine and his sexy self if I thought he and I would damage the great and unique relationship that he and Nicky shared.

"You're pretty quiet, babe," Nicky said, facing Antoine. "Is something wrong?"

"Nope," he answered. "Just happy to be here with you both."

I glanced over at him. He looked so content. I noticed Nicky's expression. She appeared annoyed, but the expression quickly disappeared. She still was not feeling me too tough, I thought. There was something else added to her look, not about me though. I couldn't put my finger on it, but it had me worried.

"So what's been going on in your neck of the woods, Nicky?" I asked.

Her eyes widened and she looked from me to Antoine before speaking. "Nothing much," she answered, plastering a smile on her face. "I've been busy with catering jobs, and getting things together for a rather major event that's popping off soon."

I watched Antoine glance at Nicky, love permeating his eyes. If I didn't know she was a lesbian, I could have easily mistaken his glance as that of a deeper, more sexual type of love. It warmed me; it was endearing. I never had that type of relationship with anyone before, male or female, and I felt a stab of jealousy watching the silent interplay between the two.

"Nicky is going to blow up any day now," Antoine said. "She and my mom are the only two women who can cook anything that I would happily eat and love."

"What a promotional tool. Ever think of having Antoine as your spokesperson, Nicky?"

"Believe me," Nicky said, "he's that and a whole lot more. Half of my clients came from him and his artsy acquaintances. This man keeps food on my table…literally."

We all laughed.

"With all the eating I do at your place, I better keep food on the table!"

"Roxy, Antoine tells me that you're looking for a place to live," Nicky said, changing the subject.

I nodded and sighed. "Yea, I am. I have to be out of my apartment in about a month. I've had some leads, but nothing that's been wowing, you know? I'm not looking for a mansion. I just want something that is for me and that's close enough to Visions. And of course, you two." I didn't glance Antoine's way, but I could feel his eyes on my cheek, and that made me blush.

"Well," Nicky began, as if thinking about whether she should spill the beans or not, "there is an empty apartment or two in this complex…"

I jumped up in my seat, clapping my hand. Antoine was beaming at

Nicky's attempt to befriend me. "Now don't get excited yet," Nicky said, "but, uh, I think I could call the super and have him let you see the apartments, talk money and all that stuff. That's if you don't mind me butting in a bit."

"Girl, please!" I squealed. "Please, please, please, by all means, put a holla in for a sistah. Lord knows the only thing he can say is no, and that's nothing." I looked at Antoine who winked at me, and then at Nicky who surprised me by actually looking pleased. "Thanks for looking out, Nicky," I said, "I really appreciate this."

"Eh, I know what's it's like to find that first New York apartment. Besides, any friend of Antoine's is a friend of mine."

My right hand instantly went up to my heart and I actually broke a cheekbone from smiling so hard.

"Okay, okay!" Nicky laughed. "No need for a damn Kodak moment. Let me clear up the dishes."

"No, no, no," I said, jumping up from the table. "You made this wonderful dinner. The least Antoine and I can do is dump these into the sink until someone decides to wash them."

Nicky sat back down as Antoine and I piled dishes and marched into the kitchen.

I ran a hot sudsy sink full of water, placing the dishes in there to soak. I turned around and found Antoine staring at me. This man was a cornucopia of things, like how light–shone in different angles–could bounce different rays off a stained-glass window. With one glance, he was a young, boyish man, full of whimsy; and in another glance, he was this sexual being, dripping with appeal from the tip of his black locks down to his feet. Now, he had all qualities rolled up into one, standing there in his staple outfit: jeans and tee shirt. He ran his fingers loosely through his hair.

I wondered what it would feel like to have his soft silky hair teasingly moving along my torso, over my breasts, my nipples. My face reddened, and it was my turn to stroke my fingers through my own hair.

"What was that thought?" he asked, taking a step toward me.

"Nothing," I responded back quickly, turning back to the sink and picking up a scrubber.

"It was something." I could hear Antoine's soft footsteps coming closer and soon I could feel his chest against the top of my shoulders, his imprint pressed close to me. I sighed. "I saw your face redden," he added. I jumped, almost out of my skin when he whispered in my ear, "I saw a look of lust pass over your eyes. Lust for whom? Me?"

Without asking, he slipped his long arms around my waist, pulling me even closer to his front. He groaned, as did I. He kissed the lobe of my right ear and I shuddered, whimpering, "Antoine, behave…what has gotten into you?"

"You," was all he said before kissing my ear again. I could feel the wet lines of his tongue move from my ear lobe to the back of my ear. My knees buckled, and I held onto the sink. How could I scream out to him that it had been a long ass time since I had looked at a man let alone had one make me feel like I was on cloud infinity. In fact, no man had ever made me feel like that. Until then.

I was about to turn around to commence to kissing Antoine deliriously when the phone rang. We stood, frozen in our position, Antoine's arm tightly around me, his breath ticking my ear and neck, and my hands secure on the sink.

"Antoine!" Nicky yelled. "Phone. I think it's that white chick, Sabrina or something."

"Samantha," I whispered.

Antoine's hands dropped like lead from my body, and I moved away from him, needing to add distance from my body and my heart. He looked at me as if he wanted to apologize, but I turned away, focusing on the job at hand, washing dishes. Besides, what did he owe me? We kissed a few times. I lied a few times. We felt a few things, nothing worth admitting to, right?

CHAPTER *Twelve*

ANTOINE

Monday afternoon, I was heading up the elevator to Samantha's penthouse. She had told me that one, she had a surprise; and two, we needed to discuss the financial arrangements for my art line with her galleries. As always, she was waiting at the elevator with open arms.

"Hello, handsome," she crooned.

I kissed her softly on the cheek.

"Hey, Samantha. Sorry I'm a bit late," I apologized. "You know how the traffic can be."

A knowing look ran across her fair features. She was looking as lovely as ever, with her light blond hair pulled up in a pageboy upsweep, her handsome yet feminine face heavily made up. Now I didn't have a problem with ladies and makeup, but I couldn't help thinking about Roxy's natural non-pretentious beauty, and the light makeup and lipstick she always wore compared to...well, Samantha's. Thoughts of Roxy and what I hoped I could have with her made me feel really uncomfortable with Samantha, even though we really hadn't spent much private time since dinner at Houston's.

Samantha and I sat in her beautifully decorated office. She was showing me some figures that were blowing my mind. The set-up with her galleries was different than with Lincoln, in that with them it was a one-shot deal.

I would have a certain amount of paintings available, and they would pay me one set price, regardless of sales. With Samantha's galleries, I'd get an advance and also, I could comfortably look forward to monthly royalties according to sales, with me grabbing thirty-five percent.

"Whoa! This sounds great. Now if only I can get busy enough or enough in demand to keep me painting through the night."

"That's what we're hoping for," she agreed. "Really though, Antoine, we don't expect to have a hard time selling your work. That is the reason why we are willing to gamble with this large of an advance for you."

She handed me a white envelope as she spoke. I opened it, gasping at the sum.

"Da...dayum! This is more than I expected, way more!" I exclaimed, staring at the huge numbers typed on the check.

"That is just how good we feel you are, dear. I mean, I know how good you are, but that's another subject there," she joked with a wink. "We already have three clients asking about you and the portrait you put up. The one you call *Mystic Maiden* is sold, and get this, for ten grand!"

I was thrilled. Ten thousand was a lot for an almost unknown like me.

"I can't believe it. I never expected things to roll so fast."

I was beaming like lightning. I couldn't believe dreams were finally starting to come true for me. I automatically grabbed Samantha for a hug. My mother was a hugger, and her affectionate ways had rubbed off on me.

Samantha squeezed tight, pressing herself against me. "I've missed you, darling," she said softly, standing on her tiptoes and pressing her lips against mine. I kissed her lightly, then moved away slightly.

"You okay?" she asked curiously, then jumped right into her next thought before I could answer her. "I got another surprise for you, Antoine. One that I really think you will definitely love. C 'mere..."

I followed her reluctantly, knowing that somehow I would have to let her know that I didn't want to roll like that with her anymore, that I had someone else that I wanted to get real with. But, at the same time, how could I do that without insulting her? Plus, my work being so tied up in her galleries. Samantha Lox was a jewel indeed to have in the art business, but she could be almost death to an artist's career as an enemy.

"Look," she said, catching my attention again. I walked over to the big picture window where she was standing. She pointed toward a navy blue Jeep Cherokee, gleaming in the afternoon sunlight.

I looked over to her in puzzlement. "Wassup?"

"Wassup? Wassup is that that Jeep is yours, darling. I got it for you as a gift, no more taxis and trains for you, lover. Here are the keys." Samantha's smile was as wide as the Eiffel Tower was tall, standing there waiting for my reaction. And what reaction could I have? I was still trying to focus my vision on the gleam of that Jeep!

"Well? Do you like it? I thought, Cherokee, because of your Cherokee line. Get it?" she buzzed.

"Samantha..." I looked from the Jeep to the new keys in my hands. I was trying to find the right words to say. "I don't know what to say. I mean it's tight, I love it, but I can't accept it."

"And why not?"

"Because I can't. I mean that's not like, a little present. It's a car, for God's sake. I mean, I'm not a..." I looked at her, trying to find the right words to explain. She jumped in.

"If you are thinking that I'm trying to buy you, don't, because I got it as part of your advance. And let's face it, Antoine, you didn't have a car and you needed one. Now you have one. You are going to make me big money, honey, so I'll get it back ten-fold." Samantha grabbed both my hands, caressing them with her own. "Trust me, it's nothing to do with our personal relationship."

"I, I do trust you but..."

"No buts. It's yours, darling, paid and in the clear. If you want, I'll put it in the records as an advance. But I really don't want to do that."

I sighed, looking out the window at the Jeep again. It was sweet as hell.

"I think that would make me more comfortable, to be honest with you. Will you do that then?" I asked. My back was still to her.

It all felt funny, too funny, but if it was part of my deal then...I felt

Samantha come up behind me, reaching her hands around me. She started unbuttoning and unzipping my jeans. *Dayum, she wanted to kick it…*

"Anything you say, baby," she whispered in my ear, stroking me up and down. I stiffened. *This ain't right,* I thought to myself. *It's just not right.* My inner thoughts must have registered to her somehow because she stopped suddenly, turning me around to look at her. "You don't want to play anymore, do you? You haven't enjoyed what we've had? You feel pressured, forced?" A hurt look coated her face.

"No, no, it's not that!" I lied, speaking up quickly. *Why don't you just tell her,* I thought, silently wanting to kick myself. "It's just that all of this has been overwhelming, and I'm also dealing with some personal shit. It's not you." I grabbed Sam's hand, bringing it to my lips. "I just haven't felt too good today." I cleared my throat.

"You mean you're coming down with something? Why didn't you say so?" she asked, feeling my forehead.

Great, now let me lie and tell this chick I'm sick, or maybe I should tell her "*This* is making me sick."

"I'm just tired and a bit stressed. But happy, too," I assured her. "Sam, I hope you know I appreciate everything you've done for me, I really do."

"I know, baby, and it's okay. How about a rain check?" she asked with a pout, running her nails up and down my thigh.

"Yea, yea, we'll do a raincheck."

I drove my brand-new Jeep Cherokee home, with mixed feelings, of course. But there comes a time when a brotha has to just go with what comes, at least that's what I tried to convince myself.

I got home, showered and decided to do a relax night for Antoine, chilling with some juice, trying hard not to think about my new Jeep not having a Club on it, or the thought of some fool jacking it before I had a chance to even seriously power it up. I jumped out the shower and slipped on a pair of shorts. I fixed myself a tall glass of iced tea, grabbed my laptop and popped in a CD.

Welcome, you got mail! "Junk mail," I said out loud, clicking "delete" at all the ads and advertisements on my AOL account. I was about to sign off when suddenly, Roxy's work e-mail popped into my mind. Maybe it would put a smile on her beautiful face to know I had her on my mind. I couldn't deny the fact that rarely an hour had passed without my thinking of her. I clicked for new mail, and started typing.

To: roxywinters@visions.com

Roxy, surprise, huh? Just a little something to let you know you've got a brotha in Manhattan thinking about you. But then that shouldn't be a surprise. I think about you a lot. I hope you enjoyed yourself last night. Nicky can cook her ass off, always has. And more than Nicky's cooking, I enjoyed you, period, especially holding you, for that brief period that I was able to.

Can't get you out of my mind, Roxanne…I hope you're thinking of me. Email me back when you get a chance.

Antoine…

All right, here I go. "Spell check, pushing send." I sighed, put my laptop aside and lay back sipping on my tea. I wondered what she was up to. And try as I might, one thing I wrote to Roxy in the e-mail was definitely true; I could not get her out of my mind. I closed my eyes and could almost feel her, taste her mouth moving over mine. "Dang…" I groaned. Keep this up and I'd soon need another shower, but this time on the cold tip.

You got mail! I almost ignored my new message, having forgotten that I was online. My daydreams of Roxy were far better than the unreality of the Internet. But curiosity got the better of me. "Probably more junk mail," I said to myself, clicking the yellow AOL mailbox. It was from Roxy!

What a surprise. I was thinking about you, too. I'm just about to leave for home, trying to get some odds and ends wrapped up for Charlise. She really is a cool boss. Seems like great minds think alike. I haven't been able to get you out of my mind either…funny how much easier it is to say that to you here, huh? I'm going to sign off now, but guess what? I got a huge smile when I saw your name on that email:O)

Sweet Kisses

"And if she could see my huge smile, she would think I'm some goo-goo fool," I said aloud. I was slowly but surely going nuts over this girl. So much that without even a thought, I clicked over a link that said, FLOWERS, GIFTS, BALLOONS AND YOU! And ordered special delivery, to Miss Roxanne Winters.

Nicky

Business was picking up, booming actually. Finally, I was beginning to feel like I could actually get somewhere feeding these mickey flickies. I had a dinner scheduled to cater a ladies book club that was having a birthday celebration for one of its members, and wanted to big it up, catered and all. It was really only twenty- five ladies, so this time I didn't need any help, meaning…(fingers crossed) I should make out pretty good moneywise, without having to pay a helper.

While I was packing up the last of my things and waiting for my stuffed crab hors d'oeuvre with crackle shell, a dish that I'm quite famous for, it hit me that I had forgotten to call Miss Thang. Okay, Roxy. I guess I'd have to relent and say she doesn't seem as bad as I first thought she was, but still, if she were to fuck with my baby's mind I would mess her up, period. During the dinner with her and Antoine, I tried really hard to be cordial, almost failing at the sight of Antoine shining up in her face like she was a freaking Quarter Pounder from McDonald's or something. I haven't had a chance to talk to him much since, but next time I do, I'm gonna have to tell him, don't be so dangone obvious, damn it!

"Ouch!" I exclaimed, burning my finger while placing the stuffed crab shells on a tray. I ran cold water over my fingers, then picked up the phone to call Roxy.

"Roxy?" I said, after she picked up. "This is Nicky."

"Hi, Nicky, how you doing?" she said cheerfully.

"Oh, I'm fine, but I wanted to let you know that I talked to my landlord this afternoon. He said to let you know that he does have an apartment available. It's one bedroom, living room and a small kitchenette, too."

"Yes!" she screamed.

I pulled my ear away from the phone to avoid hearing her shout. I mean girlfriend was happy, that was without a doubt.

I made a face and jokingly said, "Girl, that's my ear you're hollering in. Anyhow, he said to tell you to come around tomorrow, anytime before six and he can show you the place. Y'all can talk about it and what not. So I'll talk to you later, okay?"

"Thanks, Nicky, I appreciate your looking out," Roxy said.

After hanging up I looked around, trying to remember the last bits and pieces I needed to take care of before leaving. I was known for leaving something behind, no matter how small. I had put most of everything in the living room, except for my hotplate dishes that I wanted to take out last. The phone rang again.

"Damn, who is that? I got to go!" I fumed. I walked back to my kitchen. "Hello!"

"Wassup, dyke…"

"Excuse me?"

"You better watch yourself, dyke. Pussy-eating bitches like you end up cold and laid out at the morgue," said the whimper, husky male voice.

I slammed the phone down hard, bringing my hands to my mouth for a moment. *What the hell…*

It took a moment to gather my wits about me, and for my hands to stop shaking. Things were getting weird as all fuck around here. First, I'm harassed at the club. Now some sick muthafucka is calling and threatening me *in my own home!* I shook myself, opening the front door to start taking the food and drinks out to my car, when the phone rang again. I paused and looked around, as if someone else were in my apartment. I slowly picked up the receiver.

"Drive carefully, bitch!" the husky voice said, laughing wickedly.

"Stop it! Don't call here no more, damn it! Leave me alone!"

I slammed down the phone and fell to my couch in a shaken heap. My hands shook as I gathered up my food dishes, trying not to focus on my fear. I had no idea who could hate me so much to do this. I had always been a person who kept to herself, not ever having a lot of friends other than Antoine. When you grow up fighting the demons that tell you that your sexuality is wrong, that you aren't normal, then trust is not an outstanding attribute. It had never been for me either.

I had gotten an armful and headed out the door to my car when Leon, one of my neighbors, went past me as I walked toward the parking lot.

"Yo, Nicky, what's going on with your whip, boo?"

"Who…what?"

"Your car, shanty. It's funked," he announced.

I looked at him, trying to register what he was saying. "No…," I said, shaking my head. I walked faster, trying my best not to drop my armful. "Oh, my God…"

"See, told you. It's funked," Leon repeated. "Somebody trying to spook you or sampan'?"

My Taurus had purple paint sprayed over the top and sides, and across the front windshield were the words: DIRTY DYKE.

CHAPTER *Thirteen*

Roxy

I felt so giddy; I couldn't stop moving. All morning, I was running up and down stairs at Visions, conversing with patrons of the gallery while I checked out the sound systems in the bookstore café. The furniture would be arriving any day, and the bookstore and café stood with new paneling, gleaming floors, new and spotless kitchen appliances, and a sound system set for background music and stage performances. If this were the only thing going on in my life, I would have been thrilled enough, but no, God have given me a couple more sun moments to shine upon me.

I was already figuring out how to smooth-talk Nicky's landlord. I would definitely have money in hand and a smile on my face. It meant a lot to me that Nicky remembered to check it out for me. I knew she wasn't my biggest fan, and to know that she would find out and call me, too, it added to my sunny disposition and feelings that things were definitely on the upswing. A great job just about well done; a newly found cynic-turned-maybe-friend had me on the verge of finally having my own official digs; and then of course, there was Antoine. That man had me anxiously bouncing out of my bed every morning before my alarm clock rang because I knew that the day wouldn't go by without either hearing from him or seeing him. I figured if I got up early, the sooner I would see him. The logic didn't always hold up, but I could settle for my second rationale: getting up earlier gave me more "awake" time to think about when I'd be able to hear from or see Antoine.

Whenever I thought about him, I felt this welling fear in my heart. In Baltimore, Dee had warned me to confess my feelings for him, and while I was at it, tell him the truth about my past.

"You may be his soul mate, true love," Dee had said, "but if you don't act upon your feelings, someone else will step in and take your place."

Since that kiss on the cruise, I had wanted no other kisses but Antoine's and that thought alone had me in a tailspin. After all, I never believed in that happily-ever-after, one man-one woman shit. Never ever felt that I would be weak enough to allow those types of feelings to enter into my mind. But did loving Antoine make me weak? No...for I had never felt this strong, this sure, this purely happy before.

I felt like Julia Roberts, finally finding my Richard Here like she did in *Pretty Woman.* I was trying to convince myself that I deserved to be with someone like Antoine. I had to work on expressing it though because I knew that Antoine already had his attention thwarted with the likes of Samantha Lox. I had no idea how important that relationship was to Antoine beyond professional. Not that Samantha was unattractive, but I couldn't help but wonder why he would be so fascinated with her. When she called him the night of our dinner with Nicky, both Nicky and I had the urge to kick the phone from his hand. He could have easily told her he was busy, or something. But he didn't, and that hurt.

However, I realized, he didn't have to tell me anything about his relationship with Samantha. That, in some small respect, also kept me from saying anything about my past. It would take a lifetime to be able to explain the series of events that led up to my life as a high-class escort. If I were to have a relationship with Antoine...or any man for that matter, I would want to enjoy my time with him in the present and future, and not live my life to explain my mistakes. The idea of painting my life on canvas came to my mind. I had the fuzzy beginnings of a painting in my head, one that would embody all that Roxanne Josephine Winters had been and had become.

I mentioned to Charlise the painting and she quickly pushed me in front of her easel, begging me to paint. I laughed at the time, but she was serious. She could see the artist in me, without so much as seeing one of my strokes firsthand, except for my portfolio book. I felt that if I wanted to touch Antoine's soul, to make him understand the real me, painting…art would be my foundation for that.

"Penny for your thoughts." I looked up, finding Charlise leaning against the entrance of the bookstore where I was sitting in one of the old stuffed sofas I'd found. I was in there on a short break, sipping coffee while perusing a copy of *Chicken Soup for the Artist's Soul*, a book that was giving my inner artist the fuel it needed to hopefully come back to life.

"Girl, you know inflation got that penny up to a nickel now." I watched her saunter into the room and plop down beside me on the sofa. "What are you doing down here? What if a patron comes?"

Charlise threw her hands up as if she didn't have a care in the world. "They'll ring the bell, and voila, I shall appear."

I chuckled. "Just looking out for your interest."

"Believe me," Charlise said, "everything in here is insured. Besides, these works of art have devices on them to keep from being stolen. I'd like to see the crook who would even try to snatch 'em up." Charlise tapped against my bare knee, peeking out from under a short black pleated skirt. "You know, you never told me about dinner with Antoine, or anything else regarding him. You *do* know that he is so incredibly sexy, he needs to be snatched up immediately, right?"

I laughed at the fast spewed words of Charlise. She had the same hyped speech of Dyeese when she first met him, then was alone with me to tell me just how fine Antoine was. Everybody wanted to make sure I knew how special they thought Antoine to be…that I needed to make him and me an item, and fast.

"Dinner went great." I blushed. "His girlfriend Nicky, I don't even want to get into all that, but I will say that the two have an extremely close relationship, and sex is not even a part of the equation."

"So she's not competition?" Charlise asked.

"Not in the boyfriend-girlfriend relationship way, no. But they share a very deep relationship. He would dump a woman quick before messing things up with her, I think, so you know it's almost as important to befriend her as it is to befriend Antoine."

"Does she like you?"

"At first, I know she didn't, but after the great dinner, I'm thinking she might be warming up to me. She also talked to her landlord about an apartment for me. I'm going to see him later about it."

"Congratulations, Roxy." Charlise gave me a hug.

I felt this overwhelming tightening in my chest. The love and pure excitement Charlise had for me and my joys were wowing. She was my boss but, more and more, she was becoming a true girlfriend, sistah-friend, something I had been lacking. Before Dyeese and Charlise, I had no real female friends, except for Deandra, and I realized with Charlise's hug that this type of woman connection was a definite necessity in my life. I craved it.

"Thanks, Girl. Say a little prayer for me this evening. Maybe as soon as the end of the week I could be moving my junk to my new place."

"I'm saying one now as we speak." Charlise winked.

The buzzer of the front door sounded, shocking both Charlise and me. I hopped up from the sofa and took Charlise's hand. "Let's see who wants to partake in purchasing exquisite works of Visions."

"I don't know if I can take all this happiness coming from you," Charlise said jokingly.

"Hush, and come on."

We took the escalator up to the first floor, and as we came closer to the door, I noticed the person on the other side was holding what looked like strings for balloons. When Charlise opened the door, my eyes widened. There were at least twenty-five, thirty balloons in an array of colors, hovered over the deliveryman's head.

"We having a party and nobody told me?" I laughed at Charlise.

The deliveryman looked at Charlise and then me before saying, "Hi. Are either of you Roxanne Winters?" *Who would send me such a bouquet of balloons?* I thought.

"Um, I'm she," I whispered.

The deliveryman smiled and raised a clipboard for me to sign. When I did, he handed me a bunch of balloon strings along with a card.

"Have a good day," he said before leaving.

With help from Charlise, we were able to get the balloons inside of the gallery, and standing at the door, Charlise giggled.

"Open the card, open the card," she squealed. "This is just so precious!"

With shaky hands, I removed the card from the envelope and read…and sighed…and inwardly swooned. *Meet me at Panchitos, One p.m. XOX, Antoine.* My free hand rose to my heart as I sighed. "They're from Antoine," I whispered.

"What does the card say?" Charlise asked, leaning against me to read it. "Ooh, he wants you to meet him at Panchitos?" I nodded and felt my eyes swell with tears. Charlise must have noticed them and the emotionally ravaged expression on my face.

"What's wrong, Girl? Talk to me."

"I…" I raised my hand to wipe the tears that had trickled down my face. "It's stupid, Char. I don't want you laughing at me."

"I would never laugh at you, Roxy. Come on, tell me what's wrong."

"I've never received anything like this from a man before. Flowers, candy, Valentine's Day, birthdays, Christmas, a nice piece of jewelry, a 'thinking of you' card? None of that…never met a guy who felt I was worth it…unless they were getting something out of it."

"Getting something out of it?"

I shook my head. My tears and golden happiness mixed with yesteryear sadness overwhelmed my thoughts, allowing things to slip out.

"You know how guys are," I added, snickering and trying to play it off. "They never want to give unless they think they are making an investment."

"True." She laughed back.

"Anyway, I'm just totally taken aback by this…want to like find Antoine, kiss him and tell him how crazy I am about him."

"Well, *do that*, Roxy," Charlise said, with a strong assurance in her voice. "He's one of the good guys. I can feel it in my bones and it's obvious he's got a love jones for you."

Charlise was really trying to be a diverse somebody with her "love jones" comment.

"Okay, Miss Love Jones," I said. "I'm in agreement. I think Antoine is the real deal, too, and when I see him at Panchitos this afternoon, I hope I can use the sweet feelings I have right now to tell him what he does for me."

Panchitos was a quaint yet festive restaurant. I had been there once before and fell in love with their enchiladas, even stepped up to their baby-grand piano and offered to belt out a tune. I sang *Someone To Watch Over Me.* As I waltzed into the restaurant, I felt that God Himself had heard my song and decided to create this path for me, a path to Antoine. When the hostess approached me, I told her I was there to meet Antoine Billups. She quickly ushered me to the table.

I saw him before he saw me, watched his eyes move along with the entrees and drinks in the menu, his hair glistening beneath the soft lights of the restaurant. His navy-blue V-neck top went so well with his coloring and, at that moment, I wanted to profess all my feelings with no remorse. Three steps before reaching him, he looked up. His eyes were shining yet his expression was questionable, as if awaiting my response to his balloons.

He rose from his chair and took me into his arms for a hug. I looked at him and whispered a "hello" before kissing him on his lips–a soft, lingering kiss that left me as hot and achy as I know it did him. When we were both seated with our drinks and lunch ordered, Antoine reached across the table and took my hands.

"So, you liked my little surprise?"

I nodded. "It was the best thing I have ever received." My thumb stroked the patch of skin between Antoine's thumb and index finger. "I loved it, Antoine." *And I love you*, I thought to myself, wishing I could open my mouth to say the words out loud.

"I'm glad you liked them. After getting your e-mail yesterday, I saw the link for ordering balloons and flowers, and thought it would put a smile on your face."

"You've done more than that, Mister Billups."

"Oh, really?"

I smirked, blushing. "Oh…yes."

The waiter returned with a mineral water for Antoine and a margarita for me.

"So, what's been going on with you, Roxy?"

"Well, your girlfriend has hooked me up nicely," I gushed.

Before Antoine could ask what girlfriend and what hook-up, I spilled forth Nicky's assistance in getting me in to talk to her super. Antoine smiled brightly. I could tell he was pleased to see Nicky and I getting along.

"That is great," he said, winking across the table at me. "Have both my girls living in the same complex." My eyebrow rose at the words "my girls," and Antoine knew I caught them but continued to sip on his mineral water, refusing to acknowledge my questioning glance.

"It might be a good thing to have you there," Antoine added. "Lately, I haven't spent as much time with Nicky because of my work with Samantha." I cringed, hoping it was all internally. "I'm worried about my girl, and with you around, and with you two growing and perhaps becoming good friends, she can confide in you."

"I thought she told you everything?" I asked.

"Normally, yea, but sometimes, we get 'human,' too, acting like we can't share, like we'd be too embarrassed to tell the other things."

Like me telling you I love you, I asked myself. *Or wanting to know about your relationship with Samantha*?

"Well, I think Nicky is a really cool sister, and if she'll talk to me, I would be there for her."

"See, you make it so hard to not like you. Everything you say seems to be dipped in a can of love and warmth."

I squelched an "ooh, ahh" and a sigh that erupted from my throat and knocked on my lips, begging to be let out. "Just telling the truth," I picked up my margarita and began drinking.

"You're looking beautiful today."

My eyes closed briefly as I tried desperately to fight all the warmth that seeped under my skin. "I'm sure you say that to all the women in your presence."

"No, only you. You know, if you allow me to paint you, I can keep you in my life forever."

"Wow, you're creative with the pick-up lines, huh?" I chuckled.

"I keep it real with you, Roxy," he said, a serious tone to his voice. "I told you once before that you should be painted. Your beauty, your essence should be on a canvas in all its colorful complexity."

"I have a colorful complexity about me?"

"You try to act as if you're one hundred percent together, as do most people in the world," Antoine explained. "But I can feel you, Roxy. I can feel all the inner crevices of your soul, and even though you like to keep yourself to yourself…I hope someday you can open yourself up to me."

For the second time that day, I tried to keep in my tears. This time I was close to succeeding. At this most pivotal moment in our conversation, the waiter came back to the table, with our dishes: chicken paella for him, shrimp paella for me. We planned to share, but would we eventually be sharing more than lunch together? *That's* where my mind was right then.

"So, um, what's going on with you, Mr. Billups?" I asked, drinking down my margarita in gulps.

"Actually, life is almost great," he said, his serious expression moving into the joyful stage. "My Cherokee line has been picked up and I received a nice royalty check…and a new car. I'm on Cloud Twenty."

"Wonderful, Antoine. You just go, boy! I'm so proud of you."

I wanted to kiss him so bad, to express my joy for his happiness in more than just smiles and congratulatory words.

"Thanks. I'm too happy about it."

"So who picked you up? Who is going to make you a star?" Antoine lowered his gaze. I swallowed hard, instantly realizing who supplied Antoine with money and a car, maybe more? "Samantha?" I asked, failing to remove the pain in my voice.

He nodded. I felt him stare at me while I focused on the shrimp paella. My tongue felt numb as I ate the spicy flavoring of the rice, peas, and shrimp. All I could think about was what Antoine and Samantha must have done together. My year-long celibacy streak had been weakened by the thoughts I had of Antoine...of what I wanted to have with Antoine, more than just sex. A best friend, a lover, a companion–all the things my parents embodied.

After swallowing a mouthful of paella, I asked, "So, do you care for her?"

"She's a very dear friend, yes," Antoine answered, his eyes never leaving my face.

"You know what I mean, Antoine."

"Okay, tell me this. Do you want me to want her, Roxy?"

My eyes told him no, dump her; my lips remained silent. Eventually, Antoine spoke with, "I want you, Roxy."

I looked into his eyes and saw the love, the lust, the sexual tension brooding beneath them. I opened my mouth to speak, to tell Antoine that I was feeling him the exact same way, but instead, fear clenched at my throat, and I reached for my water.

I was pacing from foot-to-foot in front of Visions. Antoine insisted on coming back to the gallery with me. This was a date and he wanted to drop me off at a doorstep. He was hoping for my apartment door, but beggars couldn't be choosers. Besides, he had a new ride. Why travel an hour via trains or pay a fortune for a cab when he was right there? Antoine was mere inches away from me and, in a second, he had that space closed in, his chest lightly brushing against my blouse, and my awakened nipples straining against the fabric. I stifled a moan.

"Thank you for the balloons, and for lunch," I whispered, watching Antoine's eyes fasten onto my lips.

"Anything for you," he whispered, his hands finding solace against my hips.

"Mmm," I moaned reluctantly. My hands sought out his, and our fingers intertwined. Before I knew it, I had leaned in even closer and kissed him, not a soft dainty kiss, or one full of maybes, but one that said, *Yes, Antoine...I want you, too...so much.* I swear I could feel his heartbeat resonating in my right breast as mine flowed into his chest, like a circular respiratory of love flowing between us.

The kiss ended...way too soon in my opinion, and I looked up into Antoine's eyes, still finding that safe, warm loveliness within them. "Call me?" I asked, my voice soft, tentative.

"Oh...yes, most definitely," Antoine answered, dropping one last kiss on my mouth before walking back to the sidewalk, hopping into his sparkling navy-blue Jeep and pulling off.

Seeing him leave, still feeling his heat, his lips still on mine, I raised my fingertips up to my mouth to capture his taste. I couldn't fight it anymore. I wanted him...and I was going to fight my demons in order to have all he had to offer.

Hot Damn! I was batting a thousand today! Blessed to have a wonderful job, received the bouquet of balloons from Antoine–a man whom I had kissed just hours earlier and still had embedded into my brain. And now I was leaning against the island that separated *my* living room and kitchenette as I signed my lease!

I felt as if my face was about to break off from smiling so much. Mr. Davork–my new super–laughed at me while I jumped up and down and read through the contract. I rambled on and discussed some things with him before handing him over first and last months' rent and signing my year-long contract.

When Mr. Davork left with funds and contract in hand, I walked slowly around my new apartment. Yes, it was small, but it was all mine. The floors were hardwood and the living room was big enough for a sofa and chair, coffee table, my entertainment system, all of which I had in my NYU apartment. The bedroom was large for my dresser and king-sized bed and stationary bike. The kitchenette was just the size for a woman who *could* cook, but didn't divulge in it too often. The bathroom sold it for me. It was quaint with one of those huge oval tubs with the claw feet. I could quickly envision lying in it with the bubbles up around my neck.

After about fifteen minutes, I got tired of doing the happy dance solo and went in search of bothering Nicky. My apartment was 3E, so I bounded up the flight of stairs stopping in front of door 4B. I rapped on her door to the tune of *Happy Days Are Here Again*. I knew that would get her out there with a scowl on her face. "Nicky," I sang, "come open this door before I put on a Broadway performance in your hallway."

Nicky opened the door, and I stepped back, eyeing her up and down. All other times I had seen her, she seemed to exude this cocky bravado but, this time, I was hit with a sullen feeling from her. She looked the same, her Queen Latifah-*Set It Off* type of dress, baggy jean shorts and a red Polo tee. Her hair was in fat cornrows, but her eyes were dull and her skin looked drawn.

I continued to smile cautiously anyway. "Girl, don't hit me, but I have to give you this." I hugged her hard, not only for the apartment hook-up, but because I also felt she needed one. "I want you to know I appreciate what you did for me, you know?"

Nicky leaned out into the hallway, glancing up and down it before saying, "Come on in. No need to be loitering up the hallway."

I followed her inside.

"The apartment thing is no prob. I know my Antoine digs you. I promised him and myself that I would be cool with you…until you showed me I shouldn't be."

"That's decent of you, Nicky, because I like Antoine, too, and I would like to be cool with you as well."

"Go ahead and tell me your version," Nicky said, falling back onto her sofa.

"What version?" I asked, confused.

Nicky guffawed. "He called me right after your lunch date." I tried to look stunned, even though I shouldn't have been. "So, did you enjoy yourself?"

I sat in the chair opposite the sofa and shrugged, though I could tell Nicky wasn't buying it. "Do you even want to know? If this is going to make you uncom..."

"If my baby is happy, I'm happy, so go ahead."

Before I knew it, I had poured the whole balloon/lunch day to Nicky, waving my hands animatedly as I talked. She looked preoccupied, as if she had some other place to go or that she really didn't care about my version of the day's events. I was beginning to think that Nicky wasn't as cool as she pretended to be about whatever Antoine and I were up to. But then her phone rang.

Nicky's eyes grew huge as she jumped up from the sofa and snatched up the cordless. She listened for about three seconds before hanging it up and reaching behind the phone's base to unhook the cord. "I swear, you would think I owe people money." She returned to the sofa. "Phone been ringing off the hook, and I've been trying to do some meditating today."

Her hands were shaking and her voice had a quiver to it. "I know I may be crossing a line," I said, eyeing Nicky, "but I don't believe a word you just said. What's wrong?"

Nicky remained silent for a good five minutes, and I continued staring at her, waiting for her to speak. "Look, you know I'm a lesbian, right?" she asked, her voice slightly annoyed. I nodded. "Well, some things have been going on lately that have me nervous. I don't know what to do about them."

"Things, like what?"

"Like the other night I was harassed coming from a bar with this sistah. And I've been getting a lot of phone calls from the same man saying nasty shit to me, been getting hang-ups, and then last night..." Nicky stopped, shaking her head, anger flushing her skin. "Last night I was on my way to an event that I was catering when I found my car totaled, spray painted purple and on the hood, someone wrote '*Dirty Dyke*'."

I moved from the chair to the sofa, giving Nicky a hug. "Girl, I am so sorry," I sighed, scratching the back of my head. "What did the police say when you reported your car?"

"I didn't go to the police."

"Nicky! Please, please promise me you will. There are a lot of wackos out here who get their rocks off from fucking with people, just because they have hang-ups. Maybe this sicko is doing this to other women—men, too, for that matter."

"I don't have much faith in the police around here," Nicky said, with an almost defeatist tone.

"So, you're telling me you want to keep going through this," I pointed at her unhooked phone, "or even worse?"

I sat there with one hand around Nicky while she thought about what I said. In the back of my mind, I was wondering how much of this Antoine knew...and if he didn't know, how would he act once he did?

CHAPTER *Fourteen*

Nicky

I sat in my car for about fifteen minutes outside of the NYPD 48th precinct. I knew that what Roxy said made good sense but, on the other hand, reporting the harassment somehow made it more real to me. I wanted to believe that this was just a nightmare, or even a bad joke maybe. But I had received another threatening call this very morning and was getting fed up. Something had to give.

I finally got up my nerve and walked inside the busy precinct, looking around for someone who could possibly help me or at least lead me in the right direction.

"What can I do for you, miss?" a tall white fella asked me.

"Umm…I want to report an incident," I said nervously. He looked toward a counter with a line of people standing alongside it.

"Right over there, but it may be a wait," he said.

"Thank you." I got in the line. Looking around I caught sight of a woman, maybe about my age. Her face was black and blue and swollen, her lips fat and bleeding. She glanced back at me with a weak, lost look in her eyes. I looked away after a moment, wrapping my arms tighter around me. *I did not belong there.*

Finally, I was standing at the front of the desk with a police officer asking my name and information. "So what can I help you with?"

"Well, I've had someone harassing me. At first, it was outside of a club. Lately, it's been at my house. Someone's been calling and hanging up, and calling me names, stuff like that."

The police officer looked at me blankly. "That's it?"

"What do you mean, that's it?" I exclaimed, looking at him as though he were crazy. "I want to report this. I'm a single woman, I live alone, and I'm very upset and nervous about this. It hasn't just been phone calls either. The other day when I came out to my car, someone had spray-painted dirty words on my windshield."

"What kind of dirty words?"

I hesitated, not sure if I wanted to reveal to this cop that I was lesbian, but at the same time wanting and needing their help. "They had sprayed *Dirty Dyke* across it."

"Ahhh, I see." He looked at me knowingly. "So you think this is a gay bashing?"

"I don't know. I mean anybody can be harassed, gay or straight." I sighed.

"You said you were first harassed outside of a club. What club was this?"

I paused. This was getting ridiculous. "It was the Viper, off 44th and 3rd."

"The lesbian joint?"

"Yes."

"Whoa..." He shook his head. "Look, miss, I think I'm finally starting to get a picture of what's going on here. I mean, yes, I do believe you are being harassed, but it could be an ex-lover or something, couldn't it? Some woman you pissed off in the past? Can't you find out who it is and straighten it out with her? Kiss and make up or something?"

"What does it matter what type of club it was? Harassment is harassment, and it wasn't a woman. It's a man and he's been calling me 'bitch' and 'whore' and 'dyke,' saying for me to watch my back. It's not a pissed-off lover thing!"

"Just calm down, okay?" He looked at me with a smirk. I swear his black, ashy ass was pissing me the fuck off. "All I'm saying is that I know how you ladies go at it sometimes. I'm here to help you figure it out. But with so many serious crimes going down around here, we also don't want to make a big deal out of something that may be small. I mean, think about it, phone calls? Your car spray-painted? A gang could be responsible for that. You have to have proof before you start swinging accusations. You understand what I mean?"

"No, I don't understand what you mean. I have no idea how other women or ladies, as you said, act, nor do I care. All I know is that I want the harassment to stop. I even have an idea of who it may be."

He cocked his eyebrow. "And whom may that be? You have a name?"

"A friend of mine's husband. His name is Winston Greer."

"And why would he want to harass you?"

I was silent a moment, thinking that I'd put my foot in my mouth with this one. It didn't take a genius to see that this cop was biased and thought my being a lesbian was amusing. So now what do I say? That I thought my harasser was the husband of my on- again, off-again creeping lover? I looked at him and sighed, shaking my head.

"Look, this was a mistake. I'll handle it myself, okay?" I backed up and started to walk out of the precinct.

"So what you're saying is that you don't want to file the report?" he called out.

I turned around and looked at him. "I'm saying, what's the point? I can do better getting rid of my little problem all by myself. Thanks for nothing."

I got in my car. Holding my fingers against my temples, I could feel a migraine coming on. It was just too crazy. "I don't know why I even bothered going in there," I said to myself.

My pager buzzed against my hip just as I was about to start the engine. I looked at the number. It was Belle's, a small café that I baked breads and tarts for. I had quite a few small restaurants and cafés that I contracted with. All of them combined made up my monthly income, outside of the catering jobs I did, of course. I grabbed my cell phone and dialed their number.

"Belle's!" came the high-pitched voice of Lisa, the owner.

"Lisa, what's going on? This is Nicky."

"Hi, Nicky. I'm glad you called. I just paged you. Listen, we had a little problem this morning. Some guy came by looking for you."

"Looking for me?"

"Yes, he came in basically making a scene at one of our counters. Asking for Nicole Carter, and saying some really awful things," she continued. Her voice was stiff.

This was starting to sound worse and worse. "What kind of things?"

"Well...telling the customers not to eat the tarts you brought by, that they were poisoned. Screaming out that they were made by a crazy lesbian, and all kinds of obscene things. A few of our customers walked out and we eventually had to call the police. But he had already left, so nothing came of it."

"Lisa, I am so sorry." I fought hard to hold back my angry tears. Now this bastard was messing around with my clients.

"I know, Nicole, and I'm not blaming you. But you know that we have been in a slump as it is lately with business, and I would hate for some rumor to get around about our food. My husband is livid, and he says he doesn't want to do business with you any longer. I'm really sorry," she said sincerely.

"But why?" I cried. "You two have always ranted and raved about my tarts and breads. I had no control over some lunatic coming in and making trouble!"

"I know that, Nicole," she said quietly. "Listen, maybe you should watch who you have as friends. This person seemed to know you. He certainly knew enough about you to come here and make a scene. Like I said, we are already struggling with our business. We can't afford rumors like this. We can finish out the contract. It's like another month I believe, but that's it. Again, I'm very sorry."

I stared at the phone for long minutes after she hung up, feeling a knot in my throat growing at an enormous rate.

I had the windows down and the radio up as high as I could possibly stand it all the way home. Anything to get the shit out my head. I was starting to feel more than scared; I was starting to feel straight up pissed!

The pissed-off feeling intensified when I opened my apartment door, and there stood Mya, naked as a jaybird.

"What are you doing here?" I said. I observed her nude form, high breasts and shapely hips, and felt totally unmoved.

"My goodness, aren't we friendly today," she said sweetly, walking up to give me a kiss. I drew back. "What's wrong, Nicky?"

"Mya, does Winston know about me?" I demanded.

"Why would you ask that? I'm leaving Winston. He knows that much, but he doesn't know about us." Mya tried to put her hand around my waist, still trying for a kiss. I pulled back again. "Come on, Nicky, why are you acting all stanky danky?"

"Because, I believe your husband has been harassing and making trouble for me. For the last week or so, I've had hang-up calls and my car spray painted and all kinds of whack shit happening."

"And what does that have to do with Winston?" she asked defensively. "I mean, I know he can be a bit of an asshole sometimes, but he is no crazy person who'd be harassing someone. He doesn't know about you anyhow, just like I told you. The only reason I'm even considering leaving him is because I'm tired of sneaking. I want you and I to spend more time together. I want things to be more solid between us. Don't you want that?"

What in the world was she talking about? I just knew this chick wasn't thinking I wanted some one-on-one thing with her. That was not my cup of tea, and she already knew that. I didn't need some girl hanging all up on me. I had always made my position and feelings on relationships picture clear.

"Listen to me, Mya," I said slowly. "I'm not the one for that. I mean, I've been completely happy with things as they are. You know what I'm saying? And as for Winston, I know for a fact that he has been harassing me. I saw him at the Viper."

"The Viper? When? And what were you doing there?" she asked.

"What do you mean what was I doing there? I was doing what everyone else be doing: chilling and meeting people. And when I left with a friend, there were two guys waiting outside, calling us dykes and stuff like that. I had to pull out my blade to get rid of 'em. But then as I was starting up my car, there was your Winston, high-fiving one of them, and parked right beside them. He *knew* them."

A look of jealousy coated Mya's face. It was pretty obvious to me that she hadn't heard anything I had just said about her husband. "So you are seeing someone else now?"

I sighed deeply. "Girl, that ain't even what this is about. Are you even hearing me?"

"Yes, I heard you!" she screamed. She walked toward the couch, grabbing her jeans and slipping them back on. "I don't believe this shit. I mean you just don't care who you fuck, do you? While I'm home thinking about you, looking forward to the next time I can be with you, planning how I can finally settle things with Winston so that I can make that break, you're out at the Viper picking up bitches!"

I shook my head, staring at her in disbelief. To be honest, my entire day had been one of disbelief. Any worse and I'd think it was really Friday the 13th and someone forgot to tell me. "I think you should leave. Mya, it's pretty clear that you and I aren't on the same page right now. And I see whomever I want, okay? If I'm out picking up bitches, it's no different than how I picked you up at the same damn club! And do me a favor, tell your husband to back the fuck up, 'cause I've already clued five-O on his ass, and I'm not joking."

"Nicky, I love you! Why are you being like this?" Mya cried, big tears streaming down her face.

"Stop it! We ain't never been about that, and you know it. I care about you, Girl, but I'm not seeking no love thang. Not right now, not eva! I've always been honest with you. I told you how I felt from the start. Back then the fact that you were married was no problem for me because you said you weren't looking for more either. So don't come to me now with this change of plan talking about you're leaving your husband and want to be with me, 'cause I'm not even hearing that!"

The room was quiet after my drawn-out words. Mya stood completely still, tears still flowing. Me, I felt like shit as I walked over toward my window blinds, closing each one to the Manhattan sunlight.

"Now what do I do?" Mya asked quietly. "You don't want to see me anymore all because you got this crazy idea about Winston?"

I looked at her somberly. Mya was a sweet person, a good friend, and a fantastic lover. But my sense of calm and well-being was being threatened, along with my business and reputation. I had done business with Belle's for a year, a whole year, and now all because of Mya's sick husband, that was gone. And I knew it was him. I knew it. There was no way I was ever going to get anywhere if he started going through my clientele like that.

"We'll talk later, Mya, okay? Let's just leave it for now. I'm tired and I need a bath. I have deliveries to prepare for tomorrow."

Mya put on her bra and blouse, and left quietly, without another word.

ANTOINE

Rise and shine are not always the operative words, not when your crib looked as unkempt as mine. Then again, I hadn't been spending a lot of time in it lately either. It's funny how busy a brotha can get once his work is actually in demand. Those are smiling words there: "in demand"…those are the words that every artist, singer, writer, actor or anyone in the field of selling their talent wants to hear. And I was finally hearing my song.

I got up kind of early, wanting to get a head start on for the day, but at the same time I needed to clean up my place. Now with things seemingly warming up between Roxy and myself, I didn't want to chance her stopping by and getting a glimpse of what a slob I could be. I flopped down in my La-Z-Boy, taking what I felt was a much needed break. I couldn't help but smile, thinking about Roxy, the look on her face when she walked into Panchitos. Things were looking up, moving faster, although not nearly fast enough for me. I was biding my time, waiting until it seemed the "normal" time to give her a call. The longer I looked at the clock, the less obscene it seemed to be dialing her up at seven forty-five a.m., so I picked up the phone.

She picked up on the sixth ring, right before I was about to hang up and give myself a swift kick in the ass for seeming too anxious. “Yea,” she said sleepily.

“Roxy, how are you?”

“Antoine? I’m fine, boo. How are you? Is everything okay?” she asked.

“Yea.” I laughed. “It’s just that I hadn’t talk to you in a few…hours, and I missed you.”

“Hold up,” she said, putting me on pause.

Great, I thought, remembering what Nicky had told me about begging and appearing desperate. But somehow I couldn’t help it. I was really feeling her, that *all-I-could-think-about-is-you* type of feeling.

“Sorry, I wanted to wash my face real quick. You got a sistah straight out of dreamsville, boy,” she said. I could hear the smile in her voice.

“Dreaming of me, I hope,” I pressed.

“Mmm…maybe.”

“Maybe, huh?”

“Yep,” she joked again, “maybe.”

“What if I told you I dreamt about you?” I whispered.

“And what did you dream?”

“I’ll tell you next time I see you.”

She sighed. Hmm, I was getting to her, good. Maybe now she could feel a bit of how I’ve felt from the moment I first saw her on that ship. “So, are you working today?”

“No way. I have my new apartment to piece together, and Charlise gave me some time off to do it. I’m going to take advantage of every single free moment.”

“So do you want some help?”

“Well, my furniture, the little I have that is, arrives this afternoon. My sister Deandra is giving me her old set, and it’s arriving from Baltimore. A few friends from school are going to help me pull that in, so really all I’ll have are boxes and a bunch of junk, but I’m just enjoying having my own place, you know?" She breathed in deeply. "There's no place like home."

I felt warm, picturing her again. She was so bubbly and happy, reminding me a lot of my mom in that way. "Is this your first apartment?" She paused for a long moment. "Roxy, are you still there?" I asked.

"Yes, I am. And yes, it's my first real apartment. When I was in L.A., I was just staying with my girlfriend. It wasn't really my place."

"So when you worked as a nanny, you didn't do live-in?"

"Umm...I lived with my girlfriend, and I would go over to baby sit in the mornings. It was really weird, not at all ideal, which is one of the other reasons that I quit and started dancing."

"Damn, girl, what have you not done?" I shook my head laughing. A thought hit my mind. "What kind of dancing did you do?"

"Hold up, Antoine," she said again.

I waited patiently, thinking that she was acting kind of weird. Or maybe it was me and my seven-thirty a.m. willies. A lot of minutes passed.

"Hey," she said on her return, "sorry I took so long. Someone was on the other line."

"Oh, okay...So, do you want me to come over and help you a bit? I'm free for you."

"Maybe tonight? Around six?" she asked. "Maybe you can tell me about that dream," she whispered.

"Six it is," I agreed. "And, baby, I'll tell you anything you wanna hear... Maybe we can *live* that dream."

"Mmm...chill bumps!" We both laughed, feeling kind of goofy.

"Later, baby."

"Lata..." she whispered.

Hours passed and I was just about to head out the door after having a rather upsetting conversation with my old man when the phone rang again. My mood had definitely changed from the morning. Seemed like

I'd spent the entire day on the phone. First, my call with Roxy, that was my uplift for the day, 'cause let's face it, the lady warmed me inside out. Then there was the disturbing news from my father. Tests had revealed that a pacemaker was probably the least of his worries, but he also might be looking at a double bypass. I felt a mixture of fear and anger talking to him. Fear of what could happen, and anger at his know-it-all, trust in the Lord and nothing could or would ever happen to him attitude. If there was one thing I knew for sure, no one was protected from health problems, or could escape if the angel of death came a knocking, not even Reverend Billups.

I answered the phone hurriedly, wanting to leave and pick up some groceries, and maybe something for Roxy's apartment, a housewarming type of thing.

"Hello!"

"Antoine, this is Samantha. How are you, darling?"

"Hey, Samantha. Listen, I'm on my way out, okay? Can I call you back later?" I felt frustrated.

"Okay, but listen, hon, I need you to pop by here tonight. I have some news for you, and it's too good to give you over the phone. Besides," she said seductively, "it's been too long. I need you, Antoine. I want you..."

I sighed, feeling the stress building to an even higher level. I had to tell her, regardless of the consequences. I had to get this out in the open. Risking losing Roxy was not an option for me...I was slowly coming to realize that I was feeling something real and lasting for her.

"Samantha..." I said slowly. "Can we meet tomorrow? We really need to talk."

"And what's wrong with tonight?" she insisted. "Be here at say, sixish? I'll be waiting with my news, and some Moet. Buh bye, handsome."

"Damn it!" I said out loud after hanging up the phone. I had my plans with Roxy, had made them myself, and now this! Thing is I couldn't just not show with Samantha. She said she had news and it could be pertaining to my art line. But it was final. I had to tell her I didn't want to deal anymore outside of business and friendship; I had to. And if she was the woman I'd always respected and admired, she would accept that.

I hope...

I called Roxy up about an hour before I was supposed to be there. I had been hoping against hope that Sam would somehow call me and cancel, but of course she didn't. I didn't even have to wonder if Roxy was upset. I could tell by the sound of her voice.

"You have to work, with who? Samantha Lox?" she had asked, quietly. "Okay, no worries. I'll talk to you later."

"It's just that this was an unexpected meeting, Roxy, but you know I'd much rather be with you. You know this," I pleaded.

"One thing I've learned in this adventure called life, Antoine, is that a person is usually where they want to be. But like I said, no worries. I'm not stressin'."

"Roxy..." There was a stilled quietness on the other end. I sighed. "I'll call you tomorrow, okay? I'll contact you as soon as I can. Goodnight." She hung up without a word, but I felt even more determined to end things with Samantha.

That determination hadn't faltered while I was going up the elevator to her penthouse.

"Guess what?!" Samantha said, after giving me the big squeeze.

"What?"

"We've scheduled a showing for you. It's in two weeks. It's going to be at the gallery, and it's going to be big!" she exclaimed, smiling broadly.

I admit, despite my determination about ending it with her, I was pleased. An art showing at a prestigious place like Samantha Lox's Galleries was like a dream come true. It was like a coming- out party to an artist, and it was already rolling around in my head, exactly what pieces I wanted to display.

"We want you to show everything you've got," Sam said, reflecting vocally while I was thinking to myself. "Not just the Cherokee line, but everything. It's good to let art buyers see how diverse you are. And, Antoine, darling," she cooed, "your name will shine! There is a market now, as you know, for new artists. And there will be buyers there all the way from France."

All I could do was shake my head in wonderment. Things were getting overwhelming, but in a good way.

"How can I ever thank you, Samantha?"

"You don't have to." She sat down comfortably on her white couch, with me following to sit down beside her. "Just keep doing what you're doing. You're going to make it, darling."

I sat quietly, letting it all soak in. "Okay, now," she said in a breezy tone. "You said that we had to talk?"

"Yea…we do…"

"Well then, shoot." I looked up at her and her eyes were dancing. She reached out her hand, tracing my facial features. "With your handsome self…I think your dark, exotic, good looks are going to sell your paintings along with your talent." She laughed at my expression. "Sorry, go on, go on!"

"It's just that, Samantha, you know that I care about you…" Samantha started to break in, then paused as I put up my hand. "I love working with you. I appreciate everything that you have been doing for me, more than you could ever know. And I've enjoyed the brief sexual relationship that we've had. I won't deny that. But…"

"But? Lord, please don't tell me that you're gay?" she asked in horror.

"God no!" I exclaimed. "No, it's nothing at all like that. Believe me, I'm into ladies only."

She giggled. "Sorry, it's just that you know how the business can be. Whoa! What a relief though." Samantha focused on me again. "Okay, so what is it then?"

"The other day when you asked me if I didn't want to play anymore, I wasn't completely honest with you about my feelings. I don't want to anymore, but it's not you. It's just that I'm in love with someone, and I'm hoping to have something with her."

She was quiet, looking at me somberly. "The girl from Houston's, right? Roxy something? She was on the art cruise."

"Yes."

"And why didn't you think you could tell me? I had no illusions about us, Antoine." At my silence, she answered her own question. "You thought that my support to you as an artist was dependent on or because of our intimate relationship, right? You thought that if you told me that you didn't want it anymore, then I wouldn't want to run your line?"

"In a way, yes," I admitted. "Samantha, you of all people know that it's hard getting a break in this business."

"Yes, it is, but I've told you numerous times, Antoine, that one had nothing to do with the other. Hopefully, you've found me attractive, and our working together was not the only reason you've slept with me..."

"Of course not! You're a beautiful woman, Samantha."

"I hope not, because that *would* upset and hurt me. But see, I am a very astute businesswoman, and artist; I know a good catch when I see one. And while I will admit that I've been partial to you, I would never have risked my reputation and money on an artist that I felt had no talent, or put so much into you, if it was just because you have a purty dick and know how to use it."

I felt myself flush inwardly. *Damn, she didn't mesh words, did she?* "So, um...are we okay now?"

"Do you really love her? Does she love you?"

I sighed. Reality was hitting. "I don't know how she feels about me. But I've never felt this way about a woman before."

"Then you tell her that, sweetheart," Samantha encouraged, touching my cheek. "I will say this though. She's a lucky girl." She sniffed. "And yes, we–me and you–are fine. I'll pout and lick my egotistical wounds for a while, of course. But I like you, Antoine. You're a sweet young man. I want you to be happy, and that Roxy couldn't possibly *not* love you back." She kissed me softly on the lips. I kissed her back deeply–for gratitude, for being one terrific lady and because she was one of the most likable and caring people I'd ever met.

"Mmm...baby," she moaned, "keep that up and I'll be fighting this Roxy girl for you, and I won't be such a swell loser."

"Thanks, Samantha."

She touched my cheek again, mouthing quietly, "No problem, handsome..."

CHAPTER *Fifteen*

Roxy

He stood me up. That's the only thing that stuck in my mind during this supposedly happy day of moving into my new place. As soon as the sun rose, I was up packing boxes. To top off my already depressed, angry mode, in the midst of packing, I came across my journal, the one that contained every horrific moment of my life. Most people would have thrown it away, to finally put the past in the past. But to me, it was a record of how through the grace of God, I had managed to move on past my rape, past my days of being a call girl, leaving the country with Thomas, and watching him die at his own hand. I quickly dropped the journal into an empty box, wanting it buried deep…I may have kept it, but seeing it tore me apart.

I called Charlise, reminding her that she would be helping me and, by the stroke of luck, my girl, Dyeese, came to town the night before from Baltimore for a meeting with a prominent art buyer who was interested in her work. She thought she could come holler at me and hang out a minute before the meeting. She was here, so why not put her to work? By eight a.m., the girls and I were boxing up my junk and transporting everything to the rented U-Haul I had downstairs.

We had managed to move out everything in my bathroom, kitchen and living room, minus the sofa. Steve said he would be over to get it and help us move the things in my bedroom. For now, us girls passed out on my bare mattress, catching our breaths.

"Girl!" Dyeese moaned. "When you get settled in, you'll have to invite us over for a gourmet meal!"

"Uh-uh," Charlise added, "I want cash!"

I laughed in between heavy pants of breathing. "I'll hook you guys up. You know I appreciate this, seeing that you two and Steve are my only real friends here in the city."

"What about Antoine?" Charlise and Dyeese asked in unison.

I rolled my eyes and sucked my teeth. "Like I said, I got *three* friends."

"Whoa!" Dyeese yelled, rolling over on my left leg. "What's going on? You and Antoine aren't cool anymore?"

"Just a day or so ago, the man bought you a gorgeous bouquet of balloons," Charlise said, equally confused. "I saw you guys having one of those *love* moments outside the gallery after your lunch. What's up?"

"Honestly, I don't even know why I'm worrying about him," I said, more to myself. "So what we met on a cruise; so what we shared an incredible kiss; so what I've been fighting him off like the damn plague; so what he creeps into my mind like the wind through the sky; so what, so what, so what?"

I slid Dyeese's head off my left knee so that I could get up off the mattress. I was antsy and jittery, and couldn't stand still for too long. Once up, I smoothed down my cut-off jean shorts and absentmindedly tugged at my white tee shirt that was tied up under my breasts.

"So, are you going to leave us in suspense or what?" Charlise asked, swinging her legs off the mattress. "What did he do?"

"Okay, see, it's like this," I said, my words coming out fast before I stopped myself. "Antoine called me yesterday, which was great because I was missing him…" I momentarily stopped and shunned my girls for awing at me. "…and I was still swooning after the balloons and lunch and the kiss. Gawd, the kiss," I whispered, raising my hand up to my forehead to farce a dramatic swoon. "I've never felt like this for anybody," I said, afraid of actually saying the words. "Anyway, he called, saying he would come over last night, help me pack up my boxes and all, but lo and behold he called me back, telling me he had to go to Samantha Lox's place…for work."

"Are you serious?" Dyeese asked.

"Girl, I mean, does he take me for BoBo the Fool or something?" I asked, hands thrown onto my hips. "He said he would get back at me as soon as he could, and I haven't heard from him since."

"It's been what, not even a day?" Charlise laughed. "Don't condemn the man yet."

"Whateva, Char, for real, going to someone's house, a *someone* you kicked it with at night? No, unh unh, *nope*, I don't and won't believe that mess–especially when he made plans with me first."

"Grant it, I haven't spent time around him like you and Dyeese have," Charlise began, "but I mean just in general, what type of guy would say the things he's said to you, or do the things he's done for you, if he didn't care?"

Dyeese and I glanced at each other before shaking our heads.

"Okay, I'll let that slide, because you're a white sistahgirl." I plopped down beside Charlise and wrapped my arm around her shoulder. "Even though, just as a woman, you come in contact with those men who are just dogs, who will do any and everything to get the skins…even if it's buying someone a nice lunch, paying bucks for a beautiful scarf or surprising her with balloons. It's all about getting her to soften up, to get her to succumb to his charms."

"So, you mean to tell me that you honestly believe that Antoine is using you?" Charlise asked. "White or not, I know the game, too, sistahgirl, and I know that there are good men in the world. And hell, Antoine is sexy! Why would he continuously pursue you when just about any woman would die to have a stab at him? Uh, not saying you aren't beautiful or anything, Roxy."

I fell back on the bed, holding my belly and laughing. "I get what you're saying, Char, I do…just right now I'm pissed, because first, he tells me he's all into me, tells me he's going to be there for me, and then he disses me for his lover? That hurts."

"Then tell him that, instead of condemning the brotha to hell," Dyeese suggested.

Before I could respond, a hard knock resounded from my door. It was Steve. I quickly gave him a hug. "Thank you so much for helping me, Steve," I said.

"You know anything for you, Roxanne." Steve brushed back his blond hair. "I was wondering when you were leaving this place. I'm finally outta here tomorrow."

"Well, let's get me outta here today, okay?" I asked.

My NYU apartment was spotless. Steve and us girls removed everything in record timing, and Steve stayed to help mop the floors and clean appliances before I left. When the last sponge was tossed in the U-Haul along with everything else I owned, I wiped my hands along the back of my shorts and smiled toward my moving crew.

"I'll never be able to repay you guys." I gave them each a hug and continued to hug onto Steve. Throughout my last year there, he had been a sounding board when I became frustrated with classes or with life. Living right across the hall from me, he was the best choice. He was the only man that I felt I could trust, aside from my father.

"You girls are getting a gourmet meal and love and hugs forever and always." I laughed. "As for you, Steve," I added, hugging him tighter and planting a kiss on his cheek, "what can I mail to California for you?"

"Well, you know," he said, his gray eyes twinkling, "when I went to visit my family in California, I found an apartment for me and Kat."

"Yea, yea, yea," I said. "You told me. I'm jealous. It's gorgeous. What do you *want*?"

He playfully shoved me. "Remember the art class we took as an elective, and that painting you did and absolutely hated?"

I laughed, remembering vividly. The exercise was to draw your future and, for some odd reason, I painted the canvas black, with a perfect white circle in the center. "Why in the hell would you want that piece of crap?" I asked.

He laughed. "To put up in the apartment."

"But it's *crap*," I reiterated.

"To me, it was the light at the end of the tunnel," he responded, "and it reaffirmed for me that you and I both went through some things, and that light was indeed at the end of our tunnels."

Instantly, I teared up. I rubbed my eyes, wiping the tears before they had a chance to fall. I gave Steve another hug, this one harder, tighter, before whispering, "I love you, man."

When I opened my eyes, I saw a dazzling blue Jeep pull up behind the U-Haul and froze in Steve's embrace. *Antoine*. He jumped out of the car, eyeing Steve and me suspiciously, as if he had caught me in a compromising situation. I loosened my grip on Steve as Antoine walked up to the gang and me.

"Hey, Antoine," Dyeese said. "How are you doing?"

He turned to Dyeese, offering a wide-eyed look and a smile. "Dyeese," he said, giving her a hug. "Wow, haven't seen you since the cruise. What's going on?"

"Well, supposedly, I'm here to talk to an art buyer about purchasing some of my paintings," Dyeese began, laughing, "but when I showed up on Roxy's steps last night, she quickly enlisted me as a mover and a shaker."

They laughed. Even through his small talk with Dyeese and then Charlise, Antoine's eyes hardly left me or Steve for that matter.

"Steve, this is Antoine," I said in a clipped voice. "Antoine, this is my classmate, Steve. He was cool enough to help a sistah out and move all the big things."

Antoine sized Steve up before they shook hands. Out of the corner of my eye, I could see Steve smirking, as if he knew what was up and made no qualms to correct them.

"I'm gonna go," Steven announced, supplying me with another big hug. "I need to finish up my packing so I can head back to California. Don't forget to send me that painting, okay?"

"As soon as I unpack it, you got it, babe. Thanks!" I watched Steve jog back into the building and noticed Dyeese and Charlise back away from Antoine and me.

"Hey," Antoine said in a soft voice.

"Hey."

I felt Antoine's eyes move along my body quickly, before settling back to my eyes. "Um, can we talk?"

"Actually, I'm about to go, but you know, I can get back with you as soon as I can."

Antoine's eyes pleaded with me. "It's really important," he insisted. "I'm sorry about last night."

"No reason to be sorry. Samantha's your girl and all…who am I to be upset over that?"

Antoine glanced at the girls who had moved near the front of the truck where their own vehicles were located. He leaned in close to me, close enough for me to be intoxicated with his manly, natural scent, and his berry fresh breath.

"Roxy," he whispered, causing me to lightly shiver, "please talk to me…let me explain."

I bit my lip before raising my eyes to meet his. I was lost. Sighing, I responded, "Okay, Antoine, fine. I really do need to get going, but how about you swing by my place tonight, so you can talk?"

His positive expectations made my heart flip. "I'll be there," he said before planting a soft, wet kiss onto my lips and hurrying back to his Jeep. I stood there, watching him leave and damn it, I felt light like a gentle spring breeze.

"Yes, Miss Thang, my own place!" I squealed into the cordless phone. My apartment was in mass trashdom, with boxes piled in the bedroom, the living room, the kitchen and my bathroom, waiting to be unpacked. Before they left, the girls, along with Mr. Davork, helped me get everything into my apartment and helped situate my sofa, chair and bed, so that at least, I'd have a place to sleep. While I conversed with my sister, I opened boxes in the kitchen, taking out pots and pans to place in the cupboards.

"I'm so proud of my little sister!" Dee screamed into the phone. "Got yourself a nice job, now a new apartment. What's next, a man?"

"So, how are you and Step doing? How are the wedding plans going?"

"No, see." I could hear Dee chuckling. "There's already a man in your life, isn't there? 'Fess up, I'm your sister. You can hold nothing back from me."

"If you really must know, nosey girl, I'm *talking* to a guy, yes."

"Is it the guy you mentioned when you were down here? Anthony…"

"Antoine."

"Ooh, so it is him? Hmm, how is that going?"

I leaned against the island before letting out a scream.

"Damn, that good, huh?"

"Better."

"Dang, I wish I could dish more dirt with you, Lil' Sis, but there's an O's game tonight, and Step and I are headed there shortly."

I dropped a pan when someone knocked on my door. "It's the welcoming committee!" Nicky yelled on the other side of the door.

"Okay, Dee, you can get all the dirt you want later. Tell Step hi for me and give big ol' hugs to you and him both. Love you."

"Love you back, babe. Later." I ended the phone call and jogged to the door, opening it to Nicky who was holding a bag.

"What's this?" I asked.

"Dinner. I knew you would be too tired to cook after moving, so I got you some orange chicken and lo mein. I hope you like."

"I love orange chicken, Nicky. Thank you so much because for real, I'm starving. Come on in."

I grinned at the swaggered way Nicky walked into the apartment. This girl didn't care who knew she was into women and loving it. I wasn't mad at her for it either. Nicky followed me to the kitchen, where I found two plates and forks, and pulled out two glasses. In the fridge, I had a bottle of white wine chilling, something I had put in there as soon as I entered the place, so I could have a celebratory glass for getting this apartment… now was as good a time as any.

"Have a bite with me?" I offered, already piling orange chicken and lo mein onto two plates.

"Sure," Nicky answered.

I examined Nicky's face while I piled the plates. She was smiling. But I detected something not as happy under the surface, and it wasn't like me to keep my thoughts to myself, so I opened my mouth.

"Did you go to the police, Nicky? I asked. She nodded, grabbing her fork and digging into the lo mein. "Okay, so what did they say?"

She shrugged. "Nothing really."

"You know, if you don't want to talk about it with me, that's cool. I know you and I ain't tight like you and Antoine, so I won't be offended or anything."

I poured two glasses of wine as I watched Nicky chew the food, more because she had to than because she was hungry.

"They didn't do shit," she responded, her voice low, anger evident. "The cop I talked to was one of those motherfuckers that get off on the thought of lesbians. He didn't give a shit about my complaint, telling me it was probably some lover pissed off at me, that he knows how we can be. How the fuck does he know?"

"I'm sorry, Girl." I pouted, genuinely upset. "Stupid ass cop. I hate it around here, like you have to damn near die before they even look your way, or try to help."

"Yea." I walked around the island to Nicky, giving her a hug.

"So what are you going to do?" I asked.

"I'll just have to handle it myself," she answered, shrugging. "I think I know who's behind it, and if I can just catch him harassing me, something, I'm going to turn his ass in."

"Be careful," I warned. "Don't do anything that will get you harmed."

"That's the last thing I need." She sighed. "I've got an event tomorrow night that I'm catering, and after what happened with Belle's, I need to stay alive and out of harm's way so I can pay my bills."

"What happened at Belle's?"

"That stupid asshole went there, slinging out accusations, causing a scene, had the patrons really upset. The owners decided to let me go as their caterer of pastries and breads. It wasn't the biggest contract I had, but it was big enough. I can't lose business like that…not because of some jealous husband…I just can't."

I wasn't even about to ask about the jealous husband, or the apparent wife she was kicking it to. I just continued to keep my arm wrapped around her, our foreheads touching. It was odd. Not too long ago, Nicky couldn't stand the ground I walked on…or maybe that was jealousy. I knew she didn't like me one way or the other, and now there we were, comforting and being there for each other. It brought me back to my feelings of the sisterly bond. I knew that Antoine was Nicky's heart and soul, and that she loved women, but I was thinking she needed a woman...to love her…as a friend, and if that position was open, I just might have to apply.

I was lying on my bed in the dark listening to Babyface's *For The Cool in You* album, listening to him croon out how beautiful I was to him. After Nicky left, I'd unpacked a couple more boxes and taken a long hot bubble bath and dressed in a white tank top and cotton shorts. The only other thing I managed to do was make my bed and plug my stereo up. Since then, there I lay. When the door sounded, I continued to lie on the bed, taking deep, even breaths, calming the racing of my heart.

I got up from the bed and flicked on lights along the way. I opened the door, and on the other side stood Antoine. There were no hellos; he simply walked right up to me, slipped his arms around my waist and drew me in for one of his heart-stopping kisses. I floated back, allowing him to enter the apartment and closed the door behind us.

The bedroom light was a dimmer, and I had it set for just above dark, making it light enough to see the shadows of people. Antoine and I were lying on my bed, on our backs, not touching. I listened to his worries about Nicky, and I filled him in briefly about what was going on, not wanting to tell all of Nicky's business if she didn't want it out there. I could tell, just from his sighs and breathing pattern, that he was really concerned about Nicky. I wanted to tell him I was scared, too, but didn't want to frighten him any further.

Up to this point, the whole convo had been about Nicky, as if we were avoiding the real topic…us…and where Samantha Lox fit into that us. "My dad's sick," Antoine blurted out of nowhere.

"What's wrong?" I turned to face him, feeling the bed move as he turned to face me.

"His heart. He's being so damn secretive about everything, and he hasn't told my mom a single thing about it."

"I'm sorry, Antoine." I reached my left hand out to stroke his cheek. He took my hand and pressed it to his lips. "I can't even imagine how you must feel, because I know I would die if my dad fell ill."

"I need to go see him." Antoine's voice went tight. "I need to see how he and my mom are doing."

"Sounds like a good idea."

"Will you go with me?"

I looked at him. I could see the whites of his eyes, and knew he was staring directly at me.

"Wouldn't you prefer to take Samantha?" I asked, not out of spite, but of curiosity.

"She and I are finished…romantically that is."

My heart skipped a beat, my brain felt fuzzy, and my mouth almost instantly went dry. "Are you serious?"

"That's where I was last night." Antoine's hand slipped from mine. I could feel it moving toward me before resting upon my thigh, bringing him closer to me. "I had to tell her that professionally, we could work together until we both were living as large as possible, but romantically, my heart was somewhere else."

"Where?" I asked in a whisper.

Antoine responded with a kiss, actually several kisses as he moved his lips around my mouth and then planted them firmly on mine. His hand moved from my thigh to the small of my back, gently pushing me closer as he stroked me there. I moaned.

"Right here," he spoke in between kisses. "Ever since that kiss on the cruise, Roxy, I've been so gone in you."

"Antoine," I whimpered, my hands stroking his cheeks as our kisses intensified. I rolled onto him and eventually, we rolled again, with him slightly lying atop of me.

"I love you, Roxy." His words caressed my lips and, with those four words, I cried silently. "Do you love me, too?"

My mind flashed through my life–what led me to not care about my body; my selling of my body; Thomas whisking me to Paris and refusing to let me leave; my sister and her soon-to-be husband rescuing me; and Thomas killing himself. All these secrets swam through my head with that question. How could something so beautiful and sweet, such as this moment, be marred with the pains of the past? Would he love me if he knew these things?

I closed my eyes and banished my past into a tightly locked box, only wanting to feel and experience the *now*, as I kissed Antoine, and whispered, "Yes, I love you…so much, I can't think of anything else but you, Antoine."

I could feel his smile on his lips as they pressed against mine. I had never told anyone I loved them before. I cared for Thomas, but the feelings I felt for Antoine were all-consuming, involving all my senses and emotions. At this most euphoric moment of my life, there was only one thing I wanted.

"Hold me tonight," I choked out to Antoine, still silently weeping. I turned until my back was to him, and he hugged me, pressing his arm against my stomach. He spooned me. I could feel his manhood hard against my backside; hear his groan, hell, my own, too. But tonight, I needed, and I felt that Antoine needed it, too, what it felt like to be loved and held and to feel safe. We had every night to fulfill our sexual needs. This night, I just wanted to be safe and warm. Antoine gave me that and so much more.

CHAPTER *Sixteen*

ANTOINE

"They're gonna love you, just as I do. You watch," I insisted to Roxy.

We were five minutes away from my parents' home in Queens, having fought some rough traffic along the way. Not an unusual thing from Manhattan to Queens, but then again, I hadn't had a vehicle in a while, and had gotten used to riding by either Yellow Cab or the train.

"You think so?" Roxy asked timidly.

She had been nervous the entire morning about meeting them. Why, I had no idea, or maybe I was just biased. To me my parents were the easiest-going people in the world, and Roxy was this beautiful young woman whom I had fallen in love with and was sure they would love, too.

Roxy sighed. I looked over at her, seeing the nervous tension on her face as we waited at the stoplight. She was looking so beautiful. Her light brown hair was pulled back away from her face showing its beautiful shape. Her eyes were lovely and sparkling as ever. She wore a dark blue jean skirt, a mini, and a matching jean vest. I reached down and placed my hand on her thigh, squeezing lightly.

"You're so beautiful," I told her, warming at the love expression that filled her eyes.

"So are you," she said, winking back at me.

I could feel myself blushing even with my choco skin. "Okay, enough of that. We're here." I pulled into the tight driveway and parked. Roxy bounced out my Jeep even before I could with her regular hipping and hopping and bouncing ways, and I loved it. Mom and Dad were waiting for us at the door.

"Oh, my goodness! She's lovely, Antoine!" my ma squealed. "Come on in and give me a hug!"

Roxy laughed at my ma's enthusiasm. I looked at her like, "I told you so!"

"You did good, son," my dad said, giving me a punch on the arm. I looked at him closely. His eyes looked weak, not himself, although he was the same vocally, overruled by my ma, that is.

"It's so nice to meet you both," Roxy said. She looked at me and her eyes sparkled. I reached over and took her in my arms.

"Yep, ain't she fine, dad?" Roxy elbowed me. "Ouch! Well, you are." I laughed.

"She certainly is, son, a beautiful young lady," he agreed warmly.

I chuckled at Roxy's blush. She would have to get use to the Billups' warmth and outspokenness.

"Well, you two have got to be hungry," said my mom as she headed toward the kitchen. "I've fixed lunch, so just go wash your hands and then Daddy can bless the table."

Roxy followed me into the half-bath in the hallway, as my dad followed my ma to help out in the kitchen.

"They are so nice." Roxy was beaming.

"I think so, too," I said proudly. "We're very close, and they love you; in case you didn't notice?" I winked.

"Yada, yada, yada! You don' brainwashed your poor parents. What in the world have you been saying about me?" she demanded, laughing as I flicked water on her.

"Well, I told them that one, you were beautiful; and two, that we met on the love boat; and three, that you had captured my heart…"

Roxy reached her hand out, tracing my lips with her fingers. "Like you've captured mine, boo."

"Children, come on eat!"

We looked into each other's eyes. Roxy pressed herself against me slightly before we exited the bathroom. Her lips worded to me, "Lata, boo..."

Lunch was great. It felt so good seeing my parents welcome Roxy so warmly, although I never really had a doubt that they would. I had only ever brought one other girl home to meet them, the one who had insisted that I cut my hair and do the fade thing back in art school. And although they had not seemed to genuinely like her as well as they did Roxy, they were nothing but warm and polite and welcoming. That was the type of people my folks were. They wanted to know all about Roxy, of course, and about how we met. About her family, and yep, my dad asked her what faith she practiced.

"Well, I've never been a big-time church-goer," she admitted, "but I was baptized at the AME church back in Baltimore when I was twelve."

"Well, you'll have to come to the temple, dear. Doesn't matter what denomination you were baptized into. It's just important that you worship," my mother said. "Maybe you can help bring Antoine back to the fold," she perked.

Oh, oh, I had to find a way to change the subject and fast, 'cause once my mom got started with religion, there was no turning back.

"Roxy used to be a model," I said proudly. "I got an ex supermodel—a regular Tyra Banks over here!"

"Whateva!" Roxy rolled her eyes, smiling, although she gave me a warning look.

"Really, dear? Have you been in any magazines?"

"Umm...no," Roxy said, looking at me oddly. "I mean, I've been in them, but not the majors. Like I told Antoine, it was only something in passing."

I kind of got the feeling from the look on her face that she didn't want to talk about her modeling. I couldn't understand why she would feel that way, but in order to appease her, I changed the subject over to me.

"Nicky sends her love, and guess what? I have an opening, a showing in two weeks, at Samantha Lox's Galleries. Miss Lox said that art buyers from all over are going to be there."

My mom clasped her hands together. "That's wonderful, honey. Roxy, you know that Antoine came out the womb painting."

"I think this is my exit," I said, knowing my ma was going to start bragging on her only child. I stood up. "Dad, can I holla with you for a minute?"

My dad nodded at me as I exited for the living area, leaving my mom and Roxy to their conversation.

"So are you going to need a bypass?" I asked my dad in a low tone.

"Shh, I told you, your mother doesn't know, Antoine."

"I know she doesn't, and I think she should, Dad!" I insisted.

"Shh!" he looked nervously toward the kitchen door. "I won't have you upsetting her, Antoine, I won't! Now when..." My mom called out from the kitchen for us to come have some parfait. "Okay, listen, I'll call you next week. You can go with me for my last set of tests, okay?"

I sighed. I really didn't have much of a choice where my father was concerned. He had always been the rock and foundation of our family, and the thought of losing him scared me shitless.

We spent the rest of the day in Queens. My mom thoroughly enjoyed showing Roxy my old bedroom and baby pictures, some of me dressed in the traditional Cherokee war paints. Roxy got a big kick out of those, even talking my mom into giving her one. The four of us even kicked it with some Scrabble after the light dinner my mom and Roxy fixed. As we were leaving, my parents seemed sad to see us go, but I assured them that I would be bringing Roxy back and often.

Both Roxy and I were quiet on the way back to Manhattan—me, thinking a bit about my father, and she, lost in her own train of thoughts.

"So, should I take you home now? Or did you want to check out a movie or something?" I asked her. "We've missed the seven o'clock ones, but it's only eight thirty now. We could grab a nine o'clocker?"

"Hmm...I don't know if I'm in the mood for a movie."

"I, I just really don't want the day to end, Roxanne..."

"And I don't either...," she said softly.

I looked into her eyes, then made the turn for my apartment.

Nicky

"Everything was absolutely delicious, Nicole!" Lenora James exclaimed.

She was the mother of the soon-to-be bride, whom this joyous event was sponsored for. I had gotten so fuckin' lucky with this one. Now I'm talking the kind of money that be doing what Mase said back in da day, money coming out ya anus! That was these peeps fo sho. They paid me nine hundred dollars in advance, plus fronted the food cost, which most people didn't and wouldn't do. I found a new helper named Nia to replace ol' Jennie, who was never up to par. Nia had to bounce out a bit early, but that was okay. She worked her cute ass off. I even went so far as to do the skirt thang to impress these rich heads, which paid off. They also ended up hiring me to do the wedding, so I was H.A.P.P.Y!

"Thanks, Mrs. James. I'm glad everyone enjoyed the food, I take pride in the art of cooking, as you can see."

"And that you should. You do an excellent job. I'm still tasting those stuffed mushrooms, yum!" she hummed.

I cleaned up the last of the dishes that were mine.

"I'll be in touch with you about the menu for the wedding, okay? And again, thanks a zillion. I'm going to spread the word about your culinary skills."

I thanked her. She and I were the last to occupy the hall. Soon she herself left, leaving me to close up, which was okay with me. Everything was cleaned up, and all I really had to do was get the last of my dishes in my car trunk.

It was a warm, crystal clear night. The parking lot, although not well lit, had the look and feel of the upstate well-to-do New Yorkers who frequented the area. I slammed down the trunk of my car and then headed back to lock up the hall and get my purse. Now a purse wasn't something that this sistah was used to carrying, but I couldn't do the dress thang without the purse, ya know. As soon as I walked back into the reception hall however, I got a funny feeling that I was not alone.

"Mrs. James?" I called out.

Nothing. Hmm…maybe I was just tired and hearing things, I thought. I grabbed my purse, clipped off the last remaining light and turned, landing smack into a hard chest. "What? What the fuck!" I jumped, feeling a hand grab me around my throat, throwing me to the floor.

"Shut the hell up!" the man's voice demanded.

I hurried to get to my feet, trying to reach inside my purse for my switchblade. *Somebody was gonna mug me!* Oddly, I could see the image of the guy who had pushed me down on the floor but felt someone else punch me hard in the back of the neck from behind. I fell forward, feeling an aching pain in my head.

"Yea, you dyke bitch, you ain't so cocky, now are you? You pussy-eating ho, we gonna give you the fuck of your life. You won't ever want a woman again, bitch!"

The familiar voice shook me to my very bones. The same voice I had been hearing over the past week with repeated phone calls and hang-ups.

"Oh, my God, somebody help me!" I screamed.

Someone punched me hard in the face. I tasted my own blood filling my mouth. Just as I was about to scream again, scrambling to get up, I felt pressed down. I couldn't see anything! Only the dim light from the outer hallway.

"Hold her still, dawg! Get her panties down," I heard another voice say.

I felt heavy hands pressing my cut lip into my teeth, almost suffocating me with how hard he was holding my mouth. His hand held my arms over my head. I was not a small woman by any means, but I was also not a big girl. I cried inside when I realized the helplessness of my situation. I felt a third guy ripping my underpants down, and holding my left leg high up. I wasn't even able to move it. Another guy loomed over top of me, pushing his stank growth at my vaginal entrance. Everything seemed to happen in a daze, as one after the other of these faceless men violated my body.

"Take dis dick!" one yelled, thrusting hard into me.

"Turn her over. Flip her ass over!" I heard another voice shout later, after the one had ejaculated inside of me.

Tears rolled down my cheeks. I cried hard, the way I did when I fell and broke my leg as a child, but my pain was more intense. My body became racked with even more pain when someone took me from behind, pushing his hard penis roughly inside of my ass. I screamed, almost passing out from the agony. The laughter of the three rapists filled the reception hall. I mumbled over and over in my mind, *help me, somebody, help me...*

I came to, not really knowing at first where I was, but cried out once it came back to my mind what had happened to me. I tried to stand but couldn't, falling back in a heap on the hard floor. But I was alive; thank God, I was alive! Wetness was all around me. Blood, tears, semen. I searched around in the darkness for my purse, and surprisingly found it. Grabbing my cell phone, I dialed.

ANTOINE

I could not get the key to work. My hands were shaking as I fiddled with it at the doorway.

"Want me to get it?" Roxy asked softly.

"Um, I got it." I glanced at her. Was she feeling at all as jittery as me?

When I finally got the door open, I breathed a sigh of relief, gesturing for Roxy to go inside. I walked in behind her and tossed my keys on the key ring that was tacked onto the door. Roxy stood with her back to me, looking around my apartment as though it was the first time she had been inside. I was glad of that. It showed that she was nervous also, meaning I was not alone with how I was feeling.

"Do you want anything? Soda, juice, I have some Kool-Aid, too," I quipped. I instantly wanted to bite my tongue at my juvenile reference to Kool-Aid.

"No, I'm okay."

We caught each other's eye. She licked her lips, putting her hands to the front of her vest and slowly loosening the buttons. As always, my sofa bed was still out. I flopped down on the edge as I watched her, not able to look away as she revealed the light mocha swell of her tiny but perfectly formed breasts. She was braless under her vest. Her berry-colored nipples were hard and erect. I moaned as I looked at her, feeling my breath catch.

"Come here..." I choked. I buried my face in her midriff with a cry.

"Oh, Antoine, I love you so much."

"I love you, too..."

Roxy's fingers roamed through my hair. I began kissing her belly, moving my tongue in a wet circle around her bellybutton. "Mmm..." I heard her moan.

I looked up at her. Her face was thrown back, and she was kneading and playing with her nipples as she moaned again. I could feel myself straining against my zipper, hard and ready, paining to get free. I lifted her jean skirt, rubbing her lightly between her legs.

"Yes, yes, boo," she whimpered. As I loosened her skirt from the back, it fell to the floor. She wore a black thong, leaving nothing to the imagination. That came off next.

"Ohh, babe," I kissed her belly lower, her hips, thighs. Her breathing and mine quickened as I met at the Y of her love, tracing her lips with my own, parting her with my tongue.

"Antoine!" she screamed out.

I probed deeper, sucking her, licking her. Roxy sighed and gasped, swerving back and forth against my mouth. I continued the oral loving. Gripping her backside, I fell back on my sofa bed, pulling her forward in a sitting position. I locked my mouth in a tight suction, suckling her, nursing her tiny swollen bud. Roxy's thighs started quivering. "Oh, God!

Do it." I flicked my tongue rapidly against her clit. "Do it!" she screamed. "I love you, yes! Mmm…Antoine! Uh..uh..uh..!"

She purred, grinding down against my tongue. I knew when she hit her pleasure; her tiny body was racked with spasms, with her filling my mouth with her sweetness. She fell forward, breathing harshly. We both lay there for a moment as her breathing labored.

"Are you okay?" I whispered. Instead of answering, Roxy started unzipping my jeans quickly. I swallowed, working to help her. I was shaking before she even touched me there, but when her tiny hands moved and stroked me up and down, I gripped her hand, already feeling the pressure building. "No," I said, hardly able to catch my breath. "Sit on me, baby. I wanna be inside you."

"Oh, you do, huh?" she whispered, her voice quivering. Without warning she sat down on me, taking me whole in one movement. I gasped out weakly as I felt her heat envelop me. Gripping her hips, I began working to start the thrusting motions that would take us both to Never-Never land. She shook her head, holding tight around my waist. "Don't, boo, let me do it. You just keep still, okay?"

I lay still shivering as Roxy began to clench me internally, barely moving, just squeezing and releasing, squeezing and releasing in a vise grip. My mouth flew open as she expertly rode me. I tried to moan but dry squeals came out instead. She started indulging her hips, squeezing and releasing, then finally gripping me so tightly inside of her that I couldn't move. She squeezed again and again and again. I felt tiny needles pricking all over my body. She squeezed again, tighter.

My body moved in involuntary jerks and I came, screaming her name with every spasm. "Roxy! Roxy! Roxy!" Stars exploded behind my eyes.

"Where…did…you…learn…that…?" I choked.

She giggled, and then kissed my neck as shivers still quaked through me. "Did you like it?"

"God, yes…"

"Then that's all you have to worry about."

She kissed me, exploring my mouth. I kissed her back deeply. We both lay quietly for long moments, me fighting hard to catch my breath.

"Mmm..." Roxy sighed. "I'll be right back, okay?"

"Okay," I whispered. Finally getting my bearings again, I watched as she walked toward the bathroom before turning to face me again.

"I love you, Antoine," she stated before disappearing into the bathroom.

I smiled to myself, letting out a deep exhale. The sound of the phone ringing jarred me. I reached over and grabbed the ringer.

"Hello?" There was nothing at first, just the sound of someone crying. "Hello? Who is this? Hello!"

"Antoine...Antoine, help me...Antoine..."

It was Nicky!

I was instantly alerted. "Nicky, what is it? What's wrong?"

"They hurt me, raped me," she cried. "Help me, please...I hurt..."

A scared electric volt surged through me, almost akin to pain. "Where are you, babe! I'll be right there! Where are you?!" She weakly panted out the address. "I'll be right there!"

I hung up, looking aimlessly for my jeans. I slipped them on and was grabbing for my shirt when Roxy walked back in.

"Where are you going, boo? Why are you putting your clothes back on?" she asked, looking confused.

"Nicky, Nicky needs me. I've got to go. Now!"

CHAPTER *Seventeen*

Roxy

Five minutes of sleep. Ten minutes pacing around. Thirty minutes of sleep. Five minutes pacing around. I sat in Antoine's bed, baffled as he fled from his own apartment to go to Nicky. Nicky, the love of his life—well, the non-sexual love of his life. She needed him, and he was with her, which left me there alone in his place after a sensational evening of lovemaking. This was a time when I should have been snuggling up close to Antoine, getting to learn the feel of his body. Instead, I was learning the feel of his mattress against the springs...how thick and firm it appeared to be.

I questioned leaving, but thought it best to stay there to give Antoine a piece of my mind as soon as he stepped through the door. As I lay upon Antoine's sofa bed, I could still smell the scent of our recent sexual tryst. My mind immediately went to the visions of him and I connected so perfectly, and how good it felt to be loved and made love to by a man who loved me, wanted me.

I did wonder, however, if I had gone too far with Antoine. As I rode him, I got so lost in the feelings, the sensations of having him inside me that my body went into overdrive, pulling out a suction move I learned from my escort days. I just wanted him to feel as euphoric as I had, but afterward, when he asked me where I had learned the maneuver, I was at a loss for words momentarily, not sure how to respond. Even though I had contemplated telling Antoine about my past, I definitely didn't think the right time was just as the two of us converged in mind-exploding sex.

But I did want to tell him, needed to tell him. I squeezed a pillow close to my naked chest, wishing it was Antoine. The way he looked at me, talked to me, touched me, God, made each pore on my body open up and sing hallelujah. "I love him," I whispered into the pillow, tasting the salt of my tears as they trickled into my mouth. I tried to think about the opposite sex as it pertained to my past. Not even one ever truly loved me, not even Thomas. He just wanted someone he could control.

Losing my virginity at fourteen was a rebellious act, and something I had regretted since day one, something I kept only to myself. To me, sex was always something you just did. There was no meaning behind it. I never got the chance to love someone and make *love* to them. It was all about positioning, timing, squeezing, moaning at the right moment, and climaxing. Antoine made me feel like the kid I was before I gave up my precious cherry. I cried into the pillow, wishing that I had saved myself...for this one special person. But now that the past was the past, I wanted to strive to be the best Roxanne Josephine Winters I could be. That is what Antoine deserved.

"He loves me," I said, still crying into the pillow. I kept that thought and his warm, wet kisses in my mind as I hugged the pillow tight and closed my eyes to catch the next ten, fifteen minutes of sleep.

My breathing had just gotten long and deep when I heard a key being turned in the front door. When the door opened, I immediately jumped up from the sofa bed, butt naked and all. Antoine's face was ashen, and my heart sank. I spotted a tee shirt of his, and I quickly placed it on before going to him. "What's wrong?" I asked, hugging him. He held on to me as if for dear life, his embrace crushing my ribs. I winced, whispering, "Baby, loosen up, and please tell me what's wrong?"

Antoine looked into my eyes, and I could see his coal black eyes swimming in a sea of tears. "Antoine?" I asked, raising my hands up to his face to catch the tears.

"Nick…" he tried, but his voice betrayed him. "God!" His legs weakened, and with an added strength, I helped him to the sofa bed, sitting us both down. I turned his face to mine and repeated, "What's wrong?"

"Nicky's in the hospital."

My jaw dropped and a small cry of pain filtered from my mouth. "Why? What happened? What's wrong?"

"Some guys…I'm going to kill them!" he growled, jumping up from the sofa and repeatedly punching his hands against the wall near the front door.

I began to cry because I was scared for what had happened and for my baby. His anger hit me in all directions…didn't know he possessed the ability to be violent, but whatever happened gave him that possession.

"Baby!" I cried, pulling at his arms. "What's wrong? Talk to me, damn it!"

"Nicky was raped!"

I stumbled back, my knees turning to buckets of water as I poured myself onto the floor in a silenced heap. Raped. God, a word I hadn't heard since…since…

Antoine knelt down on the floor beside me, and we hugged each other for what felt like hours. We cried and hugged each other, and I stroked his hair from his face, kissing his forehead and whispering, "I'm so sorry, Baby…where is she? Can we go to her, please?"

"I wanted to get a few things at her place," he whispered, his eyes never leaving mine. "I don't know how long she's going to be there…it was... pretty bad."

I patted his hands, gave them a squeeze, along with him and a kiss. "Lemme go shower real quick, and we'll head ova to her place and pick up some things."

Antoine nodded. He had a quiet, reserved expression on his face. I rose from the sofa bed and grabbed my clothes that were sprawled on the floor. "Okay," was all that came from his mouth.

As soon as I had the bathroom door firmly closed behind me, I crumpled onto the floor and crawled alongside the toilet bowl. My stomach was convulsing, and my head was spinning. I wanted to throw up, throw up my past, throw up this whole entire scene. But I couldn't throw up, only lie against the coolness of the porcelain bowl and cry. I raised myself up enough to turn the sink water on to drown out my sorrowful tears. "God," I whispered, looking up to the ceiling but seeing so much more than just tiles, "I need you to help me.

"I need you to help me open my heart and my past and to help Nicky get through this. I need you to provide me with the strength to tap into some bad things in my own past in order to do this." I pulled toilet paper off the roll, blowing my nose. "I know I haven't talked to you in a while, and I beg your forgiveness for that, but you know I've been lost and confused on so many things, but this...Nicky, I need you, 'cause she's going to need someone there for her, and I want to be the person who *wasn't* there for me."

Antoine and I crept up to Nicky's room, both feeling afraid of having to be brought back into the realization of this moment. How could something so beautiful, so highly wonderful end with the most horrific experience ever imaginable? I was beginning to think that there was a curse on me and anyone who came within my presence.

On the drive over, I used the silence that a tearful Antoine supplied me to contemplate my own young existence. If I were smart years ago or had someone who truly cared about me around to call on, I could have gotten medical attention, gotten those pricks put behind bars, gotten therapy, learned to love myself. If I had just known right off the bat that this wasn't my fault, that someone deserved to pay, my whole life could have been so much different. That realization rocked me to the core because no matter how much I knew this, the past couldn't be changed. This was just a painful acknowledgment I had to shelve before I went crazy over it.

As we reached the hall to Nicky's room, my mind had reached four days after my rape. I had returned from my trip, my face healed but my body broken. And even though my "friends" bitched about where I had run off to, I had managed to provide a story that made them forgive me.

At Nicky's door, I took Antoine's hands, pressing them against my lips. "Baby," I said, "can I go in there alone for a minute?"

He had a perplexed look for a moment before asking, "Why?"

I kissed his lips, stroking his cheek. "Nicky and I are cool with each other. And we're women. I think it might help if I talk to her for a bit, see if she will open up to me. Besides, I want her to know that I'm here for her."

For the first time since this painful experience, Antoine smiled. "I love you for being so caring to my sister," he whispered.

"Any sister of yours is a sister of mine, too, Baby," I responded. "I care for Nicky also, and if I can help her...then that's what I want to do." I gave Antoine a hard hug, kissing him once again before turning toward Nicky's hospital room.

I was scared, so scared as I peered into the window of Nicky's hospital room. My own body felt violated, destroyed, and I didn't have to imagine what Nicky looked like or what she felt...I had known firsthand. With the silence of a thief in the night, I opened Nicky's hospital room door and stepped inside. Fortunately, she wasn't hooked to any machines, but even from the ten-foot distance from the door to the bed, I could see how small Nicky had become. Nicky wasn't fat, but she was a thick-boned sistah. And in one night, I could see from how the blanket wrapped around her, how she had lost something in herself...like her spirit disappeared, and left the remains.

One...two...three very small steps toward Nicky's bed, the fear climbed in my throat and sprouted through my limbs, making it painful to walk. Reaching the bed, I closed my eyes briefly, saying a prayer to God before looking down at Nicky. "Oh, my God," I whispered, choking back a river of tears.

Nicky appeared to be sleeping, but how she could sleep with the swelling to her face was beyond me. Her right eye was sealed shut and the size of a baseball, and the rest of her face was covered in cuts, dark purple bruises and abrasions. This pain...the face, was nothing compared to what must have been wreaking havoc in her body, I thought, silently weeping.

"What...what you down' here?" My eyes sprung open, finding Nicky looking at me–well, barely looking at me with her one almost good eye.

I pulled the chair behind me up to the bed and sat down, leaning toward the bed. "Antoine told me what happened, Girl," I choked out, raising my hand up to the bed to take Nicky's. She jerked away...I understood.

"How did he tell you so fast?" she inquired between thick- slitted lips.

"I was...um, with him tonight, and uh, he came back...devastated." Nicky briefly looked in my eyes, realizing what was meant by my staying over Antoine's house.

"Where's he at?" she asked, trying to look around.

"He's out in the hall. We went by your place to get a few things, and came here. We didn't know how long you were going to be here."

"Why didn't he come in?" she asked, a tear leaking from her good eye.

I smacked at the tears that fell from my own eyes, trying my damnedest to be strong for her, and for myself.

"I wanted to talk to you alone, Nicky," I whispered. I looked at Nicky's left hand, the one I had attempted to hold. It was scratched up and bruised and shaking badly. In fact, Nicky's entire body held a tremor. My heart broke. "I know you and I aren't really tight, Nicky," I began, trying again to grab her hand, this time succeeding, "but I wanted you to know that I'm here for you, too...and that I know what you're going through."

Even through the bruises and swelling, I could feel the anger rising in her. "How the fuck you know how I feel?" she asked in a low, raspy voice. "You ain't nuttin' but a lil' bougie princess, Roxy...you don't know about no damn hard knocks."

I allowed her to rant. In this situation, I expected nothing else, but I continued to hold her hand tightly as she tried to snatch it away. "I do know," I whispered, leaning over to her, briefly glancing toward the door. "When I first started college, I was gang raped."

This dull, excruciating throb resonated from my heart, but I didn't howl, I didn't die. Only one other person knew about this, and that was Steve. I had never found the courage, never saw the reason to expel my pain to others, but tonight it felt like a dire necessity.

"You were raped?" Nicky asked, slightly disbelieving.

I nodded, biting down on my lower lip as if starving. "I had just finished my first year of college in California. Felt I had the world in the palm of my hand," I began. "My girls and I went to this club to celebrate finishing our first year, and there, some guys tried to pick us up. They were relentless and wound up calling us bitches and whores, even dykes when we told them to fuck off."

I could feel my heart pounding tightly against my skin, and I swallowed hard to attempt to catch my breath. "After a while, they left us alone, and we were able to calm ourselves down. As the night drew late, my girls left. We had all driven separately. I met this dude, and thought he was cool, was hoping to get his number, so I stayed.

"I hadn't met anyone that first year of college, and foolishly thought that this guy could be my gift for persevering through." Nicky was an interested audience, her breathing replicating mine, hard and heavy. "He walked me to my car, didn't even try to kiss me, but when I went to place my key in the lock, he hit me, and I fell to the ground. I felt like a football player 'cause instantly, I was bum-rushed by at least two other men...the men from the club."

"No one came to help you?" Nicky whispered, crying more vocally now.

I shook my head. "I screamed, kicked, punched, any and everything I could, but Girl, I'm not much bigger than a peanut and these motherfuckers were huge. All I could do was allow my spirit to just float above me, protect me, help me to live."

By now, I was hyperventilating, no longer able to fight the tears that flowed. Nicky clasped onto my hand, giving me strength and taking mine for herself. "I never told anyone," I cried. "I went back to my dorm, packed up some things, got money out of my bank account and went away for a few days, waiting for the wounds to heal so no one would know."

"Why? Those bastards deserved to be put in jail!"

"You know, now my original personality is back. Antoine and you helped to do that, but when *it* happened, I just didn't give a fuck about myself anymore. And I especially hated men. God, I was beyond bitter, and that bitterness and self-hatred had me doing some fucked-up shit, Nicky. It was so easy to manipulate men, to take from them, to..." I stopped. I could tell that Nicky was scared of the anger and hate that filled my voice. Besides, my remembrance of the past had my mouth telling more than was needed. I took a breath and closed my eyes, opening them again. "I'm fine now," I continued, failing at a smile. "You're only the second person to know...and I told you because I care about you and wanted you to know that you aren't alone. I'll be here for you, Girl, I promise."

"So, Antoine knows?"

"Oh, God, no," I answered. "I wouldn't know how to tell him this, Nicky. I'm dying inside just telling you."

"You have..." Nicky began, but fell into a coughing attack. I raised her slightly from the bed, patting her on the back.

"You okay?" I asked, worried.

"I'm cool," she winced, trying to get comfortable again. "You have to tell him, Roxy. You really do, and I'll tell you something," I noticed a strength push through the pain of Nicky's body as she spoke, "if you try to manipulate or hurt my BooBoo, you will have to deal with me."

"I would never hurt Antoine," I said, shaking my head. "I love him, Nicky. So much."

"You better," she muttered, clutching my hands in her left one again before closing her eyes and eventually drifting back to sleep. As she slept, I continued to cry, feeling agonizing pain over my past, Nicky's present, and my future with Antoine if I ever told him any of this.

CHAPTER *Eighteen*

ANTOINE

I felt extremely solemn the next afternoon while I drove Roxy home. She had come back to my place, both of us trying to get some sleep, although the sun had been up a while by the time we got settled. It's amazing how one's mood can change. One minute you're in the midst of sexual heaven with the woman you've dreamed about, and that had finally become yours–body, soul and spirit–and the next minute, you are looking at your very best friend, your homie, sis and first ace, crumpled in your arms. I was dying holding Nicky, her weeping and shaking, barely able to speak. An anger I did not know I was capable of had started growing and festering in me ever since.

I slept fretfully with Roxy wrapped in my arms, but woke up after a few hours, thinking back to some things Nicky had said. And even while driving Roxy home, her words hadn't left my head. When I first got to her, I asked if she knew who had done this to her. I remember her saying she thought it was some dude named Winston, and then she mentioned Mya, someone who I didn't know a lot about but whom she had mentioned to me a couple of times. Enough for me to know it was someone she was dating or seeing. I also knew where Mya lived, having been with Nicky a couple of times when she dropped her off at home.

Roxy was talkative, trying to ease the tension, I suppose. She jumped when I suddenly swirled my Jeep around, making a right turn.

"Where are you going, Antoine?" she asked.

"Just want to check on something real quick."

"Ahh…okay, check on what?" she probed again. I stopped in front of a row of houses on the East Side of town, jumping out swiftly.

"Stay here, all right? I'll be right back. I just want to holla at someone for a minute. Stay in the car," I commanded again. I heard Roxy calling my name as I hurried toward the front door of Mya's house. She opened in two knocks.

"Hi," she said, looking at me with surprise. "Antoine, right?" she looked behind her, as if uncomfortable.

"Yea," I said. "Listen, I know we don't know each other that well, but can I come in for a minute? I need to talk to you. Something has happened to Nick…" A guy, about my height, a bit stockier though, slid in front of Mya, cutting into our discourse.

"Wassup? What can I do for you, my man?" he asked me.

"Winston, this is just a friend of a friend of mine. I can handle it, okay?" Mya said hastily.

The name she called him stuck in my mind, suddenly making a rush of heat flood over me. "Winston?" I asked. My eyes narrowed as I looked at him. "You're Winston?" I pushed the front screen door open, rushing at this Winston mofo.

"You raped Nicky?" I shouted. His eyes got huge as saucers, as did Mya's. "I'm a kill you, nigga!"

Mya screamed as Winston and I began a cat and mouse chase, his punk ass running all over the house, in the closet, anywhere to get away from me.

"I didn't touch her! Mya, do something! This fool is crazy! Do something!" he screamed. I caught up with him in the kitchen, slamming him hard to the kitchen floor. My fist connected with his face again and again, hardly hearing nor caring about the female screams and cries behind me. All I thought about was Nicky, lying in that puddle of blood and the look of devastation and fear in her eyes. I connected to teeth, skin and bone again and again, until finally I heard Roxy crying, begging me to please stop.

"You're going to kill him, Antoine!" Roxy cried. "Don't do this! It won't help Nicky, please!" I fell back, my fists aching and covered with his blood, my own face, wet with angry tears. Roxy cradled me in her arms. "It's gonna be okay, baby; it's gonna be okay; it will, I promise you..."

Neither of us saw nor paid attention anymore to the pitiful piece of shit that lay on the kitchen floor, whining to Mya over just having gotten his weak ass kicked. All I could think about was my Nicky...

Three days later, I was wearing my *"it's all good"* face, welcoming Nicky home. We had decided, even though she had argued about it, that she should stay at my place for a few days until she felt better. She looked much better since her attack, but still her normally pretty face was covered with black and blue bruises, and her lip was still swollen. She also had a sprung neck, which was in a brace. Her eye that was swollen to the size of a baseball was still looking just out and out whacked, but not quite as closed shut.

"You are so messy, I swear," she said as we put her things away. She lay across my sofa bed, breathing deeply after the stair climb, which had been a bit hard for her.

"What did you think, I was going to become Mr. Clean over the time you were in the hospital?" I joked.

"Never. I think you are going to have to marry a clean freak in order to have any order in your house, 'cause your mama spoiled your tail rotten, boy!"

I laughed, a little surprised at her upbeat mood, or perhaps it was an act. Either way, she had been acting like her regular old self ever since we departed from the hospital—all except for physically that is.

"I can't help it if my ma is from the old school. I got to find me a woman like that, who takes care of her man." I grinned.

"What about Roxy?"

"What about her?" I blushed.

"Hmm…guess I don't need to ask, just look at ya," she observed. "So y'all hit da skins, huh? Was it good?"

I choked, putting the last of her clothing in a drawer. "Girl, you trippin' asking me something like that."

"Oh, puhleasse, nigga; it was either good or she sucked. And don't front. You knew I was gonna ask you." I flopped on the bed beside her, looking at her with a laugh. "So, you love her, huh?" she asked.

"Yea, I do. Nicky, you know it's more than just physical with her. I'm crazy about her, and yes, it was good. *Lawd, have mercy…*," I crooned, closing my eyes thinking back to how it felt to be with Roxy. I made a mock shuddering motion.

Nicky gagged. "Mmmmmm…look at you!" she said.

"Seriously though, she's the one."

Nicky put her hand to her swollen mouth for a second, then looked at me warily. "The one? Like, *The Matrix* the one?" I shook my head laughing. I swear it was hard to be serious with Nicky; she was a walking comic.

"Naw, not like *The Matrix*. I swear you're a trip!" Nicky raised the eyebrow of her one good eye. "Vacation!" I relented.

"Sho ya right, homeboy," she said. "I know this much, your Roxy princess better treat you right. I've told her that, too. I'm glad you've found someone who makes you feel good, BooBoo. You deserve it…"

"Love you, Nicky," I said, looking at her seriously. She deserved better, too. She definitely didn't deserve the pain that was written across her face despite the way she tried to mask it.

"I love you, too…"

Later in the day I opened the door to two NYPD investigators who informed me that they had gotten my address from the hospital when searching for Nicole Carter. I let them in, watching the look on Nicky's face as they questioned her.

"Why were you at Johnson's Recreation Center alone?" one of the police officials asked her.

"I told you I had catered a dinner for a client. I'm a big girl. I didn't feel any danger so I told everyone they could leave. After I was finished all that I had to do, I grabbed my purse and left. That's when I was jumped."

"And you didn't see either of the men?" he asked.

Nicky sighed. "I recognized the voice. Winston Greer."

"Yes, you mentioned him before. We have good news in that regard. We brought Greer in for questioning. He looked like he'd been in some type of bar brawl."

I kept a straight face at that comment, but almost smirked, knowing that the bar brawler had been yours truly.

"Now we still need your identification of his voice. We picked up a couple of guys who, according to witnesses, had been bragging about teaching some lesbian a lesson. Someone who called us at the station about it clued us in. They identified Greer. But like I said, we need your ID also. It should be an open and shut case. That happens sometimes when people can't keep their mouths shut like these guys."

Ten minutes later the police detectives left. I was glad to see them go. Tension was written all over Nicky's face, but resignation, too. At least it wouldn't be a case where they had to look forever for attackers who really were right around the corner. I looked at Nicky, giving her thumbs up. She attempted to crack a weak smile. Nicky was one of the strongest people I knew. It hurt to see her this way, but I knew that her strength would be the one thing that would help her get through it. That and good friends and prayer.

Once I got Nicky to lie down and get some much-needed rest, I went on my lunch date with Roxy. Although I knew she understood everything that had been going on, I felt that maybe I had been neglecting her. Still, our love was too fresh and new for me to neglect a woman like her for long, regardless of the circumstances.

Although I had wanted to take her out for lunch, she insisted on fixing it at her place. She wanted to show me her other talents. She did that from the second she greeted me at the door with a kiss.

"Hi."

"Hey, babe." I kissed her back softly on the lips.

I slipped my hands down her hips, pulling her close against me, moaning a little at how good she felt. She smiled slightly, touching my cheek. We went inside her place, which she had *laid* out! Made me feel a bit embarrassed at how plain my apartment was, but then again she was a decorator, so I didn't feel too bad.

"How is Nicky?" she asked.

"She's fine. Investigators came by today. They said they felt it may be an open and shut case. Now they're mainly working to get that shithead Winston Greer. The other guys who were involved did a lot of talking around their neighborhood and are in custody now. Nicky may soon have to do some voice identifying though."

"Well, I'm relieved to hear that. It's just awful…"

"Yea, I know."

I noticed Roxy had gone all out. She had fixed up an indoor picnic on a blanket on the floor, with fried chicken, potato salad and pickles, along with fresh-squeezed lemonade. Basically we chowed down. I was hungrier than I had thought. I told Roxy she had an appetite of a full-figured woman. This caused her to slap me on the arm.

"I skipped breakfast, okay?" She laughed, wiping her mouth after finishing her third piece of chicken.

"That's all right. If you get fat, it will just be more of you to love. I don't mind a thick woman," I said with a wink.

"I'm not getting fat, thank you!" She rolled her eyes at me, sliding into the cradle of my arms with a sigh.

Even with our little jokes and laughs, Roxy seemed a bit down, and I felt really guilty. She put her arms around my neck, burying her lips against my throat.

"I'm sorry."

"For what?"

I traced the feathery shape of her brow with my fingers. "You know, for not giving you much attention. I've been so worried about Nicky, focusing on that. I know that I haven't been around much."

"No, Antoine. You don't have to apologize. I knew you had to be there for her. She needed you. I would have been upset if you hadn't been there for her," Roxy whispered into my neck. "I really wish that she would have let me, or felt comfortable enough to allow me to be there for her also. But the most important thing is that those who love her show her, and be her backbone right now. I love you for your sweetness, Antoine..."

My heart felt so full listening to her. From the moment I first saw Roxy, I knew that she would have significant meaning in my life. Almost love at first sight. I lay my head back against the brick of her fireplace as she kissed my neck, running her hands under my dark blue tee shirt, tracing my abs. My breath quickened. I pressed her to me.

"I love you, too. I love everything about you, Baby. But...I know it was kind of screwed how the first time we're together intimately and all this happens. Almost like a curse."

Roxy's hands were still making the rounds, caressing my lower stomach. She unbuckled my belt, unzipping my jeans. Her lips followed her hands, tracing the outline of my manhood. I jerked, moaning again.

"It was good, wasn't it?" she asked in a heated whisper, coming back up to nip at my neck again. "I loved being with you. I love you."

"You know it was good." I lifted her chin to look her in the eyes, and I saw tears, which alarmed me. "What's wrong, baby girl? Why are you crying?"

She averted her eyes, trying to look away. "I don't know."

"Is it me? You really are upset, aren't you?"

"No, Antoine. Can't a sistah just have a rotten day?"

"You know if you have a rotten day, I'd want to know what was up. I haven't asked how things have been going with you at all. I've really been one track. How are things at the gallery? How is Charlise?"

"I don't want to talk about that, Antoine. It's not that, really it isn't. Everything is fine, and I don't go back to work until tomorrow anyhow.

Remember I told you she gave me a few days so I could unpack and get my place together?"

"Yea."

Roxy had her hair pulled back again in a barrette, and I unsnapped it, letting her hair fall to her shoulders. I pulled her close to me again.

"I'm sorry I'm so temperamental. I just wanted to enjoy lunch, relax, and make love to my man. That will cheer me up just fine. Is that okay?"

I blushed slightly at her words and the heat in her eyes. "Yea, it is," I said softly, placing my lips over hers for a deep kiss.

The goings-on outside were muted in our minds as we buried ourselves in the intensity and warmth... of our afternoon lovemaking.

CHAPTER *Nineteen*

Roxy

I was feeling closed in. I could feel the walls of my apartment strangling me, cutting off my air supply. So many emotions were welled up in me that I didn't know whether to cry or jump out of one of my apartment windows. *That's* how paranoid and deranged I was feeling. It started out slowly, beginning with hearing about Nicky's rape. I felt a part of me shut down and, with no one to talk to, I tried to keep it to myself. Even when Antoine *saw* the tears in my eyes the other day while we had our indoor picnic lunch, I told him it was nothing. There was nothing else I could say, so I did what I do best–I made love to my man, fully and completely and lovingly that day. I had hoped the pleasure would wipe my mind from the growing pain, but it only reminded me of the intensity of it.

Charlise wondered what my problem was, too. The last couple of days at work, since returning from moving into my new apartment, she had been asking questions galore. How did I like my new apartment? Had Antoine and I *christened* it yet? How were Antoine and I doing? Was I getting along with his girl, Nicky? Did I open my easel and paint something yet? I smiled at her, playing coy, when actually I just didn't want to talk about me. Luckily, Charlise and I were gearing up for the opening of the Visions Bookstore & Café, which was two days away.

Personal talk was kept to a bare minimum, which was fine for me...my personal talk might have brought her to tears.

I kept replaying back in my mind just how life made a one hundred-eighty-degree turn on what was beginning to look like a fresh start for me. I got my degree; got a great job at Visions; was beginning to form wonderful sistahhood-type relationships with Charlise, Dyeese and Nicky; met and damn it, fell in love with a beautiful man; and finally professed those feelings to him and then, head-on collision.

I felt as if God were hovering above Antoine and me as we came together in a loving tryst. Just as Antoine and I consummated our feelings with climax, He brought about tragedy—a tragedy so severe that it rocked my gentle foundation and made me realize that everything I held dear could be taken away from me so quickly. Maybe it was payback for not telling Antoine or anyone else for that matter about my past. These thoughts were constant and rampant in my brain, and I cried relentlessly, feeling overwhelmed and ashamed. Nicky was irrevocably changed because of her rape, and I sat wondering how *my* life went down the tube. The realization of my selfishness made me more upset, more irritable.

Since then, I hadn't been right. Nicky's pain, Antoine's anguish and my lies combined left me in a state of disarray, and the only thing I could think to do was draw. Not call someone, see Antoine, be around positive people. I needed to get out, breathe in air, take in the sun, and draw.

That's what led me to Washington Square. After finally dragging my sorry butt into the shower, I dressed in an Orioles baseball jersey and black, baggy denim shorts. I grabbed a black baseball cap and flipped it to the back before slipping on my Ray Bans and white Reebok Classics. Grabbing my already packed bag, I headed out the door.

Washington Square was always packed, full of people checking out the free music, the old and young playing chess, and each other. In the crowd, I felt disconnected, as if I was traced into the background and allowed to observe...something an artist loved to do anyway. Finding a spot away from everyone, I slipped my sketchpad and pencils out of my bag, propping the pad up onto my knees. My sketches were dark, distorting the brightness of the day and the people who were about. I wasn't sure if this was because of the sunglasses I still wore, or the blackness I felt squeezing out my light.

The bright sun kept it warm outside, but I felt the cool tracks of tears gliding from under my sunglasses while I sketched. The sound of my cell phone ringing in my bag brought me out of a melancholy portrait I had begun sketching of an old man sitting back, thinking out a move from a game of chess.

"Hello?" I sniffed into my phone, not able to hide the tears from my voice.

"Roxy? What's wrong?"

"Steve," I whispered into the phone, holding my pad close to my heart. "You always seem to be there for me...even 3,000 miles away."

He chuckled. "I'm psychic. I told you that before."

"So what do I owe the pleasure?" I asked. Hearing his voice made me feel so much better.

"Just to let you know I received the painting today. Still looking good."

"Thanks, Man. Happy to have someone who actually loves my work want to have it in their home."

"Okay, now that my real reason for calling is out there, what's up with the sadness I hear in your voice? Don't try to hide it. Remember our moviethon and drinking to the break of dawn?"

I laughed. "You know I do."

"You can't hide anything from me, hon, so spill it."

"This call would cost a fortune if I told you everything that's going on, Steve."

"Well, it's my fortune to spend, so just come and spill it."

"You sure?"

"You shouldn't even ask that question. Come on."

I didn't want to rehash all the craziness, but having Steve on the phone, and so in tune to my pain, I let it rip. I spilled everything, from meeting Antoine on the cruise, not wanting to pursue anything with him, my job at Visions, keeping lies from everyone, Nicky's rape, my reaction to it, and my inability to cope with keeping my secrets as they festered inside of me. By the time I finished my long-winded tale, I was breathing hard and had received four tissues from passersby who saw me crying.

"Hon," Steve said, in a soft, lulling tone, "I know this has got to be hard."

"So, so hard," I whispered, shivering though well heated from the sun. "I feel like I'm losing my mind."

"You have to tell him," Steve began, hushing me when I tried to protest. "I know you're worried about what a church-bred man who's relatively good would find in you. That he couldn't possibly love you, but that's not true, Roxy. You have so much more to offer, and you've already shown these assets to this Antoine guy.

"I can't see him leaving you if you told him. My God, Roxy, being raped was not your fault. You were scared and unsure. You didn't know what to do, where to turn. You made a mistake."

"Yea, but sometimes mistakes have terrible consequences and are unforgivable," I said nodding, understanding Steve's positive spin on the situation but realizing the dark reality.

"Then you should let him see if he can forgive your past transgressions. And while you're at it, tell your sister, too. She loves you like nobody's business, and she deserves to know the truth. Besides, you need the support system."

But would I really get support? I asked myself as I sat on the marble stoop wiping at the tracks my tears had left behind.

After my talk with Steve, I sat at the Square until the sun held a purple haze in the sky about to descend for the night. I tried to collect my thoughts and my tears before making my trek home. Well, my thoughts were in check…one out of two couldn't be bad. I almost laughed out loud as I strolled up the sidewalk to my apartment complex. I could only imagine what people were thinking as they saw this girl, who normally dressed to show off her assets, clad in baggy clothes, hat to the back and a bounty of tears streaming down her face. I still hadn't checked the tears that continued to flow. I was starting to believe that the tears hidden from years ago were beginning to emerge. At the most *opportune* time.

"Who the hell dressed you today?" I jumped back as I hit a sharp right to trot up the stairs leading to my apartment complex. Perched atop the steps, clad from head to toe in black and looking ever the chic hot mama was Dee. She came racing down the five steps and practically threw herself into my arms, almost toppling us both over. I hugged her with the same hardness, loving the feel of something real in my arms, someone who loved me, even with my flaws.

I pecked her cheek. "Sis, what in the hell are you doing here?"

"Thought I would pop in on my sister. See how she's doing." Dee smiled as she leaned back to look into my covered eyes. She frowned, removing my glasses to find watery pools for eyes beneath them. "What's wrong?" she asked, wiping the tears from my face and kissing my forehead.

"We need to talk," I croaked, biting my bottom lip to keep the tears in. She nodded and we both held on to other, making our way to my apartment.

"Roxy…God, why didn't you ever tell me this?" Dee asked, taking the box of tissues I handed her to wipe her eyes. Sitting beside my sister on the sofa, I took her hands into mine, stroking them softly.

"Because I felt so ashamed," I responded with a calm voice. "I was so scared and so lost and just so unbelieving of it all that I just wanted it to go away.

"If I had told you or Mom and Dad, or anyone else, I would have been probed and prodded over and over until the men were caught, a trial occurred, and a verdict rendered. I couldn't go through with feeling as if I was raped yet again by a long court trial."

"But I'm your sister," Dee cried, hugging me to her. "I could have been there for you…wiped your tears, held your hands, let you know that none of it was your fault…that you didn't have to make such drastic choices in your life because you felt used and damaged."

I couldn't allow myself to think about what could have happened.

Those thoughts were just as painful as reality. I could have *had* a loving hand to pat my shoulder or someone's arms to hold me. I could have had *one* person to tell me I wasn't broken, that I was worth more than I thought. With just one person I might have thought I was more than just a piece of ass that could be taken, but, instead, I allowed them to take it as I gave it to them...for a price.

"Well, I need you here now, sis." I wiped my eyes with the back of my hand. "I truly feel like I'm beginning to unravel, and I don't know how to stop it."

"Maybe you shouldn't stop it."

"What? I have to. I can't hit rock bottom again and have to climb back out of it. No." I shook my head, warm tears continuing to trickle down my face. "Life is like so good right now, Dee. I got Antoine, a great job, great friends, and I definitely need to be sane around Nicky...to help her get through this ordeal."

Dee sighed. "You got all that, and you know I'm so sorry about Nicky. Rape is a devastating thing, and she is going to need you. But, baby, who's gonna be there for you while you're living inside your hell?"

"I've been doing it for yours," I answered, trying to sound strong, but failing.

"No, you haven't," Dee retorted, a slight anger in her voice. "I always thought you were flighty after you went off to college, gallivanting all over the damn place." She stopped to catch her breath. "But it wasn't that...you were running away from yourself, the rape, running into any arms that would have you...except the ones you truly needed–mine, Mom's and Dad's."

I looked away from Dee. The pain in her eyes was unbearable, and hearing her speak words so true ripped at my soul. I took a deep breath at the same time someone knocked on my door. Hopping up from the sofa, I went to answer it, and standing before me was the light of my life: Antoine.

"Hey, Babe." I practically threw myself into his arms. "Wow, this is quite a welcome." He chuckled. I kissed his lips and when he looked into my eyes, he became worried. "What's wrong? Why are you crying?"

I motioned myself away from the door, allowing him in to see my tearful sister on the sofa. "This is your sister, right?" he asked, not sure if the tears from us were happy or sad.

"Sure is," I said, faking a smile. "Surprised the hell out of me, just sitting on the stoop out front."

Antoine hurried over to Dee, who rose from the sofa. He collected her into his arms and gave her a soft hug. "I feel like I already know you. Your beautiful sister is the spitting image of you."

Dee blushed. "Well, the way my sister goes on and on about you, I feel like I know you, too."

"Hush now." I sauntered up beside Antoine, who wrapped his arm around my waist. "I don't want his head to get big and all...can't do ego-tripping."

We all shared a laugh, but I didn't feel anything funny or happy.

"I hate to run," Dee said as she checked her watch. "But I dropped my bags off at the hotel earlier before getting here, and I have an old friend who's supposed to be meeting me for dinner."

"Do I need to call Stephen on you?" I questioned, chuckling. "Having dinner with an eligible bachelor?"

"Girl, shuddup! No, it's a girlfriend that used to work on the paper here with me. You know New York used to be my old stomping grounds."

"Yea, yea, yea." I laughed.

She waved her hand at me, dissing me. "It was nice meeting you, Antoine," Dee said, hugging him again. "I'm sure I'll see you again before I leave. I'll be here for a couple of days."

"Great," he said, grinning, "I look forward to seeing you again."

I took Dee's hand, guiding her to the door before opening it. We hugged, long and hard.

"I can tell," Dee whispered to me, "just from looking at that beautiful man's face that he loves you, Roxanne. Don't destroy that by being afraid to open up."

I kissed Dee on her face. "Love you, Dee."

"And I love you too, Boo...always."

The hour was late. Antoine and I lay naked in my bed. Cuddled close, the only motion in the room was our breathing and Antoine's hand softly stroking my hair. I sighed, thinking this is what Heaven must feel like. Every negative thought was banished from my mind. I could think about nothing except Antoine and my feelings for him, which seemed to exponentially multiply with every passing second. I was in love with this brotha, for real, and I prayed to God fervently that he would always love me, too.

I turned to face Antoine, lightly kissing along his nose before dropping a soft wet kiss onto his mouth. He moaned. As he stroked my hair and I ran my fingertips through his silky locks, I could see the shadowy silhouette of a smile on his lips.

He kissed me back. "You feel so calm tonight. I was worried about you the other day, Baby."

"I know." I trailed my fingertips along his muscled back and over his backside. "I was just feeling sad, and didn't know how to act about it…I just knew that I needed you beside me. I needed to feel your love."

I whimpered when Antoine leaned me back onto the bed and viewed me in the darkness as he rested upon one arm. His fingers traveled along my legs, taking slow sweeps of my inner thighs and a few along my heated passion, causing me to purr in the back of my throat.

"Roxy, you'll always have my love." I crooned when his fingers met my swollen nips and playfully pinched each one. "I'd be crazy to let you go."

"I love you so much, Antoine. If anything were to…"

Antoine cut me off with a shushing sound before kissing me hard.

"Nothing's going to happen." Antoine blew his sweet breath onto my neck, kissing down between my breasts. My hands flew to the back of his head when he took one of my nipples into his mouth, suckling it. I could feel tiny explosions shooting into Antoine's mouth from the pleasure he was giving me. I just wanted to stay like this forever. Our warm bodies, lovingly giving to the other's needs and pleasures. It felt so right, so needed, so true.

After Antoine kissed over to my other peak and lavished me there, he looked at me and asked, "You love me, don't you?"

"Desperately," I whispered back.

Lying back down on his side, he rolled me onto my side, pressing our bodies tightly together. He stroked my right leg up over his left thigh, meshing us tighter. He didn't enter me, but I felt woozy from the feel of his need rubbing along my wetness.

"I love you, too. And I know...there are things you haven't told me." I tried to protest, but he cut me off. "I know there are, but I also know that the past is the past, Baby. Whatever closed you off back then has opened you to me now. I hope someday you can talk to me about the pain."

"I will try. I promise."

"As long as you and I are truthful now, in our hearts and feelings for one another, I'm the happiest man in the world."

"Are you serious?" I asked. I did not know that my heart could ever expand as wide as it was at that moment.

"Very." He kissed me with a deepness I never knew existed. With his words, that kiss, our bodies, Antoine removed my fright and tears. I knew that this was the man who would be my husband, the man I would have children with. He was *mine*, always.

CHAPTER *Twenty*

Nicky

I was bored, more than bored. I was going out of my freaking mind. But in a way, I felt safe. I hadn't allowed myself to venture outside of Antoine's apartment since I had gotten there. Somehow the surroundings of him made me feel untouchable, as if no one would dare come there to ever harm me. I hated feeling that way, the fear. But it seemed to be woven deep inside of me. My mind flashed back to the laughing faces of my attackers. Damn them!

I finally dragged myself out of bed, getting a quick shower in. Antoine had left an hour earlier to pay some bills. Seemed like all I was doing lately was sleeping, even though Antoine would constantly remind me that I had to heal. He had no idea of the healing that I needed. I had not told him in depth of all the horrible things that were done to me. Even thinking about them made me sick to my stomach. Although I was no goodie-two shoes, I could never imagine what other humans do to hurt one another. Or that anyone would ever hurt me that badly.

I wrapped a big soft green towel around myself, catching my breath as I looked in the bathroom mirror. I saw the same face I had always seen. Yet. I was different somehow. It wasn't just the bruises that were fading slowly but surely. It was my eyes, the strength that had once been my anchor that had helped me survive high school, those horrid days when being mocked and picked on had been my daily portion. My solace had been in Antoine, the short, dark Indian boy with the braces and big thick eyeglasses. He had been my old friend who I had played cops and robbers with as a child growing up in North Queens. His artistic, quiet streak had made him the object of ridicule, and my gayness had made me one as well. We united in making sure that our high school years were not as miserable as they could've been. It wasn't that I didn't look like a girl. My clear brown skin and large, slightly slanted eyes were purely feminine. I had curves, but I had always been a tomboy. I had always preferred Tonka trucks and cars to Barbie dolls.

Although Antoine had grown out of his so-called weirdness, I never grew out of my preference, my identity as a gay woman, nor had I ever wanted to. I had tried my hand at quote unquote *normal* one time. Like others I wanted to be accepted, wanted to prove to myself that there was nothing wrong with me. So I started dating this one guy, Larry, in tenth grade. Larry was what the sistahs called foine. And really, I was surprised when he started showing an interest in me. A few guys had asked me out before, of course on the DL. Still, there were things about me. My ample breast size for one—at least I was ample in comparison to the other girls. Those little things brought me attention. Most of my ridicule came from other girls. Larry, however, who was a senior, showed an outward interest. My dates with him stay forever in my memory because he was the one and only guy I ever had sex with. I had so much to prove, or at least I thought so.

"Oh, Nicky," he had crooned on our second date. "Baby, can I suck those puppies?" His eyes rested on my chest. I was quiet as I let him lift my sweater and loosen my bra front. We were in his grandma's basement, music low, kicking out a Jodeci love song. Before I knew it, I was laid spread eagle with Larry thrusting hard in and out of me. Forget the fact that when that nigga put his big dick inside of me, he didn't even try to be gentle. After the initial sting wore off, I was waiting—waiting for the fireworks and oohs and ahs that other girls always talked about having during sex, but all I got were grunts and his sweat. After about sixty seconds, he screamed out and fell limp atop of me. I saw Larry a few more times. Every time it was still the same. He did nothing for me sexually and I still desired the touch of a woman.

I blinked, coming back to the present. The rape just reminded me once again that men and I did not mix sexually and never would. Not that I considered what those beasts did to me as sex, because I knew it was a violent assault. I had never been a man hater like some lesbians. Even after the ordeal, I couldn't see myself blaming the entire male sex for what a few animals had done to me. But the experience certainly taught me to appreciate even more the warmth and softness that only another woman could give.

My face was wet, letting me know that I was crying. "This is the last damn time," I said aloud to myself. "The last time I'm going to cry over this shit!"

I brushed my teeth, dressed as quickly as possible, snapped my neck brace back on–which I was getting tired of, by the way–and settled in the kitchen to see what I could cook up.

I missed *my* kitchen.

I had just finished whipping up an apple crunch pie and started on a pot of spaghetti when the chime of the doorbell shook me to my very bones. My heart palpitations had to increase ten- fold, if not twenty.

"Okay, Girl, get it together..."

I grabbed a big kitchen knife before walking slowly toward the door. Taking a deep breath, I looked out of the peephole. Mya! I opened the door in a rush.

"Hey, Girl," she said right away, reaching out to give me a hug. "How have you been? I'm sorry I'm just getting by to see you. So how you been?"

I stood watching her for a minute, trying to calm my anger. I knew she was not responsible for what her husband had done but still, she was his other half, and that alone was enough for me to wanna beat her ass!

"So is that bitch husband of yours locked up yet?"

Mya's eyes widened. "Come on, Nicky. I came by to see how you were, not to get ugly. Why are you so adamant that Winston was one of the guys who did this to you?"

"Who told you there was more than one?" I asked, my eyebrow rose.

Mya exhaled loudly.

"Baby, I've been all worried about you, and now you are going to get suspicious of me?"

"Mya," I looked at her quietly. "Mya, why are you only now coming to see me? It's been over a week since I was attacked. Where were you? Pampering your husband's guilty conscious?" I asked sarcastically.

Mya's eyes narrowed. "Actually, Nicky, you have no proof that he did anything. I'm a woman. I would never side with a rapist, whether it was my husband or not. But I've known Winston for over five years. He would never do anything like this. I wish there were some way I could make you see it."

I walked over to the kitchen, leaving Mya to shut the front door behind her. Up until then I hadn't even realized that it had been left open. The water for my spaghetti had started bubbling, and my sauce was already in a simmer.

"So...," Mya said nervously, "what's that you have smelling so good?"

"Spaghetti," I said quickly.

"Hmm...okay..."

I could feel Mya's eyes burning at my back. For some reason the longer I stood, the angrier I became. I can't even be sure who I was angrier with—Mya, or her punk-ass husband.

"Why do you defend him?" I whispered, turning to look at her sideways. Diligently I fought the tears that were threatening to spill over. Mya, however, was not so lucky; the tears were already spilling from her eyes to her cheeks, running toward her lips as she quickly wiped them away. "I thought you said you didn't love him anymore?" I reminded her.

"Nicky, it's not an 'in love' thing. I'm in love with you. Can't you see how torn I am? You are my girl, and I love you. But Winston, he's my man, and I feel like I have to support him, too. But even outside of that, I know Winston and there is no way I could be so wrong about the character of a person I have known and been with this long. It's just like if someone was to say that you did something unsavory. I would defend you to the very death because I know you."

I swung around wildly and looked at her. "So if you know me, then you know that I would never accuse someone of something that I wasn't one hundred percent sure was true. I've seen him, Mya, parked outside of my apartment, following me around to my clients' businesses. I've heard him. I know that voice. He's been constantly calling me, threatening me, and I know it was him. And most of all, that night? I knew his voice then. It was totally recognizable because he has a gruffy, different type of voice. And he said some of the same types of things to me that he had been saying on the phone and the same words he sprayed on my car." I paused for a minute to catch my breath.

"Mya, no matter how much it may hurt you to believe it, your husband, the man you have known for years and the man you married, is a rapist, and he *raped* me and he *beat* me, and he *sodomized* me! And he's going down, however long it takes me to get him there..."

Before Mya could respond, the phone rang. I looked at Mya again, sadly and picked up the ringer. "Hello?"

"Nicole?" It was the district attorney. "We just picked up and booked Winston Greer."

It took me thirty minutes to get rid of Mya and get to the downtown precinct. Antoine, bless his heart, was already there. I had called him on his cell phone and he agreed to meet me there. I was so relieved because I needed all the moral support that I could get.

The district attorney, Mark Wilder, and Antoine met me as soon as I walked through the doors.

"Nicole," Mark Wilder said, "we've got some dynamite news. The DNA results for the two suspects we have were ninety-eight percent conclusive. They were definitely your rapists. And they are willing to testify against Winston Greer. *That's* what enabled us to pick him up. But being that we don't have a physical ID on him, we need you to pick him out voice-wise in a voice lineup. Now you won't get to see any faces. That would defeat the point because a prosecutor could say you were biased against Greer and use the no-physical ID as a defense in court. But, of course, we are going to do a DNA test on him also. With that and Gerald White and Lonny Matthews, the other suspects' testimony, and a positive voice ID from you, I can almost promise you he will be convicted."

"Yes!" Antoine exclaimed.

But I suddenly felt unbelievably cold as if a stiff arctic wind had come through. My attackers were in the same building that I was in and that knowledge was almost paralyzing me.

"Okay," I said slowly, "so what do I do?"

Antoine and I sat with a Lieutenant Eastman in a dark, quiet room with only four speakers on each end of the ceiling. I took a couple of deep breaths when Lieutenant Eastman motioned for the first member of the voice lineup to start.

"Okay, would you repeat the line you see on that slip of paper in front of you, please," Lieutenant Eastman commanded the suspect.

A masculine voice shouted out, "Bitch, you ain't so cocky now, are you?!"

I gasped at hearing the words that had been so viciously spat out to me while I was attacked just a week prior. Lieutenant Eastman looked at me; I shook my head in the negative. Over and over again different voices speaking the same words were heard over the loud speaker. One, however, got my total attention. "Bitch, you ain't so cocky now, are you?!"

"Oh, my God!" I cried. "That's him! That's him!"

"Are you one hundred percent sure?"

"Yes, I would recognize that voice anywhere."

I was breathless, feeling myself get the shakes. Antoine squeezed my hand tightly. I looked up at him, noticing the slickness of his cheeks. He was crying. Lieutenant Eastman stood up again and walked out the door for a moment.

"Are you okay, Nicky?" Antoine asked me.

"No, but I will be. I won't let this defeat me, Antoine. You know that, don't you?"

"Yea, Babe. I always did..."

A few moments later, Lieutenant Eastman and Mark Wilder walked back into the room. Wilder smiled and surprisingly gave me a big hug. "Nicole, guess what? You positively identified Winston Greer."

I looked toward Antoine and got his forever thumbs up.

Now, if I could only start to really heal...

CHAPTER *Twenty One*

ANTOINE

I was kind of sad to see Nicky go, but at the same time, I was happy that she finally felt well enough to move back to her apartment. Roxy had promised to keep her eyes wide open and to knock at Nicky's door often just to let her know that she was loved, which I appreciated. A lot of women would not understand or be able to deal with their boyfriend having the kind of relationship with another woman that I had with Nicky, but Roxy had never once complained or showed any jealousy. However, she had asked why Nicky's parents had not been around at all after she had been raped. Nicky had never been close to the mother who raised her. After she openly began to express her lesbianism, her mom had thrown her out. Nicky had come to live with my family, where she stayed holidays and some weekends while she was at culinary school. She never really dealt with her mom on any level after she moved out of her house.

My father was the kind of man who felt that God judged all so that made his job easier. He said it wasn't his place to judge–only to lead. Love was the main ingredient, and love is what both he and my ma showed Nicky by becoming her second family. However, I knew that she would not want my folks to know about what had happened to her, so I didn't even contemplate telling them.

Although my mind had not wavered from my sis or my baby Roxy, something else was on my mind, too. This was the day of my father's final set of tests to see if he would need a bypass. My mother knew I was with my dad but thought that we were simply having a father and son day, something that wasn't at all unusual for the two of us.

The test was actually an outpatient mini-surgery. They were going to slip a small tube through a tiny hole in his thigh and run it up to his heart. I didn't understand any of what they were actually looking to find, but I did know that the whole procedure scared me. I sat quietly in the outpatient waiting room while they worked on him. I flipped through old medical magazines, trying not to stare at the elderly white lady who sat across from me crying. She looked heartbroken. We were the only ones in the room besides a young couple who were caught up in their own conversation. After a moment I decided I couldn't take it anymore. I got up, walked over to the elderly lady and took her hand in mine.

"Are you okay?" I asked her softly.

"Yes..." She sniffed, holding my hand tightly. "Yes, young man. I will be okay." She suddenly looked up at me, bursting into tears again. "No, I'm not okay. I don't know what to do. My husband just had a heart attack. I don't think he's going to make it. I don't know what to do!"

"Is he in outpatient? Wouldn't he be in critical care?"

"He's in ICU. I couldn't stand being in their waiting room any longer...there's so much sadness there. So I told our doctor I was going to go for a walk around the hospital. It was quiet in here, so I came and sat down. I hope I'm not disturbing you," she asked suddenly, looking at me with damp, clear blue eyes.

"No, not at all. My father is in getting tests run on his heart, too. But you seemed so distressed. Why don't you call someone to come be with you? Your daughter, son?"

"We were never blessed with any children, dear. It's just Clifford and me. Oh, Jesus, if he doesn't make it, I don't know what I'll do." She caught her breath as she put her hand over her heart. Having the right words of comfort for people had never been one of my strong points. I was lost as to what to say to her so I just sat there, quietly listening as she talked about herself and her husband, and their sixty years of marriage together. Oddly enough, she didn't bore me at all.

"Do you have a sweetheart?" she asked me.

"Yes, I have a girlfriend."

She grabbed me by the chin, making me look her in the eyes. "Do you tell her you love her? Show her affection, dear?"

I smiled at her words and actions, thinking about Roxy's beautiful face.

"Maybe not as much as I want to, and should do," I confessed.

"Then next time you see her…tell her. Overflow her with love, dear, because life is so short. Before you know it, all the years will have passed and all you'll do is sit and wonder if you loved enough. If the one you loved knew the depth and width and enormousness of that love..." She sighed, and closed her eyes. "It was only yesterday that my Clifford and I were young and vibrant like you. And now I don't know if he will ever hear me say 'I love you' again. I can only hope…I can only hope…" Her voice trailed off in a whisper. She seemed to go into her own world again, tears streaming down her thin, porcelain white cheeks.

The door to the waiting room opened. A nurse called out, "Mrs. Thermion?" She got up and I stood to help her toward to the nurse, who thanked me.

After she left, I sat quietly thinking about my father and about some of the things Mrs. Thermion had told me. I hoped that I had said "I love you" enough for my father so that he would always know it.

The doctor came out about thirty minutes later, informing me that my father's test had gone well, that he didn't think he would need a bypass, but that a pacemaker was a definite. He wanted to talk to my father about being admitted the following day, when they would have a bed ready for him, but that he could go home to rest from this procedure in about an hour. I closed my eyes and gave a silent prayer of thanks.

I got home around six p.m. and went down to do some picking up in my studio. I had been so busy lately, trying to put out the portraits that Samantha needed for my art line that I hadn't paid a lot of attention to the neatness of my workplace. So a cleaning overhaul was in need big time. I thought about my mom a bit, too. She was pissed, totally pissed at my dad, and me, too, actually. Of course when we got him home, we had to tell her where we had really been, being that he had to go back in to the hospital the next day for his pacemaker implant. He also would need a special diet for the rest of the day, and extra rest and a stress-free environment. She fussed for about ten minutes, and then she fussed around him–doing what she does best–show him the ultimate love. I left after a while and told my dad I would come back on the next afternoon to see how he was doing.

I had just about gotten everything cleaned up when the bell rung to my studio. I looked out the door to see Roxy outside, winking and throwing me kisses.

"Hey, Baby," she sung, giving me a big hug and soft kiss on the cheek.

"I know I forgot to call when I got home, but I just came right down here and started picking up a bit. Things have been so hectic, Roxy."

I hadn't really seen her in days, with her working at her gallery, and me busy working on my line. Other than phone calls we had kind of spaced out a bit. What that lady at the hospital had said made a lot of sense though. You never knew when would be the last time you could say "I love you" to the one you love, so one should never take anything for granted.

"I've missed you," Roxy said. I lifted her up, sitting her on the counter edge by my paints. Slipping my hands around her waist, I buried my face in the crook of her neck.

"Missed you, too. What have you been up to?"

Roxy ran her hands through my hair as she talked. "Well, we've been really busy at the gallery this week, trying to get everything ready for the opening, but we're almost there. Charlise is so excited."

"Oh, and what about you?"

"Well, I am, too! This is almost as much my baby as hers. And, I've been working on my piece, of course."

"Which you won't let me see!" I inserted, looking up at her with narrowed eyes. She laughed.

"I told you I just want to get it finished before I show it to you. I'm not the famous artist that you are, Antoine. I mean, I'll probably change it a zillion times before I even say, *It's done!*"

"Okay, okay, but see I know you have great abilities, and in more ways than one." I winked, as she turned plum red. "I can't wait to see it, though. Get a chance to see inside of you, 'cause you know what they say."

"What do they say?"

"Looking at an artist's work is like looking inside their soul. And I'm dying to see the secrets inside of yours."

Roxy averted her eyes, looking away from mine suddenly. "You okay?" I asked her.

"Yes, I'm fine." She fixed a smile on her face. Clearing her throat she suddenly asked me, "Antoine, what is the worse thing that someone has ever done to you?"

"Shit, I had some whacked things done to me in high school."

"Like what?"

I grabbed Roxy's hand, leading her to the black Lazy Boy that sat in the corner of my supply room. I sat down and pulled her into my lap. "No different than what anyone else dealt with I guess. I was small, kind of quiet. Didn't really care about sports or things like that. I cared about painting, drawing, anything that had to do with art…that was my passion. I was no different from what I am right now. It's just that when you're in school being different from what is considered the norm leaves you open as a target. Plus the fact that I was short," I explained.

"Well, how tall are you now?" She smiled mischievously.

"I'm five nine. So what you trying to say, I'm still short?" I licked at her neck, biting softly. "Well, check this out. I got *length* where it matters, a hear?"

"Yep, you sure do, Baby." She licked her lips, wiggling a little in my lap.

I groaned. "You better cut that out before you start a fire, Miss Winters."

Roxy giggled again, then sighed.

"What?" I asked her, feeling a bit curious at her sighs.

"Well, what I was really asking is what is the worse thing a person could do to you *now*, like what would make you stop dealing with someone."

"You mean like in a relationship?"

"Yea..."

"I haven't had a lot of relationships. But when I was in art school, I was with this girl, Belinda. She was always trying to change me. I guess I wasn't black enough for her. Homebody enough, you know? Sometimes she would say I talked too white, too proper. Then she had this thing where she wanted me to get my hair corroded. At first, she tried to do it, and of course it wouldn't stay. Then she wanted me to get a fade, and being the dumb and whipped fool that I was, I did whatever she wanted. She was my first real girlfriend. I didn't start dating until I graduated from high school, and kind of had a growth spurt, finally started looking and sounding older than a fourteen-year-old." I laughed as Roxy's eyes widened. "Yep, and you know I'm still carded to this day."

"But you're so cute!" She put her finger to the tip of my nose.

"Yea, whateva. What brotha wants to be called cute?" I made a face.

"Well, I like the goatee you're growing. It's definitely you!" She winked.

"It is, isn't it?" I glanced cockily over at my reflection in the mirror across the room. Roxy punched me in the arm.

"Go on, fool!"

"What, what?" I laughed. "Oh, you mean what happened with Belinda and me? Well, she was two-timing me. Had been all along. That shit hurt me, too. But now that I think about it, I realize that I only thought I was in love. Now that I'm really in love...with you, I know the difference. Besides, you and I, we have honesty and realness. I didn't have that with her. She didn't have an honest bone in her body."

"Yes, honesty is important," Roxy whispered, looking at me with glassy eyes.

"It's the most important thing," I pressed. "That's another reason why

I'm glad that you and I became friends first because you get a chance to get to know a person outside of the passion. Although, there was never a time that I didn't have passion for you. I really love you, you know that?"

"I know."

"And you love me, too, right?"

"So much."

I sighed happily. "Then we don't ever have to worry about anything bad happening to our relationship. We have the two most important things: love and honesty. Always, Baby."

"Always, Antoine," she whispered.

I parted her lips with mine and pulled her close to me as I deepened our kiss.

"My God, you have been busy!"

Samantha was beaming as she looked at all the work I had been doing. I had finished many of the paintings that I had worked on, or started years ago, finally having the inspiration to complete them.

"Antoine. I knew that you were the one!" Samantha exclaimed. "Your exhibit is going to be a smashing success! Four weeks and counting, baby! Are you going to be ready?"

"I think so." I laughed nervously. In actuality I was ready. I just felt like I wanted to double-check and cross all my artistic Ts, so to speak.

"We have about a hundred fifty people on the guest list, with your family included of course, and the friends that you put on the list. So it's going to be your night, Antoine. Really, I want you to finish up your pieces and then take some time to yourself. The last thing you need is to feel panicky or rushed the last couple of weeks. You want to make a good impression, not just with your work but also in your demeanor."

"You know, Samantha, if someone told me that 2001 would be my year, I would not have believed them."

I shook my head in wonderment, thinking about all the good things that had happened to me since the spring. Meeting Samantha on the cruise and Roxy, who turned out to be the icing on the cake.

"Well, it was your destiny, darling. I knew it when I first saw your work, and only good things from here onward will happen. So, tell me." She patted a spot beside her on the striped couch in her office. I sat down beside her. "How are things going in your personal life? How is your father? I know you had mentioned before that he was having heart problems."

"Well, this morning he had a pacemaker put in. It went well. He's fine now and resting. As a matter of fact, I'm just coming back from the hospital. I left my mom up there. She's going to spend the night, so they kind of told me to get lost."

"So your parents are still the lovebirds, huh?"

"Sure are. Disgusting, ain't it?" I scowled.

"No, it's cute as hell!" Samantha cooed. "If everyone could love forever like that, the world would be a wonderful place."

"True," I agreed, thinking about my parents. They did look kind of cute, all cuddled up in that hospital bed together.

"So, how is *your* love life? How is the little Roxy treating you?"

"We're fine. I've been busy and all painting, but all is okay..."

"So she's been taking care of all your needs?" Samantha asked pointedly. She leaned closer to me, whispering, "You want a blowjob...? That's not really cheating, you know."

I squirmed. Samantha was a trip! "Ah, naw, thanks though, Samantha." I smiled at her hesitantly. "I better get going. It's kind of late."

"Oh, okay, but remember if she doesn't keep you satisfied, my door is always open for you, darling..."

"I'll remember that."

CHAPTER *Twenty Two*

Roxy

"I am so freaking happy!"

I glanced over at a gushing Charlise and broke out into loud laughter. To say she was beaming was an understatement. Girlfriend looked as if she was just popped the question and received a platinum, 10-karat diamond ring. I watched her as she floated into the bookstore and ran her nimble, alabaster fingers along the sleek black wood of the bookcases up and down the spine of books. A flash of something negative passed before her eyes instantly and her normally beautiful face scrunched up into insecurity.

"This is going to go well, right?" she asked.

I sunk deep into a plush plaid sofa, flipping through a book by Bacon and Daniels. My mind drifted in and out of hearing Charlise and reading the book, really getting into the steamy interludes and crazy characters.

I looked up from the book and asked, "Huh?"

"You're not even listening to me!" Charlise cried, throwing her hands up over her face and slipping them through her blond locks.

"I am." I dropped the novel onto the sofa and got up to walk toward Charlise. I gave her a long, hard hug and threw an arm up over her shoulder. "The café, the bookstore; both are going to be wonderful, Char. We've found some great employees for them. They're inviting and cozy and will be the hippest places to chill and wax artistically. You just watch!"

"You really think so?" Charlise asked, still seemingly unsure.

"Come on now. After you don' put all this money into the place, you best believe it!"

For emphasis, I gave Charlise a playful swat on her backside that ignited giggles from her.

"You are so dumb!" She laughed, shaking her head at me.

That's all I had wanted to do…get her to smile, to forget her problems for just one second. It was too late to think about the negatives now, for in a few short hours, we would be showing off our hard work to the masses.

"I thank you for the compliment." I smirked, bowing deeply at the waist. "My job here is done and I hope my check is in the mail."

Charlise smacked at me, and said, "Keep acting up, and you'll have no check."

I turned to head back to my awaiting novel. Suddenly I saw a figure outside of the bookstore door. It was Dee. I smiled when I saw her. Even when she is in a bum mood the girl never comes out the house looking short of spectacular. She was dressed in a white, crisp cotton shirt tied at her slender waist; a pair of black, fitting jeans; a pair of Armani slip-ons; and dark glasses to give her an air of importance.

I trotted over to the door and hugged Dee. "Hey, Girl. Glad you could make it. You said you were in New York to see me. Yet I haven't seen much of you the last day or two."

Dee laughed as we trekked over to the sofa where I had been sitting.

"What can I say?" Dee asked, whipping her glasses off. "I'm in demand, Baby!"

"I'll be sure to tell Step then. Next time I call home."

"Long time, no see, Miss Deandra," Charlise said. She came over and gave Deandra a hug before settling down beside me on the sofa.

"Your gallery is awesome, Charlise."

"You should be so proud of Miss Roxy for that."

"I am," Dee responded. "This girl is so talented, and I'm happy to see she's found a niche to show off her abilities."

"Okay, okay!" I yelled. I leapt from the sofa. "You two need to stop. I get it, you're both proud, I'm proud, everybody's proud, the end."

We all laughed.

"I got something else that will make you exuberantly proud," Charlise whispered, a glint of a grin etching along her lips.

My eyebrow instantly shot upward as Dee and I both waited for Charlise to let us in on the secret.

After several seconds, I sighed. "Okay, you gonna tell me, or do I have to beat it out of a?"

Charlise clasped her hands together. "Well, you're going on a trip soon."

I looked at the wide-eyed expression of Dee and back into the joyful glee of Charlise.

"Come again?" I responded.

"You know, you've been like the best thing to happen to Visions in a while…you came along, I had thought, to just help with the creation of the bookstore and café, but your artistic knowledge and talent helped me to get new artists into the gallery, as well as sell some major pieces."

"Well, I like to do my job thoroughly," I stated, still waiting for Charlise to fill me in on the trip part of this conversation.

She continued. "A great opportunity has popped up, and I could go, but I think it would be a better idea for you to go."

"Charlise," I said calmly, "stop talking in riddles and tell me what's going on."

Dee admitted, "Even I'm on pins and needles over here."

"Okay, okay, sheesh. I swear, I can't let suspense linger around here." Charlise rolled her eyes. "I've been secretly eyeing a hot new artist on the West Coast, and after several hard sells, he's finally interested in talking to us. I want you to be Visions' representative."

I jumped in the spot where I stood, clapping my hands. "Are you serious?" I asked, smiling at Dee who was beaming back at me.

"Very serious," Charlise responded. "I have a meeting scheduled with Dakota for two days from now. I think that's enough time for us to get you acclimated with whatever you need to know, so you can wow him."

"Are you talking about Dakota Prinz?" I asked, damn near drooling.

"Yep." Charlise nodded her head.

"Oh...my...God. I saw a print of his in *Art Life* magazine just a couple of days ago."

"And I want that print, and all his other prints. Are you game?"

"Are you freaking for real?" I hopped over to the sofa, falling into Charlise's frail lap. She squealed. "Where's my ticket? Can I bring Antoine? Are they first-class tickets? How long can I stay?"

"Twenty questions, I see." Charlise laughed. "Tickets are first class. I assumed you would want to bring Antoine, and you'll be in Sunny California for a day or so, enough time to snap up Dakota and get back to Visions."

My laughter and smiles and excitement were strangled from me with just one four-syllable word. I had read the article on Dakota in *Art Life*. I had known he was in California now. But it didn't register until Charlise spoke the word...California. I was going back to my old stomping grounds, and the images of the past that ran rampant in my mind gave me chills and pains I had thought were gone. Antoine helped to erase all the negativity the other night when we shared that existential night together, and now, with just one word, California, I felt violated.

I could see Dee's eyes glaze over with the knowledge of what I had gone through. She, too, had her excitement diminished somewhat. For her, for myself, and for my career, I hugged Charlise, smiled brightly and offered, "Thank you so much, I promise, you won't be sorry."

I just hoped I wouldn't be sorry either.

My earlier negativities had vanished momentarily. I stood, looking at my reflection in a full-length mirror hanging on the back of my bedroom door. I had to admit a sistah was looking very good. I wore a brown, spaghetti-strapped dress that clung to my short, curvy frame and color platform sandals. My manicure and pedicure dazzled Frenchly, and my two-toned hair was twisted into a knot in the back of my head. I applied a small amount of mocha berry lipstick and light eye shadow and winked at myself.

"Looking good, Girl," I said to my reflection in my full-length mirror. I had briefly talked to Antoine earlier and we agreed to meet at Visions for the opening. I was eager to tell him about my trip–and hopefully his trip–to California. I was dressed, my man was waiting for me; there was only one more thing to do before I made my way over to the opening.

"Look, I told Antoine I didn't want to go, and now I'm telling you, I don't want to go." I stood at Nicky's door, my sad, pouty mouth in place.

"Nicky, why don't you want to go?" I asked, leaning against the door frame.

"I'm tired."

"What have you been doing today?"

"Nothing."

"So why are you tired?"

"Damn it, Roxy, just go away."

I gently pushed Nicky aside and entered her apartment, shutting the door behind me.

"You know I ain't going anywhere." I laughed. "Especially when someone wants me to go away. Now tell me why you can't go, and make it believable."

I watched Nicky plod over to her couch and sit down. She was looking cute that day, even though she was feigning irritation. She had gotten her normal braids taken out, her hair cut and was wearing twists. They were long enough to gently lap against the frame of her face. She was still dressed in her normal ghetto girl gear. Her face looked lighter...but did she feel lighter?

"I'm tired," Nicky stated simply.

I sat beside her on the couch and looked directly into her face. She was lying, if anything. Her eyes were way too vibrant.

"Give me another."

"What do you want me to say?" Nicky asked, frustrated.

"The truth, Girl."

"The truth is I haven't been out this apartment but once since I've been here, and that was to get my hair done," Nicky said, exasperated. "A friend of mine has been doing the shopping while I sit here afraid of my own damn shadow!"

My heart thud for Nicky. I raised a hand, gently stroking her arm. "Nicky, I know it's hard...you know I know this, but you can't let them bastards win, for real."

"They didn't win. Any day now, all that will be put behind me. And they will be placed in jail for a while."

"Sure, the men will be in prison, justice will have been served, but you will continue locking yourself up and living like a criminal. You don't deserve that, Girl. You really don't. You need to get out, live your life, cook up a storm, because I know you miss doing it out at your events."

"I do," she responded, her eyes becoming damp.

I sidled up closer to her. "Look, please come with me today. This is a very special day for me, and I would love for you to be there...you, Antoine and me, my sister, Charlise, everybody I love there. You know Antoine and I would never allow anything to happen to you."

Nicky grabbed my hands as if I were her sole lifeline. I could see the raw fear in her eyes masking the well-hidden pain I held deep in my heart. But I could also see the strength there as well, and I knew that Nicky would pull through this. Her being wouldn't allow her not to.

She swallowed hard, nodding her head slowly. "I don't have anything to wear."

I smiled brightly, raising from the couch and taking her hand and guiding her to the bedroom. "Come on. We've got a while, and we'll find something."

"Come here!" I didn't have time to react before I felt Charlise's hand grip mine and drag me from my circle of peeps: Antoine, Dee and Nicky. I had to walk swiftly to keep from tumbling over. When she found a secluded corner, Charlise stopped, let out a small squeal and hugged me close to her. I raised my champagne flute high to keep it from spilling onto us.

"This is so," Charlise began but the excitement inside her cut her voice off. "Wonderful! I truly did not think so many people would come, I mean a bookstore and café with a gallery. How does it fit, you know?"

I laughed, patting Charlise on her bare shoulder. She had a way of rambling when she was excited and this time was no exception. Her skin was flushed—the color of a pink rose—and her champagne-fragranced breath tickled me with her closeness to me.

"I told you it was going to be awesome." I smiled, sipping my champagne. "I contacted the press, art magazines, sent press releases to the news stations, any and everything. I told you before, I work for my keep, and I wanted this to be a success, too–not just for me, but for you and Visions as well."

"It's a screaming success!" Charlise responded, prompting me into a high-five.

I laughed. With champagne flute in one hand, she draped her other over my shoulder as we leaned back against the wall. The bookstore and café were brimming with people—art critics and buyers, college students, Wall Street types—all perusing books, ordering Cappies and light entrees at the café. It was a definite success, and I don't think I had ever been prouder of myself as I was right that instance.

As I surveyed the room, I smiled, watching my baby talk so animatedly with Dee. Even Nicky seemed to be in the swing of things, especially standing next to her baby…i.e., my baby.

"Hey," Charlise said, once she shook the hand of at least five passersby. "I'm sorry about earlier."

"What happened earlier?" I asked, tearing my eyes away from Antoine.

"You know, with the trip and all. I could tell you were a little apprehensive."

I shook my head in the negative. "No, actually I feel so blessed that you would trust me with something so major," I said truthfully.

"But I could see something that made you rethink about accepting."

I closed my eyes, counting down from three to curb the edginess that began to ferment inside of me.

"Char, for real, I'm terribly excited about this opportunity, and I'm grateful to you for trusting me with it."

"But?"

"But," I dragged out, "California isn't a state that I have a lot of positive memories of, and realizing that I'm going back just brought some things to the forefront of my mind."

Charlise carefully examined my face, instantly detecting the twitch in my right eye; something that occurred whenever irritation or tears were imminent.

"I won't pry," she whispered, rubbing my arm, "but you know you can talk to me about anything, right?" I nodded. "Just answer me this, are you sure you want to go?"

It's funny how something so great could be tainted with so much badness as well. A trip that could actually make a career, and a past that could instantly destroy my present, and equally, my future. The bad greatly outweighed the positive with this situation, but I was tired of hiding, tired of running away from my life, so I nodded and smiled at Charlise. "I would be crazy not to go. Besides, Antoine will be right there with me the entire time."

"What entire time?"

Charlise and I were so secretive in our corner that I hadn't noticed Antoine sneaking up to us. My eyes swept him in one smooth swoop. I inwardly chuckled at our color coordination, him matching my brown dress as he donned a pair of brown slacks and a long-sleeve beige pullover that clung to his slight yet muscular frame. He wore his hair out, black satin ribbons of hair lacing his shoulders.

"Oh." I leaned in to kiss his cheek. Quickly, he turned his face, with my kiss landing upon his waiting lips. I sighed. "Behave," I whispered with Charlise chuckling in the background. "How would you like to take a trip with me?" I asked Antoine, raising my free hand to his face, lovingly stroking his cheek. *He looked good with the goatee*, I thought to myself.

Definitely could be the man on the cover of a romance novel.

"I would love to go anywhere with you," he answered simply.

I blushed. "Are you serious, because I know that your opening is in a few weeks."

"First, tell me where we're going, how long we'll be there, and all that stuff."

As I began to explain, Dee and Nicky sidled over to our corner.

"Well, I'm going to California on behalf of Visions to acquire about a new fabulous painter," I said, smirking at my professional tone.

"Really?" Antoine smiled, hugging me to him. "That's my baby girl, a mover and shaker."

"Anyway." I pushed him away playfully. "It'll be only for like two days, enough time to talk with the artist and maybe..." I stopped, eyeing Antoine intensely. I didn't want to publicly say that I wanted him entirely to myself to devour and savor, but my eyes told him exactly what my mouth couldn't say right now.

I watched his Adam's apple bob up as he swallowed hard, stroking his goatee in a way that had me ready to attack him. He knew I found the thinking pose while slowly stroking the goatee to be extremely sexy, and I knew this was his cue that he was feeling me.

"So, will you come?" I asked, clearing my throat to remove any wanton residue that lay dormant from our silent exchange. "We'll be leaving in about two days."

"I think I can definitely work something out." Antoine smiled. "I'll let Samantha know what's going on, and it'll be fine. Everything on my end is finished anyway for my opening."

"Yay!" I whooped, not caring if anyone caught me hugging Antoine, or kissing his lips, or jumping up and down. My joy diminished somewhat when I caught sight of Nicky. "Are you going to be okay?"

Surprisingly, Dee wrapped her arm over Nicky's shoulder and smiled. "Your sister had already told me about the trip," Nicky said, shyly smiling, "Congrats."

"Thanks," I said, still unsure about her feelings.

"I asked Nicky if she would like to come to B'more with me, spend a couple of days until you guys get back," Dee stated, "to kind of get away from the commotion of New York for a while."

"And I told her I'd think about it," Nicky finished...now smiling fully. "I don't know. I think it would be good to gain a clear perspective away from the drama."

I couldn't stop my eyes from tearing up. My sister had pulled the biggest sister move ever, and my heart was overflowing with love for her act of kindness. I only hoped Nicky would take her up on her offer. I hugged Dee fiercely, whispering into her ear, "You don't know just how happy you have made me."

She looked into my eyes, smiling and giving me a wink, answering, "Yea...I do."

I was wrapped into my sister's arms; Antoine was smiling, hugging Nicky; and Charlise was standing, just in awe of the love flowing around our little hub. "If this isn't a Kodak moment," she whispered, pressing her hand to her heart.

"Don't we look loving?"

All five pair of eyes looked forward to see Samantha examining our close-knit circle. Instantly I felt the hairs on the back of my neck bristle, and the only word in my head at the time was *fight*.

"Samantha," Charlise cooed, moving toward her to shake her hand and partake in small talk.

Throughout the entire conversation, Samantha's eyes were glued to Antoine. Nonchalantly, I slipped myself from Dee's embrace, walking into the bond of love that Antoine and Nicky shared and hugged them both. I kissed Antoine on his cheek, giving him an extra squeeze.

"Hello, handsome." Samantha smiled, marching to Antoine and kissing each side of his face slowly and deliberately. Just knowing that at some time she and Antoine had been intimate made me want to physically get ill. "So, this is your little girlfriend, Roxy? It's been a while since I've last seen you."

Antoine wrapped his arm around my waist. "Yep. This is Roxy. Roxy, this is Samantha Lox."

"How do you do?" I asked, slithering out a hand to her.

She examined it before sweeping back her long mane. She shook my hand, lightly and proceeded to take Antoine's free hand, stroking it.

"Can I borrow him for just a second?" Samantha asked, already removing him from beside me and draping her own arm around his waist. She had an air of snootiness about her, an air I wanted to smack right out of her lungs.

But instead, I smiled and replied, "Sure, no problem."

Antoine winked at me. "I'll hunt you down in a bit."

Samantha looked less than amused. As she turned away from us and began towing Antoine to wherever she was headed, I called out, "Don't forget to tell Samantha about the trip!"

I heard Samantha ask him, "What trip?" as they walked off.

"You are so bad," Dee said.

"Please. She don't want to see bad, okay? For Antoine, I'll be sweeter than sugar, but I have my antenna up on that chick 'cause she ain't up to no good."

CHAPTER *Twenty Three*

ANTOINE

"This is really nice how Charlise's opening has turned out. I'm almost jealous," Samantha said with a smile. "But of course, I had *more* people at my opening years ago. She has a nice little place here though."

"Yes, she and Roxy have been working hard," I responded. I had been a bit surprised to see Samantha show up for the Visions' opening—being that Visions would be competition for Lox's galleries; at least I knew that Samantha saw it as such.

I looked around, noticing Roxy looking in our direction. "So, wassup?" I asked Samantha.

"Just wanted to let you know that all is set for your night. We just need those last couple of paintings from you that you promised, and we're good to go."

"I'll have them at the gallery tomorrow, okay?"

"That will be fine." Samantha looked at me oddly, reaching up picking an imaginary piece of lint from my hair. I looked uncomfortably toward Roxy again, who was still looking at us.

"Wow, she is a worry bug, isn't she?"

"What do you mean?"

"Well, she hasn't taken her eyes off you since we got over here. Does she think I'm going to devour you publicly?"

I shifted a bit, avoiding Samantha's eyes. She was being catty, something that I really hadn't ever seen in her before.

"No, it's just that she knows that you and I used to hook up, so it's only natural that she would be a bit unnerved, you know?" I explained. "As a matter of fact, I think I should go on over there and see what she's up to." Samantha eyed me silently. "Sam, you remember that I told you how I felt about her, right? And you do understand?"

Samantha gave a little giggle. "Aren't I allowed to feel the little green-eyed monster from time to time, darling? Anyhow, yes, you should go on over to your little lady, but I did want to ask you, what is this about a trip? It won't interfere with your exhibit, will it?"

"No way; it's just for two days. We'll be flying to Los Angeles. She's meeting an artist friend for Charlise, I believe. But I want to go. I would hate for her to be traveling alone like that."

"You're always the gentleman, aren't you, handsome?" Samantha said. She suddenly then reached out and kissed me softly and soundly on the lips, lingering for a moment. "I'm going to go mingle for a minute, then head on home. I've been feeling woozy all day. I think maybe I'm a bit sleep-deprived and need to play catch-up. Buh-bye for now," she said, running her fingers down the edge of my hair.

"Bye..." I spun back, moving away quickly to find Roxy. She and her sister Dee were looking right at me, neither looking very happy. As I made my way toward them, I bumped right into Nicky.

"That was not cool," she said.

"What?"

"Don't play dumb, boy! You know what I'm talking about. You're here at Visions' opening, *Roxy's* Visions, and there you are kissing on Snow White. Who the fuck does she think you are, Prince Charming?"

"Look, Nicky, don't go there, okay?"

"Don't go there? Don't go where? Fuck that! You know I speak my mind. And you are wrong, Antoine, 'cause Roxy would have every right to be pissed. Look, I'm talking to you as a friend, okay? And I don't care if you don't like it or want to hear it. That wasn't cool, at all, and you need to go on over there and explain that shit."

"All right. Okay, you're right," I conceded.

"Damn right, I'm right," she spat, narrowing her eyes at me before storming off. One thing that was always true about Nicky; she was never lost for words when it came to speaking her mind. That was good and bad in a way, but for me, it was always good. What can I say? My sis always kept me in line.

Roxy must have had the same idea that I did. We were walking toward each other at exactly the same time. She with a hurt, angry yet questioning look in her eyes, and me with an "I'm sorry" look in mine.

"It was nothing, okay? Trust me?" I said, taking her hand in mine as I met her.

"You know I do, Antoine. It's just that she is so obviously and openly after you, and she doesn't care who sees it either. I swear I can't stand that bitch!"

"She's not after me, really. You just need to know her ways. She's like that with everybody."

"No, she isn't, Antoine. She's like that with you," Roxy insisted. "I've seen her work ever since the art cruise. And yes, I know she is helping you and I know how important working with her is for your career, but you should tell her to shove off!"

Time to reason, I thought to myself. "I can't and won't talk to her that way, Roxy. Women talk to other women like that; men don't."

"Whateva! Tell her, Antoine, or I will…"

"Roxy, you heard me tell her exactly how I felt about you a while ago. I'm not hiding my feelings for you, from her or anyone else." I sighed, bringing her hand up to my lips for a kiss. "Let's not fight, okay? You and Charlise have a beautiful place here. Let's celebrate it."

Roxy sighed deeply, getting her bearings together, it seemed. "I know, and you're right. We have good things to look forward to also."

"Like our L.A. trip." I winked to her.

"I can't wait, Antoine," Roxy whispered, her face getting a heated glow. "It will be like our first romantic getaway, although I am going there for a reason. You know what I mean though. I love you so much, Antoine…"

"And I love you…"

I love you were three words that Roxy and I were one hundred percent sure about.

Nothing else really mattered...

Nicky

"Are you sure you don't want to come, Nicky? You are honestly welcome, and it would be good for you."

Deandra smiled at me with warmth and sincerity. I appreciated her offer, and had thought at first that I wanted to go. But I had thought about it ever since she had first mentioned it. Roxy and Antoine tried to coax me, saying it would be good for me. The truth of the matter was I didn't have a reason to go to Baltimore. I didn't know anyone there. I *barely* knew Roxy's sister. And the most important thing was that I knew that running away from New York was not going to solve my problems nor make what happened to me go away or heal me any faster. It was time to deal with myself and put it behind me, not run away. Perhaps Antoine being away for a few would force me to lean on myself and face my own demons.

"I know you mean well, and I do appreciate it, Dee. Honestly, but my place in the world is here in the Big Apple. I have responsibilities here. I have clients who have been put on hold while I'm dealing with my personal drama, and I know they won't be holding forever. I can't afford to lose my business."

"Are they aware of what happened to you?"

"No, not at all. Just that I had to take a brief leave. A few think I was in an accident. It's not something I'd like to broadcast, a know."

"Oh, but of course not," she said quickly. Changing the subject, she said, "I wanted to thank you by the way, for being a friend to Roxy."

"Why would you thank me? Roxy is a nice girl, and Antoine loves her. That's good enough for me."

"Well, we were a bit worried about Roxy being here in New York without knowing anyone, didn't want her to get mixed up in any kind of trouble..."

I looked at her curiously. "What kind of trouble could or would Roxy get into? You and her seem to be upscale-type of chickadees," I said, laughing good-naturedly.

Deandra had asked me to come to Beck's for a drink, after Roxy and Antoine had made their getaway after the opening. She was fun, *very* cute, too, but um...I knew she didn't roll that way. Besides she had been talking about some brotha she was goo-goo over named Stephen who was a PI in Maryland. It was getting way into the early morning, and I was starting to feel the effects of a long ass day.

"I wouldn't say we're upscale. I've mostly been an educated sports buff forever. But, Roxy...well, she's been searching for a long time...," she said evasively.

I looked at her oddly, trying to feel her tone out. "Searching for what?"

"I guess what we all are searching for. Happiness, and maybe feeling that whole, emotionally secure feeling. Roxy has always been or reminded me of a kaleidoscope, you know that thing that twirls colors and looks like a telescope? She has always been searching, getting mixed up in everything. But from what I can see, she seems to have finally found her way, her place here. And I know it has a lot to do with her new position, and it definitely doesn't hurt that she is connected with good people like you and Antoine."

I hesitated a moment before speaking, but finally took a deep breath, and said, "Dee, I will admit that when I first met Roxy, I didn't really like her. I know that I may have just been feeling the twinges of jealousy, although Antoine and I have only always been good friends. But I was worried that she would be someone who would hurt him.

"I told her, and I'm telling you, I won't have him hurt. Antoine means a lot to me and I love him from the bottom of my heart. But I also know that he is a bit naïve when it comes to women and relationships." I paused for a moment, taking note of the rise in color to Dee's face, and also her concerned look.

"Nicky, Roxy is a good person," she broke in.

"I'm not saying she's not."

"She also is not out to hurt Antoine," she said defensively.

"But she is hiding something, and you know what it is, too."

Dee's face reddened even more at my announcement. That told me that one of two things was going on—either she was getting pissed, or I was touching close to the truth. "If she is hiding something, Dee, which I have felt for a while now, my only concern is how it will affect Antoine cause see, I don't even want him hurt like that. Please tell me you understand?" I pleaded. "I feel the same way about him that you do about Roxy. You wouldn't want some dude hurting her heart, and I don't want any female hurting him. He's one of the good ones. Roxy couldn't have picked 'em betta."

Deandra leaned close to me. "Nicky, she loves him, okay? I wouldn't get involved in her situation no matter what because I know she loves him. And you know he loves her. So let them work it out? And let her show him all of herself, in her time?"

I heard her. Hmm...did I really? One thing I did know was that after my late night convo with Dee, I had a gut feeling that something bad was about to happen. And what was worst, I would be powerless to stop it or to help brace the pain that it might inflict upon Antoine...

CHAPTER *Twenty Four*

Roxy

"Buckle your seatbelt."

I was in a daze and had been since Antoine and I took our places on the plane for our trip to California. I spent the night before online, printing out driving directions from LAX to the Secret Garden Bed & Breakfast where we were staying. I also got them to a restaurant in Glendale where Dakota asked us to meet him. I printed out any and all directions we would need while we stayed in California for the next two days. And when our flight took off at exactly six thirty, I was red-eyed and wired, not having gone to sleep.

My mind didn't want to think about California, but now that we were in the air, I could do nothing but think about it. I played back the last two days in my mind, how cheerful and energetic I had been, masking my fear from Antoine, wanting to protect him from my shameful past. He was just happy to be able to spend a few days alone with me, like I was with him. I felt I had successfully made it through the acting stage, but Nicky caught me off guard. Even though she didn't say anything with her lips, her eyes held questions, and the thought of Deandra fluttered through my mind. Had she told Nicky something about me? Did Nicky know about my past? I kept those questions in my mind...still had them there in fact, swimming around in a sea of confusion.

I told myself, begged myself to calm down. In no time we would be in California, freshening up at the Secret Garden before heading out to Charles Billiard to meet Dakota for lunch, which would be the chance of a lifetime for me. I closed my eyes and whispered to my mind to relax.

"Roxy, buckle your seatbelt." My eyes fluttered open as I took into focus the concerned eyes of Antoine. He leaned over to me, gently stroking my cheek and planting a delicate kiss on my lips. *God, how I didn't want to lose those lips.* "Are you okay?"

I nodded, sitting up in my seat and fastening my seatbelt. I inhaled deeply, exhaled slowly. "I'm fine. Why do you ask?"

"I told you three times to buckle your seatbelt, and you were in another world."

"Just psyching myself up for the meeting with Dakota," I lied, giving him an award-winning smile. "I'm a little nervous, and I'm preparing myself not to stutter or say the wrong thing."

Antoine took hold of my hands and brought them to his lips to kiss. "Roxy, you are going to knock him dead...this I know. Just be your beautiful, outgoing self, and make your spiel. He'd be a fool not to jump at the chance."

"You always know the right things to say to me." I sighed, feeling my heart tremble with love.

"Because I know you, and I know what you need."

Someday you'll know all of me...and when you do, I hope you will continue giving me what I need...you.

I winked at Antoine and turned my head to glance out the window. We were descending into LAX and I felt my heart pick up speed at an Olympian runner's pace. I prayed to God for safety and love, and added reassurance that this entire trip would go smoothly.

Antoine and I had arrived at the Secret Garden Bed & Breakfast, marveling at the cotton-candy pink of the exterior. We were greeted by the two friendly owners, given a rundown of the happenings at the B and B and were escorted to our bedroom, which held all the comforts and solitude that I had wanted for this trip. After dropping our bags in the room, we freshened up and ushered ourselves back into the car for the twenty-minute drive to Glendale.

"Show time!" my mind said as we drove through L.A.

Charles Billiard was far from where a "normal" meeting would be held. It was a sports bar-restaurant where one could have a decent meal and take a break and play pool or hockey.

"Dakota suggested this place?" Antoine asked, chuckling as we walked up to a host and informed him that we were to meet Dakota Prinz. The host pointed in the pool room area.

I stopped at the entranceway, eyeing the rows of pool tables and the quiet yet happy atmosphere that enveloped me. Out of the corner of my eye, I saw Dakota, his hair screaming individuality and his clothing screaming in unison. Dakota was…how should I say it? The exact opposite of what his name connoted. He was wild and free-looking, with his wheat-colored hair in dreads that hung at least three inches past his shoulders.

I felt overdressed for the meeting, sporting a crimson, two-piece business suit and matching pumps. In a phone call, I had informed Dakota of my attire so he saw me instantly and came over in long, quick strides. Instead of the usual handshake, he took me into his arms and gave me a friendly hug.

I looked from an amused Antoine to Dakota, whose bubbly personality appeared as a beacon to me. My eyes perused his torn tee shirt, his multi-colored jeans and black Converse All-Stars. I suppressed a laugh and told myself that this might be easier than expected.

"It's so great to meet you," he said, his voice thick of Beach Boy flavor.

"Likewise," I responded, taking Antoine's hand. "This is my..."

"Boyfriend?" Dakota laughed, looking at Antoine, who in turn laughed.

"Yes," I responded, blushing.

"Look, can I call you Roxanne, Roxy…?" Dakota asked.

"Roxy is fine."

"Roxy, there isn't a need for the formalities." He reached out and shook Antoine's hand. "How about we get ourselves a beer and you can wow me with talk of Visions?"

I looked up at Antoine, who winked at me. "I think I'll play some pool. You go wow him."

He dropped a kiss on my cheek before sauntering over to a pool table. I eyed Dakota, who stared at me intensely. An amused and lackadaisical smirk on his face. If he wanted me to *let my hair down*, that was definitely something I could do. Instantly, I felt myself loosen up and I slipped my arm around one of his. Heading toward the bar, I began, "Okay, Dakota, let's get down to business...you have awesome work that deserves to be noticed in a major way, and with your vision of art, and our...Visions, I think we can make beautiful music together."

To say I was feeling on top of the world was the understatement of the year. I had never felt as free, as sexy, more confident, more important... more anything! With my laid back, true self, I had managed to sign Dakota to an exclusive contract with Visions and in only fifteen minutes to boot. I had found out that Dakota was being romanced by two other galleries in L.A. as well as one out in New York. He said it wasn't just about money which was great because out of the four galleries vying for his work, Visions was the smallest and less money-endowed. He wanted a place that matched his tenacity, that held his fire and love for art and could propel him to artistic heights not yet tapped.

I quickly went into my spiel about the short yet celebrated history of Visions, our recent acquisitions–many of which I had acquired–and also raved about our new additions–the bookstore and café. Excitement itched under my skin and I could feel the heat of my body rising as I whipped my business jacket off and sipped from my second bottle of Corona. I felt as if Dakota and I were schoolmates, locked together in a funny secret that only the two of us knew about. We both held a joy discussing our accomplishments and wants, so much so that before I could continue, Dakota swallowed the last of his Corona and bellowed, "I want you!"

I jumped, startled by his loudness. "What?" I laughed.

"I felt it…that fire and love for art…I want Visions to represent my artwork…besides, any place that has a hot and spicy chick like you has got to be banging!"

I was tickled by his words and allowed them to sink in. I had snagged him and the success of that was sweeter than anything I had ever tasted, aside from Antoine's kisses.

This joy, this excitement, this wonderful news is what led Antoine and me to Café Club Fais Do-Do to celebrate. We had driven back toward the Secret Garden and spotted the place on our way. Once we returned to the B and B, showered and dressed, I had a feeling that Fais Do-Do would be the right spot to celebrate, and I wasn't mistaken.

Whites, blacks, Asians, Latinos...any and everybody filled up the club, dining and dancing the night away. The black and white checkered floor tiles brought out the vibrancy of the red furniture in the dining room. I ordered everything, hush puppies for appetizers, jambalaya for my entrée and chocolate mousse for dessert. When I was happy, not even a diet mattered!

"I am so proud of you." Antoine offered me a bite of his dessert, and we both sat there googly-eyed like teenagers.

"Baby, I am so proud of me, too. I felt like Dakota and I were kindred spirits and his uniqueness drew me to him…we clicked."

"I know about the uniqueness thing…that's what drew me to you."

I blushed as the waiter came with the bill and Antoine slipped him his credit card. My fingers were drumming to a salsa beat that rang out from the dancing area and I closed my eyes, letting the sound take over me.

"Let's dance," I whispered in a husky voice, the euphoria of the day radiating through my body. With an equally hungry glance, Antoine took his card back from the returning waiter and we practically ran into the dance room.

"Who's the woman?" I screamed at the top of my lungs to a laughing Antoine. "Oh, I said, who's the freaking woman?!"

Sweat trickled down my neck sloping into my cleavage as the frenzied pace of the music controlled my body. What little I had on…a tight, short, spaghetti-strapped, black number felt glued to my skin from the moisture that clung to my body. My hips swayed directly to Antoine's connection with his body. His hands ran down the curve of my back and rested firmly against my backside, drawing me closer. We groaned in unison.

The lights were low, but even if they weren't, we wouldn't have cared. Our eyes held wanton desires and our closeness, and we didn't care who saw us at our most primal. Gently I pulled on Antoine's silky hair, drawing his head back as I licked at the warm flesh of his neck, hearing him sigh. I could feel him rising against me, making me all the more on fire for him. Greedy hands squeezed at my ass. I looked up into the dark pools of Antoine's eyes as he lowly growled at me, "We need to go…now." There would be no argument from me.

We tiptoed into Secret Garden and found the owners relaxing in the living area—one reading, the other stroking a cat. We politely whispered "goodnight" and with silent urgency ran to our bedroom. Antoine unlocked and opened the door, ushering me inside. In one swoop, he shut the door and pulled me to him, loosening my hair from its twist before weaving his fingers through it. We kissed. His fingers pressed my lips closer, tighter to his as we breathed in each other's moans.

When we finally broke, we panted like dogs. "God, I want you so bad," he whispered, using his nimble fingers deftly to remove my slip of a dress.

In between kisses, I managed to strip him of his shirt, tossing it onto the floor. My hands moved down to his slacks, unbuckling his belt and unzipping his pants. Fervently, he kicked out of his pants and pulled his briefs off as we kissed our way over to the bed in a tangled heap.

With hungry eyes, Antoine looked down onto my sweaty, hot form and kissed my lips, my chin, licking a line to the swell of my breasts, which were freed once he removed my bra like a magician. I oohed when his warm tongue flicked across my swollen nipples. I had never been this aroused, this in need of anything or anyone. My entire body was literally in pain for Antoine and as he slowed his pace and took his time to devote equal time to my aroused peaks, I became hotter and wetter and more hungry for him.

"You taste so sweet," he whispered in between bites and licks and sucks.

"Antoine," I cried, whimpering. "You're killing me."

His fingers replaced his tongue on my nipples as he gently pinched and tugged on them, his mouth deciding to move down south to pay a visit. "Oh…," I moaned, when his hot breath laced the crotch of my panties. He kissed my entire clothed mound, sucking at my panties before demanding me to raise my hips so he could strip them from me.

His smooth fingertips parted my legs as he tucked himself between them, his mouth devouring my most sensitive of areas. My hands clutched at the back of his head, refusing to let him move as I shuddered and shook and cried out. "Oh, Baby...please don't stop," I encouraged, offering myself to him by rocking my hips upward. His hands roamed up my body, tweaking my nipples, stroking my hips, cupping and massaging my ass as his mouth and tongue continued to lavish me.

I began to feel dizzy, lightheaded, the sensations causing an overload to my mind as I let out a pitiful scream, not wanting to disturb others. "Baby…baby…baby," I panted, "I'm about to come!" With those words, Antoine stroked my ass and slid his hands up the backside of my legs, raising them up. Ducking his head further down, he licked a slow, wet, lazy line down my crack, back to my engorged clitoris, before sucking it like a baby's bottle. I gasped and cried out, "Antoine!" before my eyes rolled into the back of my head and I came. The sounds of Antoine's licking of my juices made me come a second time, and as he kissed up my three-alarm body and kissed my mouth, I didn't know whether to faint or beg for more.

In the blink of an eye, Antoine went from crazed man to romantic leading man as he kissed me softly, my taste still on his lips. He rocked himself against me, his hardness nudging at my wetness. My legs enveloped his waist and he buried himself slowly, deeply inside of me.

"I love you so much, Roxy," Antoine groaned as he stroked me with the smoothness of a violinist with his bow. We rocked with our own rhythm, a rhythm that filled me with so much pleasure, so much love, and such a deep connection with Antoine, I felt as if we had been created to fit for only...him and me.

His lips felt like rose petals falling against my nipples as he kissed them, steadily filling me with full, rocking strokes. My hands slid down his wet back and gripped his ass, bringing him as close as he could be to me. Our lovemaking was silent and bonding and with each stroke, we were so close to solidifying the bond between us.

"Roxy," he groaned in my ear, kissing me. "Feel so good…so hot…so tight…God."

I could feel the pressure rising in my body, in my being as Antoine's strokes intensified. The skin on his face tightened, his eyes never closed, boring into mine as we stroked and rocked ourselves to an orgasm that dotted Is and crossed all Ts in our contract. Antoine rolled onto his side and pulled me to him, rubbing my back and kissing my forehead. We lay there, tightly together and breathing deeply until our bodies resumed their normal heart rates and well beyond that.

Before I fell asleep, I heard Antoine whisper into my hair, "I'm going to make you my wife, Roxy…I love you."

I didn't know if he knew I was still awake or not, but I kept silent, my heart bursting in my chest and happiness running through my pores.

The owners of Secret Garden smirked as we came from our room later the next afternoon. With the deal signed with Dakota, all I could concentrate on was Antoine and the heat and passion we created the night before. We reluctantly got up out of bed and showered and dressed. Dakota had invited us to an artwork opening of one of his closest friends. Before that, I wanted to pay a visit to my friend, Steve. I dialed him up on the phone in the bedroom and he answered with a soft, "Hello?"

"Hey, babe, guess who?"

"Roxy, how the hell are you?"

"I'm in California, happy as a clam, and anxious to see you!"

"Oh, shit." He laughed. "We gotta hang out, but I'm on my way to work."

"Nooo, we're only here for today." I whined. "We go back to New York tomorrow."

Steve sighed. "Damn, I'm sorry, Roxy. I really wish I could see you...I miss you, bud."

"And you know I miss you, too."

"Fear not, I will be in New York in a week or two, so maybe we can hang out then."

"Okay." I pouted into the phone.

"Uh, Rox...who's we?"

I whispered into the phone, spilling in a conspiratorial tone about Antoine being with me, and why I had come to California.

"So, did you tell him about..."

"No," I answered, cutting him off, "but I will."

"When?"

"When the time is right."

"And when will that be?"

I looked at Antoine who was brushing his hair in the bathroom. "When the shit hits the fan," I responded.

Before we made it to the front door of the B and B, I heard someone say, "You two must be honeymooners."

We turned to find a couple, about our age, coming down the hallway and about to exit the door with us.

"Why do you say that?" I asked.

The woman smiled at her significant other and they both blushed. In turn, realizing why she had made that comment, Antoine and I looked at each other and then turned away.

"No," I said, trying to hide a laugh, as we headed toward the front door. "I think we got just a little loud last night...this morning." I hugged Antoine to me.

He kissed my forehead. "That's okay. Next time, I'll tie a scarf over your mouth."

I swatted at him. "Look at you with your kinky ass!" I squealed. "Come on before I drag you back into that bedroom. Let's act like we really want to see art today...instead of each other."

Dakota's friend, newcomer Sonya Kingston, had fabulous work. No matter how many flirty looks and devilish winks Antoine and I slid to one another during the evening, I still found the time to truly appreciate Sonya's drawings. Eyeing one particular piece called *In the midst...* I became lost in thought, wondering what the lady in the drawing was in the midst of. It looked like contemplation, but contemplation of what, I hadn't a clue.

I jumped when Dakota sneaked up behind me and whispered, "Hey there, good-looking."

"Hey there, yourself," I said, turning to face him. "Where's Sonya? I want to tell her how fabu I think her pieces are."

"She's schmoozing," Dakota replied dryly. "Sonya and I were wondering if we could treat you and Antoine to dinner tonight...kinda like a 'thanks for stopping in, come back and see us sometime' thing."

"That would be cool," I said. "We didn't make plans for tonight anyway...we'd love to."

"Love to what?" Antoine asked, popping up alongside me.

"I was just asking your pretty woman for you two to join Sonya and me for dinner." Dakota checked his watch. "Actually, this gig will be wrapping up shortly and Sonya can take her artistic leave of the gallery."

"Okay," Antoine said, kissing my cheek. "I'm going to hit the men's room, and I'll be right back."

"I'm gonna find Sonya," Dakota replied, departing.

I continued to stand in front of the drawing, rocking back and forth.

"Well, as I live and breathe." Death crawled along my back. My mind told me that as long as I didn't turn around, I was in a dream world. The moment I made eye contact with the voice behind me would be the moment my life as I knew it would end. "I would know that backside anywhere, Roxanne Winters." The Grim Reaper's sickle sliced through my heart as I turned around. "Damn, you look just as beautiful and sexy as you were...before," the man said. I couldn't speak; my tongue had swollen to the size of my mouth, if not bigger; and I feared if I opened my mouth, a scream would come out instead.

"Don't play shy now...Foxy Roxy, you were never the shy type."

"Hello, Clark," I responded in a monotone voice. I bit my lower lip to keep my moans inward. Clark was the exact duplication of his brother, Thomas. I stuttered, "What are you doing here?"

"I should be asking you that," Clark answered. As he smoothed down his shimmering gray-black hair, he added, "I'm an art buyer, always on the lookout for fresh talent." I grimaced at his words. "Speaking of talent, what's the going rate today for a trip down memory lane?"

"I wouldn't know," I said coldly. "I left that far behind me."

"Oh," Clark said, chuckling. "Trying to go the straight and narrow, I see." A choking silence enclosed around us. "I've been dealing with the loss of Thomas, as you know."

I simply nodded, refusing to let the pain of my fatal reunion with Thomas come to light.

"You know I begged him to leave you be." Melancholy swept over Clark's face and vanished. "I told him that you could move yourself in...and out and in and out of trash," Clark howled, "but you should never move trash in with you." I shuddered as his lip twitched and an evil glint sparked his eyes.

Before Thomas, I had spent one brief night with Clark, strictly professional. He always hated that I connected with Thomas beyond the job and left him to find a new piece of meat.

"Fuck you, Clark," I growled, closing my eyes into thin slits.

"It hasn't been that long, Foxy Roxy, remember? You did that once before."

"Look, I'm not an...escort anymore, so you and I no longer have an interest in the other. Leave me the hell alone."

"What, someone picked up the trash that you are and cleaned you off and tried to make you look presentable?" Clark hissed.

I reared my head back as if slapped. I tried to straighten up as Antoine sauntered over to Clark and me, a perplexed look on his face.

"Are you okay?" he asked me, but looked at Clark. My acting skills ran into high gear as I stood up straight and smiled at Antoine.

"Yes, Baby," I cooed, "I was just saying hello to an acquaintance of mine. Remember, I used to live out here years ago."

"Oh," Antoine said, still unsure. "Well, hi, I'm Roxanne's boyfriend, Antoine Billups."

Clark eyed my shattering self before moving his cunning eyes to Antoine, raising his hand to shake Antoine's.

"I'm Clark Dugué. I'm an art buyer and was a friend of Roxanne's when she worked out here as a..."

"Model," I said, filling in the missing noun of Clark's venomous sentence.

I saw Sonya and Dakota motioning for us at the gallery's entrance. "Honey, we need to get going," I said, taking hold of Antoine's hand. "Dakota and Sonya are waiting for us." I turned, glancing briefly at Clark before saying, "It was nice seeing you again."

"The pleasure was all mine," he responded, smiling. As Antoine and I walked away, I could feel my future leaking from me like a gaping wound. My days were numbered, and it was only a matter of time before the wonderful existence I now lived in would be a thing of the past.

CHAPTER *Twenty Five*

ANTOINE

Two weeks later…

Twenty-three hours and counting until my showing, and I was sweating. An artist waits all his life for this moment, and although I had always dreamed big, my moment was far bigger than I ever imagined. I busied myself during the evening before. I didn't really have any plans. Roxy was working late at Visions and Nicky had a catering job; something I knew she was big time worried about. That and the fact that the pre-hearing had been scheduled for Winston Greer. She said she was happy about it, but, at the same time apprehensive. She had been warned that usually the victim would be on trial as opposed to the rapist. The defense attorney found a way to blame the person for his or her suffering. I could only hope that this kind of crap didn't happen to Nicky. That would piss me off.

I fiddled around, doing the last bits of things to my apartment as if I were having my exhibit there. Or maybe my designer boo was having a huge effect on me and turning me suddenly into a clean freak. Thinking about Roxy took my mind back to our California trip. It had been good, really good. And it helped me seal some things inside of myself concerning her, too. I wanted her in my life and not just on a temporary basis either. Both of us had a lot of unfounded goals ahead of us, and it would be a while before we could commit to legalizing our love, but I most definitely wanted her to know how committed I was to her, and how much I loved her.

Her business had been successful, too. She had signed her artist and we had a beautiful time in California. But ever since we'd been back in Manhattan, she'd been a bit funny. I couldn't quite put my finger on it yet, but it was there. Maybe it was a keeping to herself type of funny, as if she had something deep on her mind. And every time I asked her what was up, she would always smile, give me a kiss and say, "*It's nothing, baby.*" Now I have never been one to dig too deep when someone wanted to be left alone, but when it came to Roxy, she was my baby, my everything, and whatever affected her affected me even deeper.

I sat for a moment, thinking about everything that had happened since I met her. I knew she was working but wanted to connect with her somehow. Suddenly an idea hit me. I got up, put on my old Sisqo CD, and dialed her number at Visions.

"Hello, Visions!" Roxy exclaimed. I put the phone against the speakers of my stereo system, turning up the sounds of the old summer hit of Y2K, "Incomplete." I put the phone to my ear, listening as she said, "Hello? Who is this? Hel..loo!" I chuckled. Finally, not wanting to scare her, I began singing along with Sisqo about finally having everything and my life feeling complete.

"Antoine…" I heard her whisper. "I love you, too, Baby."

I quieted, turning the music down to a softer flow, listening to her breathing.

"I know you're working, but I was thinking about you. Did you feel it?" I asked her.

"Feel what?"

"Feel me thinking about you? It was tangible, Roxy," I said earnestly.

"Antoine, your love is always tangible to me. Even when we aren't together, and I'm working and you're painting at your studio. I feel like I'm your easel, and I can feel you drawing me with your love, painting me with your touch. I feel you that much…"

My heart beat fast at her words, and I was speechless. We were both quiet for a moment. "Can you tell me what's been bothering you?" I finally asked her.

She sighed before answering with a question of her own. "Can you tell me that we have a no matter what type of love?"

"Of course," I insisted. I knew something was wrong. Why wouldn't she talk to me? "Has anything changed, or happened since L.A.?"

"No, Antoine…Look, you have your exhibit tomorrow. I'm a moody chick and you know it. I don't want to ruin anything you have coming your way with my silliness, okay? I'll pop by tomorrow morning. I still have some things to tally up here and it will be late before I'm done."

"I could come help you," I offered.

"Goodnight, Antoine, luvyalotz." She hung up. *Can't get anymore final than that*, I thought to myself. "Hmmm…"

Later as I had finally completed my mental to-do list, the doorbell rang. I jumped up quickly thinking Roxy had changed her mind about seeing me.

"Hey, suga!" Nicky chimed, giving me a hug.

"Hey there."

"Well, dayum, you look so pleased to see me, I think I'll just turn around and go right back where I came from." Nicky spinned around, making a mock exit. I grabbed her, laughing.

"Get back here, crazy girl!" I smiled.

"Unh-unh, you wanna be all funky and shit. Who were you expecting anyhow, or need I ask?" She raised her eyes with an amused grin on her face.

I blushed, walking away from her to get a Pepsi. "I was hoping it was Roxy." I offered Nicky a pop, which she accepted gratefully. "She's just been acting a lil' weird since we got back from the West Coast. She worked late tonight but I thought maybe she would just come by anyhow and talk to me about what's on her mind. I do know this dude approached her in Cali, and she seemed weirded out by him. In fact, she seemed upset. Then when I approached them she suddenly acted like they were old friends from when she lived and modeled in L.A." I leaned against my soda bar, sipping my drink slowly. "This cat seemed creepy though, I don't know, I just wish whatever is up, she would talk to me, you know?"

Nicky had a thoughtful look as she listened to me, as if she were lost in her own world a bit.

"Wassup? What you thinking?" I asked.

"Um…nothing. It's just that…well, Antoine, I keep getting this feeling…"

I let out a slight laugh. "What kind of feeling? Come on now, don't you start acting all evasive, too."

"Well, just that I had this conversation with her sister, Dee? And now with what you just told me, and with how Dee talked, things are just starting not to seem cool with Roxy. Like, I like her and all, but just how well do you know her, I mean, know all there is to know about her?"

"I know her, Nicky. See, now all this time she's been there for you…" Nicky cut me off.

"Don't you even go there, Antoine. I know that I didn't seem to like her at first, but now I can genuinely say I do. At the same time, I can sense things. You know I'm almost psychic." She winked, probably trying to ease the tense air a bit.

"Yea, you're psychic all right." I punched her playfully on the arm.

"I wish I had been psychic enough to stay away from Mya," Nicky suddenly said, changing the subject, which I was glad.

I really didn't feel like analyzing how much I knew Roxy. I also didn't want to even contemplate that she could ever possibly keep vital things about herself from me. I turned myself back toward Nicky's attention, listening solemnly as she said, "If I had been psychic, then none of this bad stuff would have ever happened, and I wouldn't be the funked-up bitch I am right now."

"Do you hear from her anymore?"

"No…," she answered solemnly. "And I miss her, too. Ain't that a trip? I mean this bitch's crazy ass husband rapes me, she dips out, straight up showing what she's about, and here I am actually missing the chick."

Nicky talking about things so casually or freely really told me one thing. She was finally healing. And even though she still had sadness in her eyes, she had life again, too.

"So what are you going to do?" I asked.

"Do?"

"Yes, about Mya."

Nicky closed her eyes, breathing in. "Antoine, I'm not going to do anything except what I'm doing now, pushing it until her husband is where he belongs. Because see, I'm not like some of these wimpy women who hide and cower in fear forever." She ran her hands through her medium-length twists. "I'm going to fight, 'cause I was wronged and abused, and too many dogs get away with it, and one thing's for sure? These dogs won't—not this time."

Even through her strong valor and words, I could sense how this entire situation had killed a part of her. Yet, one thing I had always loved about Nicky was her strength. I knew from the start that she was not the kind of woman who was going to let this hold her down, or at least, not keep her down.

I reached out for a bear hug, with Nicky hugging me back tightly without another word. When you're as close as she and I had always been, words weren't always needed.

CHAPTER Twenty Six

Roxy

"Tag, you're it!" I squealed and turned around from the easel that stood perched in Antoine's living area. I had been up since the crack of dawn, restless and too excited for my baby, whose showing was tonight. Unlike me, he slept like an infant. I crept out of bed and in my state of awake, I tiptoed into Antoine's makeshift art room and pulled out a blank canvas. Placing it atop the easel, I began mixing colors on his palette and was soon engrossed in a painting of the pre-dawn sky and skyscrapers that could be seen out of the window.

At least two hours had passed, and I was now in a zone, quietly and meticulously painting the exterior of the buildings, totally oblivious to all around me until, "Tag, you're it!" When I turned away from the easel, I found Antoine, clad in white boxer briefs and a paintbrush dipped in electric blue paint. Before I could move out of his way, he slashed the brush toward me, blue streaking my right cheek.

"Are you crazy?!" I screamed. I cracked up at the bright smile and crazy look in his eyes.

"Come and get me." He laughed, backing away and circling the sofa as I motioned toward him, my own brush in hand.

"You are so bad," I called out after him, lunging across the sofa at him, nipping his hard stomach with red paint. I cried out as I tried to backpedal on the sofa to make my getaway, but Antoine jumped from behind the sofa, landing atop of me.

"Uhhh!" I groaned from the weight of him landing on me. "Get off of me, you nut!"

I dropped my paintbrush and gripped his hand, trying desperately to take the brush from his hands…all for naught. In a flash, he pinned my hands above my head and began doodling a blue mustache above my upper lip.

"I didn't think you could look more beautiful," he began, chuckling, "but the mustache is definitely the finishing touch!"

"Screw you!" I batted the brush from his hands. We wrestled for several minutes until we both were panting and out of breath. Our wrestling evolved into stroking and touching which turned into my pressing Antoine's face close to mine, drawing him in for a deep, wet kiss.

"Now we're twins." I smirked, eyeing his faint blue mustache. "Connected in mind, body, soul…and moustache." You must be on Cloud Nine today, Baby." I kissed his soft lips.

I watched Antoine's eyes sparkle within their blackness, and my heart glowed with happiness for him. My fingers wove threw his silky black hair, pulling him ever closer to me. "This is the happiest day of my life," he confirmed, kissing along my neck. "I have the woman of my dreams in my arms, the showing of a lifetime tonight, and my dad is doing great. I don't know how it could be better."

"You deserve it, Boo. Your work is magnificent. It was only a matter of time before it would grace a gallery."

"And Samantha's at that," he added. My exuberance waned slightly at the mentioning of Samantha's name. Yes, she had given my baby what he could only dream about, but for me, she represented some looming problem, and I couldn't stop the gnawing feeling in the pit of my stomach that she would do whatever it took to pull me and Antoine apart.

"You okay, Roxy?" Antoine asked, looking down at the semi-pout on my face. I nodded yes and maneuvered myself from under him. "I'm great, if you're great."

"Don't act like that, Roxy," he chided me, pulling me onto his lap. The look in his eyes begged me to just spill my thoughts as he stroked up and down my bare thigh. "I know you're not Samantha's biggest fan..."

"*That* is the understatement of the year," I moaned, rolling my eyes.

"She's been so good to me..."

"I know," I answered, nodding my head, but turning my face away from Antoine. "I can't seem to get out of my mind how good she's been to you, Antoine."

"I know you're not talking about the cruise because that's ancient history."

I gave him a look that told him I believed him...on his part anyway. "It's true," he insisted. "Besides, I never loved her, held those deep, caring for feelings for Samantha."

"Ahhh," I replied. I couldn't explain why I couldn't let this go. Maybe because I felt our relationship being threatened, like impending doom, but I took a deep breath and let out, "Look, I'm a woman...a woman who knows women, and Samantha can't be trusted, point blank. I know she tried to kick it to you on the cruise, may have succeeded as well. You and she were an item after the cruise, too, and I know she still digs you, Antoine, I know this."

"But you know I don't dig her. Not like that. You do know that, right?" I slipped my arms around his neck, kissing him daintily on the lips.

"I'm sorry, Antoine." I sighed, stroking his cheek. "Jealousy is a bitch, and I guess I feel threatened by her...she can do so much for you."

"Yea, artistically she can help me big time," Antoine explained, "but love-wise, heart-wise, you are my soul mate...there's no one else in the world for me, and you can take that to the bank, Baby."

When he kissed me, I could feel without a shadow of a doubt that he was sincere, so I dropped the subject. But deep down, I felt insecure, unsure of how Samantha could mess up what seemed like a perfect life for me.

"Hey, what are you doing here?" I peeked my head into Charlise's office. She looked stressed. "I came by to check up on you, make sure you're being a good girl."

"Who me?" Charlise ran her fingers through her blond hair. "What kinda trouble could I possibly get into here at the gallery?"

"Oh, I dunno," I responded, waltzing into her office and plopping down on the leather loveseat in the corner. "You could meet some extraordinarily sexy man down in the bookstore or café. I read in a magazine that the number one place women meet men at is the bookstore." Charlise jumped up from her seat, smoothing down her chocolate-colored slacks.

Charlise took a seat beside me on the loveseat. "Well, let me get down there now. Lord knows I haven't had a date in many a month. So tell me why you're really here."

"I was feeling closed-in at my place, and Antoine is over at Samantha's gallery, preparing for tonight."

"And you were lonely?"

"Yea." I nodded, resting my forehead on her shoulder.

"Are you sure you're okay?" Charlise prodded, rubbing my shoulder. I closed my eyes. After I left Antoine's apartment, I didn't even go to my place. I needed to be out in the light, around people to perk myself up for that night. Antoine was going to be showered with praise and love all night long, and if I was going to be by his side, I needed to place my best face forward.

"I'm cool," I answered, sighing. "Geeked about tonight...everybody is going to be there, and Antoine will get his night in the limelight."

"His career is going to be set in stone after tonight," Charlise gushed. "Hell, I wish I had snapped him up first, but Samantha is far more ensconced in celebrity and will have Antoine's star shining fast and bright."

"Yea, Samantha is definitely the woman to ignite Antoine's artistic embers," I conceded.

"Now Roxy, don't even let that woman get under your skin. I know she was extremely high on herself the day the bookstore and café opened, but all you have to remember is that you and Antoine are the item...she has nothing to do with you two."

"I know, I know," I moaned. "My heart knows that, but my mind, well, it's playing tricks on me. I might have to pull a trick or two from my sleeve tonight if she gets full of herself."

"Well, just remember, no tricks can harm true love. You and Antoine were meant to be."

Yeah, I thought. Meant to be...

"I'd like to propose a toast to my son," Antoine's mother said. Her flawless brown skin shone in the lights of the gallery, her long hair pinned in a chignon, her black strapless gown melded along her thick yet curvy frame. I chuckled to myself. It seemed that whenever there was a gathering, "we" would form our own clique. Charlise, Antoine, his parents, Nicky, even Dakota, and myself were in a tight circle as Antoine's mother began her toast.

"From the day Antoine was born," she began, "painting surged through his blood. His artistic spirit flowed so deeply within him that he knew...we knew he was destined to do wonderful things." Her husband lightly draped his arm over her shoulder as she began to tear up. "I'm sorry," she whispered, clearing her throat. Antoine's eyes were glazed over, too. In fact, we all were waiting to let the tide flow from our eyes as his mother finished. "God gave me and Charles the gift of Antoine, and now God has given Antoine the gift of art. May he forever release it to be admired and cherished by all."

"Here, here," I chimed in, wiping the tears from my cheeks. Antoine took his mother into his arms and hugged her tightly.

"I love you, Mom," Antoine whispered, kissing her cheek.

"And you know I love you, too, Baby," she whispered back.

"This is where Antoine gets his loving spirit from," Samantha broke in. My eyes ran over her slim frame clad in a while silk dress that clung to her, giving her the allusion of an angel, especially with her long, blond hair flowing over her shoulders. Instantly, I thought *good versus evil*—her in white, and me in a racy red number that dipped below my mid-thigh and hung to my skin as if holding on for dear life. Criss-cross straps left my back bare, and the bodice of my dress properly lifted and presented my breasts in all their brown glory.

I stood up as straight as I could possibly stand, not wanting this woman to think I would ever bow down to her and let her simply take my man from me without a fight. She promptly walked up to Antoine, slipping her slender arm around his waist like she normally did. His parents eyed me, questioningly, but I simply smiled, sipping my champagne.

"Tonight is a glorious night." Samantha's eyes moved from Antoine to me before giving a quick acknowledgment to everyone in our clique. "Actually, it's approaching unveiling time and this beautiful man's coming out into the stratosphere!"

"God, she piles it on thick, doesn't she?" Nicky asked, leaning close to me. "I swear, I don't know how you stand there and not smack the shit out of her. She's so damn obvious."

I nodded, not saying a word. I didn't want to let my annoyance of Samantha fester inside…this was Antoine's night, not an opportunity for my green-eyed monster to rear its ugly head.

Samantha rose her champagne glass before speaking. "Attention, everyone," she began, taking Antoine's hand and leading him along a wall that contained hidden paintings, his paintings. "Tonight is a very special night." Samantha's look at Antoine said that she loved him and that he was hers. I choked back a gallon of contempt. "It's going to be okay," Charlise whispered, rubbing my back.

"The talents of this young artist will be seen here tonight, but come tomorrow, he will be in every art magazine and in every art section of a newspaper in New York…even the country. Yes, he is that good," Samantha cooed. "I was lucky to have met Antoine on a cruise earlier this summer, and in doing so, I was able to tap into his energy. And when I realized how much power his work exuded, I knew he would be the next best thing to grace my gallery and the art world."

I felt a prick in my left shoulder, as if someone were picking my skin with a sharp blade. I flinched, and out of the corner of my eye, I saw him, and motion stopped. Everything became blurry and hazy, and all I could think was…this is it. He smiled my way, raising his glass to me and then towards Antoine who was basking in the glory of the wondrous words that emitted from Samantha's mouth.

I couldn't hear the rest of Samantha's speech, or hear the empathetic words from Nicky or Charlise, or receive the concerned glances from Antoine's parents…to me, they were things of my lovely past, for now…my future was getting dimmer by the second. I blinked rapidly as Samantha dramatically revealed the first of seven paintings from Antoine's Cherokee line. I could barely make out the figure in the first painting, the lone Cherokee woman in her regalia, standing proud, looking strong and formidable and representing the strength that resonated from a culture of proud people.

Bulbs flashed with the speed of popcorn popping, and the sounds and lights dizzied me. "Are you okay?" Nicky asked. I glanced at her, but saw through her as I excused myself. "Wait, where are you going?" Nicky called out. I could hear Charlise asking her what was wrong as I retreated from the scene. I had planned to escape into the bathroom, to get away from the crowd, from him, but when I felt a cool hand take hold of my bare arm, I knew disastrous fate was knocking at my chained door.

"Trying to get away?" Clark asked, his sneer in place. I whipped around, removing my arm from his grasp. "It's a small world, isn't it?" he continued. I shuddered with repulsion as Clark's eyes devoured my body. "You know, I received a call from Samantha a couple of days ago, and she couldn't stop going on and on about her new find, Antoine Billups. When I told her that I ran into him in California, we had a long talk about him…and you."

The first tear slid down my face like a shard of glass cutting through me. "Me?" I asked, my voice faint. "What would you two have to say about me?"

"Oh, come on now." Clark's voice was full of hatred and bitterness. "Samantha went on about the cute and sweet girlfriend of Antoine's. I told her she had to be mistaken, because the Roxanne Winters I knew may have been sugar and spice, but she was not everything nice. She was frisky and sexy and so many more delectable things."

"You bastard," I seethed, silently crying, dodging glances from the clique. I could see Samantha's gaze through the crowd, honing in on me. *Was that a glint of a smile I saw on her face*, I asked myself while in the midst of a life breakdown. "Why? Why would you do this to me?" I cried. "What did I ever do to you?" Thunderous applause echoed through my body as Antoine stood forward from his embrace with Samantha and began to speak. He was so in the moment that he hadn't glanced my way yet, but Nicky, Charlise, even his parents were eyeing me, and I needed to make an escape.

I stepped away from Clark who leered at me, whispering, "I'll be right here waiting for you." I clutched my stomach and raced for the bathroom, into a stall, where I released the champagne and finger foods I had partaken throughout the night.

"Roxy?" It was Nicky. I heard two sets of footsteps, so I knew Charlise was in tow, too. "What's going on? Are you okay?" I hadn't locked the bathroom stall door, and Nicky and Charlise easily spotted me kneeling at the toilet hugging against it.

"Oh, my God!" Charlise cried, moving toward me and helping me from the floor. "What's happened?" she asked. Nicky handed me a wet paper towel, and I wiped at my mouth. Then the sweat formed on my forehead.

"I gotta get outta here," I whispered.

"Who was the guy, Roxy?" Nicky asked, her voice sincere yet tinged with the neutrality that only a serious, true-blue friend to Antoine would have.

"Guy?" I asked, holding on to my stomach.

"Don't play games, Roxy," Nicky said, this time her voice hard, firm. "I saw you talking to a guy…or rather him talking to you…you looked scared shitless."

I felt a tremble in my lips, and warm, salty tears cascade down my face. Time had run out. In a matter of seconds, my past would be present. But I hoped, I prayed that this was all a dream, and I wouldn't have to tell them, anyone.

"I'm so sorry," I cried out, running out of the bathroom, head-first into Clark.

"I told you I would wait for you," he said.

"What do you want from me?" I asked desperately. The cheers and applause had ended and now everyone was back into mingling, admiring Antoine's work and clamoring to get a word in with him. His eyes were wandering, I knew in search of me.

"Why do you think you deserve to live a good life?" Clark asked, his voice menacing. "You whored around for years in California, you pulled my poor brother into your web, and he killed himself. Thomas meant everything to me, and now he is dead because of you. And now you think you deserve to live happily ever after?"

"I didn't weave a web to lure Thomas," I responded. "He begged me to come to Paris with him. He told me he loved me. I thought he wanted to be with me forever. I never thought he was going to keep me captive in France. I never planned to do any of this, to be ...what I was in California..."

"Yes, I know...the rape," Clark said dryly. "Thomas told me about that, very tragic indeed, but I doubt your sweet, God-fearing mate will find that excuse plausible...after all, isn't that the sad song for every whore who raises her skirt for cash?"

There was a gasp behind me, and when I turned around, I found Nicky and Charlise behind me, startled, having heard what Clark had said.

I was frozen in place, but Clark's words, so venomous, seared through my heart and burnt my soul. "All of these people here should know what you are, Roxanne Winters—nothing but a fancy call girl, all decked out in your red. And how long did you think it would be before your Antoine found out, hmm?"

"Please stop," I croaked, my eyes still looking into Nicky's unbelieving ones. She could hear every word Clark was saying, as could Charlise, yet at this point I was too weak to even care.

"Please stop? Please stop? You bitch! You destroyed him! Destroyed a good man, and you tell me to please stop?"

"What the hell..." I looked up to the sound of Antoine's voice at the doorway. He was walking toward Clark and me in record speed. Pushing Clark hard against the wall, he shouted, "What are you doing talking to her like that. Who the hell are you?" His dark eyes lit up as he suddenly recognized Clark. "You...you're that dude from California!"

"Antoine, please, I don't feel well. Let's just go," I pleaded.

I felt Charlise and Nicky walking up beside me, Charlise's eyes filled with confusion and sadness, Nicky's brimming with anger and disbelief. Antoine, however, ignored my request; he seemed to be focused totally on Clark for now, to my dismay.

"I ought to kick your ass for talking to her that way. Get the fuck outta here before I get security to throw you out. I knew there was something fishy about you," he said to Clark with narrowed eyes.

"Oh, don't worry, I'm leaving.," Clark laughed sarcastically. "But your *lady* over there? She's got a nice little maneuver with them hips, doesn't she?" I never moved my eyes from Antoine as I waited for the words that were sure to come. "She was nothing more than a fuckin' high-priced whore in California, and now here she is, masquerading as a lady. Yeah, you have quite a jewel there, mister big-shot artist. A lady of the night, that is! Ain't that right, Foxy Roxy?"

Antoine seemed to growl as he lunged forward, giving Clark a solid uppercut to the jaw. Clark howled like a woman, grabbing his bleeding mouth and running off. And I was numb as Antoine swung around looking at me with a shaken expression. "It's not true...," he almost moaned. "Please tell me it's not true..."

"Antoine..." Nicky tried cutting in, but once again, Antoine asked, "Is it true? You...you, slept around, for money?" I kept hearing Antoine asked me over and over if it were true, and finally I cried, "Let me explain, Antoine. You don't understand..."

"Oh, I understand," he said, pushing me away from him. I fell back into Charlise's arms and cried as the man I loved looked at me with hurt and disdain. "This is the nothing you couldn't tell me," he stated, more than asked. "You were never a model in California...," he whispered with his voice cracking. "You were *fucking* for money." I cringed at his unusual vulgarity. When a tear slipped from his eye and down his dark cheek, I prayed for God to strike me down then, to end my pathetic life right then, but fate wanted me to be in pain. "I can't believe, can't believe I fell in love with a...with a..." He choked, as if unable to even say the word.

I was dead. His words leaked breaths from my body, leaving me beaten and discarded. "Antoine, you don't understand. Please, let's talk about this..."

"Oh, now you wanna talk?" Antoine laughed, without mirth. "All these months I begged you, Roxy, begged you to talk to me. Begged you to tell me about your past, and you didn't. And you know what? I don't even want to know anymore; I don't care about it now."

"You don't care about me?" I cried frantically. "You don't love me?"

"You don't want to know the answer to that, for real." I touched Antoine's arm and he jumped back as if burnt by a flame too hot to handle. He turned away from me and rushed through the crowd. I could feel Charlise's and Nicky's eyes on me, and as I ran through the crowd after Antoine, I could see the perplexed looks on his parents faces and Samantha smugly watching the theatrics.

The crowd was mildly interested, glancing our way in between drinks and bites. Samantha appeared before us, grabbing Antoine as he reached the door. "Darling," she cooed, "where are you going? This is your night."

I felt as if I were in a hospital bed, and my respirator was turned off for me to slowly die.

"My night is over." My heartbeat faded in and out as I heard the pain in Antoine's voice. "I can't be here. I'm sorry, Samantha..." He looked at me again, contempt written all over his face. "But hey, you've got a professional right here to help you entertain the masses. Make sure you pay her handsomely."

With those parting words, he left, and I stood staring out into the empty night.

Flatlined.

CHAPTER *Twenty Seven*

ANTOINE

I was running, running for my life, running for my sanity, running away from the nightmare. This was my night. This was my reward for years and years of hard work and dreams and striving. It was a rare thing that my father's Biblical training and words came back to me. But for some reason I kept hearing his voice, reciting the words of wisdom, *vanity, all life is simply vanity, and a striving after the wind.* It was so very true, and I was running in that wind, from everything, from nothing.

After the shocking revelation at my exhibit, I drove home blindly, changed into my jogging clothes and left. Now that I was done, there were no more feelings to feel. It's what I needed, wanted so badly, 'cause I be damned if I was going to fall to my knees over this, although that's exactly how I felt when I left my exhibit–on my knees. Every time I've loved, I've been fooled. The first time I counted it as just being young and dumb, and a naïve idiot. This time, it's just a plain "love is blind" scenario. How could I fall so deeply, so completely in love with a woman I knew absolutely nothing about? All I could see after hearing those words, "She's a whore..." was Roxy, talking to me, telling me about her modeling and baby-sitting and all her other lies she wove throughout our relationship.

"No wonder she was so damn good in bed," I said to myself as I climbed the stairs leading to my apartment, mumbling words with every step. When I got to the last one I felt rather than saw Roxy curled up in a ball at my door.

"Excuse me," I said coolly, working to get past her to unlock the door. She stood up. Her eyes were glued to my face, looking for a reaction, I suppose. I wasn't prepared to give one. When one had a reaction, that meant they were feeling. I didn't want to feel anything. Especially for a woman, especially for her.

She walked in behind me. I took off my Nikes at the door, hung my keys on the door hook, and walked into my kitchen, ignoring her. I opened up the fridge, grabbed a bottle of milk and began washing the acidic taste from the back of my throat, which was slowly closing up on me.

Long moments passed with neither of us saying anything, until finally Roxy broke the silence. "So, where do we start?"

"We?" I looked at her with wide eyes. "There is no we; Roxanne, there is me and there is you. And as for me, I had nothing to do with what you chose to do with yourself in California. Let's get that straight."

Tears sprung in her eyes. "Antoine, I'm sorry, okay? I know sorry doesn't change things, but you are so cold and so bitter. You won't even stop for one moment and try to understand why I would do what I did. I had a reason. Maybe no reason is good enough, but at least hear me out?"

"I don't want to hear what you've got to say. I'm sorry..."

Something inside of me had shut off that reasonable, warm part that had always been a part of my personality. There Roxy stood, her eyes red and swollen from crying, her nose looking as if someone had punched her in it. Yet I didn't want to feel the concern and love that usually flowed through me whenever I looked at her. I watched her lips as she spoke, begging me to give her a moment, a simple moment to explain. But all I could think about and wonder about was how many dicks she had sucked with those beautifully shaped lips.

She continued talking, I continued thinking. Had she seen me as one of them? Had she seen me as of her customers? Had she faked with me, acted with me, like she did with them? Was I a john, too, given a freebie? I felt nauseated, sick. I looked away from her.

I heard her sigh. "Please talk to me, Antoine. What we have is too special to just let it die like this. Please?"

I wondered how much she charged an hour. How many men had there been? Did she even know? I said nothing…

"Say something, Antoine, *please!*"

I looked far away from her, tightening my will, tightening my heart. I heard her crying—a deep bawl like a hurt baby. I felt my eye twitch and forced myself to ignore her tears. I couldn't, wouldn't give in to her!

"Then if…if you won't talk to me, I'm just going to go."

"Okay."

"Okay? Damn you!"

I broke. "What do you expect me to say, Roxy? My God! How could you sell your soul? And you expect me to understand it?"

"I expect you to give me a chance to explain. But no, you're too busy being self-righteous and good to do that, aren't you?" she cried.

"Ah, naw." I laughed sarcastically. "Don't put this on me. You did this. You did this to me and you did this to yourself. You did this to us. So don't try to switch the blame now in order to soothe your conscious." I looked at her, shaking my head in disgust. "All those lies, Roxy, how could you love someone yet lie to them? How?"

"I wanted you to love me!" she cried again. "I just…wanted…your love…"

I was unable to stop the array of emotions and pain I felt from showing on my face. If I looked anything like she did though, we were both destroyed by the lies.

"You already had it," I whispered brokenly.

"Yes, I *had* it," she replied as she rose to leave.

I never budged. I just watched as she walked to the door, her back to me.

She opened the door, then stopped. Without turning around, she said, "We all sell ourselves in some form or fashion, Antoine. I may have sold my soul for money…" She turned around, looking at me with hollowed eyes. "But when you slept with Samantha, weren't you selling yours for your career? Think about it."

The following morning, I had a mission. I showered, dressed quickly and made myself coffee, which was horrible as my coffee usually is. I dumped it in the sink and left. The traffic was pretty busy for a Sunday morning, but then again, in Manhattan it doesn't really matter what day it is. I got to Samantha's apartment, only to have her doorman inform me that she had left for the gallery an hour earlier. I turned around swiftly, and got back into my Jeep. I was definitely going to talk to her today!

The one thing that did stick to my mind was Roxy's parting words. She was right; I had sold myself. Maybe not totally as she had, but that first time I had sex with Samantha it wasn't just desire talking; it was my wanting so badly to impress her, my wanting so badly for her to help me get where I had finally gotten. Was it worth it? I really couldn't answer that question, even to myself.

My cell phone rang as I was crossing the Manhattan Bridge, which was surprising. Usually it wouldn't work until I was already across. "Yea?" I hollered.

"Antoine?" It was my father. "Where are you, son? I've been trying to get in touch with you all morning."

"I'm on my way to the gallery. I need to talk to Samantha."

"Oh, okay." There was a pause, as if he were waiting for me to say something.

"Washup, Dad?"

"You know what's up, Antoine. Your mother and I didn't call last night because we wanted to give you time to deal with whatever it was that happened there, but you know we want to know what's going on. Why did you leave the gallery like that?"

My heart heaved in my chest, reliving again what I felt when I heard Clark's words. "So you didn't hear…see anything then?"

"No, so why don't you tell me?"

As I got to the end of the bridge, I pulled over to catch my bearings. My parents were no-nonsense type of people, however warm and loving. "Dad, sometimes you can love someone and think you know that person and really not know them at all. I found that out the hard way last night."

"What happened?"

"Roxy was not what she told me she was. She lied to me about so many…things." The last word got caught in my throat.

"Like what, son?"

I could hardly get it out, the embarrassment for her, for me, the shame that my Roxy, my baby could... "Dad, remember at dinner that time, when I told you that she had been a model in California?" With his grunt of remembrance, I continued, "She was never a model; she was a call-girl, a hooker. There was this dude at my exhibit who we had seen when we were in California a couple of weeks ago. She had told me then he was an old friend from when she'd lived there. That was a lie. He was one of her johns. Actually, the brother of a man she flew to Paris with. And last night, right in front of her, he told me everything, everything!"

There was a moment's pause before Charles Billups spoke. *Probably thinking how stupid I am*, I thought to myself. "Son, I don't know what to say. This is just awful..."

"What is there to say?" I cried. "I made a complete fool of myself for a woman, again."

"No, not again, Roxy loves you," he insisted.

"How could she love me? She lied to me, Dad. You don't lie when you love someone. You've always told me that."

"I've also always told you that people make mistakes, son. All of us make mistakes. It's what makes us human. If we didn't make mistakes, we wouldn't have any reason for Jesus, now would we? If he died for our sins and there were no sinners, his death would mean nothing, right?"

I sighed. "Dad, I don't need a sermon, not today. I really don't need this."

"This isn't about a sermon, Antoine! Come off of that high horse you're on and see yourself, *really* see yourself, because you know that young woman loves you! And I don't care if she had a slew of johns or customers from here to the West Indies, it wouldn't change the depth of that love that shines so clearly in her eyes every time she looks at you. She's open with it, honest with it, for everyone to see."

My heart was hurting. I knew he was right; I knew I was so wrong. I could forgive myself, excuse myself for my goings-on with Samantha, but I didn't even want to hear Roxy's reasons for why she did what she did. To hear it would obligate me to forgive her, and I didn't want to, not yet. I was hurting too much to want to see, understand, or forgive anything.

"Dad, I gotta go," I choked out.

"Don't betray her, son. Can you imagine what she must have feared all these months? Afraid of you finding out the truth about her? Can you imagine how devastating it must have been to her, to have you find out as you did? *When* you did? *How* you did?" he stopped, breathing deeply before adding, "Don't be her Judas, Antoine...hear her out."

"I gotta go," I replied, and hung up.

"Darling! How did you know I'd be here today?" Samantha smiled.

"You knew, didn't you?"

She looked at me with a lost, blank expression. "Knew what, sweetie?"

"You knew about Roxanne. You knew that Clark dude and his brother, Thomas. All of it. That's why you invited him to my exhibit. How could you, Samantha? How could you do it me?" I demanded. I stared at her with hurt confusion.

"Wait, hon." She put her hand up, as if putting me on pause. "It's not how you're thinking. Yes, I knew Clark Dugué, but of course, I didn't know about Roxy! And I would never ever have invited him to your exhibit if I had known he was going to make a scene as he did. All of this has been just as important to my galleries as to you. My money was invested, remember?"

She sounded convincing, but still...

"How did you know that he knew her? And why was he here anyhow?"

"Antoine, Clark is one of the buyers from Los Angeles that I had told you about. When I called him up to remind him about my new artist, and how he should come to check out some of your work, he mentioned that he had actually met you. And then when I asked him had he met your beautiful lady also, he then told me how he had met her years ago, and also about her prostitution."

I cringed when she said "prostitution." Samantha exhaled, looking at me with sad, sorry, gray eyes. "I'm sorry, darling, I knew this would be hard for you to take. She lied to us all. I'm glad you've dismissed her.

You deserve better than a woman like that." I cut her off, not wanting to hear her putting down Roxy.

"Samantha, then why did you still let him come? You must have known what he was going to do once he saw her again."

She laughed in amazement. "How would I have known? You said yourself that he saw her and you out West. If he didn't have a reason to tell you, then why would I have thought he would do so at your exhibit? Really, this is all Roxy's fault, not mine, not yours, and not Clark's either. She's the one you should be sore at."

I stared at her solemnly, deciphering if I should believe her words. There was something not quite honest in her eyes, but then again I could barely trust my instincts at that moment as to who was honest, and who was not. I got up, looking around her office before taking my leave.

"You believe me, don't you, Antoine?" she asked anxiously.

I looked at her with sadness, and strength. "Samantha, I thank you from the bottom of my heart for all that you've done for me. I really do. But at this point, belief in anything or anyone is not something that I'm feeling real strong right now."

I looked her in her eyes again, still examining if I could trust her. I could not. Something told me, she *knew*.

"I want to keep working with your galleries, of course, but I think we should ease up on the social stuff that has nothing to do with work for a while. I'm not feeling very social."

"But, Antoine..."

I shut her door, firmly.

"Don't betray her, son. Don't be her Judas." Was I being her Judas? Listening to Samantha tear Roxy into shreds made me wonder again and again. *That* kind of woman, she had said. What kind of woman? I knew exactly what kind of woman, kind of person she was, regardless of her past, didn't I?

Was I judging her unfairly, not thinking about how it may have been for here–not taking another route inside of her heart? I loved her—totally, completely. I needed to talk to her. I wanted to know, needed to know why, why she would ever do what she did.

I got home as quickly as I could, and picked up the phone to call Roxy. Her phone rang and rang. Her answering machine picked up. My mind snapped. All I could think about suddenly was her, with another man, touching him, loving him, for money.

"Where are you, damn it!" I screamed at her answering machine. "With some dude, some dude? Fuck!" I hung up, slamming the phone hard against the wall.

CHAPTER *Twenty Eight*

Roxy

"I should be home by this evening," I spoke into the phone as I dumped clothes into a duffle bag. The sun was barely shining in the sky, but it could have been nighttime for all I cared. I hadn't slept a wink all night. I cried, wandered the streets, and I realized that Antoine wanted nothing to do with me. It was over. He made that so plain the previous night, and without him, I couldn't be here.

I was determined to leave New York, wander back to Baltimore and try to restart my life there. I had always been good at leaving the scene of a crime. I ran from my normal, loving family to go to college. I fled college after my rape. Dumped my career as a call girl to be with Thomas, and then finally, I was rescued by my Step and Dee from Thomas to come back to the States, hoping to get my life back in order again. I failed, desperately, and now it was time to flee the scene. Dee was the first human I cried to once getting my bearings. The first thing out of her mouth? "You can come down, sure…but to visit. You've worked too damn hard for what you have in New York to leave it because of this disaster, a disaster that will blow over."

"Blow over?" I had asked. "Antoine will never forgive me for this. I embarrassed him, lied to him, and he made it clear we are no more. The *situation* may blow over, but the ramifications of the situation will live on forever." I began weeping hysterically. The pain of the previous night was hitting me every five minutes like clockwork. I had finally managed to calm myself and, after several minutes of talking to Dee, told her again, "I should be home by this evening."

"I told you, honey," Dee whispered, "you are welcome here, but this isn't your home. I'm not going to let you give up on all your dreams."

"Fuck dreams," I moaned into the phone, digging through boxes to find clothes and other items to take with me. At the bottom of a box, my fingers caressed a leather-bound book, and I jumped up and kicked the box back into the closet. I stumbled onto my bed.

"Sis," I croaked into the phone, "I have to go…yea, I'm okay, I'll call you to let you know the exact time I'll be in…love you, too."

I clicked off the phone and dropped it to my side. With my back against the bed, I sat on the floor and eyed the box in the closet as if it were a demon about to leap out at me.

"It's your fucking fault!" I cried. I crawled toward the closet and dug inside the box. I removed the journal.

"I was doing so well, keeping all my dirty secrets so well hidden, but you just wouldn't die, would you?" With speed, I flipped through each page, my tears splashing onto years of pain and hurt and misuse of my own body. I cried for every time I wanted to have someone there to hold me, tell me that the rape wasn't my fault. I screamed for every time I begged those guys to leave me alone and to not hurt me. I cursed for every time I allowed a man to impale me with more lies and more dirty deeds, cheapening me, making me nothing more than a body to screw.

I hated myself and right at that moment, I realized why Antoine could never forgive me because I never forgave myself. I probably didn't deserve forgiveness from myself, him, or God.

I got up from the floor and walked over to the desk in the corner of my room. After digging through a desk drawer, I pulled out a padded envelope and slipped the journal into it, sealing it. "I don't need you anymore," I whispered to the envelope. "I have all the memories right here," I added, tapping a finger to my head. "There is one person who might learn something from you."

I quickly zipped up my large duffle bag and roll-on and dragged them to my front door. I returned for my backpack and made sure everything was turned off in the apartment, and then I retreated to my bedroom to grab the envelope. Staring at it, my eyes grew misty. "I know you don't love me anymore, Antoine, but I hope this helps you understand why I funked up."

I stood outside her door, feeling the need to explain myself once again, knowing that my words would be ignored. "She's not going to hit me…I hope." I took a deep breath and knocked.

"Who is it?" I heard Nicky's voice on the other side of the door.

"It's me, Roxy. Can we talk?" In a flash, her door swung open and she greeted me with an evil glare.

"What the hell do you want?" she asked. She leaned against her door and didn't offer me a chance to come into her apartment.

"Can we talk…just for a minute, please?" I begged. Her eyes roamed over my tear-stained face, and the dishevelment of the baggy jeans and wrinkled tee shirt I had on, and after a few silent moments, she let me in.

"Nicky, I know you hate me right now, but…"

"You know, I oughta beat your ass, Roxy!" Nicky screamed, slamming the door behind her. "I knew there was something up with you the moment I laid my eyes on you, but Antoine kept insisting that he knew you. He didn't know shit!"

"I am so sorry, Nicky, I never meant to lie. I didn't." I stepped away from the fury that moved Nicky. "I tried to explain it to Antoine last night, but he…"

"Did you really think he would listen to you? He continued to ask you what was wrong, to talk to him, and you always said *nothing's wrong*. He trusted you, Roxy. He loved you more than anyone could ever love a person."

I wiped the tears from my face. "I don't know what I thought," I whispered. "I know now that Antoine hates me. He has every right to, and so do you."

"Don't tell me what I have the right to feel," Nicky sneered. "Because I love Antoine, I kept my opinions to myself…I even befriended you, Roxy."

"I love our friendship, Nicky. I know you hate me. I know this, but, Girl, I love you so much, and our friendship has meant a lot to me."

We stood, staring down the other, me in love, her in hate…maybe a step down from hate. "Say what you came to say," Nicky said, her voice less venomous.

"I never meant to lie…to anyone, and that's the truth," I began with a sniffle. "You remember the night in the hospital, when I told you about what happened to me?" Nicky's eyes slightly glazed over, remembering our talk…and her pain. She nodded. "Back then…when it happened to me? I wasn't nearly as strong as you are, Nicky. Being raped changed me forever. I blocked it out of my head like it never happened, but my soul and my spirit were dead, and I hated myself.

"I think I still hate myself. To me…being…sexual with those men was nothing, because my body was a rotten carcass. Ironically, I felt strong, like getting the money and making those men nothing more than a body part made me feel strong…crazy now that I think about it…," I said, wandering off in my mind.

"Antoine was my first shot at real love," I continued, looking away from Nicky's steady gaze. "I know you don't believe it, but he is the light that lit me, made me realize that I was a *person.* Even though he doesn't know about my rape, his love made me see that it wasn't my fault, and that I deserved to be loved and to give my love. I love Antoine, but I do know that it's over between us." I nodded. "He hates me, you hate me, everyone hates me…and that's my fault, so I'm not whining or complaining."

I rubbed the pain that ebbed in my heart, hoping that the intense stabbing would lessen…someday. "That's all I really wanted to say," I ended, walking toward the door. "It was really nice getting to know you, Nicky. I hope that you continue to grow stronger, and get through your situation. I want only the best for you guys." I opened Nicky's door.

"You sound like you're leaving?" Nicky asked. I turned to face her.

"There's really nothing here for me in New York," I stated simply, not saying I was leaving for good, and not saying I would be back. "Gotta pick up the pieces and move on." I was halfway out the door before I said, "Take care of you, Girl…and Antoine."

There was only one more person I had to see before I left the wreckage that was my life. "Hey," I whispered, before sticking my head into Charlise's office. "Do I still have a job?"

Charlise leapt from behind her desk and came to me, hugging me hard. "You will always have a job here," she answered. "Come in here." Charlise sat me down on the sofa and followed, wrapping me into her arms. Her open act of care brought the tears forward again. "Oh, don't cry, baby," she said. "It's going to be okay."

"Nothing will ever be okay," I replied, laying my head on her shoulder. "Antoine hates me, Nicky hates me. I feel like there's nothing left for me here, Char."

I let out a long, drawn-out breath.

"You are a strong woman," Charlise offered.

"Yea, right."

"Shut up, you are. It's going to hurt like hell for a while, but you're going to make it through this. I'll help you…so will your sister."

We sat, my head resting on Charlise's shoulder. I sniffed and swallowed hard.

"Rox," Charlise said, stroking my hair, "why didn't you tell me about this? You and I are friends, right?"

"You know we are," I answered. "I love you big-time, Char. It's hard to explain why I didn't tell people, other than to say I didn't want people to think less of me…less than how I thought of me, anyway.

"It's true, I slept with men for money, but there's a whole backdrop to how that happened, starting with me being raped while in college."

Charlise's eyes watered. "Oh, my God, Rox. I didn't know."

"That's how I wanted it to be, Girl," I responded. "I've been away from the rape and the prostitution for a long time now, and I tried to tell myself it never happened. Being in New York, meeting you, falling in love with Antoine, befriending Nicky, I was finally getting my life in some kind of order, and I prayed that my past would stay in the past. Now that the shit has hit the fan, I gotta take a breather from this madness."

"What?" Charlise asked incredulously. "You're leaving? You can't go, Roxy, you have a great job—I should know—you have friends who love you..."

"Correction, one friend, you. Not that you're not a great friend because you know I love you to death."

"Roxy, don't leave. I need you, and believe it or not, you need me *and* New York. We helped to restart your new, better life. Don't throw us away so quickly."

"I just need some time away," I pleaded. "I've already been told by Dee that I'm coming to Baltimore for a visit, so if I could just get two weeks off, so I can lick my wounds in peace, please?"

"If it's only two weeks, I can do that," Charlise answered, sighing. "Don't lie to me and leave and never come back."

"I'm through with lying, Char," I said in all honesty. "The pain that comes from lying is so harsh, so deadly...I never want to feel like this again."

"So, you talked to Antoine?" Charlise asked.

"It's over," I answered, calmer than I thought possible. "Tried to talk to him last night, but he didn't want to hear a word from me. I don't blame him, so I'm chalking our relationship up to my stupidity."

"You weren't stupid, just in love."

"In my life, same thing."

"Your sister asked me to come up here and see if you wanted to come down and hang out a bit..." I turned away from my easel and faced Stephen. He wore the same worried look that Dee had on when I came home a couple days earlier. Neither had been able to get me out of the attic where I had been living since I arrived. I found solace in finishing the painting I began in New York...a painting that symbolized my love for Antoine, and what that love had done to me. Now, I finished it just to complete it, so I could discard it. The love was gone, and these last couple of days helped me to realize that.

"I'm straight," I answered, trying my best to smile.

"That's not going to be good enough," Stephen said, his tall presence infiltrating the attic, approaching me. With delicacy, he took my paintbrush from my hand and placed it on a clear spot of my palette. Taking me by the hands, he led me from the attic and down the stairs to the main living area of their huge, Victorian house.

"Stephen," I begged, "I just want to be left alone."

"You've been alone for the past three days," Stephen said. "It's time for you to come out into the light...it won't burn you or anything."

"Ha, ha, ha, very funny."

"Besides, someone's here to see you."

My heart instantly bounced in my chest, stupidly of course, thinking that Antoine somehow found his way back to me. I quickly pushed those wishes out the back door of my mind as we wandered into the living room and found Dee and Dyeese sitting on the couch. For the first time since leaving New York, I smiled.

"Hey, Girl." Dyeese rose from the couch and hugged me tight.

"Long time, no see," I offered, my voice soft, resting from days of crying and dying over my life.

"Yea, and your black ass been here in B'more for three days and haven't called on me once," Dyeese chided. "You should be lucky I don't beat you down right now!"

"Would you guys like something to drink?" Stephen asked.

"Aww, see, my baby trying to be so nice and host-like." Dee smirked. I gave a half-smile, trying my best not to let the jealous bile rise in my throat. It was true. I kept myself hidden because I just simply didn't want to feel a part of something right now, but another reason for my seclusion was because I didn't want to see the lovey-dovey atmosphere between

Stephen and Deandra. Hell, they were in major love, planning their wedding. Lies, none. Deception, none. I knew I would never have that, and seeing it made me die that much more inside.

"We have tea, soda, coffee," Stephen added, laughing at Deandra.

"I'll have a glass of tea," Dyeese responded and Dee seconded.

"How about you, Roxy?"

"Yea, that sounds cool, thanks."

Dyeese pulled me down onto the couch between her and Dee. "Your sister told me you over here living like the Hunchback of Notre Dame, all up in your sanctuary."

"Yea, well, I just want solitude right now."

"You start having too much solitude, you'll get used to it, and I will never get you out of my attic."

My eyebrow arched skyward. "So you want me to leave?" I asked. "I mean if that's the case, I can find someplace to get my bearings..."

"I didn't say all of that. Damn, you can't be biting my head off every time I say something. I know you're hurting, and I'm dying seeing you in so much pain, but you can't let the pain dictate your life."

"Tell me," I began, moving from the couch to the chair that sat directly across from them, "what's the worst thing to ever happen to either of you?" Neither spoke. "I remember you being with this guy, someone you loved majorly, Dee, and you two broke up...painful, yet amicable. Dyeese, what happened to you?"

She didn't respond. "See, you two have never lived through what I'm going through, so hearing that 'the sun will rise tomorrow' shit gets a bit old after a while. For years, I have lived a lie so that I could try to find a normal life. I had that, and lost it, and now I have to learn how to live again. It's like learning how to walk as a baby, and I'm stumbling all over the damn place."

I bowed my head into my hands. I didn't cry. My eyes had been dry and itchy all day. It was probably phase one of my healing process.

"I'm not asking for people to hold my hands, to walk me through this. I just need space so I can learn to like myself again."

"You should love yourself, Girl," Dyeese demanded, tears in her eyes. "You are beautiful, caring, loving, giving, and stronger than the Rock of Gibraltar. I remember you on the cruise. You were spunky and witty, so in the moment. That's who you are, Roxanne. Don't let this crush what you have worked so hard to do for yourself."

"I embarrassed myself, my family, Antoine, Nicky, Charlise, and most importantly, God. He never wanted one of His children to wind up in the state of destruction that I have. I can't see how He could love me, so how could *I* possibly love me?"

"Did you ask to be raped?" Dee asked bluntly, pain in her face.

"Hell no," I cried.

"But you blamed yourself. You hated yourself, instead of the bastards who hurt you. That blame? God never bestowed that upon you, sis. He loved you...and even through that painful time, He was there, protecting you, keeping you alive, and hoping that you would reach to Him for help."

I felt my eyes grow watery. "After the rape, God didn't exist in my life. I couldn't believe in a world where God would allow someone to be brutalized, having their self stripped from them. Even now, it's hard to keep the faith."

Stephen stepped quietly into the room, holding a tray with four glasses of tea. He didn't breathe a word.

Dee knelt before me and took my hands. She gazed deeply into my eyes before saying, "Sis, God loves you, and all He's waiting on is for you to reach out your hand to Him. Let Him heal you, show you that you deserve love."

I wanted to be happy. I had been happy with Antoine, but I had to put that in the past with the rest of the pain. I looked over to Dyeese and Stephen, and I could feel the concern and love they had for me. When I took hold of Dee's eyes with my own, that sisterly bond reverberated through my entire body, and I cried inside, and secretly asked God to give me one more chance to prove that His love wouldn't be wasted on me.

CHAPTER *Twenty Nine*

NICKY

The clock ticked angrily on the wall in front of me. I sat in my navy blue starched dress suit, uncomfortably so. Mark Wilder sat on my left; Antoine sat on my right. Winston Greer's attorney sat across from us, and the judge at the very end of the oblong-shaped table. This was a very important pre-trial meeting, an effort to avoid a trial, something I wanted to do if at all possible. Anything to end the chance of my personal life and sexuality being aired out in public, something that could totally ruin my business.

"Ms. Carter, we want to make this as easy for you as possible, and we want to put an end to this mutual nightmare for both you and my client," Winston's attorney said.

"Mr. Kelly, I'm sorry, but I'm sure you realize that Ms. Carter's least concern is how her rapist feels," Mark Wilder said quickly.

"And you understand that with your client's background and sexual history, getting a rape conviction is almost impossible!"

My face grew hot. I knew my lesbianism would be an issue. Why it should be shows the unfairness of this world, yet, there it is, something that is not even a choice–something that I simply am. There it is, coming back to haunt me, even when I am the victim.

"Well, this isn't about Ms. Carter. It's about a crime that has been committed against her person."

"*Alleged* crime," Winston's attorney said pointedly.

Antoine sighed, looking at me and shaking his head in disgust.

The judge jumped in. "Gentlemen, are you prepared to settle this issue right here and now or do you want to take it before a jury?"

"I want this concluded now if possible, but to my client's satisfaction," Mark said.

All eyes went to me, waiting for a word. I paused briefly before saying, "I simply want justice. That's all I've ever wanted."

"And that is all Mr. Greer wants, too, Ms. Carter. My client is willing to plead guilty to aggravated assault."

"Aggravated *sexual* assault," Mark resounded.

"How about rape!" I cried. Antoine squeezed my hand again, but was silent.

"We will fight a rape charge, Ms. Carter. My client vehemently denies it. Now if you want to take it to court, then…"

"We can take it to court then, you starch-neck muthafucka!" I shouted angrily.

"Mr. Wilder, would you please get control of your client!" the judge demanded.

Mark looked at me, motioning for me to quiet myself. "Nicky, don't," he began, before looking toward the judge and saying, "Your honor, can I confer with my client in private?" The judge quickly nodded his approval.

Mark Wilder and I left out of the room to stand outside of the heavy oak door. He looked at me solemnly, as if understanding what I was going through, which of course, he had no idea. He wasn't a woman, and he hadn't been raped.

"Nicky, I'm not even going to say I know what you're going through because frankly, I only have to look in your eyes to see what your response would be to that. But I will say this much; you have to calm down in there. You don't want to alienate the judge." He looked at me and sighed. "Now we have two choices here. Mr. Kelly in there, Greer's lawyer, knows we have a lot on his client, but by the same token I've told you before, you will be on trial probably even more so than Greer will be. The other two guys who raped you have changed their testimony so many times that they are barely reliable witnesses anymore. So except for the physical evidence, which of course is strong, it would be your word against his."

"That is so fuckin' unfair," I responded, closing my eyes tightly to hold back my angry tears.

"I know it is, and I have to deal with the unfairness more often than I'd like to admit, but I wouldn't be honest if I told you that I was one hundred percent sure we could get him on rape. Frankly, I'm more doubtful on that than anything else. However, we can get him on aggravated sexual assault, which carries the same stigma but not the same jail sentence."

I shook my head as he spoke. "How much jail time?"

"Ten years max."

"And how much time would he serve?" I laughed, sarcastically.

"About three to five..."

"Wow, so that's the price tag on a woman's dignity these days?" I asked, eyeing him with an empty expression.

"I'm so sorry, but it's up to you. You know what the cost could be if we take this to trial. I wouldn't try to dissuade you in any way. If you want a jury trial we can have it. If you want to settle, we can do that, too. But I want to make sure that you have a clear understanding. If this goes to trial, we may lose and he may get away with even less time. But with a settlement, at least you would have some type of victory and your privacy, which you said was vital to you."

I looked at Mark Wilder. He was an honest-looking man, if there was ever such a thing. At this point the only man I knew for a surety that I could trust was Antoine. "I don't want my whole life ruined because of this monster," I said. "I'll accept the plea."

An hour later, Antoine and I stood outside of city hall. He was watching me closely to see how I was handling things I knew, and as for me, I was feeling some sense of closure, and no sense of justice. Mark Wilder was just inside the rotating doors, shaking hands with Winston Greer's attorney as if they were old friends from law school. He walked out afterward, reaching out to shake my hand.

"It's over, Nicky, finally," he announced.

I looked at him and nodded my head in the negative. "No, it's over for you, and it's over for them, but me? I have to live with what happened to me for the rest of life, and I have to live with the knowledge that justice for crimes committed against you is according to whether or not the law finds you *worthy* of justice. And that's the sad truth."

Later, Antoine and I shared a banana split at Friday's on Broadway. I could see he was sad for me, but I was done with being sad. At least now I could go on with my life without the worry of a trial, and the shame my sexuality would bring on my mom, and my family, and also Antoine's parents, who had always kept me as their own. Although I felt no shame about who I was, sometimes it was more about shielding the ones you love.

"There is no point in dwelling on this rape thing any longer. Mark was right. It's over, and you know I'm a strong black woman; I'm going to get over this," I said, smiling brightly to disguise my solemn mood.

"I don't know any woman who is stronger than you, Nicky," he said.

Antoine had a weak look in his eyes. For as much as I knew that he had tried to be there for me, especially doing the pre-trial, I also knew that he had a lot of shit on his mind. Number one being Roxy. I hadn't talked to her myself for a few days. I knew she was chillin' in Baltimore, hiding more likely from her shame. I also knew I had been hard on her, really tough on her when she came to visit. It just burnt me to see Antoine hurt as he was, and as much as I had grown to really like Roxy, I knew she was responsible for his pain. But at the same time, I also knew what she had gone through, and I knew that Antoine hadn't a clue. I figured I would give it a few days, then call her at Dee Dee's, and let her know that I understood. I could never condone pain brought on my suga of course, but woman-to-woman I could understand how she could have lost her dignity as she did. I also didn't hate her, and I had to let her know that.

"So change of subject. How are you dealing, babe?" I asked Antoine.

"I'm aight," he said, avoiding my eyes.

"Yea, right, this is me, okay?" Both of us were quiet. I was waiting for him to open up, without pushing that is. But push come to shove, I needed to know what was going on in that cute little head of his.

"I haven't heard from her. I suppose she's moved for good," he said finally, after a few moments of silence.

"Have you talked to Charlise? You know she's at Dee Dee's, right? I have the number. I could give it to you."

"Naw, what would be the point?"

"The point would be maybe you could get over some of this pain you're feeling, and some of this stress." I made small circles on the backside of Antoine's hand. "I know you feel guilty because you didn't hear her out. Maybe it's time you did?"

Antoine breathed in deeply. "Man, she *sold* her body. Can you even believe that? Sold her body to strange men. It doesn't even seem like Roxy. I can't even picture her doing anything like that."

"That's because that is not her, not the Roxanne you know, and that I know. I will admit, Antoine, I don't understand the whole thing either, but I do know that she is a different person now." I leaned a bit closer, looking in his eyes. "Sometimes women do desperate things. Sometimes it's desperation because of being financially destitute."

"And that couldn't have been her reason because her family was not and is not poor," he cut in defiantly.

"Okay, but also sometimes there are emotional reasons behind why we do what we do. See, baby, listening to you now, I know that you will never be content; you won't be until you know and understand why she did what she did. Whether or not you still want to be with her after you get those answers is yet to be seen, but you won't find closure until you do...I can promise you that much."

Antoine looked straight ahead, a stubborn look still coating his face. "Well, I can't find anything out right now while she is in Maryland. If she comes back to New York, I'll hear her out."

"And if she doesn't?"

"Then I'll fight like hell to get over her, and chalk it down to another lesson learned."

ANTOINE

After dropping Nicky off and driving back to my studio, I felt emotionally drained. It had been exhausting at the hearing, listening to those lawyers bickering back and forth, and knowing the turmoil that Nicky was going through. Yet at the same time it was comforting to know that at least the legalities were over for her.

Outside of all of that, I hadn't been getting any sleep lately, and I hadn't painted a stroke. I missed Roxy, and I felt angry with myself for not hearing her out. I felt angry at her for leaving so quickly and not giving me a chance to come to terms with what had happened. Maybe I was looking for reasons to validate my confused feelings, but at this point they were all I had to feed on. I had pretty much closed myself off to anything else.

I walked upstairs to my apartment after checking the mail in my box and found a package sitting at my door. I picked it up without really looking at it, stuffed it under my arm and went inside. I needed a shower, and a shave, and some wine. Yep, I had developed a taste for wine, not a huge one, but still it was amazing how things changed.

I placed my mail and the package on my wet bar, stripping my clothes off piece by piece as I headed for the bathroom. The hot water was like stinging needles but it felt good, and was doing wonders to help me deaden the hurt that was rolling around inside of me. I wondered what Roxy was up to, remembered the last time we had shared a shower together, the way she touched me, moaned against my skin. Flashbacks of her sitting on the edge of the tub making love to me with her mouth, telling me she loved me, devouring me until I was too weak to stand. All of the memories rummaged through my mind. She was so good at loving, an *expert.* I groaned, remembering just *why* she was so good and professional at it.

"I've got to stop thinking about her. I've got to stop thinking about the past," I said out loud, jumping out the shower and toweling myself dry. I slipped on some boxers and a pair of jeans and made my way to the kitchen to tear into the day old chicken I had chillin' in the fridge. As I passed the wet bar, I caught a glimpse of my mail and the package that had been sitting at my door. It having at first slipped my mind, I was suddenly curious as to what could be inside of the fat, sealed envelope.

Instead of red wine, I grabbed an A&W root beer from the fridge and sat at the bar, tearing the package edge. It was a shiny, black book, what appeared to be a journal. The name Roxanne Winters was encased on the outside in gold lettering. My breath caught as I slowly opened it…unsure if I really wanted to read its words, but some outside force seemed to be pushing me, some karma. I opened to page one seeing the date of February 15th, 1999 in broad black ink. I began reading.

I'm so dirty, ugly, used. This was all my fault. Deandra always warned me that my flirting-ass ways would get me into trouble! I hurt so badly...I can't tell a soul, who would believe me? Oh, God, did I bring this on myself? God, I can only write this to you on this paper, because I can't bring myself to my knees to even pray…

I felt confused as I read, but yet still my heart was beating wildly. It was as if I were listening to Roxy's voice, and I could feel her pain as I read, cutting me sharp as a knife.

I showered, washed away the evidence of my rape, but still it's so deep in my mind. I can still feel them, one after another thrusting inside of me, laughing with one another, high-giving as each took turns.

"Oh, my God, Roxy," I exclaimed, my throat feeling suddenly dry. I continued reading, an hour went by with me still sealed to my chair, unable to move as I walked through the life of my baby, and read her pain.

April 19th, 1999…

The art studio job was a fucking joke; men lie so damn much it's a shame. Now that bastard Michael wants to offer me a deal, as if I don't know what his deal would be. I'm nobody's fool…

April 20th, 1999…

He wanted to fuck me; now tell me please why I shouldn't have been surprised? I shocked myself when I agreed to it, for a price. Hell, men take it anyhow. I may as well get paid…

July 30th 1999…

He's a nasty stank man; I don't think I can deal with this anymore; I need Dee, but God! I can't tell my family what I've become. Thomas is good to me, isn't he? But he's still buying me. I'm so confused. I don't know who I am anymore. Maybe he's my ticket, my way out of this hell I've created. I have to go to Paris…

The days, months went on and on, each telling the when, how and every personal detail of Roxy's life as a call girl. But most importantly, I began to understand, to know her inside. She had been hurt so badly, and unable to trust that there was anyone she could turn to. So instead she turned on herself and became her own critic, punishing herself for something that was not even her fault, her rape.

"And I've punished her again!" I said, closing her journal and wiping my own tears that shamelessly covered my face. "I'm her Judas just like Dad warned me not to be."

Even through my shock, I knew Roxy, knew the type of woman, person she was, but I didn't want to see it. Instead of me listening and giving her a chance I shut her out. I was shaken, thinking about all that must have gone through her while that snake muthafucka Clark exposed her at my exhibit. He had been one of the monsters that had used her, abused her body. And he abused her still while I watched. Too blinded by my own pain to see hers. If only she had trusted me months ago with her secret. But in hindsight, after the way she explained her feelings in her journal, I knew she would never have been able to do that.

I jumped up, grabbed the phone and dialed.

"Hello, what time is your next flight to BWI in Baltimore, Maryland?"

I had to right this. I had to see her. I had to let her know that I loved her still, and always would.

CHAPTER *Thirty*

ANTOINE

Catonsville, Maryland

"Keep the change," I told the Checker Cab driver as he let me out in front of a big house in Catonsville, Maryland. I double- checked the address that Nicky had given me. It was all in the clear, so I grabbed my overnight bag from the car, thanked the driver, and walked toward the front entrance. I was nervous. I also wasn't expected, and didn't know what type of reception I would get. But I swallowed all my misgivings, and rang the doorbell.

It was a cozy place, kinda didn't look like the type of place I would picture Roxy's sister living at though. She appeared like Roxy, to be more of the city girl, upscale type of lady, probably even moreso than Roxy.

A big, tall, baldheaded dude answered the door, speaking out in a deep voice, "Yeah, what can I do for you, my man?"

I looked again at the address on my paper, wondering who this brotha could be. Does she live here?"

"She does. What can I do for you? Are you some business client of hers?"

"No, I'm a friend of her sister's, Roxy? Is she here?" I reached out my hand. "I'm sorry. I'm Antoine Billups, from Manhattan."

Suddenly I heard Dee's unmistakable voice call out. "Antoine? Baby, let him in. That's Antoine, Roxy's boyfriend."

The cautious look left the tall brotha's face, to be replaced by a warm smile. He moved from in front of the door, inviting me in. "Sorry, bruh. I thought for a second there you were the *other* man."

"Whoa! Naw, man, ain't nothing up like that!" I exclaimed.

Dee laughed, punching the guy on the arm. "Antoine, don't pay him no mind, Step is a fool and a half!" The guy who I now knew to be Step smiled warmly down at Dee. Looking at the two of them, I suddenly felt short again. They were a tall couple.

"Stephen, this is Antoine;, Antoine this is my soon-to-be slave driver, Stephen Lewis," she cooed with a wink.

"You got that right, Shanty, just a matter of time before I put you to work," he smiled back, slapping her lightly on the ass. I raised my eyebrows, clearing my throat to kinda remind them that I was there. There was definitely a *Love Jones* going on here.

"It's nice to meet you, man," Step said, giving me daps. "So you're the guy Roxy's all devastated over, huh?"

"Um, well, I guess I am..."

"Step," Dee cut in, giving him a warning glance.

"Is she here, Dee?" I asked anxiously.

"She left about an hour ago to get some art supplies. She's been doing a lot of painting since she's been here." Dee led me to their living room, the classy design that was her all the way. "I'm sorry about everything that happened with you two, Antoine, I had never seen her happier than when she had been with you in New York. And now..." She sighed. "Now she won't eat; all she does is paint." Before I could get a word in, the phone rang. Dee excused herself.

"Have a seat, bruh," Step insisted.

I sat down, putting my bag between my ankles. I still wasn't sure how welcomed I was. Step mentioned Roxy being devastated, and Dee said she wasn't eating. It ate at my heart that Roxy had gone through pain without me being there to help her through it. Especially when I was probably the major cause of it.

"Hey, Antoine, it's cool, man. We're all family here," Step said. I looked at him and saw genuineness to him. That put me at ease instantly.

"Really, how is she?" I asked. "Roxy?"

"She's all right, I guess, but she's not herself, of course. I never really got to know her that well before she moved to New York, but we have a slight bond between us."

I swallowed, looking at him to see if I could measure how much he knew. "So she told you guys everything that happened?"

Step nodded. "Yes, we know. I mean, of course, Deandra knows more. They talk and all, but Roxy kind of told both of us when she came a few days ago. I guess finding out about her was a shock, huh?"

"Man, shock ain't the half of it..." I looked at him again. "So you know about her being a...a, you know?"

"Call girl? Yep. I'm a private detective, and you could say, rescuing Roxy is how I got with her sister. She hired me to get Roxy from this sick muthafucka in Paris, Thomas..."

"Dugué."

"Yea," he said.

"I didn't know any of this, Step. When I met Roxy, she gave a totally different story of her past. When I found out the truth last weekend, I know I reacted badly, but I was shocked out of my mind!"

"Look, you being here in Baltimore says a lot. I mean any man would have taken that shit hard. I know I would've. But, Antoine, regardless of the things she has done, I don't think I need to even tell you what a beautiful person Roxy is. She's just had some horrible circumstances that have shaped her past, but it doesn't change who she really is..."

"I know," I said, cutting Step off. "I read her journal."

"Then you know about her getting raped?"

"Yea." I closed my eyes for a second shutting out the pain of those words associated with Roxy. It killed me even to think about someone hurting her like that. I could understand more now how and why she related and empathized so well with Nicky when she was attacked.

"I just heard about it myself, man," Step was explaining. "I never understood completely why a girl who appeared to have it all would turn tricks either. But in her mind, I guess she felt she had nothing."

"I know, but I want her to know she still has me, and that I want to be here for her," I said with a certainty. Step nodded in understanding. It was a trip how I had just met this guy but was bonding the way that we were. But each of us loving sisters gave us an automatic connection, I suppose. Just then Dee walked back into the room.

"Sorry," she said, smiling at me. She then looked toward Step. "That was about that ex-minor league player they signed on. He wants me to interview him Monday."

"So how long do you think Roxy will be?" I asked. I felt rude changing the subject, but I needed to know. Dee parted her lips to answer me but just then, the sounds of a car pulling up could be heard.

"Speak of the devil," Dee said. I got up, walked toward the front door, anxious to see Roxy yet still not knowing how she would receive me.

She came walking through the door with her typical Roxy bounce, throwing her purchased art supplies up against the wall before suddenly looking in my direction. Her mouth flew open, yet no words came out. I drank her in, noticing the hollow circles around her eyes, her thinness. But mostly I noticed the absence of her Roxy shine, as if her spirit and light had gone out.

Roxy

I was frozen in place, and for the life of me, I couldn't move. My right arm was still in midair where I had thrown my art supplies carelessly on the floor. If asked to paint every possible scenario of what could happen as I came through the door, finding Antoine on the other side was not one of them. My body was tied up in knots, one part of me so ecstatic to see him, and the other–a side that had been growing the past couple of days–wanting him to leave. My body, my mind, and my soul were tired, and I didn't want to go through any more drama. I *couldn't* go through any more drama.

The room was silent, Dee and Step standing beside one another and Antoine staring at me. Dee spoke first. "Rox, look who paid you a visit," she said in a happy tone, which I quickly dismissed.

"Yea," I responded dryly, "I have eyes, sis." I took a few tentative steps into the living room, moving closer to Step and Dee to distance myself from Antoine. I didn't trust myself not to jump into his arms and beg his forgiveness. I wouldn't belittle myself any longer. As if freezing, I wrapped my arms around me, cinching them around my waist. For the first time, I realized I must have looked a mess. Since arriving in Baltimore, I hadn't given a damn how I looked, and opted to wear nothing special, like today as I wore a too big denim shirt and a pair of checkered leggings. My hair was tied up in a ponytail and absentmindedly, I had brushed a few stray hairs from my face as if it would somehow turn me into the sophisticated woman I appeared to be in New York.

"Hey," Antoine said, his voice low and soft. I closed my eyes and willed myself not to cry from the sound of his voice, a voice I had heard in my dreams every night since Antoine turned me away. "Hey," I responded back, monotone, eyes still closed, begging tears to stay in.

"Um," Antoine hesitated, "I know you came to Baltimore to catch your breath, be alone..."

"Yes, I did."

"...but I think we need to talk...at least, I would like to talk to you." I finally opened my eyes having checked my tears, and sighed.

"I don't think we have anything left to say," I whispered. "You made it perfectly clear that what I did was wrong...you couldn't...forgive me, and I understand that."

"I think we should leave them alone," Dee said, taking Step's hand.

"Naw, don't leave, sis, this is your house," I replied.

"Please, Roxy," Antoine said, almost pleading, "let me talk to you."

Without saying another word, I went to retrieve my art supplies and walked past Dee, Step and Antoine. At the doorway leading to the hallway, I turned around and said, "Follow me."

The walk down the hallway to the attic steps was a silent one. All that could be heard was our breathing. Funny, even now, our breaths flowed as one, even though our lives had been thrown into turmoil.

When we reached the attic, I opened the door, letting him in before shutting it behind me. My eyes swept the room, noticing my clothes splayed all over the place, and paints and brushes laying around. In the middle of the room stood my covered easel. Antoine turned to face me, and my breath caught in my throat. He was so beautiful…and my heart just wanted to wrap itself around the beauty that was him. "It's ironic," I began, "that I'm letting you have your say when you wouldn't give me the time of day, Antoine."

I had so much bitterness inside of me, mixed with my love for this man, and right then, my hurt feelings had to be released. Before he could speak, I continued, "I'm guessing that you're here because you've read my journal." Antoine nodded. His eyes glazed over with tears and I felt my own reaching my eyelids. "I gave you that so you could finally know everything, dispelling all lies, once and for all. I didn't give it to you so you could feel sorry for me, and come rushing to my side to be sympathetic."

"That's not why I'm here, Roxy," Antoine said, taking steps toward me. I backed up until I was pressed against the door. Antoine stood three steps ahead of me, and I could feel the heat of his body jumping the distance to touch me. I tried to push past the warmth.

"The night I tried to explain to you, and you threw me away," I continued, choking up, "I realized that you didn't love me anymore…"

"No, Roxy, that's…"

"I had to leave because I knew I couldn't stand to be around you, knowing that I couldn't see that beautiful face…knowing that I hurt you. The last couple of days I have drilled into my head the truth…you don't love me, and I need to get over you…or die trying." The first tear trickled down my face and I let out a slow, painful moan. I bit down hard on my bottom lip to curb the tears. "I funked up…I'm a fuck-up, and I don't blame you for hating me, but to come here as if you care, when I know you can't stand me…"

"Roxy!" Antoine yelled, removing the distance between us as his hands cupped my face, gently raising my tearful eyes to his. "That's not why I came...and I don't hate you!"

I reached up, touching Antoine's hand, reveling in the feel of him touching me. "You don't hate me?" I asked, confused. "Then why did you come..."

"Do you still love me?" Antoine asked, his voice tight, his words rushing past his lips.

That was like asking if the sun rose in the morning and set in the evening. It was like asking if God was good...because the answer was *all the time.* I nodded my head as the tears rolled down my cheeks. "So much," I croaked. "My life wouldn't be a life without you, Antoine."

"Baby," Antoine cried, kissing my forehead, stroking my cheeks, "I love you. I have never *not* loved you. I was mad, angry, hurt, frustrated, disbelieving, but never, *ever* did my love for you leave.

"Reading your journal, God, if I could take away the pain that you have gone through, baby, I would. I wish with all my heart that you had told me this before now."

"What would you have done, Antoine?" I asked tearfully.

"I don't really know," he answered truthfully. "I don't know."

"I couldn't risk the shame to myself, my family...to you. You're my heart, and just like you want to take away my pain, I wanted to spare you from pain. I drew up a new life for myself, because I truly did not feel I could breathe if I had to be reminded of my past...and then California." I broke down, trembling, falling into Antoine's embrace. "Everything, the rape, being a call girl, everything destroyed me, Antoine...now that you know, that everyone knows, and my life has fallen from the joy it once had, I just want to put it in the past, start anew."

"With me?" he asked.

"Can you honestly forgive me, Boo? I mean never letting my past haunt you, never wondering where I'm at if I'm a little late coming home...when we make love, will you feel sick to your stomach, knowing that I've been with so many men?"

Antoine stepped back, swallowing hard. My heart plummeted into my

Reeboks and I felt my knees begin to buckle. *If he tells me he can't forgive me*, I thought, *I will crumble up onto this floor and die…there will be no other recourse.*

Antoine ran his fingers through his hair. Instead of answering my question, he pointed to my covered easel. "I'm happy to see you painting again," he said. "What are you painting?"

"Do you really want to know?" I asked, eyeing him intently.

"You know I do." I slowly walked up beside him, both of us eyeing the white cloth that covered my easel.

"I began this painting in New York," I said. "Before you and I…made love. I was in so much turmoil. I wanted you so badly, Antoine. Ever since the cruise, but I couldn't give myself to you because I felt so damn dirty.

"When I found out you were seeing Samantha, I cried inside and realized that if I truly wanted you, I would have to tell you that. The night we made love, my whole life changed. I had found a friend in you and a lover. My soul mate, and my entire existence felt reborn. You changed me, and you change me every day into a person that I love being. This painting is the artistic version of my love for you."

"Show it to me," Antoine whispered. I could see the tears welling in his eyes, and I raised my hands, removing the cloth. "Wow," he said, as we both stared at the painting. On the canvas in the foreground of a New York City background stood two lovers, intertwined as if two snakes coiled together. From the center of their connection resonated a light that grew in brightness as it rose above them, dispersing into the night. The woman in the painting had a river flowing from the length of her hair. The river held words such as rape, prostitution, lies, deception, tears, hate. "You washed away all my negativities," I cried, turning to face Antoine. "You are the light inside of me that keeps my heart warm and glowing."

With trembling fingers, my hands caressed Antoine's face, wiping away his fallen tears. "If you give me one more chance, I promise that I will never hurt you again, Boo," I whispered. "You and I could be so happy together…let me prove it to you." In an instant, Antoine slipped his arms around my body, pulling me tightly to him. Feverishly, he kissed me, my eyelids, my cheeks, before transplanting his warm lips onto mine. Breaking the kiss, we both took in a breath, panting lightly.

"Roxy," Antoine crooned next to my ear, kissing me there, "I'm never going to leave you again…this…," he took hold of my hand and placed it to his heart, "…is yours forever."

"Are you sure?" I asked in a quivering voice.

"That night…in California, I know you heard what I said," Antoine whispered against my lips. "I told you I was going to make you my wife…that I loved you. That wasn't a lie, Roxy."

"I love you so much, Antoine," I cried, kissing him.

"And I love you, too, baby girl…forever." Antoine drew me to him, into him and we held one another so tightly, I felt we had become one…and when we kissed, I *knew* we had.

eyelids, my cheeks, [illegible] transplanting his [illegible] lips onto mine. Breaking the kiss, we both took a [illegible] breath, making [illegible].

"Roxy," Antonio crooned [illegible] kissing [illegible] them. "I'm never going to [illegible] this. [illegible]" He took hold of my hand and placed it on his heart. "[illegible] words now?"

"Are [illegible]?" I asked in a quivering voice.

"[illegible] California. I hope you liked what [illegible]. A home [illegible] was going to ask you my [illegible] that [illegible] a Tee-Roy."

"I love you so much, Antonio," I cried, kissing him.

"And I love you, my baby girl, forever." Antonio [illegible] me to him [illegible] That we had become [illegible] we have had.

NICKY

"Well?"

"Well what?"

"Don't play, boy. Y'all get it together or not?" I could hear Antoine's soft laughter through the phone, could even picture his big smile shining at me.

"Well…I'm in Baltimore aren't I?" he replied.

"So what does that mean? You still haven't said if you made up. You know I got to have all the haps, negro," I pressed.

Antoine started humming. This fool was humming in my ear!

"*Antoinnnneeee!*"

"What! What!"

"Uggggggg, do not play with me!"

"Okay, okay." He laughed. "It's all good, and we're okay. More than okay actually. We talked, she's as beautiful as ever, I love her more than ever, and we fully…truly know each other now—the good, the bad and the ugly. All is good with the world, babe."

"Humph!"

"Humph? What you humphing about. It's good news, no?"

"Of course," I said, as if he were ridiculous to even ask. "It's just that you heterosexual folks are so daggone dramatic. I knew all along it would be okay. You two were destined, so why the fuck y'all waste precious time I will never know!"

"Oh, you just knew, huh?" I could feel him smiling.

"Yep, psychic as always." I smirked. "Oh, and guess what!?"

"What?"

"I met this chick at a club last night. She was so damn sexy. I was like get it, Boo! And, chile, it was on. You know I brought her ass home and served her up on a platter."

"Oh, my God." Antoine breathed.

I could tell he was fighting not to crack up, but I continued.

"Yep, had that honey rapping out moans like Lil' Kim!"

I smiled, thinking about the sweet morsel I had entertained the night before. She was my self-proof that I was going on with my life, and my life style. Whether society approved or not, I was Nicky, a woman loving, off da hook, sexy ass Chef Boyardee, and I *loved* being me. If people didn't like me, well…fuck ' em!

I sighed happily, feeling content for the first in a long ass time. Like I had told Antoine a few days earlier, I was done with being sad, I was done with being mad, I had a life to live, and I was going to live it to the fullest. And now with Antoine and Roxy having gotten their love story to a happy ending, all was good and well with the world, and when they got back, it would be happy, happy, joy, joy in the Big Apple.

Antoine laughed good-naturedly. "You're a trip, Girl. What am I going to do with you?"

"Nope, I see you getting rusty with your lovesick self. What am I?"

"Lawd…" He laughed.

"I'm waitingggg…"

Antoine took a deep breath. "Okay, are you ready for this? You, Nicole Carter, are a full blown *vacation!*"

"Sho a right, I said with a smile. "I love you, BooBoo."

"I love you, too, Nicky."

ABOUT THE AUTHORS

JDaniels is a native Virginian and is presently living and working in King William County, VA. Having a multitude of interests, writing (stories, poetry, songs/lyrics) has always been a first love. JDaniels is a staff writer, co-founder and an editor for the popular online e-zine *The Nubian Chronicles.* She is also co- founder and a web developer for TNC Communications, which is a portal on the web designed to assist new and established writers to create a web presence. JD is also a poet, songwriter and co-author of the Strebor Books International release *Luvalwayz: The Opposite Sex and Relationships* (August 2001). JD's first solo novel, *Serpent in My Corner*, published by BET Sepia Books, will be released July 2003. JDaniels is also author of the poetic, hood-rat drama: *Ballad of a Ghetto Poet*, which will be released by Strebor Books International in December 2003. *Ballad* will be released under the pseudonym, A.J. White. Contact JDaniels at http://www.jdanielsonline.com.

Shonell Bacon is the co-author of *Luvalwayz: The Opposite Sex and Relationships* (Strebor Books). *Draw Me with Your Love* is her second literary effort. She is also co-founder and chief editor of the online literary magazine, The Nubian Chronicles (http://www.nubianchronicles.net). She is currently working simultaneously on the third novel in the *Luvalwayz* trilogy, *If You Asked Me To;* several short stories, and a new novel project. A native of Baltimore, Shonell now resides in Lake Charles, Louisiana, where she is pursuing a dual master's degree in creative writing and English while she teaches English composition and literature at McNeese State University. Contact Shonell at http://www.BaconBits.com. http://www.luvalwayz.com

Special Preview

If You Asked Me To

By SHONELL BACON AND JDANIELS

If You Asked Me To **is the final novel in the** ***Luvalwayz*** **trilogy. This time around, Bacon and Daniels are bringing you** ***mature love*** **in the hot, sizzling writing that you all know and love.**

Dr. Frederica "Freddie" Kaufman is a thirty-something, full-figured sister whose two-year celibacy streak is begging to be broken. As she counsels others on their problems, especially one woman who has had her share of horrific relationship problems, Freddie realizes that she too needs to overcome her own relationship hang-ups. Enter her good friend and colleague, Shameika, who has the ***perfect*** **man for her insecure friend.**

Carter Harrison, a buddy of Shameika's husband, Joop, and the head football coach at Catons University is a single father and is ***all*** **man. Busy dealing with his HIV-positive son, he hasn't had time for a serious relationship since the death of his wife. But when he is introduced to Freddie on a blind date, things change for Carter, and he finds the door of his heart being knocked on.**

Through-out their turbulent love affair, Freddie is determined to work her way into the heart of the rough-around-the-edges yet tender soul of Carter. If only her determination to learn the deep secrets he seems to be hiding doesn't push him farther and farther away.

Carter's aloofness is weak, however, and although Freddie gets to the point of giving up, karma helps her to realize that if she asks him to, Carter just might change his mind, and let her in his life forever.

Carter...

I didn't want to look at Freddie. Every time I glanced her way I felt anger surfacing through me. What was it about women that made them think they had some right to bust up in a man's life and try to control them? It's like they give up the ass and suddenly you have a wife with no papers.

"Carter," she whispered in my ear. "I'm sorry, okay?" I felt her sigh deeply. "I know you feel I've invaded your privacy. But I just wanted to know what was going on with you. I've been in bad relationships all my life and I didn't want to chance another one."

I turned around quickly. The anger in my eyes was evident. "Maybe that's the problem here. You're looking for a superman, Freddie. I'm just your average Joe. I can't be this person you want, this person you need."

"I don't want a superman. I want you! I need you!"

"No, what you want is to control me, and I'm not having that shit! You and I are obviously too different. You spend your days rolling around in people's minds and I spend my days prepping guys who want to be the next NFL superstars. We are too different."

"I made a mistake, Carter. You seem to hide so much from me. I don't think it's so hard to understand that I would want to know what's going on with you."

"Anything you need to know about me I told you already. Anything outside of that is not your business, Freddie."

"Okay," she said. She paused for a moment. "So can we fix this? Will you give me another chance?"

"I don't know," I stated quietly. "Probably not."

"You don't know?" Freddie laughed without mirth. "O...kay...probably not. Great, just great."

"I think it would be best..."

"Okay," she said again, her voice cracking slightly.

I fought the voice inside me that wanted to reach out. I could tell I was hurting Freddie. But I couldn't allow anyone in. I knew from the start that I didn't have room in my life for a woman. There was too much to do with Trey. He had to be my focus. All the energy that I was using to deal with this situation with Freddie is energy I should be using to help my son.

"Well, I guess this is it," I heard her saying. My eyes followed her as she made her way to the door. She turned around looking at me with pleading eyes. "Carter...I don't want it to be over."

"Freddie..."

"Daddy!"

Both Freddie and I looked toward Trey's panicked voice. There was blood all over his pajama top, and even more gushing from his nose. I felt my stomach lurch.

"Trey, what happened?" I cried. I rushed over to him.

"Oh, my God!" Freddie exclaimed, rushing along with me to Trey's side.

"Stay right there, son," I said. I ran to the bathroom to get towels. Seconds later when I returned to the hallway, Freddie was behind Trey. She was trying to lift his PJ top from the back, probably to use it to stop some of the blood flow issuing from his nose. I felt instant alarm.

"Don't touch him!"

Freddie looked at me in shock. "What's wrong with you? I'm just trying to help him."

"I said don't touch him. You need to leave, Freddie. I got this!"

Freddie backed away from me and from Trey. Her face was blanched with hurt and surprise. I held the towel to Trey's nose, applying slight pressure. I looked down at him, sensing that he had calmed somewhat, then looked back at Freddie.

"Look, I can take care of him. I'm sorry, Freddie, I think you need to go now."

Without another word she grabbed her purse and made her way out the door, letting it close quietly behind her. I fell to the floor, grabbing Trey with his bloody shirt close to me. There was an aching knot in my throat that got larger and larger as we sat there, rocking. *I'm a forty-year-old man. I can deal with this*, I thought. I have to do it for Trey.

But how could I ever deal with letting Freddie go? How would I ever be able to tell her the real secret that I was hiding? How would I ever tell her why I was pushing her away; why I didn't have time for a relationship no matter how attracted I was to her both physically and mentally? How could I stop my body's reaction whenever I thought of her?

How could I ever tell her that my son is HIV-positive?

9 781593 090005

Printed in the United States
By Bookmasters